FINAL VERDICT

"I believe Mr. Miller has made a decision he wishes to announce to you, Cosima," Nash said quietly.

"Yes," said Miller. "From now on, I want you to regard Mr. Nash as your supervisor with respect to everything you do with Fang, Incorporated. You are to do nothing for the client without his approval."

She glanced hard at Nash. "I think I'm entitled to an explanation. That client had generated more than three hundred thousand dollars in fees in the past twelve months. I brought Fang, Incorporated to the firm and you can't find a mistake in my work."

"You were called in here to be *told* Mr. Miller's decision," said Nash indignantly. "Not to debate it."

"*No,*" she interrupted. "No way."

"What do you mean, 'no'?" Miller demanded. "I hope you realize what you are putting at risk. Don't say something that will leave us without options."

Cosima drew a deep breath. "You have options," she said. "I don't." She shook her head. "So. Gentleman, I will be gone before the end of the day."

"You'll regret this, Cosima," said Nash, his voice distorted by shock and subdued anger.

Cosima tipped her head and smiled at him. "I doubt that, Dan. I really doubt that."

FOR THE DEFENSE
WILLIAM HARRINGTON

PINNACLE BOOKS
WINDSOR PUBLISHING CORP.

PINNACLE BOOKS

are published by

Windsor Publishing Corp.
475 Park Avenue South
New York, NY 10016

First Pinnacle Books printing: January, 1990

Printed in the United States of America

Author's Note

This novel is a work of fiction, as noted on the copyright page. I would like to emphasize that point. In this story, a number of lawyers and judges are portrayed as engaging in unethical conduct. Members of a subcommittee of the Association of the Bar of the City of New York are portrayed as acting improperly. I have the privilege of being a member of the Association of the Bar of the City of New York, but the conduct described in this novel is emphatically not based on my observations and impressions as a member. The story told here is the product of my imagination and is not a fictionalization of any actual events. The people of the story are also fictional and are not disguised versions of actual people.

To Diana, always

One

Cosima Bernardin kissed her father lightly on the cheek and saw him wince. Leon Bernardin was not a demonstrative man. He was capable of affection; she was confident he loved her; but he had never been what he would have labeled effusive.

"I think you are too pessimistic," he said. "But perhaps you have been too aggressive. Perhaps too emotional."

"I'll try to control myself," she said.

Her father nodded. "I would hope so. If Emilie had become hysterical over the defeats she had to suffer, she would not be where she is. And Susanne did not win her every match."

"My sisters . . ."

"Achieved their goals," said her father. He turned his eyes back to the newspaper he had been reading before the car stopped. "Achieved them, Cosima. What they wanted was not handed to them."

Cosima reached for her Italian leather bag: the copious bag she carried instead of a briefcase, filled this morning as always with heavy files. She saluted her father, shoved the door shut and stepped back from the silver-gray Mercedes.

9

Frank, her father's driver, glanced back to be sure she was safely on the curb, then he pulled away.

For a moment she stared through the rear windows at her father and saw him resume his reading, something in *American Banker*. Her father did not like to waste the time it took to come in from Connecticut every morning—he had made it a reading hour, and by the time he reached his office he would be finished with the *Wall Street Journal* and the *Times*, as well as *American Banker,* and would have scanned and marked a dozen memoranda and reports. He had given her a few minutes' conversation this morning, not grudgingly, but with impossible-to-conceal restlessness marked by repeated quick glances at his newspaper.

He was not a big man, physically, but he was formidable. His gray hat was set squarely over his gray hair. His blue suit was newly brushed this morning, his shoes were shined, and he wore a small white flower in his lapel. He was sixty-eight years old, and the habits of a lifetime, which were undoubtedly an element of his success, were beyond alteration. She loved him. Sometimes she felt a bit self-congratulatory for loving him, because it wasn't easy.

As the Mercedes sped into the distance, Cosima glanced with resignation toward the revolving doors of 120 Broadway. She turned and entered the building. Inside, as she waited for an elevator, two men and a woman nodded perfunctory, distracted morning greetings. One was from her firm; the others were not, but they recognized her.

Cosima Bernardin was a striking woman, once seen rarely forgotten. She was, to begin with, nearly six feet tall: five feet ten and a half, to be exact, and, carrying a correct hundred fifty-five pounds, she was not fashionably gaunt, nor was she in the least thickset. Her shoulders, arms and legs were strong, but she was lithe and carried herself with an erect, self-confident posture. Her hands were large, and she heard more often than she wished a compliment to the effect that they would spread beautifully across the keys of a piano—and did she play? She did not.

10

She was wearing her dark brown hair cut very short: shorter than most of the men in her office wore theirs, with only disciplined wisps combed back over her ears. Her face was long, from her high forehead to her long, square jaw. Her eyebrows were dark and thick, her eyes blue, her mouth broad, her lips full.

"Good morning, Miss Bernardin." One of the paralegals greeted her as she stepped out of the elevator. She couldn't remember the girl's name, so she nodded and smiled at her. "A beautiful sweater," the girl added, and Cosima thanked her.

It *was* a rather nice sweater, she agreed. This warm spring morning she had chosen a loose-knit, loose-fitting, off-white, V-neck cashmere. She was wearing it with the sleeves pushed back to just below her elbows. She wore, too, a linen skirt of the same color, tailored and a bit short, a full inch above her knees. She wore little jewelry, and what she wore this morning was to add accents of color to her white outfit. On her right hand she wore a ring of red and black enamel set with small diamonds. It matched the enamel-and-diamond pendant that hung in the deep V of her sweater. Also, she was wearing a red leather watchband.

The paralegal fell in step beside her as she walked along the hall to the doors to the office. "We got a bad decision in the Palmer case," she said, obviously anxious to make a bit of conversation with Cosima Bernardin. "Court of Appeals turned us down. It's in this morning's New York *Law Journal.*"

"I'll try to stay clear of Heath, then," said Cosima dryly.

"So will I," said the girl.

The name of the firm and a list of its partners were emblazoned in gilded letters on the walnut paneling to the left of the entrance:

HAMILTON, SCHUYLER, DEPEW & CHASE

Hamilton, Schuyler, Depew, and Chase were of course all dead, had been since 1914 when Schuyler died, the last of them. They were listed at the top of the list of partners,

11

with their years, followed by a thin line and then the list of one hundred twenty-four active partners.

The seniormost active partner in the firm today was Clarence Paul Davidson, a bond lawyer who had managed to survive his six years in the Nixon Treasury Department without going to jail or losing his reputation—a reputation more for shrewd and aggressive lawyering than for impeccable integrity. He was sixty-nine, and next year, in accordance with the firm's inflexible rule, his name would be stricken from the top of the list and carried below the bottom line, relegated to the brief list of partners emeritus who had neither shares nor votes. But for today it was still at the top, and he still occupied a corner office behind the inner doors that separated the managing partners' mystic enclave from what many others referred to as the working offices.

The name Cosima Bernardin stood third from the bottom on the active-partners list, just above the line that exiled the partners emeritus, and well below the line that separated the thirty-eight senior partners from the eighty-six junior partners. She had been promoted to junior partner just last fall, with the class of '81, together with four others.

Six from that class had not made it. Of those, four remained among the firm's one hundred seventy-two associates, hoping to make it this year, and two were gone. She had made the cut, as they said; she had been offered a partnership; and now, unless—in the traditional phrase that was so inappropriate when applied to her—she stepped on her cock, she was welcome to remain a partner until she retired.

This was the morning she might step on her cock.

She entered the office through the reception room, exchanging nods with the head receptionist, who flipped a switch that lighted her name on several boards in the office, indicating to receptionists and telephone operators—and to senior partners who cared to check—that she was in. Having thus checked in, she went down two flights of carpeted

12

stairs to the floor where her office was, in the corporate-law department.

"Miss Bernardin," said a secretary briskly. The woman served four lawyers. She had been with the firm eleven years and considered herself more senior than any of the lawyers assigned to her. "You have some messages," she said, nodding toward Cosima's mailbox on the credenza beside her desk. "And the meeting at"—she glanced at her watch—"ten o'clock."

Cosima nodded. Through the open door at the end of the area she could see D. (David, which he did not use) Douglas Miller in his corner office, talking on the telephone. She did not just imagine that he checked his watch, mentally noting the minute when she arrived in the office. He did that to everyone, including partners only a step or two below him in the pecking order; the rumor had leaked from management meetings that at times discussion, particularly of promotions, often turned on his reports of the hours kept by junior lawyers.

Attaining partner status was no escape from the law-firm pissing contest—another phrase carried over from the days when all the lawyers in Wall Street firms were men. It had at first only made her laugh: the image of a row of dapper counsellors standing toes on a line and urinating in competition to see who could throw his stream the farthest. But it was not funny. D. Douglas Miller himself disliked encountering Clarence Paul Davidson in an elevator, particularly in the evening. Even a partner only a dozen ranks from the top was reluctant to have a more senior partner see him leaving the office as early as that more senior man. Habit of a lifetime. The law-firm pissing contest.

According to firm legend, a junior partner with five years' status once stepped on his cock at the building security station. He had chanced to come down in an elevator with the then-seniormost partner, and on reaching the lobby tried to leave the building without signing out at the security station. He did not realize the building closed at eight and that

13

everyone leaving after that hour had to sign out. The senior partner observed his confusion and concluded—correctly—that the young man had never before been in the office after eight o'clock. The next morning he was told to clean out his desk.

Inside her windowless, twelve-by-twelve-foot office, Cosima closed the door. She picked up her telephone and pressed the numbers for Rick Loewenstein's intercom.

"Loewenstein."

"Cosima. I'm going to have to put a hold on our ten-o'clock. Just before I left last night, I got a buzz from Miller. Ten o'clock with him. I have no idea how long."

"Kay, Gussy," he said. "Let me know when you want to reschedule."

She grinned as she put down the phone. Gussy. No one else called her anything but Cosima—and she had made certain it *was* Cosima: that is, COSS-uh-muh, not for god's sake, Coss-EE-muh. Anyway, Rick had tried calling her Cossy, and when that had sounded foolish adopted Gussy. She would have objected to it from anyone else.

The mail—well, it was the usual thing, most of it internal memos, most of it documents for her to read and redline. A new question for research. She'd get an associate to do the grunt work on that, most of it on the computerized research systems, LEXIS and WestLaw. When she had the printouts before her, plus maybe a memo from the research associate, she would turn her mind to a report and recommendation. When? Oh yes, sure—tomorrow.

Another client wanted to sail close to the edge of the earth. That was the firm's chief function: to tell clients just how close they could sail before they risked slipping over the edge and falling into the devouring maw of the SEC, the FTC, or some other militant bureaucratic agency. The firm's function was not to rescue clients who had sailed over the edge but to help them steer a very nice course *along* the edge. The government was a menacing enemy. The law was a threat. (Of course it was—Cosima had learned that from

14

her father over breakfast and dinner tables since she was a child—and professors at Harvard had not succeeded in indoctrinating her with her own very different view.) At Hamilton, Schuyler, Depew & Chase that was what the law meant: a set of rules to be avoided—never broken, never evaded, but adroitly avoided. A fine distinction.

It was counterproductive to philosophize about it. Rick Loewenstein did that sometimes. To no useful purpose.

Naive friends thought she was in the business of exploiting flaws in the law—what they ignorantly called "loopholes"—when in fact she and the firm were really in the business of charting courses, not through inadvertent rents in the fabled seamless web but around the edges.

Well-represented clients got away with everything they could possibly get away with. That was the point. When they paid their lawyers, that was what they paid for. (And wasn't that, after all, what the street citizen paid H&R Block to do—to show him how to limit his taxes to what the law categorically demanded and pay not a nickel more?)

From her leather bag Cosima pulled the files that she had studied in the car while her father read his papers. As always, she was faced with more work than she could possibly do in the time she had to do it. That, too, was how the firm worked, another piece of the pissing contest—keep the associate and junior partners overburdened, lest they become confident and undisciplined.

It was an ugly thing: the obsessively hierarchical structure of a big law firm, with the devices used to sustain the hierarchy, the pervasive sophomoric attitudes, the exploitation, even the abuse, of young people. The pressures . . . the demands . . .

So why did she stay? Why had she come here in the first place, and why did she stay? The simplest answer was that she had earned $48,000 her first year out of law school, and this year with her bonus she would probably exceed $175,000. At thirty-two. None of her highly competitive older brothers and sisters had made $175,000 when they were thirty-two. Little sister wasn't doing bad.

And Cosima Eighth-In-Her-Class wasn't doing bad, either. She had made partner the first year she was eligible. (It was understood that you could not make partner at Hamilton, Schuyler before your sixth year, but if you didn't make it in your sixth or seventh, you never would. Year before last a seventh-year associate had killed himself when he learned he was not on the newly announced partners list.) She had faced a challenge everywhere acknowledged to be tough, and so far she was winning.

What was more, she shared with the other young people who could call themselves exploited a sense that in this office at 120 Broadway she was sitting in a cockpit of wealth and power that could hardly be imagined by anyone who had never experienced it. The list of the firm's client corporations read like the Dow-Jones industrials. Hamilton, Schuyler was counsel to companies and men who moved the world. What a cliché!—but it was true. The firm represented conglomerates, oil companies, insurance companies, utilities, broadcasters, builders, shippers, ad agencies, publishers and six new, high-flying technology companies. Although it did not represent Bernardin Frères, it did represent two of the most powerful banking houses on Wall Street. It maintained branch offices in Washington, Chicago, Los Angeles, San Francisco, London, Paris, Frankfurt and Tokyo.

If you didn't like Hamilton, Schuyler, chances were you didn't like the fast track. All the top firms were like Hamilton, Schuyler—almost conspiratorially uniform, as if there were somewhere a committee of master partners who met regularly and designed idiosyncrasies for all top firms to share. When exhausted juniors met in midtown bars in the middle of the evening and compared the days they had just endured, their experiences proved distressingly alike.

There was no point in thinking of moving from one firm to another. In the first place, it was all but impossible to do, and in the second place, there was no point in it; nothing would be different. The alternative was to move out of the fast track.

Like to the Justice Department. Few experiences of her life had been more revealing to Cosima than to meet with young lawyers from Washington, from the Department of Justice. Second-rank graduates of second-rate schools. Bureaucrats already, after one or two years in a stultifying bureaucratic atmosphere, with nothing ahead of them but a slow and almost automatic crawl a few grades higher in the civil service.

Or look at the thousand shabby scriveners who hung around the courthouses, grubbing for drab livings. Distressing. Or the pedestrian middle-levellers in ten thousand mean offices all over town, obscurely laboring in the service of realtors, insurance agents and pawnbrokers. There was nothing inherently satisfying in practicing law; to the contrary, it was inherently depressing—unless you could be a star at it.

If Hamilton, Schuyler was infuriating, which it was, and demanding, which it was, and politicized, which it was, and if working there was demeaning, which it could sometimes be, it nevertheless had its compensations, in money and in pride. If you were there, you were a star, by definition.

There was another compensation: she worked with people whose minds were as quick as hers. One of the burdens of confronting government lawyers—and sometimes the in-house counsel corporations insisted on employing—was that it took most of them so very long to grasp anything; often, in fact, they never did come to understand points that should have been so obvious they could remain unspoken. Lawyers in the firm could be egomaniacs, they could be petty and arbitrary, but she did not know one who was anything but intelligent and capable. In the past, all the lawyers in a firm like this had shared a common background: established families, prep school, Ivy League. Now a few of them were black, a few were women, and a few were Westerners and even Mid-westerners, but all of them were alike in their talent, drive, energy and covetous ambition.

The buzzer. She picked up her telephone.

"Mrs. Bernardin on line three."

She pressed the lighted button, "Mother?"

"Cosima, I need something from town. Please. Stop by Pedelson's sometime today and pick up the piano music for Schumann's Studies after Paganini's Caprices, Opus 3. You can do that for me, can't you?"

"No, I can't."

"What do you mean, you can't?"

"I have a very demanding day ahead of me. It would take me an hour to catch a cab, go all the way up to Pedelson's, and come back here. I simply don't have the time."

"Your lunch hour—"

"I doubt I'll have a lunch hour. If I do, I'll eat. Call Pedelson's, tell them what you want, and have them send it down by messenger. Better yet, have them deliver it to father's office—I'm not sure I'm coming back out there tonight."

"Well. All right. If you're so very busy. I'm sorry to have bothered you."

"Not at all. Good-bye, Mother."

The trouble with not having a window in your office was that you couldn't get up, stand at it, draw a deep breath and say—Shit!

One adjective covered D. Douglas Miller. Colorless. Colorless in appearance, colorless of personality. He kept his few remaining front wisps of blondish hair combed over his pallid dome; his eyes were pale blue and half hidden under sleepy lids, from under which they communicated nothing; his white lips neither curled into smiles nor drooped into scowls—his oval face was, in short, bland. It was like a

18

goalie's mask, however: it concealed an adamantine intelligence and dynamic.

Cosima had guessed the subject for this ten o'clock meeting, and she was not surprised that Miller would regard it as an imposition on his time. As head of the corporation-law department, he had assumed—seized, actually—administrative responsibility, but he begrudged every minute he gave it. The meeting would be short.

"Okay, Miss Bernardin," said Miller. "Dan and I—"

Dan was Daniel Nash, a ten-year partner and one of the coming men in the corporation-law department of Hamilton, Schuyler. He had arrived for the ten o'clock meeting five minutes early, and Miller had welcomed him and closed the door—ominous signs. Nash sat on Miller's leather-covered couch, a yellow legal pad balanced on his knee, ballpoint pen poised, ready to take notes of what they said in the meeting. Typical Nash. He had probably taken notes already, of whatever Miller had said before she was called in—and if she guessed right, the sheet of notes would go in his trash as soon as he returned to his office. What was more—again if she guessed right—Miller full well knew it.

"—have been discussing this client you brought in. Uh"—Miller glanced at a note, as though he could not remember the name he and Nash had unquestionably discussed within the past five minutes— " 'Bull Dog Fangs.' Uh . . . musicians."

"We represent corporations that will gross less than Bull Dog Fangs will gross this year," she said.

"Yes, I've had to be educated to that effect," said Miller.

"So have I," said Nash.

They had, indeed. When at first she had come in and said she could bring Ruggiero Paccinelli—Jerry Patchen—and Bull Dog Fangs to Hamilton, Schuyler, she had been met with utter incredulity. A small band? Rock musicians? Hamilton, Schuyler, Depew & Chase? Surely . . .

She remembered the first discussion—

"Surely, Miss Bernardin, you don't really think we—"

19

"They grossed more than thirty million dollars last year. Chances are, they'll gross still more this year, and more yet next year. They have contractual problems, copyright problems, liability problems, investment problems, tax problems . . . they're cash-rich. Also—if it makes you more comfortable—Ruggiero Paccinelli is a graduate of Yale. It's a *business.*"

"We've never represented anything of the kind."

"We never represented a high-tech company until there *were* high-tech companies. Paccinelli needs to incorporate. He needs planning—"

"Well, I suppose we could meet the man."

"And accept a retainer," she had said sarcastically.

Fang, Incorporated, was now a Delaware corporation. Cosima Bernardin was one of its directors. Its former agent, now manager, who had been taking 20 percent of its gross earnings, was now a salaried employee, as she had insisted, taking $220,000 a year plus bonus instead of six or eight million. The members of the band, the manager, and the band's eighteen or other employees were covered by a retirement plan, with Bernardin Frères as trustee of the fund. Some potential tax problems had been foreseen and headed off. A threatened copyright suit had been settled. An employment-discrimination claim had been adjusted by arbitration. Insurance had been purchased to cover potential liability for injuries that could occur during the group's frenetic appearances.

During the past twelve months, Fang, Incorporated, had paid $311,000 in fees to Hamilton, Schuyler, Depew & Chase.

"We have a small problem with this client, Miss Bernardin," said Miller.

"I hadn't heard that," she said.

"No," said Miller. "That is why we are meeting—so you can hear it. And the problem is that we feel there has been insufficient consultation."

"Meaning . . . ?"

"Meaning that you seem to have been inclined to go forward on your own with some elements of our representation of this client. This a *firm*, Miss Bernardin, and you are a very junior partner. The client is the firm's client, not yours, in spite of the fact that you brought it to us."

"Is something wrong?" asked Cosima. "Have I made a mistake?"

"How could we know?" asked Miller. "You didn't consult with us."

Nash scribbled away, miming the taking of detailed notes of what Miller was saying.

"Actually," said Cosima, "I've consulted very widely. I referred tax problems to the tax department, the copyright problem to the copyright people, the—"

"With whom in the corporation-law department did you consult as to the organization of Fang, Incorporated, and its retirement program?"

"With you," she said. "When Ruggiero Paccinelli asked me to sit on the board of directors, I sent you a memo, asking if that was okay. When I decided Bernardin Frères should be trustee of the company retirement fund, I sent you a memo asking if you had any objection to that."

"And how did I respond?"

"You didn't. So I could only assume you had no objection. I waited a week for your response in each instance."

Miller turned to Nash and sneered— " 'If we don't hear from you to the contrary within ten days, we will assume you want a set of our encyclopedias and will begin sending them.' "

"The client was waiting for an answer," said Cosima.

Miller began to rub his hands together—with him a sure sign of diminishing patience. "In fact," he said, "I did not object to your sitting on the company board, and I did not object to your father's bank being appointed trustee. I should rather, on the other hand, not be presented with a fait accompli."

21

"You weren't," she said. "In each instance, if you had objected, we wouldn't have done it."

He rubbed his hands more firmly, so she could hear the whisper of skin rubbing against skin. "The point we want to raise is that you have acted . . . rather independently."

Daniel Nash nodded gravely. He exhibited a sign of his own tense impatience: rubbing his cheek with the top of his ball-point pen. He had to control himself, Cosima suspected, to keep from sticking the pen in his mouth; in his own office he would have been sucking on a thin cigar, letting the smoke curl up around his spectacles and through his graying sand-colored hair.

Miller continued. "I have asked Mr. Nash to review what you've done with Fang, Incorporated. He's found no errors. On the other hand, he has certainly found things where his judgment would have been different from yours."

"Maybe not, if he had talked to the client and knew what Paccinelli wanted," she said.

"Are you sure our client had been correctly advised about all the options?" asked Nash, speaking for the first time. His voice was broad and flat.

"I reviewed our memorandum files," she said. "The options presented were the same ones other lawyers in this department have presented to other clients in similar situations."

Unlike Miller, Nash was capable of a smile, of a variety of smiles, in fact: amused, self-satisfied, condescending, sardonic. The one of this moment was condescending, Cosima judged. "You covered yourself, in other words," he said.

She, too, was capable of a variety of smiles, and the one she bestowed on him now was mocking.

Nash's face colored slightly. He compressed his thin lips; behind his round eyeglasses with thin, caramel-covered rims, his blue eyes glanced at Miller and returned to her. "I believe Mr. Miller has made a decision he wants to announce to you, Cosima," he said quietly.

"Yes," said Miller. "From now on, I want you to regard

Mr. Nash as your supervisor with respect to everything you do with Fang, Incorporated. You are to do nothing for the client without his approval. Everything is to be reviewed by him.''

This is what she had expected. It was about this that she had asked her father for advice in the car this morning. What should she do when they took her client from her? His answer had been—it depends on what reasons they give you.

Now she meant to have reasons. ''In view of the fact that I brought this client to the firm—''

''And made it a *firm* client,'' Miller interrupted. ''No one who brings a client to this firm thereby acquires a proprietary interest in that client.''

''That client has generated more than three hundred thousand dollars in fees in the past twelve months,'' Cosima continued, unflinching. ''You can't find a mistake in my work, though''—she glanced hard at Nash—''you seem to have tried. I think I am entitled to an explanation.''

''Mr. Miller has decided, Cosima,'' said Nash. ''That's the explanation.''

''That is not acceptable,'' she said coldly.

Nash blinked behind his spectacles. ''Neither of us,'' he said to her, ''is under any obligation to give you any explanation at all.''

''Nevertheless . . .'' said Miller, raising his hand in a quick gesture of peace. ''A first-year partner in this firm is not allowed to handle unsupervised the legal work of a client whose work generates more than three hundred thousand in fees. That is firm policy.''

''Is it, indeed?'' she asked. ''Who supervises Bill North with respect to the representation of Koenig? Who supervises George Teague in the representation of Stimson? I'm talking about lawyers only a year or two older than I am— and about clients they didn't bring to the firm. Who supervises *them?*''

''I do,'' said Miller.

23

"Precisely," said Cosima. "As you have supervised my work with Fang. I would be happy to have you continue."

"That is not your decision to make," said Nash.

"There is another element in the situation," said Miller. "I had hoped not to have to mention it, but since you seem to want to argue, perhaps I should. I—I am not quite sure how to put this, but Ruggiero Paccinelli, better known to the world as Jerry Patchen, seems to have a reputation for—how shall I put it?"

"He has a reputation for being a predatory stud," said Cosima candidly.

Miller nodded. "Exactly. At least two of his amours have involved him in ugly litigation. The tabloids thrive on him. There have been two stories in the *Post*, one in the *Daily News*, to the effect that—well, how does this one read? Quote—'Seen tête-à-têting at Toujours twice lately—stud rock star Jerry Patchen and rich-girl lawyer Cosima Bernardin. Law business or funny business?' "

Nash shook his head dramatically.

Miller continued—"We have concluded, quite frankly, Miss Bernardin, that there is an element of risk inherent in your being thrown too much into Paccinelli's company. I mean, risk to our firm's reputation. It would be better, we think, if a male lawyer assumed most of the responsibility for personal contact with Mr. Paccinelli. I, uh . . . believe you can understand."

Cosima rose and walked to the window. This time she could stare out and spit the word she had wanted to use after her mother's call. Her lips formed it. Her back was to Miller and Nash. She did not want them to see her face.

"I tell you what, Mr. Miller," she said, keeping her back to him. "Stimson is a homosexual. I guess we all know that—I don't think you'll deny it. By your reasoning, there is an element of risk in a young man like George Teague being thrown into his company too much. So why don't you let *me* represent Stimson? And George can meet with

Ruggiero Paccinelli.'' She turned. ''Right? Reasonable? Hmm?''

Miller glanced at his watch. ''I haven't time for argument, Miss Bernardin,'' he said. ''No matter how clever.''

''Do you have any idea how offensive this is?''

Miller turned up the palms of his hands. ''Put that element of the matter aside,'' he said. ''You have been indiscreet in meeting with Mr. Patchen-Paccinelli outside the office, in bars and whatever. But I won't be accused of sexism. My decision is not based on that element, which we could have cured simply by advising you to be more discreet. The point is, that a very junior partner cannot assume—''

''But I've handled it well, dammit,'' said Cosima. ''I brought in a good client and—''

''You were called in here to be *told* Mr. Miller's decision, Cosima,'' said Nash indignantly. ''Not to debate it.''

She remained standing before the window, struggling within herself to conceal from them all her emotions but anger. ''And what of the bonus credits that come from the fees generated by Fang, Incorporated?'' she asked, lifting her chin high.

''They will be appropriately divided,'' said Miller, closing a file folder that lay before him on his desk.

''What's appropriate?''

''What is usual is what's appropriate,'' said Nash.

''In other words,'' she said angrily to Miller, ''I have brought in a client, incorporated it, organized its business, headed off potential litigation and tax problems and generated more than three hundred thousand dollars in fees— and now it becomes Dan's client, and he takes the points, leaving me with the peanuts paid to a second-string helper.'' Her voice broke for an instance. She couldn't help it. ''Is that the deal?''

''Bluntly said, you got a little too ambitious, Miss Bernardin,'' said Miller. He stood. The meeting was over. ''We keep careful watch on your work. You are not yet ready for

25

this kind of responsibility. Be patient. Avoid outside personal relationships with clients. In time—"

"No," she interrupted, shaking her head. "No way, Doug."

Miller reacted at last, in a nervous twitching along his jawline and by an abrupt flare in his eyes. Maybe it was the first time in years that an associate or junior partner had called him by his nickname. He sat down. "What do you mean, 'no'?" he demanded. "I hope you realize what you are putting at risk."

Cosima stood with her back to the window, and she rested her backside against the sill. "I could bring in other clients," she said, now rigidly controlled. "I happen to have contacts among people in the entertainment industry. But why should I? Why should I bring in important clients, only to have them taken from me and handed to lawyers who are no more competent than I am?"

"Your self-esteem is unrealistic, Miss Bernardin," said Miller. "You are not as competent as you think you are. And—I can't help noting, now—you seem to be less than totally in control of your emotions. I suggest you go back to your office and reconsider what you've said. Then let us know if you continue to feel you've been ill-treated."

" 'Run along and be a good little girl, Cosima,' " she scoffed.

"Are you resigning from the firm, Cosima?" asked Nash.

"Well, I—" she began.

"Miss Bernardin," Miller interjected forcefully. "Don't say something that will leave us without options."

Cosima drew a deep breath. "You have options," she said. "I don't. I anticipated what you were going to say to me this morning. I discussed it with my father. I asked him what I should do. He said, that depends on the reasons they give. Well . . . I've heard your reasons. And they are not valid. Or honest." She shook her head. "So. Gentlemen, I will take my personal things from my office and be gone before the end of the day."

26

Miller interlaced his fingers and regarded her wordlessly, with mixed sympathy and scorn: his reaction to a young woman who had just confirmed his suspicion that she really was not quite up to the high standards of Hamilton, Schuyler, Depew & Chase.

"You'll regret this, Cosima," said Nash, his voice distorted by shock and subdued anger.

Cosima tipped her head and smiled at him. "I doubt that, Dan. I really doubt it.

Two

Cosima closed the door of her office and sat down spent behind her desk. She had come in this morning dreading the confrontation she had foreseen, yet inspirited by the prospect, charged with resolve: sure, bold, crisp. And she had handled herself well, she thought. She had continued to think so as she left Miller's office, as she walked into her own and closed the door firmly without slamming it. Now . . . now she felt heavy and slack. She could smell stress—sweat actually, which she could feel on the skin of her legs above her stockings, and under her bra, unpleasantly damp and slippery and redolent. Had she won, or had she lost? She clenched her fists and tried to dissipate the oppressive tension in her chest.

She stared at the stack of files that had been waiting for her attention when she left this office a quarter of an hour ago—responsibilities that were no longer hers.

She put her hand on one: Baker & Company. She had developed a fascination with the benefit the harassed Baker could possibly obtain from Section 547(b) of the Bankruptcy Code, and she had written a memorandum suggesting a novel approach to the application of that section. Not her problem now.

She opened another folder and looked at her notes and computer printouts. A problem of Florida real-estate law. Mercantile was in deep trouble if it did not have secure title to the beachfront properties it had pledged as security for borrowing. Her research had produced some old Florida cases that looked good for the validity of the titles. An interesting problem.

A finding by the insurance commissioner of the state of Ohio held Master Life inadequately underwritten. Ohio law. Simplistic. So simple that the line between compliance and non-compliance was frustratingly clear—and Master Life was on the wrong side of it. Her memorandum had come back with a curt note from Marx—"Find a way around this!" Well . . . let Marx find his own way around it.

Haggard was engaged in a buy-back—that is, it was buying back its own stock from ten thousand stockholders, diminishing the number of people who owned it, in the hope that its chief managers could take absolute control. What rights would remain to stockholders who held out? This one was going to litigation unless a formula could be devised that would satisfy the recalcitrant stockholders. There was extreme time pressure on this one, plus equally unpleasant personalities on both sides. A plague on both their houses, she had said. Still . . . she had felt proud of her closely reasoned analysis and the recommendations the firm would adopt and carry to the client.

Fifteen minutes ago she had been a partner in one of the city's—in fact, one of the nation's—most prestigious law firms. Now she was . . . She shrugged. What? When she walked out of here in a little while, she would not even have a business telephone.

She drew a breath and rejected the thoughts that had been forming in spite of her determination not to let them form and oppress her. She had planned for this day; she had known what was likely to happen and had rehearsed it, not just what she might say but what she would do, how she would allow herself to react. She resented her dry mouth and the heaviness inside her. She damned Miller and Nash, but she damned her wavering self-control more.

Telephone . . . She turned and picked up the white telephone on her credenza. she touched the numbers to call her father's office.

"Betty? Cosima. Is Daddy available? Oh . . . okay. Well, tell him I'll be coming by this evening. Need a ride out to Greenwich."

Yes. A ride to Greenwich. God! what would he say?

As she spoke to her father's secretary, an idea came to her mind, and she flipped through her Rolodex to find another telephone number. The New York *Law Journal*. She touched the numbers, got an answer on the fifth ring, and got through from the receptionist to the editorial offices.

"Max? Cosima Bernardin. How's journalism? Right. Okay. Hey, my friend, I got a story for you. Guess what? Yours truly quit Hamilton, Schuyler this morning. Yup. Quit. Understand, I don't particularly care if you run it as a story, but I don't want to see one saying they fired me. Right. You know how it goes. Same old . . . yeah. No, not 'mutual agreement.' I *quit*. Me. *My* decision. No big news story, but I want you to know that's how it was. Ignore the whole deal or run it straight—I resigned. Wasn't asked to. My own idea. One hundred percent. Right. No, I don't know yet. Uh-huh. Well, lunch, I can't, but how about a drink, say five-thirty? Digger's? Five-thirty. You got it. Looking forward to it. 'Bye, Max."

Putting down the telephone, she felt better. That was *functioning*, to see to it that the story, if any, would be the way she wanted it.

She punched Rick Loewenstein's number. He answered.

"Rick? Gussy. You are talking to an unemployed lawyer."

"Technically speaking, you shouldn't be seen in my company."

"Technically speaking," said Loewenstein, "it has been, uh, forty-eight days since it was anyone's business in whose company I am seen."

"You're talking about your divorce. I'm talking about the firm."

They sat on a bench in a small park overlooking South Street Viaduct and the East River. A tug churned past, pulling a deep-loaded garbage scow against the incoming tide. Gulls circled the scow. The wind was fresh and cool but insufficient to spare the streets and parks above the river from an occasional moment of sour stench. A girl walked four dogs past Cosima and Rick, stopping occasionally to let one of them defecate, then carefully scooping up the mess with a short-handled tool and dropping it in a plastic bag. Children ran shrieking, throwing a rubber ball among them. Two mothers yelled at them to stay close. Two young Hispanics, unable not to look menacing even to two people not in the least disposed to think of them as menacing, walked by, smoking marijuana and talking rapid New York street Spanish that would have been as incomprehensible to a European Spaniard as it was to Cosima and Rick.

"I suppose it's true," said Loewenstein, "that all the big firms are roughly the same. Anyway, it doesn't make any difference—you can never get into another one. Out of Hamilton, Schuyler, you are out of them all."

"I wanted to show you the letter," she said. She folded the wrapper from the hot dog she had just finished—bought from a street vendor and delectable. Opening her bag, she took out an envelope. "Delivered just before I left for lunch."

Loewenstein took the letter from the envelope and read:

Dear Miss Bernardin:

This letter will confirm the substance of the discussion between us in my office this morning, during which we agreed it would be in your best interest as

31

well as that of Hamilton, Schuyler, Depew & Chase if we were to terminate your partnership in the firm, effective immediately.

Your accrued compensation and various benefits will be paid to you in accordance with the terms of the partnership agreement you signed when you became a partner. You have a copy. If you have any question about any element of this, please let me know.

Allow me to remind you, Miss Bernardin, both of the terms of the partnership agreement and of the Code of Professional Responsibility regarding any possible future solicitation by you of the legal business of clients of Hamilton, Schuyler, Depew & Chase.

We have been pleased to have you associated with our firm, during your years as an associate and during your brief tenure as a partner. We wish you every success in whatever endeavor you elect to pursue in the future.

Cordially yours,

D. Douglas Miller

Rick Loewenstein grinned. "Bastards," he said, chuckling.

Cosima put the envelope back in her bag. "Whatever endeavor I elect to pursue," she said bitterly.

"Hey! You're not feeling sorry for yourself? Gussy, *you could have stayed!* They wouldn't have fired you. Even after you spoke up, they wouldn't have. They don't like to have people leave the firm. It's a loose end for them, something outside their control. They'd have kept you—"

"As a serf," she said.

He shrugged. "Sure. A quarter-million-dollar-a-year peon." He laughed. "People would get down on their knees and beg for what you walked away from. C'mon, Gussy."

His good humor was notorious at Hamilton, Schuyler. Some disliked the way others caught it from him. It was hard not to catch it. It surrounded his eyes, of course, in wrinkles that deepened when his whole face beamed in the celebrated Loewenstein smile. It was a generous smile that spread and exposed his teeth, lifting his cheeks to his eyes. His lower lip was heavy and mobile. His brows were bushy. Every morning he brushed his thick, unruly brown hair back over his ears, and by mid-morning every day it was loose, falling entirely over his ears, drooping almost to his eye on one side of his forehead.

Needless to say, he was an expressive talker. He used his hands. He varied the pitch of his voice. He stood sometimes, slack-shouldered, with his hands pushed deep into the pockets of his jacket or trousers, and gently argued people out of judgments fixed so firmly they thought they would never surrender them. Six-feet-four, he looked down on most people, and bent forward over them as if he did not wish to take advantage.

Cosima shrugged and repeated—"Whatever endeavor I elect to pursue. Uh . . . you should get back. Somebody is counting the minutes of your lunch hour."

He grinned. "Hell with 'em," he said. "Hey. We came over here so we could retreat to my apartment if you'd like." He pointed at an undistinguished redbrick apartment building on Market Street. "Tenth floor. New bachelor quarters for the new bachelor."

"Why, Mr. Loewenstein," she said, mocking a southern accent. "Is this an indelicate proposition?"

His smile disappeared. Cosima knew very well that the smile was not shallow, that a complex personality lay behind it. He nodded. "Absolutely," he said quietly. "An indecent proposition. But"—the smile crept back, covering something as it often did—"It's probably the wrong day for it. I haven't checked with my astrologer, much less my shrink. A drink, Gussy, if you want. Or—a decent flat with plenty of crying towels, yours for the day while I go back to the office."

"I'll take the drink," she said.

He had a long, spare living room, with a long, steel-framed window overlooking the river and across to the Brooklyn waterfront. The furniture was new and undistinguished—the impulse purchases of a sudden bachelor. The apartment, with this room and its tiny kitchen and one bedroom, had the aspect of a suite in a Holiday Inn. He had a music system in which he took a bit of pride: amplifier, speakers, and a digital-disk player. She appraised his books, as she always did whenever she first visited someone's home. History. Biography. Science. He had made bookshelves from raw boards and concrete blocks.

He cast aside the jacket of his lawyer-blue suit, loosened his tie and opened a cabinet to show her what he could offer for a drink. She took Courvoisier.

"The daughter of Leon Bernardin," he said when they were seated on his couch with two brandies, "doesn't have to practice law with Hamilton, Schuyler or anyone else."

"The daughter of Leon Bernardin," she said, "was left a legacy by her grandmother and could spend her life skiing in Switzerland, swimming on the Riviera, and . . . and, well . . . whatever. And the daughter of Leon Bernardin, so doing, would have to live with the vocal disdain of her parents and siblings all her life—not to mention that the daughter of Leon Bernardin would wither of boredom and shame. Seriously, Rick. I mean it."

"Gussy—"

"My sister, Emilie McCarthy, represents the Eighteenth Congressional District of New Jersey, third term. My brother Charles is Erlanger Professor of Astronomy, Columbia. Brother Pierre is a vice president of Beiser & Company. Susanne, my sister married to Albert Wilkinson, was national amateur women's tennis champion. My brother-

34

in-law, Albert Wilkinson, produces "What's News?," CBS. Rick—"

"What do you want me to do, crawl under the couch?"

Cosima shook her head forcefully. "I'm sorry. Please forgive me. And please understand."

"My father sold shoes in a store on Lexington Avenue from 1938 to 1972," said Loewenstein. "I have a sister. She has three children by her first husband, who was a machinist, and two by her second, who is a meat cutter."

"Rick, please."

"I want to do better," he said.

"But if you don't, they won't scorn you," she said.

"But *your* family would?"

Cosima licked her lips. "Something like that." The thought of how her father would react to the news she had resigned from her law firm constricted her chest.

"Gussy . . . really?"

She nodded. "It's a matter of expectations. The children of Leon Bernardin are expected—"

"You exaggerate," he interrupted. "Surely—"

"Like a stable of race horses. Each one is expected to win the Kentucky Derby."

"Gussy."

"We've always had a pool table in our house in Greenwich," she interrupted. "It has always been Daddy's rule, though, that no one can touch the pool table except really to play pool—I mean, to learn to play, to practice or to compete. As Daddy always put it, we were welcome to play on the table but not to play around on it. Well . . . when my sister Susanne, the one who plays tennis, was about fourteen she broke Daddy's rule. She'd sneak in the game room when he was in the city and she thought no one was around to notice, and she'd just bang the balls around. She liked to knock the balls around hard, not trying to learn to play, just—"

"Just having fun," said Loewenstein dryly.

"Maybe. Anyway, Daddy found out, and he told Su-

35

sanne she had broken his rule—defied it, actually—and would have to be punished. He said he was going to give her a spanking. But then he told her he wouldn't spank her if she learned to play pool. He gave her a month to learn and set her a goal: she would have to play him a game of fifty-ball straight pool, and she had to make thirty-five balls while he was making fifty. He'd play her two or three games, so she would have a fair chance, but if she couldn't do it, then she would be spanked for breaking his rule."

"So what happened?"

"I was a little girl," Cosima continued. "I'd go down to the game room at three in the morning sometimes, because I could hear the balls clicking, and Susanne would be there, practicing. Practicing, practicing."

"Was she afraid?"

Cosima laughed. "No! Not afraid. He wouldn't have spanked her very hard! That wasn't the point. What counted with her was that he had set her a challenge, and she'd be damned if she'd fail to meet it. What she was thinking about all those nights wasn't the spanking if she didn't succeed, it was the satisfaction she'd have when she played him and did make her thirty-five balls. Or maybe beat him. That was what she really wanted—to beat him."

"I suppose she made it," said Loewenstein.

"No. In fact, she didn't. But she made twenty-four, I think it was, and on the second try she made twenty-eight. And he was pleased. He said she played well—well enough. This was on a Saturday morning, and he took her out afterward and bought her her own jointed cue. They played often after that, as long as Susanne lived at home. She is the only one of us who can really compete with him on the pool table. The rule still stands. None of the rest of us can touch that table—because we never troubled ourselves to learn to play."

"Do you recommend this kind of thing as a way of living?" asked Loewenstein.

Cosima shrugged. "Whether I recommend it or not

makes no difference," she said. "Anyway, don't think there was any cruelty. My father said to Susanne—'If you're going to play a game, play it well. Play to win.' So she did—she learned to play well enough to win. She was happy. He was happy."

"Do you think you'll get a spanking when you tell your father you are no longer a partner at Hamilton, Schuyler?"

"My family doesn't take defeat lightly," Cosima said earnestly. "I don't know if they'll think I've been defeated or not."

"Sounds grim," said Rick. "Judgment—"

"It isn't grim," she interrupted. "We have more fun together than any other family I know."

"Family . . ." he mused. "I love my father and mother, and I suppose I love my sister. What else can I do? They're my family, whether I like it or not. But they don't judge me. They know I'd resent it."

"You can be sure they judge you," said Cosima. "I expect they're very proud of you."

"The conversation just deteriorated. What became of candor?"

"I happen to think it's true," she replied.

Loewenstein stood. "Do you want another drink?" he asked.

"One more," she said.

He poured more brandy for her but did not take more for himself. "I'll be going back to the office shortly," he said, as if by way of explanation. "My master calls."

"I am now without a master," said Cosima.

"I meant my conscience," he said. "Whatever you call it. For me, it can't be the Protestant ethic, obviously. Anyway, I feel uncomfortable not working during working hours." He paused, smiled feebly. "To admit the truth, I don't feel entirely comfortable not working during *any* hours. That's how I lost Lydia, according to her."

"You and Hamilton, Schuyler are a good match."

37

"Not so good. Don't think I haven't been tempted to tell them off and walk out."

"Oh, but everyone feels that way, sometime or other," she said. "D. Douglas Miller himself included, I imagine. Maybe not Dan Nash."

Loewenstein handed her the glass. "So, anyway, I do have to go back. I have a stack of files—well, you know. But look, I—" He opened a drawer. "Here's a key. Think of this place as yours, Gussy. Anytime you want. You're going to need a headquarters for a while. A phone. Look, we can change the message on my telephone answering machine, so you can give this number to anyone you want and—"

"Rick, I can't just take over your—"

"Nobody calls me at home. Not during the day, anyway. You really are going to need a headquarters in the city, Gussy. You really are."

"You are a generous man."

She watched him thoughtfully as he tightened his necktie and put on his jacket. Moved by a quick impulse, she rose and went to him and kissed him: on the cheek, not the mouth, more happily than ardently, still, a fond, sustained kiss, with her arms around him, followed by an affectionate nuzzle along the side of his neck before she separated from him. He reached for her, and instantly she realized a spontaneous kiss was far more significant to him than it was to her. So would be forbidding him another kiss. She let him seize her and kiss her tenderly on the lips.

Without intending, she had breached the dam of that filled reservoir of solemnity behind his easy smile.

"Gussy . . . ?"

She shook her head. "Not yet, Rick," she said. "Not now."

After Rick left, Cosima took a shower. She let her underclothes air before an open window while she bathed and refreshed her makeup. Feeling better, fresher, she returned to the offices of Hamilton, Schuyler in the late middle part of the afternoon. She took a cab. She could not endure Rick's roundabout subway ride, with transfer.

It was better for Rick, she thought, that they had not been seen returning together, and it would be better too if they were not seen leaving together. In the office, she avoided him.

She found her personal desk things and the prints from her walls already packed in brown cartons. The stacks of files had been removed from her desk. The little room—which certainly she would never miss—looked abandoned and stark. People hurried by her in the hall; they spoke cordially enough, but they were resolutely rushed, conspicuously pressed.

Except Joan Salomon, a lawyer from Webster, Kent, Harriman & McCoy, who happened to have been in the office for a meeting with a Hamilton, Schuyler lawyer that afternoon. Joan and Cosima had been introduced two years ago at a conference for woman lawyers, a meeting that neither of them found worth her time. They had repaired to the bar to laugh about the obsessive seriousness of the conferees and had so become friends. They had lunch together from time to time, and met for drinks after work. When Joan spied Cosima sitting at a bare desk, she rushed in and closed the door.

"Hey. What's going on?"

Joan was smoking; and, knowing Cosima didn't, looked around for a place to crush her cigarette. Seeing the state of things, she shrugged and crushed it on the windowsill.

Joan Salomon was a six-year partner at Webster, Kent. She was a specialist in pension-fund arrangements, in fact that firm's number-two expert in that complex and abstruse field of law. She was thirty-eight years old, though her chain-smoking had aged her, roughening both her skin and her voice. Her hair, of an uncertain blond-brown color, fell over her forehead and around her neck. Except for her tobacco habit, she was not unattractive, but she had never married—a fact she did not choose to explain.

"Well?" she persisted bluntly. "The halls are full of rumors—every variety you could ask for."

"I resigned my partnership," said Cosima quietly. "They took Bull Dog Fangs from me and gave it to Dan Nash. I was to work strictly under his supervision. I refused."

"Jesus Christ . . . Nash. I always supposed he must be good for something, but I could never figure out what it might be. So you quit. Or they fired you. The word's around, you know, that you were fired."

"Whoever says that is lying," said Cosima. "Even the letter they gave me says agreed to separate. The truth is, Joan—I *quit*."

Joan Salomon shook her head. "They'll never acknowledge it. They'll put the word around that they asked you to quit, you quit, and if you hadn't they'd have fired you. And they've got ten thousand vague reasons, any one of which will suit the people that want to believe them. They're going to close doors for you, Cosima. I'm sorry, but they've got the word going in the office already this afternoon."

"No other big firm will ever take me," said Cosima. "No matter what word Hamilton, Schuyler circulates. You only have one chance in this divine brotherhood, you blow that one chance, you're gone, it doesn't make any difference why."

"So what are you going to do?"

"God knows."

Joan Salomon reached across the desk and put her hand on Cosima's. "Let me know," she said. "For sure. Keep in touch. I mean it, Cosima. I want to know what you're going to do. Not many of us have the guts to walk away, and I want to know how it works out."

Cosima nodded. "I'll do it, Joan," she said. "You'll hear from me."

* * *

She was a few minutes late arriving at Digger's Bar on lower Broadway. Max Wilmot, from the New York *Law Journal,* was already there. A heavy man, some ten years older than Cosima, he was at the bar with a stein of dark beer, watching the door. He broke away from two men who had engaged him in conversation and hurried toward her.

"I'm honored," he said to her. "I got to thinking about it. This is a big day for you, and you take an hour of it to see me—I'm honored."

"I'm a little weary, Max," she said. "I don't mind telling you. I'm a little tired."

"Bar stool or—"

"Sure. Why not?"

He led her to where he had been, and the two men who had been talking with him moved to make room for the tall, striking young woman. They were two young partners from Milbank, Tweed, Hadley & McCloy. Max introduced her, and once they heard her name they identified her—Leon Bernardin's youngest daughter, Harvard Law '81, new partner at Hamilton, Schuyler, Depew & Chase, and one of the most fascinating and eligible young women in New York. The perfunctory character of Max's introduction had told them plainly that he meant for them to say hello and not remain for conversation; but both of them instantly turned bright and chatty.

Max was tolerant. He was patient. While the two young lawyers essayed drollery in the transparent hope of making an impression on Cosima, he ordered her a beer; and as they began to edge away, protesting that they really wished they could stay and talk to her, he used his pudgy fingers to wipe a trace of beer foam out of his stringy mustache.

When she and Max were alone—as alone as they could be in a crowded, smoky bar—she saluted him with her heavy stein of beer and, glancing around, relaxed a measure: a measure she could use just then. Digger's was a relaxing place, one of her favorites. Beer was the favorite drink here, beer and martinis, depending on the kind of day people had

41

had. Big bowls of peanuts sat everywhere, and drinkers cracked them and tossed the shells on the floor, where they crushed constantly underfoot. The walls were hung with signed photographs of the movers and shakers who had relaxed here since the repeal of Prohibition—and even before.

"So. You bade farewell to Hamilton, Schuyler, Depew & Chase," said Max, cracking a peanut between thumb and forefinger and pushing the kernels into his mouth.

"Not exactly," she said. "It was really weird. When I left, no one said good-bye. No one said anything. It was as if I were coming in again in the morning. Only they knew I wasn't. The word was around."

He smiled sardonically beneath his damp mustache. "Were you surprised?" he asked.

"I suppose not," she said. "But . . . but it was distressing to learn how quickly—and how thoroughly—I'd become a nonperson. I mean, Max, it was as if I'd never worked there!"

"You realize," he said, "that they will try to prevent your working anywhere else."

"You are the second person who's said that to me in the past couple of hours."

"You didn't just quit a job, Cosima. You controverted the dogma by which tens of thousands of lawyers live their lives."

Cosima smiled. "Giganticism. Rhinocerosism," she said.

Max nodded. "Organizationism. Structurism. Did you read what Chief Justice Rehnquist said on this?"

She shook her head. "Not one of my heroes."

"Nor of mine. But he made a speech last summer in Indiana—said that the growth of giant firms is debasing the practice of law. I couldn't agree more. Things that used to count with lawyers don't count so much these days. Professionalism. Ethics . . ."

Cosima looked away to nod at a vice president from Bernardin Frères who was making his way toward a table in the rear. "I don't know, Max," she sighed. "I'm not sure

42

my situation says anything about the state of the profession."

"Well, it does in a sense," he said. "You have to find a new berth, and the other big firms are going to shut their doors to you."

"Oh, I know that."

"In my combined profession—putting law and journalism together, you know—I get around a lot, hear a lot. I know a dozen young partners who've left big firms in the past six months, and not one of them was able to move to another firm. Let me guess. You didn't make a booboo, you bucked the hierarchy."

"Yes . . ."

"The cardinal sin. Hierarchy is the sine qua non of structure, structure is the sine qua non of bigness, and bigness—if you accept today's business dogma—is the sine qua non of maximum profit. Ergo, insubordination threatens profit. Insubordinate juniors endanger the seniors' profit shares."

"They couldn't point to a mistake I'd made," she said quietly. "Or wouldn't."

"Insubordination is the unforgivable mistake, the one unpardonable offense. And, of course, it's the one without a name. They don't like to talk about it."

She smiled. She always enjoyed Max, even if she did not accept all his ideas. "They like to talk about quality," she said, anticipating that would inspire some further sally.

"Sure they do. Like manufacturers of automobiles and washing machines. And a client gets from them exactly as much quality as they can deliver without hurting profit. Everything is based on computerized cost accounting, which treats quality as a cost. Too much quality hurts the bottom line."

"In spite of the fact that I've just left Hamilton, Schuyler," she said, "I still think the big firms turn out the high-quality legal work."

"You were brainwashed to that effect," said Max. "For a big organization, quality is a measurable cost factor, so they dole it out sparingly. Seriously, Cosima, the giant firms do nothing that small firms can't do better.''

"You say, 'can't do better.' *Do* they do better? I don't see that. I don't see them doing it.''

"You would if you looked. Cosima, if I had a tax problem, let us say, I wouldn't think of taking it to Hamilton, Schuyler or any other giant. I could be represented just as well, maybe better, by any one of half a dozen lawyers I know personally, who practice in ten-man, twenty-man offices—and charge half the fees.''

"Then why do all the big corporate clients go to the big firms?''

"Lots of reasons. Big companies are big law firms' raison d'être. Big firms exist to serve big companies. They never disagree with them. They share a common philosophy and a common language.''

Cosima smiled as she lifted her stein of beer. "Rhinocerosism,'' she said.

Max crunched another peanut shell and shoved kernels between his lips. "Girl with your talent . . .'' he said. "I can give you a job. I'd do anything in the world to have you on my staff at the paper, Cosima—anything, that is, but pay you what it would take to get you. You decide you want to do something good for the profession . . .''

"I'll keep it in mind.''

"No.'' He shook his head. "What you ought to do is find one of those small firms, one of those I'm talking about, with ten or twenty lawyers, and practice law where old-fashioned commitment to the traditions of the profession means as much as the bottom line.''

"Name one for me, Max,'' she said.

"Are you serious?'' he asked. "Would you consider a small firm?''

"What choice do I have?''

"You have other choices,'' he said. "Really. But I'll put the word out if you want me to.''

"I can't sit back and live off my legacy,'' she said.

Three

"Your mother," said Leon Bernardin, "will join us as soon as her television show is over. Dinner will then be served—when the show is over."

"What's she watching?" asked Emilie, Cosima's oldest sister.

"I am not sure what it is called," said Leon Bernardin. "I should guess something like 'The Beach Police Helicopter Jiggly Girls.' Does that sound like something possible?"

Emilie McCarthy—she was the congresswoman from New Jersey—laughed and raised her glass in toast to her father's wit. She had never learned to compete with him on the pool table, but she shared his fondness for martinis made with Bombay gin. His eldest child, she was forty-six: a bulky, formidable woman who made no effort to conceal the fact that her hair was graying or that her face had become deeply lined. Nor did she trouble herself with the fact that she was a few pounds overweight. Dressed in the black she thought complemented her most—though it was a spring evening—she was a little uneasy for the want of a cigarette but would not smoke in her father's presence.

Cosima, who had almost failed to make it home to Greenwich without asking her father's driver to stop at a station along the road and let her relieve herself of the beer she had drunk with Max Wilmot, was sipping very sparingly from one of the martinis her father so much esteemed. She could not imagine herself taking too much to drink in the presence of her father, any more than she could have let herself ask Frank to stop the car to let her empty her bladder.

"I bought pounds today," said Leon Bernardin. "Sterling futures. At $1.648. Very good, you know. The market discounts them too much. I shall be surprised if they don't open at $1.65 on Monday and move to $1.67 by Wednesday."

Neither of his daughters could discuss this with him. They simply stared blankly. He smiled. It had been fun to tell them, but he did not continue with the topic.

"Well, tell us about Hamilton, Schuyler," said Emilie to Cosima.

Cosima glanced at her father, feeling vaguely that she needed his permission to go into that subject. "Not much to tell," she said. "I brought in a good client. They took it away from me. I refused to let them do that. They insisted. I quit."

"Will the client leave with you?" Emilie asked.

"I doubt it."

"To go where?" their father asked. "Cosima has no alternative as yet."

"Won't she join the bank?" Emilie asked.

"No," said Cosima.

None of them worked for Bernardin Frères. Every one of them could have. Cosima was not sure if her sister had made a disdainful suggestion or meant to create an option by the suggestion.

Leon Bernardin refreshed his martini from the pitcher on the silver tray. "No," he said. "Cosima doesn't want to do that."

So the option closed. It had never been open, really.

Cosima stood before the cold fireplace. The chimney had been cleaned for the season, and no fire would be lighted

46

again until fall. The room was as familiar to her as a room could be, yet it was like a hotel room she had occupied many times: too formal to be friendly.

The oil portrait above the mantel was traditionally of her great-grandfather, Claude Maurice Bernardin—though her father admitted he wasn't sure. In some sort of gaudy uniform, with epaulettes on his shoulders, he was supposedly a general in the army of Louis Napoleon. The family joke— at which others were not welcome to laugh—was that he had been ignominiously captured with the Emperor at Sedan in 1870. The furniture was Empire, some of it genuine antiques, most of it from stores in White Plains and Scarsdale.

They were drinking their martinis, though, from eighteenth-century stem crystal. Her father's joke about those was that god only knew where they came from, probably from the plunder some larcenous Bernardin had exacted from some impoverished French aristocrat in payment of a debt. If some of the Bernardins had been soldiers, most of them had been bankers, for five or six generations. It had long been difficult—another joke—to convince Americans they were not Jews.

Ordinarily, dinner would have been at half past eight. On a Friday night it might be, as it would be tonight, at nine. After her talk with Max Wilmot, Cosima had reached her father's office at seven. She had asked him to sit down there with her for a few minutes while she told him what had happened at Hamilton, Schuyler. They had left the office at seven-fifteen—a quarter of an hour late—for their drive to Greenwich. Because they arrived a little late, her mother had told them testily she would *watch* her television show instead of taping it, and dinner would have to wait.

This was no small matter. For Leon Bernardin, lunch was nothing—he didn't eat any; but breakfast and dinner were ritual occasions. Usually Cosima was not here for dinner, but her father had made it plain that if she wanted to ride into the city with him in the morning she should be here for breakfast. He read his newspapers in the car, but no newspaper was allowed at the breakfast table. Grapefruit was served every morning: halves in ice. Eggs. Ham and bacon. Toast. (Never any Danish, which her father scorned.) Coffee. Tea. Conversation was important—whoever was in the house was expected to be at the breakfast table, dressed, and ready to take part in a lively discussion, usually of the news—the main points of which would have been taken from the television sets in the bedrooms. At dinner the day's news was a forbidden topic. Over dinner one discussed books one had read, plays one had seen—rarely a television show. No business. No gossip. These rules had prevailed since before Cosima's birth. It had never occurred to her to challenge them, only to escape them.

Her father never drank until the cocktail hour before dinner. At the cocktail hour, though, he usually drank two or three of his martinis, which tempered him—as he intended—and then sipped wine with his dinner, in preparation for a restful night. He never played pool after dinner. His eye did not remain sharp.

"I have no great respect for big law firms," said Emilie. "I see a little of them in Washington. I won't kid you, Cosima, I wasn't enthusiastic about your affiliation."

"She was on the ladder to the top of her profession," said Leon.

"There must be many ladders," said Emilie.

"Actually, there are not," said Leon.

"To an extent," said Cosima, "I imagine that depends on how we define the top of the profession."

"The top of the profession," her father said categorically, "is partnership in a major Wall Street firm." (After the manner of New Englanders, he did not allow himself to say "furm" but pronounced the word "fearm.")

"How about a judgeship?" asked Emilie.

"A partner in a major firm earns five times the salary of a justice of the Supreme Court of the United States," said Leon.

48

"I'm not sure that top of the profession should be defined exclusively in terms of income earned," said Emilie. "I'd like to take other factors into consideration."

"Do so if you wish," said Leon. He tipped his glass. By that gesture and the tone of his voice he signaled that so far as he was concerned the conversation was finished.

And now Cosima knew his judgment.

"And so, a weekend, and I don't have any music," complained Elizabeth Bradford Bernardin, Cosima's mother. "Whatever could have been so important to both of you—"

"Cosima resigned from her law firm this morning, Mother," Emilie interrupted.

Elizabeth jerked her head around indignantly. "So. So, that was the great crisis."

"Just after you called, Mother," said Cosima.

Elizabeth had just come down from her bedroom, her clothes and hair reeking with cigarette smoke. She was wearing a heavy cardigan, rough knit, black and white, with a floppy collar. Her gray hair, once blond, was cut almost as short as Cosima's, but it was coarse and unmanageable, as it had always been, and wisps of the high tangle on top fell criss-cross down her forehead. Her blue eyes were hard, piercing—and weary, as always.

"Tuesday evening," she said. "I am playing the piece for the Schubert Club. I said I'd play it. Well, it certainly won't be very polished."

"You could have telephoned and had it sent downtown, as I suggested," said Cosima.

Elizabeth shrugged. She pulled her chair closer to the dining room table and with her foot touched the buzzer button under the carpet: the signal for the cook to begin serving dinner. "So on Monday . . . ?" she asked.

"I'll get your music," said Cosima.

"Thank you."

"Unless she comes to Washington with me, which I was

about to suggest," said Emilie. She turned toward Cosima. "I'm not suggesting the government. I'm thinking of a Washington firm."

"I appreciate it, Emilie," said Cosima. "But I think I'll see what doors are slammed in my face in New York before I think about moving to another city."

"Doors slammed?" Elizabeth asked. "What has happened?"

Cosima frowned. She realized that no one had told her mother anything. She could have called her during the day . . . "Mother. You remember Ruggiero Paccinelli, don't you? His music group has become a very big business, generating tens of millions of dollars a year. I brought him to our firm as a client. Today, six months later, the firm announced to me that they were taking him away from me as a client and giving him to another lawyer. I refused to accept that and resigned from the firm rather than accept it."

"Good," said Elizabeth.

Leon was eyeing a bottle of Bordeaux with a censorious eye. He poured a splash in his glass and tasted. "She walked away from a quarter-of-a-million-dollar job," he said. "An expensive bit of petulance."

"Hardly petulance," said Emilie. "A matter of principle, I'd call it."

"If one wants to establish a principle," said Leon, "one can do it more effectively after a success than after a failure."

Cosima stared at the tablecloth, holding back tears.

"Oh, well," said her mother.

Elizabeth's attention was focused now on the wine, as she waited for Leon to pour for her. Her span of attention was very short when it came to matters of business and money. Except for three calls a week to her trust officer at State Street Bank in Boston for a briefing on her investments, she had no further time for such things. Cosima would never forget what her mother had once said about money: "You know, god said, 'Let there be light,' and there *was* light.

Well, great-great-grandfather or somebody made money, and there *is* money. There just is, that's all." Leon, too, had inherited, though not as happily as she, but he had proved heir also to a genius for increase. Her bland optimism remained unshakeable.

Elizabeth Bradford Bernardin was a pianist. She was a graduate of Juilliard and had studied under eminent teachers. In her own judgment, she was an artist who might have been world-renowned, except for a girlish infatuation with the charismatic French financier Leon Bernardin, followed by marriage, followed by successive pregnancies—a prolonged interruption in her career that had robbed her of its promise. During the seasons of 1968 through 1971 she had toured and had soloed with orchestras like the Omaha Symphony, the Indianapolis Symphony, the Columbus Symphony and the Louisville Orchestra. Since she was not asked to appear with such orchestras as the Boston Symphony, the Philadelphia Orchestra or the New York Philharmonic— and it became plain she never would—she decided the concert tours were not worth the sacrifice and discipline they required. Now, at sixty-five she played nothing more demanding than solo performances for the Greenwich Schubert Club, the Greenwich Philharmonia and the Stamford Symphony, plus accompanist chores for violinists and singers.

Elizabeth tasted the wine she had waited impatiently for Leon to pour. "Matter of dignity, I suppose," she said, an afterthought about Cosima's news having apparently occurred to her. "Matter of integrity." She turned to Cosima and smiled. "Fortunately for you, Cosima, you can afford dignity and integrity."

Emilie laughed, but Leon didn't.

"I'm serious,' said Elizabeth. "They are luxuries. Mr. Nixon, for example, seems to have thought he couldn't afford them. Poor little Mr. Ford, apparently, thought the same. It was fortunate for the nation that Joseph Kennedy had stolen enough while his son was a child to make it pos-

51

sible for President Kennedy to conduct himself honorably in office.''

Now Cosima laughed.

"My father always said it was better for wealthy men to hold all important public offices," said Elizabeth, "for the obvious reasons."

"Tomorrow . . . ?" Emilie asked Cosima.

"Saturday," said Cosima. "I'd have had to go in and work. Now . . ." She smiled, shrugged.

"I'm thinking of a round of golf," said Emilie. "A weekend in Connecticut. I don't get very many."

"Are you taking the boat out, Daddy?" Cosima asked.

"Whether I do or don't, feel welcome to do it yourself," he answered.

"I'd rather sail than play golf," Cosima said to Emilie. "Could I tempt you away from the club?"

Emilie grinned. "If you promise not to work me too hard," she said.

Cosima drove a red Porsche Carrera, which had been in her parent's driveway all day. She left at eleven. She drove south from back-country Greenwich to the town itself, to "The Avenue," as locals called the long shop-lined street that sloped down to the water of Long Island Sound. At eleven-ten, The Avenue was all but deserted, except for people leaving the movie theaters and a few teenagers hanging around a pizza parlor. There were no traffic lights on The Avenue. During the day policemen stood in the middle of the intersections and controlled traffic by arm signal, also giving directions to people who stopped in mid-intersection to ask where such-and-so a store was, or which way it was to the beach. After eleven, Cosima cruised the entire length of the street without stopping. When finally she reached the bottom, the traffic light seemed to her as it did to all Greenwichers a rude violation of the traditions of the town that called itself "Gateway to New England" and that paid a heavy price to preserve a meticulously contrived New England character against the encroachment of New York City, only twenty-five miles away.

The shortest way to her apartment was by the New England Turnpike, and she turned into it, accelerated the Porsche to sixty miles per hour, and covered the two miles to her exit in two minutes.

She lived in a condominium overlooking Cos Cob Harbor and the Sound. It was a clear night, and as she parked her car she could see lights on the north shore of Long Island. She had the same view from her terrace and from her living room through the glass doors. After she had turned off the alarm system and before she switched on the lights, she stood at the doors for a moment and stared at the flashing strobes of an airplane on an approach to Westchester Airport. Then, because she wanted her privacy, she pulled the drapes.

The red light was burning on her telephone-answering recorder. She had just one message, from Ruggiero Paccinelli. He had called about ten, said the group was playing a concert in a Chicago theater, and that he would call her again later, maybe as late as two A.M. eastern time. She could let the recorder take the call if she didn't want to talk then. She smiled and shook her head. Jerry. Two o'clock in the morning. It wouldn't be the first time he had called at that hour.

She had put on a pot of coffee, which would brew while she showered. She might be awake at two, maybe not; but she would be awake an hour or so yet, anyway. A cup or two of coffee. A splash of brandy. She wanted to wind down, alone, with no necessity to react to anyone. She was in the midst of Gore Vidal's *Creation,* which she had put off reading for years and now found engrossing. She might check the Carson show tonight; sometimes she enjoyed it. Anyway, she was alone, and she was glad; it was time to be alone.

After she showered, she pulled on a pair of panties, nothing more. She poured her coffee and a sparing drink of Courvoisier, settled into a corner of her couch with her bare

53

feet up and lent her attention to the adventures of Cyrus Spitama, as told by Vidal—writing she found piquant and stimulating.

She read for more than an hour before she became drowsy and found herself losing track of the story. She dozed. She woke with a start and realized she had slept for a long time. The apartment was filled with the bitter smell of coffee left too long over heat. An astringent odor rose from the residue of brandy in the snifter that sat within her reach.

Cosima sat up and shrugged herself awake. Then she remembered bits of the dream that had troubled her sleep and had perhaps wakened her. The memory was confused; the dream had been meaningless, as all dreams are, yet it had generated emotions that persisted after she was awake. It was unusual for her to waken and find it difficult to shake off the fear from a nightmare, not unusual to find it hard to dispel the residual irritation of a dream in which she had been frustrated and annoyed.

This was more complex, and it was beyond doubt the product of what had happened to her that morning. The dream had involved self-criticism; worse, self-condemnation—in it she had damned herself for a failure.

An element of it was a recurrent chimera based on the spring when she graduated from Harvard Law. Her class rank—eighth—had troubled her. It was not a standing that would produce offers from the firms she wanted to join. In fact, she had not received offers from the firms that had been her first choices: Coudert Brothers, which she had hoped might assign her to its Paris office, or Cleary, Gottlieb, Steen & Hamilton, which also had a large Paris office. The most painful humiliation of her life had been a meeting with her father, to whom she had to confess she had no offers from the first-rank firms she wanted to join.

"Why wait for offers?" he had asked. "*We* don't wait for offers. We go and get offers."

"It isn't done that way, Daddy," she had said.

54

"Oh, no? How about Hamilton, Schuyler, Depew & Chase? They owe me a favor. I'll call for it."

Which he had done. Within two days she had received a call from Clarence Paul Davidson. Within a week she was sitting at lunch with him and three of his partners. Within ten days she had an offer.

It had been widely known at the firm that she had procured her offer that way. She had encountered resentment among other young lawyers in the firm.

You meet that, her father had said, by doing well. *Let* them resent you. To hell with them. So you got in by using a resource they didn't have. Now you use another resource they may not have—an exceptional order of ability—to climb above them. Maybe law school was an insufficient challenge for you. Maybe that's why you didn't commit yourself enough to graduate at the head of your class. Well . . . I think you will find a sufficient challenge in what you are undertaking now.

He had said something like that. The way he said it in her dreams was more vivid than the memory of what had been only a few casual comments given on the dock as they were boarding the boat. His casual words had always had more impact on her than his considered statements. They came from his feelings, and his feelings always touched her more deeply than his statements. Anyway, his words had returned in the dream, in some form or other, accompanied by a wrathful scowl that was wholly of the dream.

Also, she had dreamed she was naked in public. This too, was a dream she had repeatedly. In it she would decide quite consciously, and rationally, to go somewhere naked, only to discover after arriving that she was the only naked person there. She never panicked, never fled. She was never painfully humiliated by her nakedness, only tormented by a sense of dreadful impropriety. She would awake with a sense that she had done something foolish and should be phoning around apologizing.

Cosima rose from the couch and went in the kitchen to

switch off the heat under the coffee and pour some Diet Coke over ice, for a cool drink that would help dispel sleep and the dream. She was cold, she realized as she stood in the kitchen. Her arms, her big, heavy breasts, her belly and hips, and her long legs were dry and cool. She carried her Coke into the bedroom and picked up a peignoir.

Oh, god . . . Jerry. Yes, Jerry had said he might call as late as two. She looked at the clock. It was only a little after one. She went back to the living room, to the couch. She was awake.

Damn dreams! You couldn't come to terms with them because you could not take them seriously. Some people said they did not remember a thing they dreamed. Neither did she in any specific sense; but shreds of dreams, plus the damned emotions, remained, paroxysmally grabbing in the bowels of her subconsciousness after small shreds of memory better left alone.

Like the way she had confessed to Father Joe, and then, a year later, had told Madeleine all about it, and . . .

"Father, forgive me, for I have sinned." "How have you sinned, Cosima?" "I let a boy . . . touch me." "How did he touch you, Cosima? Sinfully?" "Yes, Father." "In what way, Cosima? How and where did he touch you?" "On . . . on . . . on my boobies, Father." "Did he uncover them?" "Yes, Father." "He touched you on your bare breasts?" "Yes, Father." "Did he just touch them, or did he . . . rub them?" "He rubbed them." "Did you like it?" "Yes, Father." "Even though you knew it was a sin?" "Yes . . ." "It is a sin, Cosima. You sinned, and you let that boy sin, too. Touching your breasts is a preliminary, you see, to the procreative act. You know what I mean by that, don't you, Cosima?" "Yes . . ." "What is it called, Cosima?" "It . . . The word . . . It's called fucking, Father." "Yes. That's what it's called. Not a very pretty word, is it? Did he suggest you let him do that?" "No, Father." "But he will, Cosima. He will. Is he of our faith?" "No, Father. I . . . I don't think he has any faith." "So you are fourteen years old and are having an intimate relationship with an unchurched boy? Do your parents know?" "Well, no, not that . . ."

"You told him *everything?*" Madeleine had shrieked with laughter. "You are a fool, Cosima! In France we have learned to say, 'Father, mind your own business!' "

Madeleine had been her roommate and best friend at Pensionnat Passy, the Parisian school where she studied for two years. Roommates confessed everything to each other, with far more confidence than they vouchsafed to their priests. Madeleine had not only been touched on her breasts; she had been penetrated by a boy, with his big, bare organ. Cosima had not experienced that. But she had seen one: Don's, the boy who had rubbed her breasts, who later had become even bolder, as the priest had predicted. She had told Father Joe how it looked, how it felt to the touch of her fingers.

"You told him *that,* too?" Madeleine had snickered.

"Well, he asked me. And he granted me absolution."

"I should think so! You made his day! More correctly said, you made his night! He spurted in his bed that night, Cosima! After hearing *that* confession! I've done it to them myself, gave the pour souls something to excite them in their lonely nights. Fibs for their jollies!"

Others had done more than she, knew more than she. They made her feel . . . *American.* She had supposed the French schoolgirls, in their modest uniforms, were innocents, that she, the American, would be the sophisticate at Passy. In some ways they were naifs; but they didn't think they were; no, they were the heirs to an enviable old civilization, as Americans were not, and they insisted on keeping the American girls in their place as supplicants come to seek a modicum of refinement at its abounding source. Madeleine was kinder than most of them, but she could not help treating Cosima as an artless child. She had been unable, too, to resist telling other girls about how an American priest had induced the guileless Cosima to divert him with confessional tales of her pubescent carnal adventures. Cosima acquired a nickname that remained with her, not just at the school but to this day among her French friends.

They called her Perle, meaning Pearl; but it was a play on words, based on what they called Father Joe: Père Lu, short for Père Lubricité, Father Lubricity.

Maybe it had been while she was at Passy that she began to have the dream about going naked in public. Anyway, in the dream she often entered one of the classrooms there, the only naked girl in the room; invariably she sat and did her lesson, while the others smiled and tittered behind their hands. Perle was, after all, only an American.

She resented judgment. She could not resent her father's, but she resented everyone else's. That was what had happened to her this morning, and what had provoked her nightmares: she had been judged—and not favorably. Essentially, as she thought of herself, she was a strong, well-integrated personality. She was reminded often enough—too often, in fact—that she was fortunate in her heritage and her inheritance, but she believed she had done well with her resources and could be commended for what she had done as much as for what she was. To be judged—

Damn! She jumped up from the couch and went to the glass doors. Switching off the lights behind her, she opened the drapes and the doors and stepped out onto her terrace. Maybe the cool night air would clear her mind of the emotional litter of the day and the dream.

She did not notice the man on the water's edge three floors below. She had no idea he was there or that he saw her and stared intently at her as long as she stood on her terrace. She never would know, for he would not mention to anyone—certainly not to her—that he had seen her. He had come out of an apartment below and had walked down to the edge of the water, he too seeking release from something troubling him. She would never know that the distraction she afforded him, just standing there, yielded him the comfort he had come out to find.

He stood still, not wanting her to see him and withdraw inside her apartment. He could not remember ever having seen a more beautiful woman. The clean, white moonlight

58

modeled her in tones of gray, like a statue, sketching her
elegant simplicity in a few lines and planes. The peignoir
she was wearing was almost modest, yet, through its sheer
veil he could see the contours of her breasts—vague in this
light, yet exquisite and provocative. He could see that she
was wearing brief panties, and he was not sure if in the
crotch he saw just a shadow of her hair through the sheer
fabric. The peignoir ended just below her hips, and he could
see that her legs were long and firm-muscled.

He knew who she was. He knew he would never touch
her, would hardly ever speak a word to her. But he was
able, when she had gone back inside, to smile, kick a couple
of small rocks into the water, and return to his own apartment, renewed by the sight of her.

The telephone rang at eight minutes after two.

"Jerry. I wake you?"

"No. I napped for an hour between midnight and one.
Been reading since then."

"Hey, Cosima, what you got on?"

"None of your business."

"Well, I like to have an image of the people I talk to on
the telephone. Tell me you're nude, Cosima."

"Want to give me a second to get nude?"

"Yeah!"

She put down the telephone, but instead of pulling off the
peignoir and panties, she took a swallow of the Coke.
Then—"Okay, Jerry. Let your imagination run wild."

"Imagination . . . Damn! Hey, Cosima, I got a telephone call from some prick at Hamilton, Schuyler this afternoon—"

"Dan Nash," she interrupted.

"Right. Nash. He told me you're no longer with the firm
and that my files have been handed over to him."

"That's right."

"I don't follow that, honey. How come? Who's Nash,

and why do I get handed over to him whether I like it or not?"

"It's a matter of seniority, Jerry," she said. She picked up the Coke and sipped again. "I wasn't senior enough in the firm to handle a client who generates as much business as Fang, Incorporated."

"So . . . ?"

"So they took you away from me and gave you to a more senior lawyer."

"But why do they say you aren't with the firm anymore?"

"I quit, Jerry. When they told me this, I told them to shove it."

"Cosima—my god! Do I bear any responsibility for that?"

"No, not at all, Jerry."

"Well . . . This guy Nash. Is he any good?"

"I don't like him, but I'm sure he's a competent lawyer."

For a moment Paccinelli was silent, though she could hear him breathing. "Uh, do I have any choice in this matter? I mean, Nash just called and said he is my lawyer now. Whether I like it or not—and I'm not sure I like it."

"You don't have to accept him."

"How do I say no?"

"Call Douglas Miller. Or Clarence Davidson. Tell them you don't want Nash."

"Yeah, but Cosima Bernardin is not an option for me. You quit. Why didn't *you* call me? I'd have said fuck this. I—"

"I'm grateful, Jerry, but there was more involved. You'd have had to take another lawyer if you want to continue to be represented by Hamilton, Schuyler."

"I paid you guys a quarter of a million to—"

"You paid more than that. But it doesn't make you their biggest client by a very long shot. You are right when you say having me for your lawyer is not one of your options.

They wouldn't have given you that option for twice the fees.''

"Well, maybe I don't want Hamilton, Schoolyard for my lawyers anymore. Fuck 'em.''

"I'd think about that, Jerry. They're good. And it's expensive to move around.''

Another moment of silence. She could hear raucous noises in the background. "Hey, Cosima. Where *you* going to be?''

"Don't know, Jerry. Not another one of the big firms. I have to find another place.''

"Start your own firm,'' said Paccinelli quietly. "I can promise you one good client. Fang, Incorporated would be client enough for a start, wouldn't it?''

"I couldn't handle you, Jerry,'' she said. "You need tax work all the time, and I'm not a tax lawyer. You may have more copyright problems, and I'm not a copyright lawyer. I—''

"Hell, Cosima. I got a gig needs an extra electric fiddle, I *hire* an extra electric fiddle. You got a gig needs a tax man, *hire* a tax man. Don't lawyers hire around? Anyway, enough business, you can put a tax man in full-time. You and I can make a partnership. You be my main lawyer, and we'll hire what we need when we need it.''

"Jerry—''

"I'm serious, Cosima,'' he said. "I don't like getting a call from some asshole who tells me he's my lawyer now. He didn't ask if that was okay with me, he just told me. I heard arrogance in that voice if I've ever heard it in my life. To hell with that. I don't need that. I won't accept it.''

"I don't even have an office.''

"Well, *get* an office. I only ask one question, Cosima. Can you handle it? I mean, can you handle the part you've been handling? And can you get the other people we need, when we need them?''

"I can handle what I've been handling,'' she said. "The rest of it—'' She sighed. "Well . . . why not?''

"Fang won't be your only client. Hell, there are other

61

guys out there who need help. You know what? They're afraid to go in an office like Hamilton. Some of them are stuck with jackleg lawyers that aren't worth a damn. Listen, we can—"

"Jerry."

"What?"

"Let's *think* about it. There are problems. There are lots of problems."

"I'll be back on the East Coast the middle of the week. Let's do think about it. You and I are buddies from way back, Cosima. That's why I trust you. I don't trust that prick Nash."

"I'll look into the idea," she said. "I'll write down all the reasons why it won't work. That'll take all the pages in six legal pads."

"Typical goddamned lawyer," he grunted. "Always full of reasons why things won't work. Save a couple of those pads for reasons why it *will* work."

"Okay, Jerry. Give me a call. Let me know when you'll be available."

"To you, I'm always available," he laughed. "Hey, Cosima. Tell me the truth—you really naked?"

"Would I lie to you, Jerry?"

Four

Cosima disliked driving her Porsche into the City. It was a thief's dream. Worse, it would be a target for the gangs of boys who hung around intersections and demanded money for washing windshields. Though she was not fond of the trains either, except during commuter hours, she walked from her apartment to the Cos Cob station Sunday morning and caught the 11:06 for Grand Central. She settled into a seat with three sections of the Sunday *Times* and tried to ignore the dozen local stops this weekend train would make.

She had almost never been so casually dressed going into the City. It was the result of her new freedom. Though she was not enthusiastic about that, she supposed she might as well enjoy it while it lasted. Anyway, she was comfortable in soft, faded old jeans and a gray sweatshirt imprinted in red with the logo of Bernardin Frères—one of the shirts given to the two score employees who competed as bank representatives in a half-marathon run two weeks before the New York Marathon three years ago. (She had not run, but neither had half the people who had been given the sweatshirts.) She amused herself briefly with the speculation that Rick might not know her when he saw her.

For a moment he didn't. Grand Central Station was empty at noon on Sunday—empty at least as compared to any hour of a weekday. Oddly echoing and oddly unlittered, it was gray, too, without the hot lights that burned on weekdays. Rick watched the file of people coming up the ramp and through the door, and for a moment he didn't know her.

"Well, Rick?"

"Gussy! My god, another facet of you! And *sexy!*" He was himself wearing a frayed tan corduroy jacket, a blue chambray shirt, and khaki wash pants. He embraced her. "Hey! Welcome to New York."

She had telephoned him Saturday, to tell him about the call from Jerry Paccinelli, to ask if he thought she should even consider trying to establish her own firm. He had said they should sit down together and talk about it; he had said, too, that his coming week was burdened by a heavy schedule. Could they meet on Sunday?

"I'm famished," she said. "Nothing but coffee this morning. Can we grab a bite somewhere? Where do you eat on Sunday in New York?"

"Best day of the week, the natives say. For eating or anything else. I know a place."

He did, indeed. Half an hour later they sat down at a table facing a broad window that overlooked the East River from the arcade floor—the third floor—of an office building on Avenue A. Rick ordered them Bloody Marys, lox, cream cheese and bagels.

"I want to know more about this Jerry Paccinelli," he said. "Do you trust him?"

"Trust him how?"

"If he would be your first big client—and probably for a while your *only* big client—you would be betting the store on him. And he is, after all, a rock musician with a checkered reputation, in spite of his thirty-million gross last year. What kind of fellow is he?"

"You'd be amazed," she said. "I have been. Always."

"So. How would I be amazed?"

"To begin with," said Cosima, "he didn't get to be the leader of a group earning tens of millions of dollars a year by being a subliterate idiot. Jerry knows music as well as you and I know law. I suppose it's true that any fool who can abuse a musical instrument can turn up the volume and switch on some strobes and call himself heavy metal. And it would appear to be true, too, that he'll find a few spaced-out fools who'll shriek for his every appearance. But—they don't make it to the top that way. Jerry is a composer and an arranger. And he imposes a tough discipline on those guys who play for him. One of his legal problems six months ago was an employment-discrimination complaint filed by a black homosexual he'd fired because the man was doing cocaine. Jerry's got the mixed reputation you mention, but he's a professional—and I don't pay any higher compliment than that."

"How long have you known him?"

"Jerry? Oh, Jesus . . . uh, I guess twenty years. He went to the public schools in Greenwich, which I didn't, but I saw him around, at parties and so on. He's Italian, of course. His family lived in Cos Cob, his father owned a liquor store and was a very big man in local politics. Everybody knew Basilio Paccinelli. Even my father, wanting to get a little zoning variation, dealt with Jerry's father."

"For money?" Rick asked with a sly smile.

Cosima shook her head. "Absolutely not. My father doesn't operate that way, and neither did Basilio Paccinelli."

"I'm sorry I suggested it."

"You've lived too long in the City."

"How could I have lived here less time? I was born here."

She could remember driving past Paccinelli's on the Post Road: a family store selling liquor, beer and wine. Always there were cars parked in front. Customers came and went all day, but half the cars belonged to men who had come in to talk with Basilio Paccinelli, about problems as widely diverse as seeking reductions of tax assessments and finding a few dollars' temporary welfare money for an abandoned teenage mother. Jerry's father sat in the back of the store, on an empty beer keg that served him as a stool, with his account books and papers spread out over shelves within his reach. He was a paunchy, bald man, almost always holding an unlighted cigar stub in his mouth. A tan-and-black German shepherd lay beside him, usually asleep but often appraising visitors with calm, intelligent eyes.

As soon as he was old enough, Jerry worked behind the counter. Cosima would stop in to pick up a bottle of Bombay gin for her father. After Basilio helped him with his little zoning problem, Leon bought all his wine and liquor at Paccinelli's. That was what Bernardin paid for Paccinelli's help. Other times Jerry came by the house in Back Country to deliver cases of wine. Cosima, sitting by the pool on summer days, sometimes thought of asking Jerry Paccinelli to come back when he had finished his deliveries and have a swim. But she hadn't. As he reminded her years later, that would have breached a line that remained inviolate in Greenwich.

Jerry played football for Greenwich High School—a team that, oddly, wore red and called itself the Cardinals. Like any brilliant, highly motivated young person, he excelled, not just at one endeavor, but at everything he tried: football, academics, dramatics and music.

Cosima looked up from the dance floor at Greenwich Country Club one night to discover that the lead guitarist in the little band hired for the evening was Jerry Paccinelli. That night she had the only date she ever had with him. Being bored with the conceited preppie who had brought her to the dance, she had sought out Jerry during a break and suggested he take her home after the dance. It was the kind of thing that intrigued Jerry, and he agreed. She had created a minor scandal by slipping away from the country club with one of the dance-band musicians, leaving the preppie to wonder where she had gone. They had gone to a nightclub across the state line in Port Chester, and she had been distinctly aware as they danced that Jerry's friends were watching and conjecturing.

"He went to Yale," she said to Rick. "I guess he had some kind of scholarship, but his family could have paid the fare."

"What'd he major in?"

"He was supposed to major in economics, but the music became more and more important."

"Did you and he . . . have a relationship? That is, if you don't mind my asking. I'm renowned for blunt questions, you know. I'm told it's a Jewish idiosyncrasy."

Cosima laughed. "A straightforward question. A straightforward answer. No. Even if I'd wanted to, he wouldn't have. He didn't like the boat."

"What? Why?"

"Daddy owns a thirty-eight-foot sloop he calls *Lafayette*. It's a very nice boat, but you wouldn't have to be a millionaire to own it—particularly if you bought it as long ago as Daddy bought *Lafayette*. I sailed it yesterday. My sister and I took it out on the Sound about twenty miles, and back. Jerry—actually, it wasn't the boat he didn't like. What he didn't like was that I could sail it, and *he* didn't know how. If there is one thing an Italian man can't take, it's seeing a female doing what he can't do. And he saw it one afternoon. He put a distance between him and me for a long time after that."

What was more—and what she did not elect to tell Rick—Ruggiero Paccinelli liked girls to fall into his arms. Pretty Italian girls, chubby and soft, doe-eyed and adoring suited Jerry better than the tall, austere, self-possessed daughter of the Back Country and private schools. She would have represented a challenge, and he could have everything he wanted of girls without having to meet any challenge—or so she as a girl had judged him and had guessed his assessment of her.

"Alcohol?" Rick asked. "Substances?"

"The former for sure," she said. "Of the latter I've never seen any evidence—or heard of it. You understand, I don't see him very often."

Rick glanced out the window at the choppy water of the East River. "Hell of a way to start a new law firm," he said. "With a quarter-million retainer."

"If it doesn't work out, it would be a hell of a way to waste a year or two," said Cosima.

He sighed. "When did you ever waste a year, Gussy?" he asked. "When did I? When did we ever have the chance?"

"You are about to tell me," she said, "that if you had my resources you'd take a year off and have a good time." She smiled at him, nodding slowly. "I doubt you would."

"My divorce cost me a fortune," he said. "I got a clean break, but I'm starting over, as you might say. You . . . it's different. You can afford to take a chance, Gussy."

"That depends on what resources you think I'd spend," she said.

"Well, obviously I'm talking about money. I'm saying you can afford to take a chance."

"I'm not talking about money," she said, "and I'm not sure I can afford to invest a year of my life in a highly doubtful proposition."

"What do you think you'd have to have to make it work?" he asked.

"Only two little things," she said, tipping her head to one side and smiling at him. "More clients and more lawyers. I can't found a new law firm on Jerry Patchen and the Bull Dog Fangs, not on that client alone. And even if that's the only client I have, I can't represent it by myself. I need a law firm."

"A lot of small firms would love to have you—bringing along a client like that."

"Are you sure? Hamilton, Schuyler will raise all kinds of hell with whoever takes Fangs away from them. That's another point, you know. Miller and Nash are quite capable of being nasty.''

"If you're thinking of your no-compete agreement, forget it,'' said Rick. "Not worth the paper it's written on—especially for a lawyer.''

"You know the answer to that,'' she said.

"Sure, I know. A new firm hires you and you bring the client. Hamilton, Schuyler can't win a lawsuit, but they'll tie you up in litigation from now to 2001. I don't think so, Gussy. Have you checked the New York cases?''

"Not yet.''

"I have. And you can bet *they* have. You look into it. It's your field.

"I don't even have a library where I can do the research,'' she said.

"Library of the Association of the Bar of the City of New York,'' he said. "West Forty-fourth Street. I assume you're a member.''

"I'm a member,'' she said, tipping her glass and finishing her Bloody Mary. "Want to go for a walk, Rick?''

They walked south, eventually to Broadway, Bowling Green, and Wall Street. These were the thoroughfares where on weekdays Cosima and Rick rushed from appointment to appointment: burdened, distracted, almost oblivious to the stuff of wealth and power that reposed in the very stones of the prestigious buildings on these celebrated streets. This Sunday afternoon, with time to savor this unique essence, Cosima became imbued with it. She strolled buoyantly, gawking like a tourist, allowing Rick to hold her hand, even interlacing her fingers with his and swinging his arm.

For a moment a vexing contradiction interrupted her cheerful mood—she remembered she no longer had an affiliation here. She stiffened, shrugged off the anxiety, tightened her hand on Rick's and dragged him past the smoke-stained stone building with the brass plaque wrapped around one of the foolish columns that supported nothing:

BERNARDIN FRÈRES, INC.

FOUNDED 1902

She was not oblivious of the subtle guiding nudges by which Rick began gradually to lead her west. His hand closed more and more tightly around hers, and she understood where he wanted to go: to the IRT stop, to the subway, to his apartment.

She was not sure she wanted to go there. She knew he would find more significance in it than she would. She knew what he had in mind, too, and she was not certain she wanted to parry him. She liked him, really, especially his sane, almost reflexive, wit. They had been friends for a long time, almost from her first day at Hamilton, Schuyler. They had been more than friends, in fact; they had become mutually supportive, alert to each other, instinctively communicative, readily exchanging confidences. She knew more about his divorce than his wife did, because she knew his agony, which he had never been able to communicate to Lydia and which Lydia had never guessed. So, suppose this afternoon he proposed to advance from friendship to affair? She could cope with that rationally. But could he?

"I trust you are not interested in a boat ride out to the Statue of Liberty?" he asked playfully.

"I really want to talk about the problems of starting a new law firm," Cosima said.

"Would you like to go to my place, then? We'll have privacy and quiet and—"

"Sure, Rick," she said knowingly. "But let's get a cab."

He turned decisively toward Broadway, where they were more likely to find a taxi on Sunday afternoon; and, perhaps unwittingly, he lengthened his stride. Cosima kept pace with him, amused and sympathetic, yet a little dismayed by how purposeful he had become.

"Max Wilmot says he knows other lawyers in my situation," she said when they were seated in a cab and were on their way east and north. She meant to interrupt the fantasies Rick might be building. "He'll help me locate them, if I want him to."

"You'll have no trouble staffing a law firm, Gussy. Will Bernardin Frères give you any business?"

"That's not wholly possible," she said. "Something to pay the office rent. But it will be grunt work."

"Then hire a grunt or two. And use your name, Gussy. The name Bernardin opens doors that are slammed in the face of Loewenstein."

Cosima heard what he said and didn't respond. She wouldn't explain. She *would* use the name Bernardin. It was hers, it was not her father's exclusively; it was a resource, she was heir to it, and she had every right to take advantage of it, whether with permission or not. At the same time, Rick and everyone else had to understand what he would find difficult to understand: that her name was a *personal* asset on which she alone would draw.

Even Hamilton, Schuyler had had to suffer that. She did use it. She knew how to use it. She had made a study of using it—hadn't all of her family done the same?—and she would use it as they had always done: shrewdly, subtly, very privately and very effectively.

Rick's Sunday *Times* lay scattered over his couch and the floor. A plate covered with toast crumbs and smears of jam sat on the table beside a cup containing the cold dregs of his morning coffee. A tattered gray bathrobe lay over a chair. The appearance of his living room suggested that he had left this morning without any thought he would ask her to come here—for he was not so crafty as to have contrived this clutter to make just that suggestion, was he? He grabbed the robe and tossed it through the bedroom door, where she saw it land on an unmade bed.

"I, uh . . . hadn't gotten around to—"

"So?" she shrugged.

"The maid comes twice a week. Friday and Tuesday. When we were here Friday afternoon, she'd just left."

Cosima grinned and glanced around. "Not till Tuesday . . ." she laughed.

He picked up the dishes and carried them to the kitchen, then stacked the newspaper on the coffee table. She sat and watched him, amused. Could it really be that he had left this morning without the least idea of bringing her here? It was possible. His divorce had astounded him; he really was an innocent. With all his practiced perceptivity, he was an innocent. She hadn't thought of him that way before. It was engaging.

"The place must look pretty poor at best, compared to what you're used to," he said.

"I don't suppose it's what *you're* used to," she said. "Though it—"

"No, I'm not used to it," he said. "Lydia and I—" He stopped for a moment. "Well. You know. We had a nice home, really. Rented for three times what this place costs. On the other hand, when I was growing up my parents would have considered this apartment luxurious. I—"

"Rick. Forget it. I'm not permanently unemployed, and you're not permanently a newly divorced man living in the digs he had to grab when he was put out of his home."

His smile returned. "Want a brandy?" he asked. "I do have clean glasses."

"Got any seltzer?" she asked. "If you do, you can cut the brandy with a splash of seltzer. Just a splash."

"I never heard of that," he said as he picked up the bottle.

"Learned it in France," she said. "A splash of *eau minérale*. When I was in school in Passy, they served wine with our dinners, but they cut it with water. At the younger girls' tables, more water; at the older girls', less. When brandy is cut a little—but just a little—it's not such a hairy beast." She shrugged. "Of course, Americans think it heresy to drink brandy any way but straight and with anything but coffee."

He shrugged as he sat down beside her, handing her a glass. He had poured a little Scotch for himself.

"I've given a lot of thought to what happened Friday," he said. "Those arrogant bastards! If it had been anybody but Nash . . ."

"If it had been anybody but Nash, I might have been able to live with it," said Cosima. "My image of his face is obscured by the stinking smoke from those little cigars he smokes—also that patronizing little smile he seems to have glued on."

"Neither of which he shows to people above him in the firm," said Rick. "I tell you, Gussy, I've been disillusioned with Hamilton, Schuyler for a long time, but what they did to you lowered them six more notches in my esteem."

"I'm going to quit talking about the firm," she said. "It's inelegant to go around bad-mouthing an organization you've just left."

Rick put his hand on hers. "I have this damned sense that they hurt you," he said softly.

"Don't let that bother you," she said.

"It does, though. I care about you, Gussy. I think you know that."

She nodded. So here was the tentative. And now was the moment to stop him, if that was what she wanted. If she didn't stop him now, she could not later do it kindly. He cared for her, he said. Well, she cared for him, too—though she doubted the word meant the same thing to both of them. What a cliché it would be to tell him she wanted him for a friend, but just a friend!

"Do you know what I mean, Gussy?"

"I think so," she said quietly. "I'm very fond of you, Rick."

The Rick Loewenstein smile bloomed. " 'Fond,' " he said. "A carefully chosen word, I'm afraid."

"No. What word would you like better?"

He tipped his head toward his right shoulder and lifted his brows. "Well . . ."

73

"You said you care about me. Okay. I care about you, too."

"What I should have said, Gussy, is that I care *for* you. I think you are a very special person. That's not original, but that's what I think."

Cosima sighed. "Rick . . . I think you're special, too. I care for you. I just don't want you to think—"

"I understand," he interrupted gently. "Nothing of any great significance. Do you care enough for me to let me kiss you?"

"Of course."

He kissed doubtfully at first, as if he were not sure she wouldn't take offense and break away; the touch of his lips on hers immediately quickened and emboldened him, and he clutched her more tightly in his arms and crushed their mouths together so hard that she tasted blood. She had not expected him to be so fervid so soon, but he was, and his ardor communicated itself to her. In defiance of her resolution to be measured in her response to him, she was already excited. The possibility of stopping short—which she had thought would remain until the last moment—receded beyond her grasp before she could form a resolution about it.

He drew back and looked at her for a moment, then pressed his face to her neck and began to kiss her throat, at first with his lips, then caressing it with the tip of his tongue. Cosima gasped, stiffening with indrawn breath.

"Gussy . . . okay?"

His hand was on her left breast. She nodded. He dropped his hand and slipped it up under her sweatshirt. He tested the tightness of her brassiere; when he found he could not press his hand under it and squeeze her bare breast, he began to stroke and squeeze it through the taut sheer fabric. Aroused, she let her head fall back, to encourage him to nuzzle and kiss her neck. He did. His whole tongue came out and licked the skin of her throat. She bent forward then and kissed him under his ear, along his cheek, and on his mouth.

He circled her with his arms and snatched at the hooks of the bra. "I want to see you, Gussy," he whispered.

Cosima closed her eyes, and when he had loosened her brassiere she raised her arms and let him pull it and her sweater over her head.

"Cosima!" He threw himself down to kiss her naked breasts, first one, then the other—pressing his face into them, knowing their rich, firm fullness with his lips and cheeks. He knew how to use his tongue, and here he applied it exuberantly to her nipples, hardening them so he could suck them between his lips and nibble on them. "So beautiful . . ."

She hadn't wanted this, but now it was too late not to want. "Rick," she muttered. "Here. Not in the bedroom. Here."

She pulled away from him. Drawing herself erect, first she ran her hands over her flushed face and through her hair; she pushed down her jeans and panties.

"Gussy!"

Her shoulders were broad, but her body was not heavy, and her breasts lay on her rib cage like two water-filled balloons set in motion with every movement of her body. Under her ribs, her belly was flat. She had no pubic hair, none at all. From her association with the French girls at Passy, to whom daily bathing and deodorants were amusing American affectations, she had gained an attitude that pubic hair was unsanitary, a tangled, sweaty asylum for a complex microbiology that generated discomfort and stench; as a part of every morning's toilet for fifteen years she had shaved off every trace of it.

She nodded at him. He understood the signal; he undressed. She lay back in the corner of the couch and watched him. His smooth skin had a dusty cast. His musculature was well formed but it showed neglect; it was slack, and he carried a little more flesh around his middle than he should have. Her eyes fell to the part of him with which she was about to have so intimate a connection. He was circumcised, of course. Except for the color, his naked glans looked something like the cap of a thick-stemmed mushroom. The notion brought to her face a smile he was bound to misinterpret.

He sat down, his hips pressed to her belly. "Gussy," he whispered. "You what me to put on a rubber?"

She nodded. "I suppose we should," she said.

He hurried into the bedroom and in a moment returned with a foil package. She watched as he took out the condom, put it on the tip of his penis, and unrolled it, covering the length of his shaft in tightly stretched thin rubber. Seeing a man do this was one of the most erotic things she could imagine. It so aroused her that she wanted him to enter her immediately, without any more preliminaries.

He didn't want them either. He turned and straddled her. She accepted him, and he entered her. She wrestled to free her legs and cross them behind him, to pin him to her and secure their connection. As he began his motion, she tried to answer his each thrust with one of her own. In a moment she knew he was no longer thinking but was driven by a more feral instinct. She surrendered and immersed herself totally in him. In them.

She was disappointed in him only in his damned questions afterward—Had it been good? Had she enjoyed it? For a moment she was afraid he was going to ask if she was sorry.

He poured her another brandy, this one without seltzer, and another Scotch for himself. Cosima lay naked on the couch with her hands clasped behind her head, smiling, placid—wondering if he would pick up the two wet condoms he had thrown on the *Times* or if he meant to leave them there like some kind of lewd trophy, laurels to what he probably considered a triumph.

"You could stay the night," he said. "We'll have dinner somewhere. While you shower, I'll clean up the bedroom."

"I'll need something but jeans and a sweatshirt tomorrow morning," she said. "I have to go back out."

"Well anyway," he said, "will you come back here and use this place as your headquarters? I'll change that telephone recorder. In fact, we can change it now, put your voice on it. I looked at the instructions and found out how to change message tapes. It's easy. We can put your tape in during the day and mine at night."

She stretched. "Okay, Rick. I accept your generosity."

"I have a motive," he said. "I may as well tell you. If you start a new law firm, and if you want a tax man, I just might quit Hamilton, Schuyler and join you. Like I said, I'm more than a little sick of being bullied . . . and seeing other people bullied."

"Don't even think of it, Rick," she said. "Over lunch you said you couldn't afford it."

"Hell, I can make the rent for this joint, can't I? Surely—and the price of two hotdogs a day."

"I couldn't promise it," she said solemnly.

"Even grunt work from Bernardin Frères, for a while," he insisted.

"I can't promise that either."

"Gussy—"

"Rick. Three hours ago you said *I* could afford to leave Hamilton, Schuyler but that *you'd* just been wiped out by your divorce and have to start over. You—"

"Start over," he interrupted. "That's the point. If I'm starting over, why *don't* I start over—*really* start over?"

"When did that thought come to you, Rick?" she asked. She reached for her panties and pulled them up her legs. "Not within the last hour, I hope."

He shook his head.

"We just made love," said Cosima. "Rick, you know we may never do it again." She shrugged. "Or . . . we may

77

do it again. Often. I don't think it would have been so easy for me to do if I had thought of you as a law partner or a potential law partner."

"Gussy—"

"To put it another way, Rick," she continued, "we just established a new sort of relationship. Whatever we may call it, it is one hundred percent inconsistent with a business relationship."

Rick rose from the couch and bent over to recover his undershorts from the floor. "Did we establish a relationship?" he asked. "I would like that, but I thought you didn't want anything significant."

Cosima put her brandy to her mouth to give her a moment to consider what she would say next. She took a small sip. "What we just did was significant," she said. "By definition. By *my* definition, anyway. You have not just enrolled in a big club."

"My god, of course! I—"

"I'm not in love with you," she said. "and you're not with me. But . . . Well, two people who make love together shouldn't be business partners. It isn't consistent. It's bad for the whole deal."

He shook his head. "Is this a choice I have to make?" He sighed. "If I want to be your partner, I can't be your lover, and if I want to be your lover, I can't be your partner. Is that the way it is?"

"Do you disagree with me?" she asked. "Do you think we can be both?"

He sighed again, and again shook his head. "Oh hell, Gussy, I don't know. I know what you mean. You are very rational. Too damned rational."

Cosima reached out and put her hand on his cheek. "One good thing, Rick," she said with a warm smile. "It's a choice we don't have to make right now. I don't have a firm you could join if you wanted to."

* * *

The club where Jerry Patchen And The Bull Dog Fangs opened during the middle of the following weeks was on Sixty-ninth Street and was called—almost inevitably—Soixante-Neuf. Jerry phoned Cosima on Tuesday and asked her to meet him at the club. He told her also that about the only time he would be free to see her was after the Thursday night show. He suggested she come and see Bull Dog Fangs perform. He suggested also she bring a man with her; otherwise she would hear more invitations and propositions than she would want. He would send her two tickets. The shows were all sold out, and without tickets she could not possibly get in. The show would be over at two A.M. He would not have had dinner. And she and her friend should plan on dining with him.

Cosima arrived with Rick, about twelve-thirty. A rowdy, jostling throng blocked the walk in front of Soixante-Neuf. It was difficult to press through to the door, difficult to get the attention of the burly man in black tie who was checking tickets. When he pulled back the rope and let Rick and Cosima through, the crowd behind them shrieked derisively, some of them angrily.

Inside, they passed through a rather shabby foyer carpeted and furnished in maroon, and from there they entered through wide doors into a cavernous, virtually dark room. Everything was painted dull black: the ceiling, the walls, the floors, the bar, the stage curtains, as well as the box-like risers on which people would sit during the performance. What little light there was came from tiny bulbs scattered over the ceiling like stars—which they were intended to suggest—and from the jarringly bright spots on the cash registers behind the bar.

"We had better get drinks pronto," said Cosima. "The show will start any minute."

The crowd was mostly young, mostly rude, pushing for the bar, pushing for seats on the risers. Some were dully stoned. Many were grotesquely dressed and coifed. Rick was conspicuously uncomfortable; Cosima, who had little patience with the uncouth, was impatient. It was she who shoved their way to the bar, fending off one drunken young man with a painful elbow to the sternum.

"Scotch!" she barked at the girl behind the bar—figuring it was not a good place to ask for a brandy.

The bar girl's hair stood up in a narrow red-and-green hedge from her forehead to the back of her neck. The rest of her skull was smoothly shaved. She wore black lipstick. Her hips and legs were squeezed into skintight black rubber pants. Her rubber vest was open, and when she moved her small breasts became visible, exposing lipstick-blackened nipples. She poured two tall glasses about half full of Scotch, pointed to the bucket of ice and pitcher of water down the bar, and waved away Rick's proffered money—the drinks were included in the price the rest of the crowd had paid for admission. Before he could dig out smaller money and offer a tip, she had moved on and was pouring liberally into someone else's glass.

Rick and Cosima pushed their way to the ice pitcher, took ice with their fingers since tongs were nowhere in evidence and began to work their way toward one of the risers. They found seats well up and to the rear, where they had to view the stage from across the bar.

"It may be just as well," Cosima said to Rick when he apologized for having found no better seats.

"LADIES AND GENTLEMEN!" The amplified voice roared through the room. "JERRY *PATCHEN* . . . AND BULL . . . DOG . . . FANGS!"

The crowd shrieked as the black curtains swept back. Blinding flashes burst from strobe lights facing the crowd. Enthralled faces were frozen in ecstasy. A series of guttural, amplified noises, like bursts of cannon fire, shook the room. Then through all this bedlam—the beat. The band was behind the strobes. No one could see them yet, except in dim glimpses; but the insistent beat of all their instruments, hugely amplified, set up an undeniable, hypnotic pulse. The crowd yelled. For a moment some tried to applaud but soon gave it up as they were drowned out by the amplifiers.

The white strobes stopped; others, flashing red and yellow and blue, erupted above the band. For two minutes the musicians were exhibited as jerking marionettes in successive fragmented instants of brilliant color as they continued to pound out the beat. Then strong spotlights from above began to pick out individual musicians, one by one. As the hot light displayed each one, the crowd found strength enough to scream through the beat and be heard.

The drummer was a majestic, chocolate-colored black man, naked to the waist—and perhaps below for all you could see—and oiled so that his skin glistened in the combined light of the spots and strobes. He pounded the drums with destructive power. In fact, Cosima knew from Jerry that Hal destroyed a drum set about once a week. His fervor was ingenuous and infectious.

The spots moved to the keyboard. It was played by a young woman. Cosima knew from Jerry that Adela was a graduate of the North Carolina School of the Arts, where she had studied piano under an eminent teacher. Her hair was cut and dyed like that of the bar girl—red and green, just a hedge of it remaining on her shaved skull. The bar girl may have costumed herself for this engagement by Bull Dog Fangs to resemble Adela Drake. The costume was the same: painfully tight rubber ski pants and an open vest that occasionally afforded the Fangs' frenzied audiences a glimpse of bare breast. No one guessed what Cosima knew: that Adela was a born-again Christian who faithfully contributed a tithe of her earnings to a small Baptist church in North Carolina. Her hugely amplified keyboard generated a counterpoint to the rhythm that moved the shrieking crowd but was appreciated by few of them as an element of Ruggiero Paccinelli's talent as a composer.

The spotlights continued their scan of Bull Dog Fangs, as the rhythm grew more complex and the thread of a theme began to whisper through the beat.

The theme was suggested at first by an amplified violin played by another young woman, dressed in a tight, thigh-length black skirt and wearing her dark hair so long, falling over her shoulders and almost to her waist, that audiences wondered at first if she wore anything above the waist. She did, a black halter, but her hair hid it most of the time. Angela Monroney.

Three amplified guitars picked up the theme. The spots shifted to them: three young white men in the black rubber ski pants and loose vests. Finally, a mandolin. The tea-with-cream black who played it also wore the band's rubber costume.

With the beat still throbbing under the powerful theme, suddenly the strobes stopped, the stage was lighted for a moment in weak rose-colored floods and then the strongest spot yet made a burning circle, stage-centerfront, and Jerry Patchen trotted from the wings and took his place. The crowd rose, shrieking and stomping. The amplifiers were turned up to overpower them, and Jerry hammered a new theme out of his authoritatively amplified guitar.

He struck a dramatic posture, with his legs spread wide, the guitar held high on his chest. The tight, thin rubber of his hip-slung pants conformed faithfully to the shape of his penis and scrotum, flaunting them as explicitly as if they had been bare and painted dull black. Behind, the rubber clung to his nates and disappeared into the valley between them. Even the amplified music of his laboring band was all but defeated by the shrill screams from the risers. Above his navel his hairy chest was hung with gold chains. A microphone rose from the floor of the stage, and Jerry began to voice the beat and melody, in words that were lost in the din.

Cosima squeezed Rick's hand. She had seen this before.

He was staying at the Hyatt Regency on Forty-second Street. It was difficult to get dinner with wine anywhere at three A.M., but he had arranged for room service to serve dinner at that hour, and he offered drinks and wine from his own bar. In the privacy of the hotel suite, with a friend, Cosima, and a man he was willing to accept as a friend, Rick, he paced the floor in his undershorts and wiped the still-streaming sweat from his whole body with a succession of damp towels.

"Pour, honey-babe," he said to Cosima. "Whatever you want. Whatever Rick wants. Excuse me a minute."

She had seen this before, too: he took an hour or more to come down after a performance. He drank nothing, not even water, for the last three hours before he went on stage, since the excitement irritated his bladder and generated an irresistible need to urinate; on stage he sweated—those shining streams of sweat that so excited some of his crowd—and came off the stage with a burning thirst. Then he drank glass after glass of cold water, a shot or two of gin or whiskey, maybe a glass or two of wine; and shortly he began to make repeated visits to the bathroom. Filled with liquid, his nerves still tight, he went again and again; only after that phase was over could he sit down and talk.

Returning from the bathroom this time, he wore a short terrycloth robe. He dropped into a chair and glanced at his watch. "Screwball goddamned way to make a living, isn't it?" he asked Rick.

"It would be if you weren't one hell of a success at it," Rick said.

Jerry nodded. "Yeah. A splash of gin, Cosima, if you don't mind. Over one ice cube."

She got up and went to the bar to pour his drink. What a contrast between Jerry and Rick! Rick would have offered to pour her a drink, would never have thought of sending her to the bar to pour him one; Jerry, perfectly at ease, without a moment's thought, called on the woman to fetch for him.

Ruggiero Paccinelli was a big, handsome man—commonly referred to as a hunk. His curly black hair had stiffened under the lights and sweat of his performance and stood above his scalp as a rowdy mop. His face remained flushed.

83

He took the gin from Cosima's hands and swallowed it at a gulp.

"This Nash fellow keeps calling," he said. "I wish I could send a five-hundred-volt shock back across the telephone line. I don't want to know him."

"I wouldn't be hasty about that, Jerry," she said.

He changed the subject. Tipping his head to one side, he grinned at her. "Lawyer lady," he said. "I like it. You look like my kind of people—blue jeans. And cashmere. That's some kind of style."

"Well, I didn't have any rubber pants," she laughed.

"You wouldn't believe how sweaty hot they are! Hey, kid, you'll bake your buns if you try those."

"It surprises me you can still get it up after baking your thing for two hours," she rejoined.

"How do you know I can?"

"You have a reputation for it," she said.

"I have a reputation for smoking, sniffing and shooting, too, and I don't do any of that stuff. Hey, you're supposed to have six pads full of notes about why you can't be my lawyer."

"I have them," she said. "I didn't bring them with me."

Jerry leaned back and closed his eyes. He began to scratch and massage the insides of his legs, just below the short robe. "Tell you one thing," he said. "I'm not going on with Hamilton, Schoolyard. I'm sorry, Rick. I know you still work there, but—"

"Feel free," said Rick.

"I've got reasons," said Jerry. "I go in that office, they stare at me like I'm something just escaped from the Bronx Zoo—from the reptile house. I get a feeling they take out any chair I sit on and have it cleaned."

"Yeah, they spray your checks with Lysol," said Cosima. "C'mon, Jerry. Don't be defensive."

"Well, I've got other reasons. My old man worked all his life in that liquor store so he could have some kind of retirement, like he wanted. Twenty years ago he bought a place in New Hampshire, a little house on a lake where he and my mother could go for vacations and go live when they retired. They like to fish and putter around in a little boat they got. Twenty years they've been making payments on this place. Two years ago they went up in the fall to do some fishing, and there wasn't a live fish in the lake. The water was so clear you could see bottom thirty feet down—bottom all white, covered with some kind of white silt. Chemicals. Paper company up the creek had dumped its chemical garbage in the stream. I went to the hearing they finally had last month."

Rick had begun to nod. "Orion Forest Products, Incorporated," he said. "Represented by Hamilton, Schuyler, Depew & Chase."

"In the person of the lyingest shyster I've ever seen. I couldn't believe what he said—that the chemicals were harmless, that only a very small amount was accidentally lost—get that, 'lost'—into the water, that the people in the neighborhood had gotten hysterical . . ."

"Brad McDonald," said Cosima, nodding.

"Right. McDonald. The lawyer for the state asked him how he explained the death of the fish. McDonald said he had no idea what killed the fish but the small quantity of chemicals that accidentally trickled—get that, 'trickled'—into the creek could not have been the cause—his company's chemical tests proved that. Goddamned liar."

"The client's lie, Jerry," said Cosima. "Bradley McDonald could only argue what the company told him."

"Oh, sure. And smooth as oil. Arrogant. Haughty. Nobody was complaining but a lot of hysterical Yankee farmers and a wop who sold whiskey for a living. The blue-suits were of course so very, very respectable, so articulate, so *right.*" He shrugged. "So the lake is polluted, ruined, and my dad's little house is worth a third of what it was. I'm going to buy him another place, but it won't be the same."

"Orion is still dumping, right?" Rick asked.

"Orion is, as they ruled, 'authorized to release measured

quantities, not to exceed . . .' et cetera, et cetera. That bastard *smirked!* If it hadn't been for you, Cosima, I'd have called Hamilton, Schuyler that same day and told them to send me my files. Now I've got no reason for staying with them, and I'm damned well not.''

''That still doesn't mean I can represent you, Jerry,'' said Cosima. ''I don't have—''

''Then *get* what you need,'' Jerry interrupted. ''You're a tax man, Rick. You gonna join her? You two take over my tax work, my corporation work . . . Christ! What's it gonna cost me? Enough for you to make a start.''

''I've been thinking of leaving Hamilton, Schuyler,'' said Rick solemnly and very quietly.

''You can't,'' Cosima protested.

Jerry paused, glanced into his glass with a hard frown. ''Well, whatever you want.'' He shrugged again. ''You don't want to . . . let me know.''

Five

Bernardin & Loewenstein established an office in Rick's apartment—which is to say, they bought two desks with chairs, installed another telephone line, ordered a small supply of stationery, and announced to the world that they were a law firm. Max Wilmot gave their announcement prominent display in the New York *Law Journal*.

In *The National Law Journal,* an affiliated lawyers' newspaper, he did more than that: he ran a feature story under his own byline, discussing the resignations of Richard Loewenstein and Cosima Bernardin from Hamilton, Schuyler, Depew & Chase as symptomatic of "a crisis of dissatisfaction" faced by many of the nation's largest law firms.

On Thursday, May 28, Cosima received a letter from Hamilton, Schuyler:

Dear Miss Bernardin,

Early this week our firm received notice from our client Fang, Incorporated to the effect that it wishes to discontinue representation by our firm and to be represented by you in the future. The president, Ruggerio Paccinelli, demands that we forward all our client's files to your office on Market Street.

We remind you that, under the terms of the employment agreement you signed when you joined Hamilton, Schuyler, Depew & Chase, you agreed not to endeavor in any way to take clients from this firm or to attempt to make them your clients. It now appears that you have violated that agreement, both in spirit and letter. We remind you, furthermore, that solicitation of clients by a former employee of a law firm is a serious violation of the Standards of Professional Responsibility.

We have advised Mr. Paccinelli of the terms of your agreement and of the consequences of your violation of the agreement. We have suggested to him that he reconsider his decision, particularly in view of the fact that a one- or- two-person firm, such as you seem to be in the process of establishing, also cannot, consistent with professional standards, accept a client that will require competent advice in a wide variety of fields of law.

We would appreciate receiving from you a letter acknowledging your receipt of this warning and a renewal of your commitment not to engage in activities in violation of your agreement with us.

Yours very truly,

Daniel Nash

Jerry Patchen answered, without consulting Cosima. His letter was delivered to Hamilton, Schuyler by messenger on Monday, June 1:

Nash—

Cosima Bernardin did not take a client from you. I took *myself* away from you *because I don't like you*. I don't like you personally, Nash, and I don't like your law firm. I brought my business to Hamilton, Schuyler because there was *one* lawyer in the firm in whom I had confidence—Cosima Bernardin. When she left you, I left you.

Cosima did not solicit my business. She is abiding by your agreement so scrupulously that I practically had to *force* my business on her—as I will testify in any proceedings you may care to initiate. As a client I have the right to choose my lawyer—a right you cannot take from me by any cheap little agreement you force on your young lawyers.

A week has passed since I notified you that I want my files delivered to the offices of Bernardin & Loewenstein. I am not a lawyer, but I don't need a lawyer to tell me that you will be liable for any loss caused for me and my business by your withholding my papers and records from the attorneys of my choice.

You get those files over there by messenger *today*, sonny boy, or yours truly is going to burn your butt.

Ruggiero Paccinelli
cc: Bernardin & Loewenstein
Attorneys at Law

A van arrived that afternoon, delivering six cartons of files to the office-apartment.

It arrived when Max was there. At Cosima's invitation, he had come over from the newspaper to see what kind of office had been established by the two lawyers he had discussed in his article. Cosima and Max were sitting on Rick's couch, Rick at his desk.

Max pretended not to notice the drama of the arrival of the cartons of files. He feigned indifference to Cosima's laughter as the two delivery men carried in the heavy cartons and stacked them between the desks. When she handed him a copy of Jerry's letter, he held his lips firm and tried not to smile as he read.

"Want to publish it?" asked Cosima.

Max handed it back to her. "I think I'll forego that privilege," he said. "I've already had a snotty letter from Nash—copy to my boss."

"We can celebrate a small triumph," said Rick. "It's after five. Drink?"

"Have any real beer, by chance?" Max asked. "I mean, no 'Bood Lat,' for god's sake."

"Beck's suit you?"

"I'll take it."

Rick was dressed in a pinstriped dark blue suit. This was the first day of the second week that his own living room had been his office, but he had made no sartorial concession; each day when Cosima arrived he was decorously attired in suit, starched white shirt, necktie, black socks, black shoes: exactly what he had worn at Hamilton, Schuyler, Depew & Chase. It was as if he were determined to make a correct appearance for the first client who rang their bell.

Actually, as she understood, that was not the point. The point was that he was determined not to surrender a mote of his accustomed prestige and dignity. He was as disdainfully aware as she was of the scriveners, tacky-clad from the racks of outlet stores, who scuttled through the streets of lower Manhattan on their little errands, like so many hyperactive water bugs, and he was determined he would not become anything like them.

Max was watching him pour their drinks, a little curious. Cosima tried to catch Max's eye. She wondered if he too marvelled at the fragile shield that guarded Rick's dignity. She had no reason, actually, to be surprised. Dignity was guarded by assorted brittle shields, and it was a rare person who could maintain it without the tokens—anything from scepters to suits. Max himself claimed his own special dignity by defying the conventions; yet, as he was probably perceptive enough to understand, his nonconformity was itself a kind of conformity.

Anyway, after only one week without affiliation, Rick was anxious for identity. It was something the firms counted on: the bleak sense of alienation that followed disaffiliation. Post departum depression.

"You kids got a big retainer already, right?" Max said.

"We have one client," said Rick. He had poured Max's beer and was measuring brandy into a snifter for Cosima, whisky for himself. "He has been generous."

It was true. Jerry had paid a fifty-thousand-dollar retainer: his contribution to the establishment of the law firm he had urged them to establish. With Fang's files at hand, Rick would spend at least the next three days reviewing the company's and Jerry's tax situation. Cosima had gently suggested he don jeans and sweatshirt and spread the files around him on the floor, reading until he understood every element of the client's business.

For herself, while Rick had remained in the office-apartment this week—pacing the floor, she imagined—Cosima had spent much time away, at lunches and cocktail hours with people who were pleased to learn of the establishment of the firm of Bernardin & Loewenstein. Her absence from the office during the day, at least doing something besides sitting and waiting, while he paced the floor and made phone calls, had intensified Rick's premature sense of futility. Twice last week she had acquiesced in his diffident suggestion that they have sex. She did it from a sense that maybe she owed him, or at least that it was something she could do to renew his zest; she found herself lying under a man whose dejection was ponderous, and for the first time in her life she failed to exhilarate a partner.

Max leaned back on the couch, making himself very comfortable. Distracted for a moment by the clatter of a subway train on the Manhattan Bridge, he sipped beer and seemed to ponder on some significant thought churning in his mind, as if uncertain whether or not to voice it. Whatever it was, he chose not to voice it. When the clatter ceased, he sipped again and rolled the liquid around in his mouth as if all he had in mind was the quality of the beer.

"I'm going to need a copyright man, Max," said Cosima. "Know anybody?"

"I do," said Max. "You ought to talk to Hugh Hupp. There's nobody better."

"What's his affiliation?" Rick asked.

Max chuckled. "You ask him that, you've handed him a straight line," he said. "He loves it. The secretary on the phone says, 'With whom are you associated, sir?' And Hugh says, 'With me.' He likes it even better when she pursues it and asks him whom he represents. He tells her, 'The Great Jehovah and the Continental Congress.' "

"Solo practitioner?" Rick asked.

"Yes, and has been for forty years. Uptown office, Third Avenue. He does a lot of copyright work. Books. Plays. Songs. If your client has a copyright problem, you could do a lot worse than talk to Hugh."

"Fang, Incorporated, has an ongoing copyright problem," said Cosima. "Once a group makes big money, every songwriter who's never been published thinks he hears his tune in their music. Every songwriter who can't get published sends his drivel to Jerry Patchen, then claims Bull Dog Fangs is playing his song. Jerry sends the stuff back unopened, but they think they hear their songs anyway."

"See Hugh," said Max. "I'll call him for you, if you like."

"I'd as soon eat at Zum-Zum," said Hugh Hupp. He lowered his chin and regarded first Cosima, then Rick, through the narrow gap between his dark, bushy eyebrows and the gold rims of his little round spectacles. This was his response to Cosima's suggestion that maybe a little later they should go to the Harvard Club for lunch.

He was not a large man, and Max had said he was sixty-six years old, yet he sat with a stiff posture, shoulders high and back, and the fit of his dark-brown suit suggested a hard, muscular body. His hair was thin, but what was there was black. Curly, coarse black hair was conspicuous on the backs of his hands. Either his face was flushed or newly sunburned, or his complexion was dramatically ruddy. His hazel eyes were fixed intently on hers.

"Don't like the Harvard Club?" she asked.

"Don't like the *Hairr*-vuds. Can't stand their constant arrogant allusions to the *'Yad.'* If I have put up with that, I'll do it where I get a better meal than you can get at the Harvard Club."

"I graduated from Harvard—and from Harvard Law," she said.

He shrugged. "You don't look it."

Rick was letting Cosima do most of the talking. He was not reticent, but their firm was, after all, Bernardin & Loewenstein, not Loewenstein & Bernardin, and besides he was interested to see how she would cope with a man Max had warned them was known for his prickly, acerb personality. So far she'd given no ground, and the sparring between these two concentrated egos was fascinating. She chose to accept Hupp's comment that she didn't look Harvardian as a sort of inverted compliment and returned him a dry smile.

In his office at 866 Third Avenue, Hugh Hupp sat behind a desk covered with untidy heaps of books and files, a telephone, pens and pencils scattered here and there and a glass ashtray containing the ashes and butt of one small cigar. On this floor of the building he was not above the reach of jarring street noises: honking horns, shrieking brakes, sirens, all muffled by the glass, yet intrusive; on the credenza behind him the hard-disk drive in his microcomputer persistently hummed an impudent monotone. For decoration, his light-green-painted walls were hung with his diplomas and the certificates of his admission to various courts, plus a small collection of spy prints from *Vanity Fair,* of bewigged barristers and judges over cryptic captions. It was a depressingly unexceptional law office, like ten thousand others in the city, including many at wealthy firms like Hamilton, Schuyler: functional, unimaginative, drab. And here, discouragingly, sat the man Max had sent them to see; it was the background for a portrait of Hugh Hupp.

"I'll take you to 21," said Hupp.

"Actually, we don't have to go out to lunch at all," said Cosima. "Our appointment was just for a meeting. A meeting is all we asked for." Rick wasn't sure she had not made a mistake. Apparently she wasn't either, for she repaired it, adding, "Of course, we'd *enjoy* having lunch with you."

"I'm not entirely sure *why* we're meeting," Hupp said. "Max thinks it's a good idea, but I'm not sure why."

"Frankly, I'm not either, entirely," said Cosima. "Did Max tell you about my law firm and my client?"

"Sketchily," said Hupp. "Why don't *you* tell me?"

"In as few words as possible, about a month ago, a little less, I resigned my partnership at Hamilton, Schuyler, Depew & Chase. I have one client. That one is enough to let me start a new firm in a small, modest way. Rick, who was also a partner at Hamilton, Schuyler, and is a tax man, has joined me."

"Your client is Bull Dog Fangs," said Hupp.

"Yes. Fang, Incorporated, to be exact. Ruggiero Paccinelli, a.k.a. Jerry Patchen, has been a personal friend for many years. I organized the corporation for him. I'm a member of his corporate board. I expect to continue to handle all of his business that I'm qualified to handle. Rick will handle the tax work. But Jerry has copyright problems. Max suggested—"

"That I'd handle those," Hupp interrupted.

"If we can work out something," she said.

"Bull Dog Fangs is a first-class client," said Hupp. It was the first positive statement he'd made. He made it blandly, his austere mien unchanged from the dour gravity he had shown so far. "Big money. Big problems."

"Right."

"And you are a couple of young lawyers trying to start a practice, based on the highly doubtful proposition it can be done with one client—no matter how rich."

Cosima nodded. "All right," she said quietly. "I accept that."

"On the other hand," said Hupp, "you are the daughter of Leon Bernardin."

"Which is immaterial," said Cosima.

"It is like hell," said Hupp.

Suddenly Rick liked this man better—and so, obviously, did Cosima. "Okay," she said. "That can never be immaterial. On the other hand, my father is not subsidizing my attempt to establish a law firm. And you're right, of course, that it can't be done with one client—no matter how rich."

"Which is none of my business, really," said Hupp. "You want someone to look into your client's copyright situation, and you want to know if I'll do it. Bluntly said, whether I'm interested depends on the fee."

"It would be the same fee Fang, Incorporated, paid the copyright lawyers at Hamilton, Schuyler, I suppose," said Cosima.

"Doesn't have to be that," said Hupp. "I don't have their overhead."

"That's what Bernardin & Loewenstein is going to charge—the same hourly fee as the major firms charge for the work of middle-level partners," Rick said. "In your case, it would be the fee for a senior partner."

"Gutsy call," said Hupp. "You may not get away with it. One reason clients will come to you is that they expect you to be cheaper than the big-name firms."

"Wouldn't that be some kind of admission?" Cosima asked. "I mean, to accept lower fees. Equal pay for equal work is going to be our policy."

"You're as good as the big boys, hmm?"

"You're damn right we are," said Cosima.

95

Hupp's expression did not change but remained sober and skeptical. With the tip of his index finger he wiped a tiny, gleaming bead of perspiration off his upper lip, a precise, deliberate gesture. *"I'm* as good as any of them," he said. "After all, what does it take? A reasonable amount of smarts to begin with. After that, it's mostly hard work." His eyes shifted from her to Rick, and he shrugged. "You don't have to be any smarter to be a lawyer than you do to be a doctor."

"What I was thinking of," Cosima said, "was something more than your just handling the copyright work for Fang. I was wondering if we might establish an arrangement, formal or informal, for us to refer to you any copyright work we get."

"You can refer anything you want," said Hupp.

"The question," she said, "is whether or not we can use your name when we talk to prospective clients—tell them you do our copyright work."

"I might turn a client down," he said. "In fact, I might turn Fang down. Are you sure your client *hasn't* stolen someone's work?"

"No. But I don't think he has."

"The worst thing about being a lawyer, Miss Bernardin, Mr. Loewenstein, is clients who lie to you."

"I've had that experience," she said.

"You may find it happens more often when you're no longer representing Fortune 500 companies," he said.

"I doubt it."

For the first time, Hupp smiled: so subtly, ambiguously, evanescently that Rick was not certain, actually, he had seen it. "I am sixty-six years old," Hupp said. "I am thinking of retiring. I suspect that what Max had in mind is that I might retire into your new little firm, so to speak. Is that what *you* had in mind?

"We wouldn't put it in quite those terms," she said. "But it's an idea worth exploring."

That the idea was worth exploring was why he had agreed

to meet them. They knew that. It had been left unspoken in the telephone conversation that arranged this meeting, but they knew what Max had said to Hugh Hupp. Cosima had come here to judge, knowing she would *be* judged; and, knowing she would be judged, however little she liked it, she had prepared for a confrontation.

Looking at Hupp's hooded eyes, Rick wondered what he was thinking—not of him, but of Cosima. He wondered if Hupp was judging her by the criteria he himself used: that she was a striking beauty in spite of being too tall, of having unstylishly full breasts, of cutting her hair forlornly short, of refusing to pluck her prominent dark eyebrows. She was wearing a tailored cream-white linen skirt and a chalk-white silk blouse with a raspberry-colored silk scarf tied loosely around her neck. She looked comfortable. She *was* comfortable. She was almost always comfortable, always poised. Rick wondered especially how Hupp reacted to that distancing patrician poise that so affronted the egalitarian-by-necessity crowd.

Cosima crossed her legs, having decided, Rick guessed, that she would wait Hupp out for a moment, see what *he* would say, what lead he would give the conversation.

"Max says you got part of your education in France," said Hupp, and Rick guessed the sniffing-out process was over.

"My family is of French decent," said Cosima. "Each of us—my brothers and sisters and I—spent one or two years in French schools. I was at Passy."

Hupp pulled off his glasses and rubbed his eyes. "I began my first visit to France on June 6, 1944," he said. "It lasted just seven hours. Seven hours after I set foot on French soil, I was on my way home."

"Wounded . . . ?"

"I was able to start law school that fall. University of Michigan. Gave me a jump on all the guys that came on the G.I. Bill. Well, so much for my autobiography. Let me take you to lunch, Miss Bernardin, Mr. Loewenstein."

When he rose from behind the desk, they saw what wound he had suffered on June 6, 1944. His right leg was an ingenious contrivance of plastic and steel. He walked erectly on it, and briskly, but with the characteristic swinging gait such devices almost invariably require.

They emerged from the building at 12:30. A dark blue Cadillac was waiting at the curb. The driver hurried out to open the rear doors. He didn't need to be told where to go; he drove them to 21. There, Hugh Hupp was escorted to his usual table. The captain asked Cosima and Rick what *they* would have to drink; he knew what Mr. Hupp would have.

"They think they've improved this place," Hupp said, glancing around the dining room of the newly reopened 21. He returned the nods of half a dozen men who had noticed him and nodded greeting. "But they haven't."

"I've rarely come here," said Cosima.

"When you reach my age," said Hupp, "you like to return to familiar scenes, be taken care of by people who know you, know how you like things done, without having to be told. You like to see the same faces, even if they're the faces of people you don't know."

"I don't think that has anything to do with reaching an age," she said.

"Are you suggesting I restricted my horizons when I was a young man?" he asked.

"No. I'm not suggesting anything."

His smile was, as before, so elusive Rick was not sure he had seen it. "Well, maybe I did," Hupp said.

"Let me ask, if you—" She stopped to smile and nod at Dan Rather, who had nodded at her and quietly greeted her by name as he passed by on his way to a table. She had mentioned to Rick that she had met Rather a couple of weeks ago at a party at her sister Susanne's apartment. "Let me ask, if you don't mind, if you are married, have any children?"

"Married," Hupp said. "Twice—and divorced twice.

Child by each wife. I have a son who's an aeronautical engineer in California, a daughter who's married to a lobster broker in Maine. I play poker once a week. I drink Scotch. I smoke three cigars a day. And I'm an opera lover. Once a year I go to Milan, then to Vienna, sometimes to Paris—to the opera. I am generally regarded as a man of steady habits and unimpeachable integrity. My curriculum vitae, Miss Bernardin."

"My own, then," she said, lifting her chin a little higher and looking down her cheeks at him. "I have never been married. I have no children. I drink whatever comes to hand, with a preference for brandy. I don't smoke. I'm not particularly fond of opera, but, on the other hand, I'm not particularly fond of what Bull Dog Fangs plays either, so I guess that balances out. I am generally regarded as a poor little rich girl, with a colossal, hypersensitive ego."

Rick smiled and opened his mouth to say something facetiously corrective, but Hupp interjected— "It was wrong to say one cannot be too rich or too thin. What one cannot have too much of is money and ego."

He spoke flatly, almost in monotone, with a slight lift of his bushy black eyebrows. His thin lips were red, and he kept them in motion, as if he were chewing a small seed between his front teeth. He did not waste his smiles—perhaps because he hadn't many—but Rick began to understand that his forbidding façade was that: a façade.

"Egos can clash," she said.

"Much good might they be if they didn't," he replied. "Miss Bernardin—"

"Won't you call me Cosima?" she interrupted.

He nodded curtly. "Hugh. What about you, Loewenstein? What kind of ego have *you* got?"

Rick grinned. "Nothing to match you two," he said.

"We'll overpower him if we're not careful," Cosima laughed. "But he could justify an ego as big as either of ours. He's a first-rate tax lawyer."

"Why don't you two do this?" said Hupp with abrupt

decisiveness. "Send me a letter, outlining whatever arrangement you want to suggest. Don't suggest I become a partner in your firm. I won't do that. I won't attend partnership meetings, and I won't serve on committees. If I'd wanted to do that, I could have joined a firm forty years ago. If you are thinking of sharing offices, tell me where it's going to be. I can't get any more space in the building I'm in, so you can't move in there. So, think it through and talk it over and let me know what you have in mind."

"Okay. Fine," she said.

"Don't count on my accepting anything. I've had these propositions many times, and I've turned them all down."

"Understood."

"So . . . where the hell are our drinks?"

"Would you believe," Rick asked, "that I am unable to drive an automobile? I mean, a Chevrolet, much less a Porsche."

"City boy," said Cosima.

"Well . . . when I was at the age when you were learning to drive, I lived in the city, that's true. If my family could have afforded a car, what good would it have done us? We lived a block and a half from the store where my father worked. We bought our groceries at a store three doors from the apartment building. We bought our clothes around the corner on Second Avenue. Weeks went by when neither my father nor mother went five blocks away from our apartment. I moved around town a lot more, but—" He shrugged. "Subways. Buses. A car would have been an exorbitant luxury."

"Even so. Years have passed," she said.

"Well, I went to NYU, then to Columbia Law. Married in the city. Joined a firm in the city. Vacations . . . Bahamas. Jamaica. Europe."

"So you never learned to drive. Don't be defensive about it."

100

"I'm not."

They were on the 5:32 express train, Grand Central Station to Greenwich and Stamford in fifty minutes. If the train was on time, they would have a little less than an hour to dress in her apartment and join two other couples for cocktails and dinner. He would spend the night with her, and tomorrow, Saturday, if the weather was good they would fly to Nantucket in a private plane, or if the weather was bad but not *too* bad they would cruise on the Sound. One of the couples they were joining for dinner owned the airplane; the other had access to the boat. The second couple were Cosima's sister Susanne and her husband Albert Wilkinson, and the boat they would take on the sound was Leon Bernardin's thirty-eight-foot sloop, *Lafayette.*

Rick stared moodily at the passing view of railroad-side Westchester: tracks, ditches filled with wreckage and litter, tenements, dirty little factories, gloomy little stations. "Never judge a place by what you see from the train," he said to Cosima.

"Or see inside the train," she said quietly.

They were surrounded by commuters on their way home to towns like Mamaroneck, Harrison, Rye, Port Chester, Greenwich and Stamford. Though the decades of the gray flannel suit were gone, conformity remained; most of these men and women were hardly identifiable from one another. A bridge game was in progress in the facing seats at the rear of the car; otherwise, almost none of the commuters spoke a word to each other. Although they saw the same faces day after day, week after week, they seemed to pretend they had never noticed each other before; they stared blankly at their newspapers, or looked out the windows, and seemed hypnotized by the sway and rattle of the car. Some had drinks they had carried in from the bar car. A few slept. Boredom and fatigue were palpable in the heavy air.

Susanne had telephoned two nights ago and suggested the dinner. She and Bert lived in a New York apartment and spent occasional weekends in Greenwich, in the Bernardin

101

home. Their mother, she had said, would be playing for some group or other and would not be home for dinner Friday night, and their father expected to dine in the city, in the club atop one of the Trade Towers. Susanne and Bert would dine with the Bernardins on Saturday evening—and. wouldn't Cosima also?—but Friday night they could party with the Craigs. And couldn't she bring someone, so they wouldn't be five? If the weather was good on Saturday, Bill Craig would fly them to Nantucket for lunch. If it wasn't, they could take out *Lafayette*.

("You *do* have somebody on the string, don't you Cossy? Hey, where's Jack Putnam, anyway? It'd be great if—well, anyway, bring *somebody* along. I mean, even if it's that Jew you took on as a partner. In fact, I'd like to meet him. Not sure the parents would, though. For Saturday night, you don't need—anyway . . . Is it a deal?")

"Cold yet," said Bill Craig. "I've had the heater on, but—" He shook his head. "I'd guess the temperature is about the same as Cosima's martini." He was talking about the water in his swimming pool. "Oh, I've been going in it, the weather having been so un-Christian this week," he continued, "but I want to tell you, fellows, it'll shrink your balls."

They stood outside on a wooden deck that overlooked the swimming pool. Immense citronella candles—fat wicks in little red buckets filled with yellow wax—scented the air and drove away mosquitoes. Although the sun was still high between seven and seven-thirty, it had descended below the tops of the tall windswept oaks that surrounded the house and pool, and sunlight frolicked in sharp effulgences across the floor of the deck.

"God forbid," said Susanne. "Shrink . . . *Jesus!*"

"Not Bert's balls, for sure," said Priscilla Craig. "Surely they're brass—and unshrinkable."

"Is that eyewitness testimony or your best guess?" asked Cosima.

"I take the Fifth," laughed Priscilla.

"Take a quart," said Bert.

Bert Wilkinson weighed two-fifty, maybe two-seventy-five, as Cosima guessed. He wore a thin mustache above a mouth with thick lips. Ruddy, blondish, the jolly fat man, he moved powerfully on the tennis court and surprised everyone with his speed and grace, as many heavy men did. It was on the court, of course, that he had met Susanne. He couldn't beat her. He never had, not even one set. No one could, among their friends. Off the court, Susanne was sun-bleached, weathered, muscular: still much the same hard, compact woman she had been when she won her championship. But she was slower. Her reflexes were not as good. But she conceded nothing and still brought to the game the passion to destroy that had carried her above most other amateurs and then sustained her in her drive for the national championship.

"I bet he's got a schlong on him," Susanne said to Cosima, apart, looking at Rick lifting a chip from a basket and delicately running it across the bowl of clam dip. "Jews have, they say."

Cosima tipped her head. "Ever see Bill's?" she asked.

"Yeah, confidentially, I have."

Cosima nodded. "Very much alike," she said, saluting her sister with her martini.

"You bitch," Susanne laughed.

Cosima had always been able to do things like this to Susanne. She had never seen Bill Craig's organ, but she had tricked Susanne into admitting *she* had—which Susanne understood too late.

The Craigs—Bill and Priscilla—were a comely back-country-Greenwich couple. He was a dark-haired young man, insufferably intense and sincere at first acquaintance, easy and whimsical once he decided you meant nothing to his business. In eight years he had increased the net worth of a few clients by ten times, trading for them in the futures markets that were his specialty. In the same eight years he had increased his own net worth by twenty times. If in the easy, personable manifestation of Bill Craig there was a flaw it was in the facile self-confidence his success had engendered. As for Priscilla, she was so happy to be married to Bill that she had submerged her personality in his. She was quick, but she held back until she was sure what he wanted. It was lucky for her—for all of them—that she read his reaction to present company as allowing her free rein. Her flaw was her conspicuous devotion to Bill, and subordination to him. She was no beauty but was a pretty, busty, young mother. Cosima guessed there was an explosion in her future.

(Susanne guessed it too—"Someday she'll circumcise him with her teeth.")

Rick had accepted Cosima's judgment that he would be overdressed in Greenwich if he appeared for this party in a necktie. She was pleased with how easily he assimilated here. In tan linen slacks, blue blazer, and a light blue Ralph Lauren polo shirt, with a heavy Scotch in hand, he was indistinguishable from the other men. Bert wore a pale green jacket and green-and-white seersucker slacks. Cosima's sister was showing the deep shadow of her navel in the wide gap between her low-slung white slacks and her knit green tank top. She was drinking Stolichnaya. Priscilla was the only woman in a skirt, since Cosima had wriggled into well-faded and soft skin-tight blue jeans, which she wore with a bright yellow polo shirt.

"Understand you're Cosima's *partner*," Susanne said to Rick, with an inflection that imposed ambiguity on the word "partner." She had managed to edge him away from the others for a moment.

Rick nodded. He read her inflection and responded with his own ambiguity.

Susanne smiled. "I hope we'll see you at dinner tomorrow night, also," she said.

He nodded again. "I hope so, too," he said, though Cosima had not mentioned any Saturday-night dinner. He had heard a subtle slyness in Susanne's voice, and he saw a too-eager curiosity on her face. "Cosima and I haven't talked about it, actually."

"Oh—"

"I'm not sure I can stay," he said.

"Well. Do you really want to go to Bec Fin?" she asked, referring to Café de Bec Fin, where they had a dinner reservation for nine o'clock. "That pool water is not as cold as he says. I know, I put my toes in it. We can stay here, drink, swim and have a ball—and order something to eat. I'd settle for a pizza."

"I'm a guest," he said.

"You have a vote," said Susanne solemnly.

"I've given my proxy to Cosima."

"Cop-out," she grunted.

In the quiet little restaurant, Susanne pushed her way to a chair beside Rick, leaving Cosima to a chair diagonally across the table from him. He remarked the contrast between the two sisters: Cosima tall, cool, and elegant, Susanne short, edgy, and—by comparison—coarse. Her hair was like her mother's: the color and texture of straw, her mouth was wide, her lips thin and pale, and even in the dim light of the restaurant her eyes remained narrowed as if she were squinting in bright sunlight. He remembered Cosima's story of how Susanne learned to play pool.

"Unless it's an unpleasant subject, tell us why you left Hamilton, Schuyler," said Bill Craig to Cosima.

"They bored me," said Cosima.

Bill smiled. "I bet there was more to it than that," he said.

"Okay, I'll tell you," said Cosima. "I overheard a conversation on the train this afternoon that dramatizes it perfectly." She glanced at Rick. "I don't think you noticed, and I couldn't mention at the time. They were sitting right across the aisle from me.''

"I heard a little of it," Rick said.

"Hang in with this story," Cosima said to the rest of them. "Two men. The one on the aisle was maybe sixty. The one by the window was maybe thirty. Except that the older one had on a hat, they were dressed exactly alike—blue suits, white shirts, the whole deal. Wall Street types. The younger man was trying to have a conversation with the older man, who didn't want to be bothered, wanted to read his paper. When I picked up on it, really got to listening, it was going like this:

'Well, I had just wondered if I couldn't have maybe a little more responsibility, and this seemed like a good time—'

'There are those who don't think you're ready for more responsibility.'

'May I ask *who* thinks that? Maybe I could—'

'That's none of your business.'

'I'd like the chance to review things. I'd like to know what people think I should do to improve my performance. If someone has a problem—'

'We'll review with you, when we think it's time.'

'When might that *be?*'

'When we think it's time.' ''

Cosima shook her head. "Talk about spoiling somebody's weekend! The old bastard buried his face in his newspaper again, oblivious, and the kid stared out the window, miserable. I could almost read his mind. Someplace a young wife was making dinner, or maybe putting together something for a little cocktail party on Friday night, and that young man was wondering if he should try to keep this talk to himself when he got home, or tell her and ruin her weekend, too. I . . . I'm not going to kid you—I was upset. That supercilious, sophomoric old bastard!''

"Maybe the kid's *not* ready for promotion," said Bill Craig, apathetically.

"Well, I'll tell you what it brought to my mind," said Cosima. *"The Witches of Eastwick.* God, I wish I'd had the power to stuff that old sadist's mouth with cherry pits and feathers."

Bert Wilkinson laughed heartily, from which the others took their cue—except Rick, who knew Cosima had not exaggerated her feelings.

"That's the real world, Cosima," said Bill. "You can't be a chief until you've been an Indian."

"Hierarchy," said Cosima crisply. "What a mean and petty thing it is."

Bill grinned. "The corporate ladder," he said. "Everybody has to climb it."

"Fine talk," Priscilla interjected. *"You* didn't climb it. You chose not to."

"And Cosima and Rick have just jumped off it," said Susanne. "So fuck it."

The word "fuck" had cut across a chance instant of silence in the restaurant and had been heard at half a dozen tables. Susanne put her hand to her mouth and grinned sheepishly. The others subdued smiles and concentrated on their menus.

They ordered. Dinner was served. Café du Bec Fin did not serve liquor, only wine and beer. They'd had champagne and now wine with dinner. Cosima, as Rick was accustomed to see, was hardly affected. Neither was Bert. The myth was that a big man had plenty of capacity and was slower to feel the effects of anything he ingested. The others—including Rick himself—were altered personalities.

"I'm going swimming when we get back," muttered Susanne. "Can't wait to get in that coo-ool water."

"You'll drown," said Bert.

"Won't," she said. She turned her chair, so as to be more nearly facing Rick. "You'll go swimming with me, won't you?"

"Why not?" Rick said with a smile.

"You know . . . I was thinking. Cosima and Bert can't—

107

You know. Can't. That'd be incest. So that means it would have to be you and me, Bill and Cosima, and Bert and Priscilla. That is, if we—you know.''

"Well. It could be Priscilla and me, you and Bill," said Rick.

Susanne grinned and shook her head. "Not interested."

Rick glanced around the table. "I suppose it requires unanimous consent," he suggested.

Susanne's grin remained, and she wrinkled her nose and shrugged lightly. "How old are you, Rick?"

"Thirty-five."

"Me, too. Cosima says you're divorced—but not because of her." She shook her head. "That's my sister. Everything always so tidy. Never leaves a mess." She turned to Bert. "I want to go swimming. Let's finish up here and get going."

Bill drove the baby-sitter home. Priscilla relit the citronella candles and did not turn on the pool or deck lights. In the cold gray light of a quarter moon that had almost set, Susanne tossed aside her clothes and splashed into the pool. Bert followed her, then Priscilla.

"We don't have to do this," Cosima said quietly to Rick. "We can leave. I don't care."

"They'll think I'm strange," said Rick, and, emboldened by all he'd had to drink, he began to take off his clothes.

Nude swimming after midnight was neither romantic nor erotic. The water was in fact cold. The people bobbed around grimly at first, and only gradually did their bodies adjust and the water come to feel less than painful. All of them were logy from food and drink, so the cold water did reanimate them a little, but it did nothing to stimulate libidos suppressed by immoderation.

The comparison Rick had made between Cosima and Susanne clothed held good for them naked—Susanne lacked

Cosima's composed grace; her breasts were flat, her nipples brown, and a white scar slashed across the lower right quadrant of her surprisingly ample belly. She would not have aroused Rick in the best of circumstances. As for Priscilla, she would have, easily. The smooth skin of her little round breasts was tight, as though stretched against a force within that wanted to burst forth and double their size. When she emerged from the water, his eyes were attracted to her abundant dark pubic hair, part of it drawn out into a point by the weight of the water streaming off it. To him it was like a stage curtain, concealing and heightening a promise.

Bert and Bill were conspicuously focused on Cosima. They had seen her before, surely, yet they stared at her as if they hadn't. Bert was a mass of muscle, covered by a layer of fat. He brought to Rick's mind Rodin's nude study for his monumental statue of Balzac, the stocky, heavy-bellied torso supported by the thick columns of muscular legs. His genitals were in proportion: as massive as those of Balzac as imagined by Rodin.

Cosima swam. She stroked smoothly from end to end of the pool half a dozen times, then climbed out and sat on the edge. "Got any towels handy?" she asked.

Priscilla climbed out. "Also, we need some coffee," she said. "I'll start a pot."

"And uh . . . bathroom?" asked Rick.

"C'mon, and you can carry the towels out," said Priscilla.

In the kitchen he dried himself on a towel from the stack Priscilla brought to the counter. He wrapped the towel around his hips and padded off barefoot to the bathroom. When he returned to the kitchen, a red light burned on the coffee maker, Priscilla was gone and Susanne stood at the counter, her hips wrapped in a towel, her breasts still bare, pouring Calvados into a large snifter.

"Drink?" she asked. "I've got orders for more than I can carry. You can help me carry them out."

"Is Cosima—"

"What's the difference? Question is, do *you* want a drink?"

"That's . . . Calvados? Just a splash."

"We drink this round," said Susanne, "there's none of us going to be worth a crap. For anything. So my little proposition is dead, and you don't need to worry about it."

"I wasn't worried," he said. "Either way."

"Either that we would or we wouldn't, huh?"

He grinned. "Something like that."

Susanne sipped Calvados. She ran her eyes up and down over his body and, consciously or unconsciously, drew back her shoulders to thrust her breasts forward. Here, in the warmly lighted kitchen, their near nakedness was incongruous and colored with a blush of the illicit, as it had not been beside the pool.

"Has Cosima warned you about our family?" Susanne asked.

"Amply," he said.

"Do you want a word of advice? Don't come to dinner tomorrow night," said Susanne. The words were spoken in a quiet, matter-of-fact monotone; they were not unfriendly, yet were harshly blunt. "Cosima hasn't told my father and mother she's sleeping with you."

"And *you* assume she is."

A cynical smile raised the corners of Susanne's wide mouth. It was a smile of the mouth only, not of the eyes. "Is Cosima dropping you off at the Hyatt tonight?" she asked.

"Sure," he said satirically.

"Well, don't answer her telephone if it rings in the middle of the night. The parents don't know about you two. They think you're just her law partner, nothing more. That's all she's told them."

"I can understand."

"I don't think you do understand," said Susanne. She turned her back on him to pour herself another drink of Calvados. Her towel slipped down for an instant, and be-

110

fore she grabbed it back up he saw her smoothly arched back and the small, taut, round tush that had to be her best erotic attribute. "My father and mother aren't so naive as to suppose baby daughter is a virgin. On the other hand, they're faithful Roman Catholics." Susanne turned to face him again. "You know what I mean?"

"Anti-Semitic?" he asked. He pressed his teeth tight together. "Hmm?"

"Don't be so fast to drop that one, Rick. It's not that you're a Jew. It's that you're not a Catholic. If you were a *Methodist* they wouldn't like it."

"So she won't tell them much," he said. He reached for the Calvados bottle and poured himself a second splash. "So they won't know."

"Oh, she will sooner or later," said Suzanne. "And before that, they'll guess. Or they'll assume."

"So I should stay away."

"Depends on how thin-skinned you are. Daddy can be a bastard."

"So can I," said Rick. "But there's no reason to be. Not yet."

"With my daddy, it won't take much reason."

"This is a *friendly* warning, I assume."

"It's meant to be," said Susanne.

Bert opened the door. "Christ, what are you two doin', having a quickie?" He stepped to the counter, his bare feet slap-slapping on the kitchen tile, and grabbed a bottle of brandy. "I've got a sincere and monumental thirst."

"Susanne is warning me to steer clear of Leon Bernardin," said Rick.

"We'd all love to be able to do that," said Bert. He reached for a towel and covered himself. "My wife will forgive me if I tell you something about her father. Leon Bernardin is like the Holy Roman Catholic and Apostolic Church. He is incapable of error. He has never erred and never can err, to all eternity. But of course we love him just the same—I guess."

"Bert—"

Bert laughed and poured himself a drink. "Cosima'd like a Courvoisier, Rick," he said. "The forecast is for low clouds tomorrow. No flying weather for amateurs, Bill says. We'll take the boat out. You a sailor? You're not, by god, Captain Cosima will put you to work in the galley."

They woke to the jangle of her telephone. It was ten o'clock, and Susanne was calling from the boat club to say she and Bert had been aboard *Lafayette,* stocked it with food and beer and were waiting for Cosima and Rick as well as for the Craigs. Half an hour, Cosima told her. She and Rick would be at the dock in half an hour.

"We can pick up coffee and some doughnuts," she said to Rick as she pulled on her panties.

"Hey, Gussy, I'm not so sure," he said. He had not moved from the bed. "Last night left—"

"Hangover? Nothing like a salt breeze to conquer that."

"How about a pitching boat?"

She laughed. "So long as you toss your cookies over the lee side. Never into the wind, sailor. Never piss or barf into the wind."

"Gussy . . ."

"You serious?"

"Also, I have to think about what train I'm going to take back into town."

"They run till midnight," she said. "We'll be back in by five or six."

So. Five or six. No mention of dinner with the Bernardins. Cosima had never mentioned it, in fact. Only Susanne.

"I think it would be better if I just walk up to the station and catch the first train that comes in," he said. "I'm afraid I wouldn't be very pleasant company today."

Cosima was busy dressing. She had chosen white shorts and a loosely knit white cotton shirt with black stripes.

112

"Well," she said. "The point is for you to have a good time. If you think you won't, then . . ."

"I think I'll run back to town, Gussy."

She paused for a moment and stood frowning at him. " 'Kay, Rick," she said. "If we had some exciting alternative, I wouldn't go on the boat, but—"

"Give my best to the gang," said Rick decisively. He rolled out of bed and began to gather his clothes.

Six

"Cosima . . . ? Hughie."

For a moment she could not imagine who was on the telephone, calling himself "Hughie." Then she realized it was the voice of Hugh Hupp.

"Oh, yes. Nice to hear from you."

"I've gone over your letter. It's not too far from something I could agree to. This call's about something else, though. Office space."

"I've got to find some," she said. "I can't work out of a living room much longer."

"Right. Right. You sure as hell can't. For one thing, it's got no prestige. What I've got in mind has prestige."

"Expensive, I imagine."

"Everything good is expensive, Cosima," he said. "Here's the deal. A client of mine has too much space and is willing to sublet enough for a small law firm. I'm talking about a reception room, and say three or four offices connected by a corridor wide enough for secretarial stations. No corner offices. Just three or four in line, with a hell of a view of the Chrysler Building and everything north and east, all the way to LaGuardia Airport."

"What building, Hugh?"

"Pan Am Building, Cosima. 200 Park Avenue. Think of the commute. In on the train, up the escalator."

Cosima was standing as she talked on the telephone, idly watching Rick musing over a sheaf of accounts he had been unable to match to Fang's 1984 tax returns. She glanced at her watch. Her father had done something astounding: had suggested on the way into the city this morning that they meet for lunch. In consequence, she had not done what she often did: changed into casual clothes for her day in Rick's apartment. She was wearing a yellow silk dress. Rick had made the concession she had urged on him and was comfortable in blue jeans and a white T-shirt.

"What's the dollar?" she asked Hugh Hupp.

"Let's say forty-eight thousand," he answered. "Four thousand a month. Let's say—just for discussion—that I pay a third, that's sixteen thou, and I'll bring along my secretary, who'll act as *my* secretary and *our* receptionist. She'll answer *our* phones and receive all *our* visitors, but she won't do *your* secretarial work. So you're going to have to have a secretary. Telephones. Stationery. Incidentals. Cosima . . . you can have an office in the Pan Am Building for, oh, let's say sixty thousand a year. I mean, figuring your secretary costs you twenty. And, let me tell you, don't skimp on that figure. A cheap secretary makes a cheap office. So . . . sixty-grand for the first year."

"I was thinking of a place downtown," she said.

"Not for the business you're thinking of going into," said Hugh. "Talent is midtown, Cosima. Money is downtown, but talent is midtown. Lots of people in the talent world are reluctant to venture into money country. They'd rather make the money people come to them."

"Have you seen this space?" she asked.

"MBC is my client," he said. "I'm in and out of their offices every week. But Xytel, as you know, bought their Trager subsidiary, and they don't need as much midtown New York office space as they used to. Look. Separate entrance. Our own names on the doors that face the elevators. We—"

"The most attractive element of this office space," said Cosima, "is that—unless I misunderstand you—it is office space you are willing to share with Rick and me."

"I don't make it a condition of our associating," said Hupp. "But I can see affiliating with a small firm in the Pan Am Building much more easily than I can see myself affiliating with a small firm working out of a Market Street apartment building."

"I can't *afford* it, Gussy," Rick protested. "There's no *way* I can afford it. Five thou—Jesus!"

"You can afford it," she said. "Equal partnership, your half is $30,000 which is $2,500 a month."

"Gussy! What the hell are we *living* on? I *know* what you're living on. But what the hell am *I* living on?"

Cosima turned her back on the narrow view of the East River from the windows of his living room. "Are you so poor you can't—?"

"Yes!"

"No, you're not. You left Hamilton, Schuyler less than a month ago."

"They owe me a big check," he said resentfully. "My partnership settlement."

"Sure they do. And they're going to as long as they think they can get away with it. They'd like you to *beg* for it, Rick. But you know it's coming. They *will* pay. They'll make you sweat as long as they can, but they *will* pay. You're not broke."

"Gussy . . . It's a hell of a commitment. For me, anyway."

"It's important," she said. "I tell you what, Rick. I'll take your note for any month you can't meet it."

* * *

116

Her father had ordered trays delivered to his office. As they talked, he nibbled on breadsticks, contemplated his salad plate with distaste and sipped from a glass of cold Graves. She had already told him of her call from Hugh Hupp.

"I had never before heard of this man," he said of Hugh Hupp.

"He's well respected in his field," said Cosima. "I've checked on that."

"He practices law all alone," her father said. "Without affiliation. If he had been really good, when he was young he would have been taken into a firm."

"Not everyone wants affiliation," said Cosima.

Her father shrugged. "Perhaps not. But you have decided to romanticize people who lack affiliation, as if failure to affiliate were a positive attribute. Believe me, it isn't."

"Hugh Hupp is a capable lawyer and an impressive man. I'm anxious for you to meet him."

"Wounded on Omaha Beach. He receives a partial-disability pension—a check from the government every month. A graduate of—uh, *Michigan* law school. Twice married, twice divorced. Over the years he's had a . . . varied reputation."

Cosima touched her lips with her wineglass, to conceal her faint smile. So her father had put someone to work to assemble a report on Hugh Hupp. In his private files there was a folder on Hugh. And one on Rick, no doubt. No surprise. Nothing less than she had expected. And good news, actually. If there had been anything materially negative in those folders, he would have slapped the report on the table between them and pounded a finger on the negative item.

"You are associating yourself, Cosima, with a peculiar group of lawyers," her father on. "This Jew . . . And now an old solo practitioner on the verge of retirement. Have you any thought that they may be taking advantage of you?"

"In what way?"

117

"Can this man Loewenstein pay his way? Can he bear his share of expenses?"

"He'll earn his share of income," she said. "And we'll take his share of expenses out of that."

Her father pursed his lips. "An optimistic view."

"I need a tax man," she said. "He's a tax man."

"And Hupp is a copyright man. But for what clients? You have only one client."

"Not necessarily," said Cosima. "I've been talking to several more prospective clients. I have—"

"No additional retainers," said her father.

"Not yet," she conceded.

"Mmm," he murmured. He munched on a breadstick with his front teeth. "So. And yet you propose to commit yourself to the expense of an office on Park Avenue."

"I can afford it."

"Of course you can. And so can Hupp. But Loewenstein?" He shook his head. "No. So why is he not an employee? Why is he to be called partner?"

"For the same reason I'm investing in an office in the Pan Am Building," said Cosima. "A first-class firm must function from first-class offices, and a first-class firm must have a tax specialist. To get a first-class man, you make him a partner."

"Your relationship with this man is not . . . *personal?*"

"It is personal. But without commitment."

"You mean you sleep with him . . . but without commitment."

"Father—"

"I understand."

She understood: understood that this topic of conversation had been curtly dismissed.

"I have inquired as to whether or not any other respectable firm would be willing to take you," he said. "You *could* enter the firm of Allen, Kennedy & McGrath. They would be willing. You would enter the firm as a senior associate, with the possibility of partnership in two years or so. I suppose you wouldn't be interested."

"No."

Her father's mouth twitched, the corners descending into an eloquent scowl. "It is a *firm*," he said.

"Two ranks below Hamilton, Schuyler," said Cosima.

"You *lost* your place at Hamilton, Schuyler."

"I did *not* lose it. I gave it up."

"So you say."

"Yes, I *do* say. So what should I do? What do you *want* me to do? Having been a partner at Hamilton, Schuyler, should I go begging for an associateship at Allen, Kennedy?"

"We do not beg for anything, Cosima."

"How did we get the offer from Allen, Kennedy?" she asked.

His scowl hardened. "Timothy McGrath telephoned on a matter, and during the conversation he asked me what you were doing. I told him. He said it is very difficult to start a new firm in New York. I asked if he knew a firm that would take you. He said his would."

"Express my thanks to him," said Cosima.

"You will fail in this venture, Cosima," her father said.

"The first time Emilie ran for Congress, she could not get the nomination. Then she got the nomination and lost the election. Did you call that failure?"

A fragile little smile appeared and in an instant broke. "Your mother regarded it a failure to have *been* elected," he said. "But no, I didn't call her defeats failures because I thought her efforts realistic. I thought she *could* be elected, eventually. I cannot believe this venture of yours is realistic. Even if ultimately you make money, you will not win respect—you will not attain dignity."

"Thank Mr. McGrath for me."

"So." He pushed his plate and his wineglass away. He did not usually eat lunch, and the whole idea of it was apparently disagreeable. He dabbed at his mouth with a white linen napkin, as though to remove any trace of the repugnant fare he had sampled. "So. You think your man Loewenstein is a competent tax man?"

"Hamilton, Schuyler thinks he is. He resigned his partnership. They can't argue otherwise."

Her father pushed a file folder across his desk. "Let him take a look at that, then," he said. "BF, our bank holding company, took a loss on the sale of its stock in Connecticut United. You remember, I suppose. We acquired control of CU, then had to disgorge. We took the loss as an ordinary loss on our tax returns, and now the Commissioner of Internal Revenue disallows. My tax people think we can't prevail on an appeal. Let Loewenstein look at it. I take it he's not so busy he couldn't give me a memo in ten days. I don't want him to represent us, just to give me a written opinion. We'll pay him accordingly."

Cosima slipped the file into her shoulder bag. She smiled. "Thanks," she said.

By late July, Bernardin & Loewenstein was established in its offices in the Pan Am Building. The gold lettering on the walnut door read:

BERNARDIN & LOEWENSTEIN
Attorneys and Counsellors at Law
Cosima Bernardin
Richard N. Loewenstein

Hugh G. Hupp
Of Counsel

On Tuesday evening, August 4, they held a cocktail reception in the offices. Among their guests were pretty much the whole Bernardin family: Cosima's father; her forty-two-year-old brother Pierre Bernardin, the stockbroker; her sisters, Emilie McCarthy and Susanne Wilkinson; and her brother-in-law, Bert Wilkinson. Only Cosima's mother and her elder brother Charles, the professor of astronomy, did not appear. Jerry Patchen came, with Bull Dog Fangs' keyboard player, Adela Drake. Max Wilmot came. Joan Salomon, the pension-fund lawyer from Webster, Kent, came in response to Cosima's personal telephoned invitation. Cosima had extended scores of other invitations, to friends and acquaintances in theater, music and dance, also to the proprietors of galleries. She had told Jerry to invite anyone he wanted. Some of Hugh Hupp's clients came: writers, composers and publishers. The space was not nearly sufficient for the number of people who appeared—as Cosima had intended when she rejected suggestions they hold the reception somewhere else—and the guests jostled each other in the corridor and in the offices, most of them hungry, thirsty, and loquacious.

"Tell me something, Counsellor," Jerry said to Hugh Hupp. "What's it mean, 'of counsel' under your name?"

Cosima answered. "It means Hugh is associated with us in the capacity of a senior adviser but is not one of the partners."

Hugh shook his head. "It means 'not liable,' is what it means," he said.

"It means if we get sued for malpractice, Hugh is not a partner and is not liable," said Cosima, laughing.

"Right," said Hugh. "If these kids make a boo-boo, I'm not stuck for it."

Adela Drake laughed. Hugh was so fascinated with Adela he could not take his eyes off her. She was dressed discreetly, in a loose white cotton summer dress. She was wearing only a little makeup, not the black lipstick she wore on stage—but her head was shaved except for the hedge of red-and-green-dyed hair that stood bristly stiff from front to back of her smooth scalp.

"I've seen your posters," said Hugh.

She smiled and nodded. The screaming posters were everywhere: in windows, on the walls of stores, on display stands—and, presumably, on the walls of dens and bedrooms all over the country. Bull Dog Fangs. She was second only to Jerry as the image of Bull Dog Fangs, and on the big Fangs poster she stood hip-to-hip with him. She appeared now even on a poster of her own: ADELA! in black rubber, in the glare of a spotlight, her right hand on her keyboard, her left hand, first clenched, in the air, her mouth open in a shriek of musical frenzy.

"Can I get you a drink?" Hugh asked her.

She looked up at him, surprised. "Well . . . maybe just a Coke or somethin' like that," she said in her North Carolina accent. "I don't drink anything alcoholic."

Hugh put his hand on her elbow. He nodded toward the bar. Adela glanced at Jerry, then walked away with Hugh Hupp.

"Innocent?" Cosima asked Jerry.

"Some ways," he said, dismissing the subject. "What are you doing for dinner afterward?"

"Family," said Cosima.

"And you're going back out to Connecticut later?"

She nodded. "In my father's car."

"Well, I want to get together with you soon."

"Sure. Give me a call."

Cosima circulated, greeting the guests. She looked into her own office. Rick was there, engaged in what looked like an earnest conversation with Susanne. Cosima was about to walk in to see what that was all about, when her father walked in ahead of her, shook Rick's hand, dismissed Susanne with a curt nod and engaged Rick in a new earnest conversation, probably about the taxation of bank holding companies.

"Coss-eee!"

She liked that even less than "Coss-*ee*-ma," and only one person knew it and still called her that. Even if he had just said it, not sung it, she would have known the voice from behind was Gunther Midlen. She turned, and he was gamboling across the room toward her.

"Oh congratulations, congratu-*lations!*" he gushed. "To have your *own* ritzy office! Really, Cossy! I love it!"

"I'm glad you could come, Gunther. Have you had a drink?"

"Oh, I've had a glass of white wine," he said, leaning forward on the balls of his feet, almost to the point of falling over. "No more. You know, I have to be careful. A pound here, a pound there, and—well, you know."

He was a dancer. Gaunt, delicate of face and hands, his body was conspicuously taut, and he wore his clothes tight to show it off. He reeked of the odor of talcum powder—baby powder, specifically—as if he had dusted himself all over with it.

"I hear good things about you, Gunther," she said.

He understood the compliment to be conversational and so ignored it. "Oh, *God!*" he groaned. "I saw Adela over there. Can you *imagine?* I am *appalled!*"

Gunther had trained for dance at the North Carolina School of the Arts, where Adela had trained for the piano. They had known each other there.

"I know you've seen the posters," Gunther went on. "But have you seen the *performance?* She plays an electronic keyboard." He leaned closer to Cosima and lowered his voice. "And, Cossy . . . she shows her . . . *tits!*"

"Ask her for a contribution to your ballet company," said Cosima dryly.

"She could fund you."

"Money . . ." Gunther breathed. He shook his head. "Cossy, you know she's a born-again. I wonder what they think. I mean, her church."

"They like her contributions," said Cosima.

Gunther chuckled. "I bet they do." He sighed, glanced around the room. "Cossy, I've got a serious problem. Maybe you can help."

"Uh . . . Well, maybe."

"The New York Ballet has a lovely little ballerina from the Soviet Union, named Svetlana Terasnova. She's a defector, walked away from a touring Russian ballet company during an appearance in Toronto. Came to the States four years ago. She's received notice to report for depor*tation*. Can you imagine? The child is in hysterics. Everyone who knows her is in hysterics."

"She needs a lawyer," said Cosima.

"That's why I mention it."

"I'm not a specialist in immigration law."

"Who *is*, Cossy? Creepy fellows, the ones I've seen. Involved in keeping loft seamstresses in the United States. Nobody has any confidence in them. None of our crowd do. Why don't you talk to Svetlana? I'd think of it as a favor."

"We're here. This is our office. Bring her in."

"*Cossy!* This is a vendetta! By those *people!* Not just the Immigration Service. The Justice Department. I mean, why the *Justice* Department, anyway? What do they have to do with it?"

"The Immigration and Naturalization Service is in the Department of Justice," said Cosima.

"Well, they're absolutely *consumed* with the idea of deporting poor little Lana."

"Bring her in, Gunther. We'll take a look."

"I'll *send* her in, Cossy," said Gunther, subdued. "I think you lawyer types can deal with her better in my absence."

Cosima's instinctive reaction was *Fine! Great! I can deal with anything better in your absence, Gunther*. Then she saw the anxiety on his face: unaffected and humane. She touched his hand. "I'll do what I can," she said softly. "Send her in. Tomorrow. Those orders have to be appealed fast."

"You're a princess, Cossy."

She eschewed the response that came to mind. Instead, she squeezed his hand and said, "So nice of you to come this evening, Gunther. Why don't you go rescue Adela from my counsel? I suspect she'll welcome the deliverance."

Susanne sided in. "How can you stand it? C'mon. I want

you to talk to Alan DeRosche. He's curious as hell as to how you relate the law business to—well, c'mon."

They sat around a long table afterward: the guests of Leon Bernardin at La Grenouille—the Bernardins and Wilkinsons, plus Rick Loewenstein and Hugh Hupp. Threads of conversation wove shifting and complex patterns over the table:

Rick: "There's a 1986 decision from the Ninth Circuit that may affect the commissioner's thinking."

Leon: "Not over dinner, Mr. Loewenstein, please."

Pierre: "Dad, did you realize that Jerry Patchen is the son of Basilio Paccinelli? Cosima tells me—"

Leon: "I wish your mother could have been there to meet that young woman with the red and green hair."

Cosima: "I don't know how to handle an immigration case."

Hugh: "Nothing to it. We'll handle it."

Emilie: "In your *office*, for Christ's sake?"

Cosima: "Well, a serigraph. Not a painting."

Rick: "Who the hell's Symbari, anyway?"

Susanne: "If you could paint like Symbari, you wouldn't have to practice law, dear."

Hugh: "I suppose you can handle a divorce? Tax man though you are . . ."

Rick: "I have a little recent experience with the divorce court."

Cosima: "Jerry would like to have Leroy Neiman do a poster for Fang."

Hugh: "She's been married three years. Her husband can't accept the Bull Dog Fangs deal."

Rick: "I suppose if it's an *uncontested* divorce."

Susanne: "He used to deliver cases of wine and gin to our house."

Bert: "Why the hell they want to *deport* her?"

Pierre: "Was that Watson Waugh? I thought I recognized him."

Hugh: "She's going to have tax problems, too."

Cosima: "You won't believe this. He wanted to know if our firm could write wills."

Leon: "I don't know exactly. Playing for some old ladies' musicale. All this is insignificant to her."

Hugh: "I lost a goddamned fortune in Brussels sprouts futures."

Pierre: *"Bruss—?* Ha! Very good!"

Rick: "Is he? You think? I mean, that could complicate—"

Cosima: "Well, if she's going to be our client, ask her."

Rick: "Potential conflict of interest in it, too, you know."

Hugh: "It was Patchen's idea. He can't complain."

Bert: "If you could land Waugh . . . Tell you what. I'll do a lunch with him and nudge him a little.

Emilie: "I'll ask. But you know what's going on—the White House is prodding the Immigration Service. Maybe we should introduce a private bill.

Leon: "The '71 was a better year than this. I put away ten cases of it."

"My name is Svetlana Nikolaievna Terasnova."

She faced all three of the lawyers at Bernardin & Loewenstein, sitting on the couch facing Cosima's desk, with Rick beside her and Hugh in a chair turned toward her.

"Usually I am called Lana."

She was everyone's idea of a young ballerina: small, lithe, exquisite. Her little face was utterly flawless, with symmetrical features and unblemished skin; she studied Cosima with big, round, solemn, deep blue eyes. Her dark brown hair was tied back tightly. Her unplucked brows accented her eyes. Her subtle smile went unnoticed at a glance and was remarked only after a moment's close observation. She spoke slowly, with a soft accent.

She had handed to Cosima the order she had received from the Immigration and Naturalization Service. She was directed to surrender to the INS on Monday morning, August 17. The order advised she should be prepared to be held in custody, pending her actual deportation. She was also notified she was entitled to appeal to the Board of Immigration Appeals.

"Has an appeal been filed, Lana?" asked Cosima.

"No. Mr. Tracy, who has been my lawyer in this matter, has said it would be pointless, that I must be deported. My friends say I should not have him as my lawyer anymore."

"Do you want us to represent you?" Cosima asked.

"Yes, please. This paper says I will be put in jail on August seventeenth. Doesn't it? I don't want to be put in jail. I am afraid."

"You are not going to jail on August seventeenth, Lana," said Hugh firmly.

"We'll file your appeal. That will hold things up for at least six months."

"My friend was deported," she said sadly. "It was very bad. He was made to stay in jail for *two weeks*. Then they put him on an airplane."

"We won't let that happen to you," said Cosima.

"I cannot return to the Soviet Union," said Lana gravely.

"What would they do to you?" asked Hugh.

"They would not permit me to dance."

Hugh frowned. "Ah . . ." he murmured.

"We, uh—We need to know why they are trying to deport you," said Cosima. "We'll get your files, but for now . . . Please. Tell us."

"I did that which was bad," said Lana soberly. "Always I have wanted to dance. Always, I have wanted to dance outside the Soviet Union, where the artist is free to express whatever . . . Well, I am sure you know. As I am growing to womanhood and must have my training, it is the time of Brezhnev and Andropov and those others, those old men from the bad times. When it is time for me to go abroad,

127

it is still their time. To obtain my training, I must always be silent. I must never criticize. To be allowed to go outside the Soviet Union, I must be *kommunistka*. You know? Communist. So . . . I am of Komsomol."

"Komsomol . . ."

"Komsomol. It is . . . Communist Party, for the young people. You have heard of this?"

Hugh nodded. "What we'd call the Communist Party youth wing."

"Yes."

"So they want to deport you because you were a Communist?"

"Yes. But more. I did the bad thing. When I came into this country, they asked me if I had ever been a member of the Communist Party or any . . . anything like it. I said no. I signed a paper saying no. I was afraid they would not let me enter the United States if I said yes."

"False statement on the visa application," said Hugh. He shook his head.

"That does make a tough case."

"I must be put in jail?"

He smiled at her. "No, Lana. We'll file the appeal. That will give us time to work on the case. On the seventeenth of August, don't go to the INS office as it says on this order. You come here that morning." He glanced at Cosima. "Just in case there's any mixup."

"I am without very much in funds," said the little ballerina.

"We'll represent you anyway," said Cosima. "You pay us when you can."

"If the court please," said Rick, nodding toward the judge: the slightest hint of the bow with which in centuries past a lawyer might have acknowledged the dignity of a judge. "I am Richard Loewenstein, of Bernardin & Loewenstein, counsel for the plantiff, Adela Drake Woody."

For a brief moment the judge raised his eyes from the file on the desk before him and regarded Rick curiously. Then he gave his attention once more to the manila folder and the few papers bound to it with an Acco fastener.

Rick continued. "The motion before the court is an application for a restraining order. The plantiff, Adela Drake Woody, asks for an order to restrain the defendant, John Woody, from interfering in any way with the plantiff's person, property and business relationships during the pendency of this action for divorce. As the affidavit of the plantiff discloses, the defendant has, by letter and telephone, threatened physical violence against the plaintiff and has threatened, further, to do all he can to damage the plaintiff in her career as a musician."

Cosima had come with Rick, to see him in action before a court. He stood erect, dignified in his dark blue pinstriped suit. His presentation was crisp, factual, polished; he had rehearsed it, at least mentally, and was, Cosima thought, a formidable lawyer who had perhaps chosen wrong when he chose taxation, not litigation, as a speciality. He was in distinct contrast to the other lawyers in the courtroom, the dozen or so of them waiting for their cases to be called. These others lounged carelessly on the benches, chatting amiably, filling the courtroom with a drone of conversation that required the judge and anyone speaking to him to raise their voices. Polyester suits. Brown shoes. Loose ties. Some of them in sport jackets and slacks. She heard what sounded like snickering.

This was the practice she and Rick did not want: routine appearances before the minor courts. Still, as she had anticipated, they could not refuse their business clients full-service representation. Every law firm knew that clients who had to go to other lawyers with part of their business often took the rest of their business with them, sooner or later. They were not likely to lose Jerry Patchen by refusing to handle Adela's divorce; but Adela, who would earn half a million dollars this year, much of it from the posters and T-shirts that featured her alone, was a worthwhile client. Rick was reviewing her tax returns for the past five years, and they were preparing to establish an investment and retirement program for her.

Rick had filed the petition for divorce two weeks ago. It should have been simple, uncontested, even amiable. John Woody had agreed to the divorce and promised Adela he would not resist it. But when he received the petition and summons in the mail, he changed his mind. He had written Adela a letter, saying he had what he called a "lean" on half of everything she owned, on half her earnings. He said he had talked to a lawyer in North Carolina, and this lawyer had told him he was entitled to half of anything his wife had and, what was more, could prevent her from working if he wanted to. When she telephoned to try to make peace, he had threatened to come to New York and enforce his claims with his fists.

"In the circumstances, Your Honor, we—"

"Okay," said the judge. He scribbled something on a paper in the file and pushed it to the front of his desk.

"If Your Honor please, I—"

"I said okay, Counsellor. Okay. C'mon. I got a hundred more of these to hear."

"I beg your pardon?"

The judge sighed and pushed the file forward until it was ready to fall to the floor. "Ya got your order, fella. I signed it. Take it to the clerk. And, incidentally, next time don't type up your papers like this. Typed stuff, I got to read it. Buy a set of the printed forms for these cases. Printed, I know what it says and don't have to read all the way through. Okay? Who's next?"

A fat, sweating lawyer pushed past Rick, grabbed his file and handed it to him, and shook his head scornfully. "Fraticelli v. Fraticelli," he said to the judge. "Same thing, pretty much. Same order."

"Husband here?" the judge asked, looking around. "No?

Okay. Here ya go." And he handed the fat lawyer a signed order.

As Cosima and Rick walked to the rear of the courtroom, past ranks of grinning scriveners, a young woman rose and rushed after them. Just outside the doors she caught up.

"Hey. Hang on a minute, Counsellors. Della Rosario. *Post.* She's *the* Adela Drake, right?"

Cosima stopped. Rick walked on a few paces, until he saw that Cosima had not kept up with him, then he returned.

"Hey, what'd he do? Threaten her? Lemme see the file, will ya?"

"I don't think I can do that," said Rick.

"Hey, it's a public record, Counsellor. You file it in the clerk's office, I can go in and look at it. C'mon. Why hold me up?"

Cosima nodded to Rock. "Let her see it."

Frowning uncertainly, Rick handed over the file. Della Rosario—a stocky young woman, broad-shouldered, broad-hipped, full-breasted, with a pretty face and dark brown hair down to her shoulders read over the application for the restraining order.

"That prick," she said. "What were they married, four months?"

"Technically, they're still married," said Cosima. "As for living together as husband and wife—eight months."

"Her bio sketch says four months."

Cosima smiled. "Giving him the benefit of the doubt."

"What's he do, this guy?" asked the reporter.

"He erects silos," said Cosima. "He's foreman of a crew that erects silos."

Della Rosario made a note. "What the hell kind of work is that?" she asked.

"Good work," said Cosima. "If you live where silos are important. Farmers buy thousands of them, tens of thousands, every year. Putting them up is a special skill."

"And he's a born-again?"

131

"So's she," said Cosima. "That's how they met—church buddies. The difference was, Adela is a prodigy—and, lucky for her, the North Carolina School of the Arts is one of the finest conservatories of music in the world, on a par with Juilliard here in New York. She went there, studied piano—"

"Yeah, right," said Della Rosario. "I know. And the rest is history. But what's going on right now is *news*. The history kind of ignored the fact she had a husband. I mean, we knew, but—he really tell her he had a 'lean' on her earnings?"

"We can show you his letter," said Cosima. "Suppose we step into the clerk's office, and I'll show it to you while Rick is filing the order."

Rick made no effort to conceal his reluctance about handing his briefcase to Cosima while he stood at the counter, filed the signed copy of the court order and got two copies stamped as authenticated copies. Cosima was not reluctant. She went through the papers in the briefcase and found the handwritten letter John Woody had written to Adela.

"Mind if I have this Xeroxed?" Della Rosario asked after she had scanned the two pages of ballpoint writing.

Cosima shrugged. "Be my guest."

The reporter summoned a clerk and had the copy made on the copying machine behind the counter. The letter read:

well you think your getting away with something well your not I talked to a lawyer here yesterday and he told me I got a lean for half of everything you got and half of everything you make so you better plan start to write some checks made out John Woody

The Book says wives cleeve to their husbands—which you never did do—The Book says wives is supposed to live where their husbands want to live and do what there husbands want to do when we got married you

132

said you love honor and *obay*—which is something else you never done

I got them papers from your smartass lawyers in New York all wrote up proper well I don't care about New York or any laws they got there John Woody follows a higher law which is the law of the Lord

I give you two choices one is to come home and live like a Christian wife the other is to send me half of everything which is mine by my lean you dont do it I send you some court papers you wont like better yet I come up to New York and beat some sense in you.

I seen you on them posters that show you with your hair cut off and what you got left colored red and green it makes me shamed I hardly show my face in church since its got around I got a wife like that I come up there and give you a nuckle sandwich Dont you think I wont

"Charming fellow, John," said Della Rosario.

"Macho," said Cosima with a smile. "You don't have to go to the Bible Belt to find them."

"Well, I appreciate the copy," said the reporter. "You let me know if anything happens."

"Don't depend on it," said Cosima. "Keep in touch."

"Call *you?*"

Cosima grinned and nodded. She glanced at Rick. "Right. Call me."

"Explain," said Rick in the cab on the way back uptown. "Be so good as to explain."

"Who's our client, Rick?" asked Cosima.

"I know who our client is. Do you think our client will be pleased to know we handed over her husband's letter to the goddamned *Post?*"

"She will if I get on the phone to the *Daily News* as soon as we get back to the office, and give a copy to them, too."

"Cosima . . . Are we lawyers or—"

"What are lawyers for, Rick?" she interrupted crisply. "To represent *clients,* right? To advance their interests. Well, it's in Adela's interest to have that asinine letter spread across the public prints. It gets her publicity, which is what she lives on. It gets her sympathy. And when John Woody finds out the whole damned country is laughing at him—which it will be after the New York papers publish that letter and a hundred other papers pick it up—he may think better of trying to send us 'some court papers' we won't like, or coming to New York and giving Adela a 'nuckle sandwich.' "

Rick shook his head. "Lawyers fight clients' battles in the courts, not in the newspapers."

"I propose to fight my clients' battles in whatever forum I can be effective," Cosima said. "Representing clients is not playing games, or, if it is, I don't propose to play by archaic rules made up by lawyers and judges who were antediluvian when they were alive but in any case are long since dead. That reporter represented an *opportunity,* and I was glad to take advantage of it. You're naive if you think other lawyers wouldn't have taken it."

"You think Hamilton, Schuyler—"

"You're damned right, Hamilton, Schuyler. Only in this forum, we're not just as good as they are—we're *better.* "

Rick put his hand on Cosima's leg and squeezed affectionately. "This trip downtown has been a learning experience," he said.

Seven

Charles Bernardin arrived at the offices in the Pan Am Building about 12:45 P.M. Cosima had asked him to lunch a dozen times, and he had decided he could no longer put her off without distinctly appearing to be putting her off. And so he arrived, on a rainy September day, and as he entered the reception room he was embarrassed to notice that his umbrella was still dripping.

The secretary-receptionist looked up. "Yes, sir?"

"Uh . . . My name is Charles Bernardin. I have an appointment with my sister."

The secretary, Teresa Idelia, smiled. "Why don't you sit down for a moment," she said. "Miss Bernardin is on the phone, but I'll tell her you're here."

Charles Bernardin was a tall man, forty-five years old. He held an endowed professorship of astronomy at Columbia University and was widely recognized as a radio astronomer. He had a deep voice, which he used as though he had been trained as an actor. A white scar on his upper lip looked as though he had undergone surgery for a harelip; actually it was the result of a boyhood accident on a motorcycle. He pursed his lips constantly, as if he smoked a pipe and was uneasy without it. In fact, he had not smoked for twenty years. His dark hair had grayed only a little and lay in fine, disciplined strands across his lofty skull.

He was curious about this law office. Their father had described it as a frivolous self-indulgence of Cosima's, from which he expected little but aggravation. Certainly it was atypical. The wall opposite the couch where he sat was all but covered by an immense and extravangantly flamboyant poster, framed behind a huge sheet of Lucite: Bull Dog Fangs, with a personal autograph by each of the bizarre performers garishly pictured. He understood that this group was a client here; even so, it seemed an inappropriate adornment for a law office.

"Charles!"

His sister Cosima. The baby of the family. They had said at home as she grew up that she didn't look like a Bernardin and certainly not like a Fitzgerald; so whence came this tall, well-put-together young woman, so much more handsome than Emilie or Susanne? So much more chic. Standing before him now, smiling broadly, her hand out to take his, she was wearing a simple blue denim dress that on Emilie would have looked like a jail uniform but that Cosima wore with a flair that was characteristic of her: with a heavy gold chain for a belt, a smaller gold chain for a necklace, and black high-heeled shoes that complemented her short skirt in showing her shapely legs.

She squeezed his hand and escorted him into her office. Here again, her style was apparent. Her desk was a kidney-shaped glass-topped table. A huge, colorful Roy Neiman serigraph hung on the wall that faced her desk: the one called *F.X. McRory's Whiskey Bar*. Two smaller ones of women tennis players hung on the wall that faced the windows. The one of Chris Evert hitting a strong backhand was the image of their sister, enough like her to have been an action portrait of the young Susanne. To Cosima's left as she sat behind her desk, she had a view of all Manhattan north of Grand Central. On the credenza behind her she had a desktop computer.

Charles sat down on the couch that faced the desk. Cosima sat down, put her elbows on the glass, clasped her hands under her chin and grinned at him.

"So, Charles. At long last. I was beginning to think you'd disowned me."

"Well, I've been to Puerto Rico, you know."

"Yes, for all of three weeks. What were you doing, looking for signals from little green men?"

"From little blue stars," he said.

She inquired of his family, and he told her his wife and children were well. He had taken them with him to Puerto Rico, and the family had lived for three weeks in a house trailer parked on the mountainside near the radio telescope. The children, he said, had picked up a crude but serviceable Spanish vocabulary; his wife had acquired a profound knowledge of Caribbean entomology.

"Where's your partner, Loewenstein?" Charles asked. "I was told to be sure to meet him."

"Who told you to be sure to meet him?"

"Father. And Susanne. He seems to have made an impression."

"He made an impression on Susanne, I know," said Cosima. "She'd no sooner met him than she tried to get him to go to bed with her."

Charles smiled. "Sibling rivalry," he said. "It was always that way between you and Susanne. Whatever either of you had, the other wanted it—at least a taste of it."

"Rick's not an ice-cream cone," said Cosima.

The deep voice rumbled out through the pursed lips. "Oh, I suppose not," said Charles. "Father says he's a competent tax lawyer."

"Dad gave him a little work, a little money," she said. "I know why."

"Sure. To get a good look at the fellow. To get a pin through him, so he could hold him down on a piece of white paper and study him."

Cosima laughed. "Whatever else we all are, Charles, you're the most expressive."

He was also, usually, the pensive, sober-sided one, the family eccentric, as their father said: the one who coped with other worlds, not with this. He had the same grandparental legacy his brother and sisters had—though his seemed somehow to have vanished, absorbed into his professorial lifestyle without a visible trace. His wife, Sybil, was a mouse who went about in long print skirts and home-knitted vest sweaters over white T-shirts. He sat here now in a tan suede jacket spotted with rainwater, dark brown corduroy slacks, and heelless, thick-soled earth shoes—surely the last surviving specimens of the type. Sometimes Cosima herself had wondered whether or not Charles' mind ever focused on the things her own was constantly focused on; and sometimes, too, she wistfully regretted she had not concentrated as he had done: on the certainties of science.

His mind was not fixed on certainties now. "Father says you sleep with Loewenstein. Not that it's any of my business, of course."

"Or of his," she said.

Charles pursed his lips and blew his breath out in a low whistle. "Right," he said. "None of our business." He did it again: blew the breath the same way. "On the other hand, I'm sure you know father's motives are none but the best. He is deeply concerned about your relationship with this man."

"Dad also thinks he can tell me how to practice law. But I think we should change the subject, Charles," said Cosima.

Charles turned down the corners of his mouth and nodded. "Mmm. Well . . . I am perhaps fortunate to have made my career in a field father utterly fails to understand. I am lucky, I suppose, that father hasn't the remotest notion of what a pulsar might be and cannot argue any conclusions I might reach about the nature of pulsars. On the other hand . . . it would be an error for us to underestimate his knowledge of the nature of human relationships.''

"Which returns us to the subject," said Cosima. "Charles—"

"The man spends weekends in your condominium," Charles persisted.

"Yes. And I spend nights in his apartment. Dad says we sleep together? That's a euphemism. We *do it*, Charles. Not constantly. But . . . from time to time, we play with each other's private parts. Okay?''

Charles had raised both hands, and his open palms faced Cosima. "Never mind that," he said. "The question is— to what purpose?''

"What *purpose?* To what—" She stopped; she had to stop, to laugh. "What purposes are there, brother?'' She held up her fingers and began to count. "Procreation. Forget that. Pleasure—''

"Cosima," her brother interrupted. "Among a few old-fashioned people, a love affair is still considered as a possible prelude to marriage. The question is—are you thinking of marrying this man?''

Cosima turned away from Charles and looked out the window. "It wouldn't be suitable. Would it? That's father's word, isn't it? Such a marriage would not be suitable.''

Charles sighed again, and nodded. "It's not that he's a Jew, Cosima.''

"The hell it isn't.''

"Cosima . . . If he were an *Episcopalian*—''

"I'm going to tell you something Rick said to me," she interjected. "His father was only a shoe-store salesman, his mother only a part-time dime-store clerk, neither of them educated, both observant Jews. And he told me he was very grateful to them for something—which was that they never tried to ram religion, or the cultural heritage that went with it, up his ass. They let him explore things like that for himself, to reach his own conclusions. They didn't constantly press—''

"But we constantly pressed you, hmm?" Charles interrupted.

Cosima shrugged. "You tried." She smiled. "Actually, of course, *you* didn't. When you went away to college, I was five years old."

Charles tipped his head to one side and smiled warmly, reminiscently. "Faith and family," he said quietly.

"Oh, yes. Only I think he's reversed it over the years. He says family and faith now."

"Yes, I guess so. Family and faith. There are no . . . conflicts in the family, you know. We are all of a kind, more or less. Oh, I know there are dramatic differences between, say, Sybil and me and Susanne and Bert, but basically we are one kind of people. Father would like it to remain that way."

"He couldn't invite Rick for Christmas dinner, I suppose," said Cosima acidly.

"You make it sound so—"

"Anti-Semitic."

"*No.* You know it isn't. I swear to you it isn't. You know we would be just as distressed if we heard you were having an affair with Ruggiero Paccinelli—and *he's* a Catholic."

"How was it that Greenwich real-estate brokers used to put it?" she asked. "In the Back Country, no property could be bought by anyone whose origins touched the Mediterranean—no Italians, no Hispanics, no Greeks, no Lebanese, no Jews. They didn't have to mention blacks—none had the temerity to apply. I should have remembered that rule; it seems to apply to my friendships."

"I think you are being unjust to your family," Charles said with heavy finality. Like his father, he closed a discussion when he was tired of it. Like his father, he disliked to be distracted from his main concerns for very long; and, in personal and family matters, away from his profession, he would not long trouble his mind with what he could not govern. "Do I understand we are to have lunch?"

As they left her office, Cosima noticed that Rick had come

in and was sitting in his. Charles noticed, too, but she was annoyed and did not offer to take him into Rick's office and introduce them.

She returned from lunch wet and exasperated. As much as Charles had infuriated her, she loved him and could not use with him the curt, harsh words he had caused to come to her mind. Indeed, she sensed she had spoken too stridently to him as it was. That was how it was with family; no matter how angry they sometimes made her, they *were* her family, and that overrode her personal feelings.

"Cosima."

Hugh spoke to her from his office. She went in. He handed her a paper.

"The Board of Immigration Appeals has turned us down," he said. "Lana's deportation order is reinstated. She's ordered to report on Tuesday."

"*Tuesday?* Why so soon? Isn't two or three weeks normal?"

"Proves something," said Hugh. "Somebody's got a hard-on about this case."

"Against *Lana,* for god's sake? Against a *ballerina?* Somebody wants to make a crusade against that pretty little girl?"

Hugh shrugged. "I don't know, but we'd better get into court toot sweet."

Cosima nodded. "Into court. *Tout de suite.* Fortunately, I've already researched the law. I know what we have to file. *Tuesday!* We can't have the papers ready this afternoon. We'll have to file on Monday."

On Monday, September 28, Cosima filed in the United States Circuit Court an application for review of the deportation order. She was not able to obtain an order fixing bail for Lana. A judge would review that application and set bail in the morning, she was told.

"An hour, Lana. Maybe two or three hours," she said

to the frightened ballerina on Tuesday morning. "We'll have your bail set and posted before noon."

"I don't want to be locked in jail. I am afraid," Lana said, sobbing.

They sat on a hard, straight, institutional bench outside the office of the immigration officer into whose custody she was ordered to surrender—Cosima and Lana, alone. Five minutes ago they had seen a smiling young man enter that office carrying a briefcase, and Cosima had guessed he was the representative of the Justice Department, come to oppose the plea she would make that Lana be released until the court set bail. Once again—as had happened when Dan Nash was called in for a prior conference with Douglas Miller—she found herself forced to sit and wait while her case was discussed out of her hearing. It promised ill.

"Miss Terasnova. Counsellor."

A grim woman in a sort of quasi uniform wearing a black skirt, white blouse and a badge summoned them into the office of Thomas Eberhard, Deputy District Director of Immigration and Naturalization. He was a big man, sitting heavily behind his desk, looking as though it might be difficult for him to force himself out of his chair. He wore a three-piece beige suit, and the white buttons of his vest formed a rough arc from his collar to his wide black leather belt. He did not rise. He pointed at two aluminum chairs covered in perforated dark green vinyl.

"Miss Terasnova. Miss . . . Bernardin. Maybe you know Layman Langley, from the Justice Department. He's in charge of your file for the Department."

Langley wore a smile that Cosima would discover was fixed, unvarying. His face was flushed, his eyes blue and bulging. Neatly combed, neatly dressed in a dark vested suit, erect, and with that fixed smile, he possessed something of the aspect of one of those missionary lads who come to your door carrying the Book of Mormon and a clipboard.

"Miss Terasnova, as you know, a decision has been made in your case."

142

"Mr. Eberhard," said Cosima. "I believe you know that we've filed an application for review in the United States Circuit Court for the Second Circuit. I would much appreciate it if you would stay your order for Miss Terasnova to surrender herself into custody until we can obtain a bail order from the court. My associate is at the court now, and there is no question but that an order will be issued. It does seem unnecessary for Miss Terasnova to be held in detention for a matter of hours, when we all know the court will certainly grant bail as a matter of course."

"Mr. Langley?" said Eberhard.

"The government will oppose bail," said Langley. "I, too, have an associate at the court right now, to argue against it. Speaking of what is unnecessary, it seems unnecessary to us to drag out administrative and judicial proceedings indefinitely, when we know that Miss Terasnova is one of those persons specifically defined in Section 1251 as deportable and will definitely be deported, sooner or later. The law explicitly provides that the court will dispose of the appeal on the basis of the evidence already taken during the administrative proceedings and will not hear new evidence. The evidence is undisputed that Miss Terasnova was a member of a totalitarian organization mentioned in Section 1251 and swore that she was not. It's clear. The matter is beyond dispute. The only purpose of court proceedings is to delay her deportation, and it is our experience that persons in custody are less interested in long delays than are persons running loose in the community on bail. The Attorney General opposes any stay and opposes release on bail pending final disposition."

Cosima turned to Eberhard. "The court will grant bail. You know that."

"I don't know," said Eberhard. "If a judge does that, it's *his* responsibility. Mine is to administer the law, and what you're asking for, Miss Bernardin, is special consideration, something outside the ordinary procedures provided for in the statutes. I can't go along with you. The young lady's case had been heard fully. She is deportable. I see no point in postponing further."

Lana understood and began to cry. Cosima squeezed her hand. Eberhard looked doleful and squeezed his hands together until his knuckles cracked. Langley busied himself at gathering his papers into his briefcase. The woman with the badge, who had stood silently apart during the brief exchange, stepped close to Lana and waited.

Cosima squeezed tighter on Lana's hand. "You and I will have lunch together," she said, loudly enough for Eberhard and Langley to hear. "Right now, you go with this lady. They're not going to hurt you."

The woman extended her hand to Lana and smiled. "That's right," she said. "Nobody is going to hurt you."

Not reassured, still weeping, Lana rose. The woman took her arm and led her from the office.

Cosima stood and confronted Langley, who seemed to pretend he had been deaf and dumb for the past two minutes. "What the hell is this?" Cosima asked him. "You get some kind of personal satisfaction from—"

"Miss Bernardin," said Langley. His smile had disappeared as he had studiously stuffed his file in his briefcase, but now it returned, measured and synthetic as before. "The young woman is a Communist."

"She was a member of Komsomol, and you know why. It's on the record."

"I know why she *says* she joined. I know why she *says* she lied about it when she entered the United States. Her *whys* don't make much difference, really. All I'm interested in are two facts—she was a member of Komsomol, an arm of the Soviet Communist Party, and she lied about it. She is precisely the kind of person we are charged with identifying and deporting. That's the law."

"That's the McCarran-Walter Act," said Cosima.

Langley nodded. "The very names McCarran and Walter may bring a bad taste to your mouth, Miss Bernardin, and cause you to grimace when you speak them, but the

McCarran-Walter Immigration Act is the law, and the Justice Department enforces it.''

"Well, congratulations, Mr. Langley," said Cosima. "Your personal dedication to protecting our country against the subversive threat of Svetlana Terasnova marks you as a real patriot."

The stiff smile remained in place. Langley nodded. "I will see you in court, Miss Bernardin."

Cosima did in fact see Lana for lunch. She picked her up in a cab at the immigration detention center and took her to 21, where they joined Hugh at his usual table at 1:30.

"They put on my wrist a handcuff," Lana said soberly. "Then that same handcuff on the wrist of a brown girl who spoke only Spanish, so we were chained together. And they carried us in a car to the prison. They took our fingerprints and made photographs of us. They made us take off all our clothes, to be searched. And then they gave us gray dresses to wear and locked us inside a big hall where there were many cells and many other women, prisoners too. They were watching television, and smoking, and they said we would stay there a long time and then be put on airplanes and flown—god knows where."

The ballerina's eyes, which were always deeply solemn, fastened now on Cosima in an earnest, almost accusing, gaze. She was like a child who, until she falls and skins her knee, believes her mother can protect her from any hurt, so that the stinging and the sight of blood seem a betrayal.

"They sent some little mouse of a lawyer to argue against bail," said Hugh.

"You should have heard the one they sent to the INS office," said Cosima. "A rat."

"They've got a hard on for sure," said Hugh. "We can string this out for a long time. We lose the appeal, we can go for happus cappus. But I think you'd better talk to your sister."

145

"I do not understand," protested Lana.

Cosima smiled at her. "Mr. Hupp says we can apply for a writ of habeas corpus. That's an important right in this country. Though you are free on bail, technically you are in the custody of the Immigration and Naturalization Service. A writ of habeas corpus is a court order, demanding that anyone who holds someone else in custody come to court and explain why—in legal terms, of course. In effect, our application for a writ of habeas corpus would call into question everything that's been done in your case and require the government to justify it."

"But your sister? He mentioned talking to your sister."

"He's suggesting that I should also ask my sister to introduce a private bill. My sister is a member of Congress and can try to get the Congress to pass a law making you a citizen of the United States."

"This is possible?"

"This is difficult," said Cosima. "But it is possible. We'll try everything, Lana. We'll try everything."

From seven thousand feet, Montauk Point, Block Island, and the Rhode Island shore were visible, though obscured by the exaggerated brightness of hazy sunlight. The white-capped waters below were vividly blue, and the white wakes of boats were distinct behind them. It was toward the horizon that visibility diminished and landmarks disappeared.

The radio in the Piper Seneca was switched through the ceiling speakers, and they could hear Nantucket ATIS—Automated Terminal Information Service.

"Nantucket altimeter two-niner-eight-niner, temperature six-eight degrees, dew point six-five, winds four-zero at ten knots, gusting to twenty, scattered clouds at four, broken at ten, runway six in use. Advise the controller on initial contact that you have received Information Papa."

Bill Craig squinted over his chart, satisfying himself about the layout of the runways on Nantucket Memorial. He glanced at the digital displays on his navigation receivers, to assure himself that the autopilot was holding the Seneca on course. Assured, he pushed back his Yankees' baseball cap and relaxed a measure.

Cosima occupied the right seat, scanning the sea below through binoculars. She was looking for a nuclear-powered submarine entering Block Island Sound and making for Groton. She had spotted submarines before, while flying with the Craigs to Nantucket or the Vineyard. She raised the binoculars and scanned the horizon directly ahead. The islands were there, but to pick them out of the haze was easier without the binoculars.

Priscilla and Susanne sat behind Bill and Cosima. Even though it was a Saturday, Bert had not been able to take the day off to fly to Nantucket. Cosima was disappointed about that, since she had hoped to talk with Bert about the Svetlana Terasnova immigration case and perhaps encourage him to do a segment on it for "What's News?" She was disappointed, too, that Rick had not come. He had talked with enthusiasm about making this flight sometime but had insisted he could not come today. Cosima wondered if he was not determined to avoid the company of Susanne.

The season for flights to Nantucket was almost over for the year. The tourists were gone now; and many of the restaurants and stores were closed. In a few more weeks. Nantucket would close in on itself, against the winter. In some ways, though, October was a good time to go for a day's visit. You could walk the cobblestone streets without justling. You could have a good lunch and good wine at the Jared Coffin House. If Rick had come, Cosima would have suggested an overnight stay.

He had responded with enthusiasm when she told him the Craigs had suggested a flight to Nantucket on Saturday morning. It had been only when she told him Bert could not come but that Susanne was coming anyway that he remembered he had promised to visit his sister. Cosima understood. She couldn't condemn him for having been offended by what Susanne said to him in Priscilla's kitchen. What she could condemn was his timid retreat from confrontation.

She had to be careful about her feelings for Rick: careful, that is, in defining them, since defensiveness could deceive, could exaggerate a comfortable attachment, a warm fondness, and give it a different name. She was being pressed by him for a new definition, to call their relationship something more than it was, by her family to call it something less. She had been surprised by the vehemence of her family's objections to Rick, also by her own fervor of defiance, finally by the bewildering evolution of her affection for him. She was not in love with him—as she had insisted to Susanne and Charles—but loving him would be easy.

What was wrong, after all, with a man who needed reassurance from time to time? His self-esteem was fragile, but what would he have been if nothing about him had been fragile? His smile and wit were more characteristic of him than his vulnerability. He—

"Vineyard," said Bill, nudging her with his elbow and pointing at Martha's Vineyard, a low, vari-colored island ahead and to their left. Then he pointed forward. "Nantucket."

Nantucket lay under a torn blanket of fluffy white clouds: a sere, brownish island that always reminded her of Herman Melville's quip in *Moby Dick* that Nantucket Island was the only place in the world where the natives sent boats to the mainland to import weeds.

In ten minutes they were on the ground; in another ten they were in an island taxi, an ancient Buick station wagon; and ten minutes after that they were strolling toward the docks, to look at the boats that had not yet left for more southerly ports. A cool breeze swept dusty dry leaves over the cobblestones.

Cosima knew Nantucket well, knew its weather, and had come prepared. She zipped her yellow nylon windbreaker to her throat. She was wearing blue jeans also, and a gray sweatshirt. She peered through the door of an art gallery she had often visited. It was closed. Most of the summer establishments were. The restaurant at the end of the street, where she liked to sit on a summer day and eat oysters and sip white wine was closed, too. The island was turning snug.

"Cosima. Am I out of my mind, or is that Jack over there?"

Cosima glanced at Susanne, then she looked across the street. Jack. It *was*. Jack Putnam. Wearing a tan nylon windbreaker, faded jeans, white running shoes, strands of his hair standing on the wind, he stood there unrecognized—except by Susanne, and now by Cosima. She strode across.

"Jack!"

His face stiffened. He was not pleased to be identified—until he saw who it was. Even then, he glanced around, apparently hoping no one had noticed. But he smiled, and as she walked toward him he nodded. "Cosima, what are you doing out here?" he asked through an honest, welcoming smile. His voice was flat, and he spoke slowly; that was an element of his stage and screen persona. "Nan . . . *tucket!* God, you never know who you'll run into anymore. How the hell are you, Cosima?"

Jack was at that stage in his career as a dramatic actor when he had begun to appear in public with his fine dark hair unsprayed and unmanaged, betraying its retirement from the forepart of his head. It was blown back now, showing distinct widow's peaks; what was more, on top of his head wisps fluttered on the ocean breeze, revealing how very thin it had become. His face was strong, broad, expressive of a wide range of emotions, capable more than his words of saying how genuinely glad he was to see Cosima.

"Flew out," she said. "You know Susanne. That's Bill and Priscilla Craig across the street. It was their airplane that brought us out here."

"Rented a house in Siasconset," he said, referring to a tiny village on the east end of Nantucket. "Had to get away

149

someplace to study a script. I knew it would be quiet out here this time of year, but . . . *man!* Hey, I'm glad to see you, Cosima. How long you staying?''

"Out for lunch, home for dinner," she said.

"Jeez, Cosima, that's a hell of a note. If you were going to be here this evening, I'd ask you to stop by the house for a drink. As it is . . . Hey, I hear you left your law firm, started a new one."

"I did."

"Still playing tennis, Susanne?"

"Play *at* it," she said.

"Me, too. Hey, Cosima. I'm sorry you're a lawyer."

"Well, thanks, Jack. I'm sorry you're an actor."

He grinned, a broad, foolish grin. "I don't like lawyers," he said. "Don't have to explain that, do I? Maybe I should have said I'm *glad* you're a lawyer. Could I get some advice for the price of a drink?"

"Sure, sometime.'

"No, I mean right now. Let me buy lunch for your group. But let you and me sit apart for ten minutes while I tell you about a little problem I've got. Uh . . . See, I don't want any hotshot lawyer turning a battle into a war. Somethin' discreet. Okay?''

"For the price of a drink," said Cosima. "Legal advice is always worth what you pay for it."

They sat apart in the cellar bar at the Jared Coffin House, taking the ten minutes Jack had mentioned before joining Susanne and the Craigs for lunch. Cosima had a martini made with Bombay gin. Jack said he had never tried one and had ordered the same.

"This is personal, Cosima," he said. "Highly personal." He glanced around to see if any of the dozen other people sitting in the bar recognized Jack Putnam. If they did, they left him alone. "A legal problem, in my personal life."

150

Cosima sipped from her martini. "A problem with the opposite sex, I suppose," she said.

Jack smiled slyly. "What other sex is there?" he protested. "I mean, Jeez, Cosima—yeah. It's the opposite sex." He, too, sipped from his glass, then wrinkled his nose and raised a finger to summon the bartender. "You shouldn't have gone to Harvard. We learned a lot more about sex at Yale."

"So you wouldn't need lawyers, whom you don't like."

"Hey, I'd like 'em if they were all like *you*. On the other hand, the person of the opposite sex has one of her own. A real bastard, that one."

"Legally speaking, what does this person of the opposite sex need with a lawyer?" Cosima asked.

"Vanessa," said Jack. "Vanessa's got a lawyer. A goddamned pettifogger."

"What's the beef, Jack? Statutory rape, or—"

"C'mon, Cosima. It's not funny. Everything was fine so long as I was poor. Now . . . Hell, you know."

"Palimony," said Cosima.

"God, I hate that word."

"Okay, Vanessa—?"

"Vanessa Kingston," he said.

"Vanessa Kingston. She lives with you?"

"She did. Like for six years, on and off. You know. A couple of kids trying to get started in the theater. We shared an apartment."

" 'A couple of kids.' How old is she, Jack?"

"Well hell, how old *is* she? Twenty-seven, twenty-eight. Like that. So okay, I'm forty-two. She was nineteen when she moved in with me. I was like thirty-five."

"Did you promise to marry her?"

"No." He shook his head. "Honest, Cosima. Nothin' like that. We lived together and did what grown-up people do when they live together. I mean, what would you think?"

"For six years."

He shrugged. "Roughly. Look, she was trying to build a

151

career, and I was trying to build a career. Mine took off eventually. Hers . . . well, she's not doing so bad. She's still in the theater."

"Doing what?"

"She's in *Les Miserables.* She was in *Cats,* too—moved over from there. She's a neat little dancer, Cosima. No actress, though she thinks she is."

"So she's got no lines."

"No, no lines. But steady employment. In what she wants to do. But she wants me to get her into films or on television, which I can't do."

"So she decided to ask for money instead," Cosima suggested.

"Would you believe ten thousand a month for the rest of her life?"

"And she's got a lawyer."

"Yeah. He says he's gonna sue me."

"In California?"

"No, in New York. My legal residence is still New York. So's hers."

Cosima sipped again from her martini. "Do you want me to represent you, Jack?"

He tipped his head to one side and grinned playfully. "You don't *look* like a lawyer," he said.

"How about sounding like one? Send me a check for a retainer—let's say five thousand dollars—and I'll contact Vanessa's lawyer and see what we can do."

"Jeez, Cosima. Well . . . you always were a tough little bitch. Okay. I guess that's what I need. You got a deal."

"Where'd you meet *him?*" Bill Craig asked. Once he had climbed to his cruising altitude for the return to Westchester Airport and had the airplane trimmed and locked on course, he was not so busy any longer. "Jack Putnam. Engaging fellow, isn't he?"

Susanne leaned forward from the rear seat and answered

the question. *"I* used to go out with him, before I attached myself to Bert. To everyone but the Bernardins he was considered a mother's dream. Doting mamas would do embarrassing things to get their daughters dates with Jack Putnam."

"He's not from Greenwich."

"No, he's from New Haven. His father is chief of thoracic surgery at New Haven Presbyterian Hospital. We used to see him at polo matches, the Harvard Yale game, around the boat docks, at Long Wharf Theater, Westport Country Playhouse . . . When he wasn't famous he wasn't busy either—and wasn't inaccessible."

"What made this underemployed actor such a mother's dream?"

Cosima answered. "Money. Family name. His grandfather was a professor of American history at Yale, also an undersecretary of state during the Truman administration. The family didn't come over on the Mayflower, but they caught the next boat. His sister was a debutante in New York and Boston."

"Big damn deal," said Bill.

"If you like that sort of thing," said Cosima. "Anyway, Jack was handsome and—"

"Rich," said Bill.

"Not really," said Susanne. "Let's don't exaggerate that. The Putnams are well fixed but not hugely wealthy. The point is, it's *old* money, and they use it quite elegantly, in a restrained, inconspicuous way."

Cosima laughed. "Spoken like our father's daughter, Susanne. The fact is, for two full centuries the Putnams lived in Congregational parish houses. The parsons married the daughters of merchants and ship owners—that is, they married money—but the restraint Susanne mentions was just innocence. They didn't *know how* to spend."

"Or wouldn't," Priscilla suggested. "Conscience and neighborhood opinion would have restrained them."

"A background not too different from your mother's," said Bill.

Cosima laughed again. "Hardly. Mother could scarcely be descended from *priests*, you know."

"I mean the New England thing," said Bill.

"Well, there's New England and New England," said Cosima. "The Putnams' Boston and the Fitzgeralds' Boston were not the same thing. The Putnams' New Haven and the Bernardins' Greenwich are not the same thing."

"There's no such thing as Bernardins' Greenwich," said Susanne. "Our family has only lived there forty years. We're not permanent residents yet."

"Neither are we," said Priscilla. "And we never will be. And we don't give a damn."

"Jack would be," said Cosima.

"What d'you mean?"

"I don't know. Something about Jack Putnam. If he moved in, he'd be old-family, permanent—right now. Whether he was an actor or whatever he was. Matter of family, maybe. Matter of *style*. Panache. People would seek him. Something about the man . . ."

"Hey—" Susanne asked in a low, suggestive voice. "You got a thing for Jack?"

Cosima looked back over her shoulders. "What? Pick up that deal where you left off? When you were losing?" She shook her head. "Uh-uh. You had a better chance than I do, and you gave it up."

Susanne grinned. "You'd love it if you could, though, wouldn't you?"

Cosima shrugged. "Frankly, I don't know what he's got that I need."

"You want me to tell you?"

"You don't have to. And I still say I don't need it."

Bill Craig switched frequencies on one of his receivers and turned up the volume. The airplane filled with sound.

"This is Westchester County Airport, Information Foxtrot at two-one-zero-zero hours Zulu . . ."

Eight

Burton Oliver rubbed his squarish bald head, puffed thoughtfully on his pipe and studied his file through the lower lens of his rimless bifocals. He took his time, letting Cosima wait. She knew what he was doing: essaying a shabby little psychological trick, suggesting the case was not important enough—*she* was not important enough—for him to have reviewed the file before she came in.

She would not let him play that game. "So far as I'm concerned, Mr. Oliver," she said, "unless you are prepared to reduce your claim very substantially, you can file your lawsuit and we'll just litigate it."

He fluttered his hand toward her impatiently. "I have to review this before I can discuss it," he said.

"You should have reviewed it before now," she said. "I did you the courtesy of meeting you in *your* office, and if you need more time to read your file, you can come to mine when you're ready."

Oliver looked up through the upper half of his lenses. "You needn't be aggressive, Miss Bernardin."

"I'm billing my client at my maximum rate," she said. "I have no intention of billing him for time *you* spend reading your file."

He closed the file. "Well, that's the point, isn't it? Your client can afford your hourly rate. Mine cannot. Miss Kingston sacrificed her career to help Mr. Putnam establish his, and now he wants to leave her to the meager income she can earn as a dancer—while he earns millions."

"In other words, you're on a contingency fee," said Cosima.

"My fee arrangements are irrelevant," the lawyer said coldly.

"Not entirely," she said. "If you are on a contingency fee, that in fact will probably have some impact on the kind of settlement we might be able to agree on."

Oliver frowned. His brows drooped over the upper rims of his eyeglasses. "I'm not sure we're interested in settling," he said. "I think a jury will award us every cent we've asked for."

"Palimony suits are a fad, Mr. Oliver. They're not much favored in New York courts anyway. Ten thousand a month for life . . . for shacking up. Pretty damn expensive shacking up. That's how a jury is going to see it."

Oliver's jowls twitched as he nodded his head and turned down the corners of his mouth. "They lived together virtually as husband and wife for six years," he said. "Then—"

"During which time she was, of course, totally faithful to him," Cosima said.

"Then," Oliver continued as though he had not been interrupted, "Jack Putnam decided to—as you put it— 'shack up' with someone else. He began to find someone else more attractive."

Cosima nodded. "And who was that, do you suppose? Is there someone you intend to name?"

Oliver raised his chin. The faintest hint of a smile thinned his lips as he pressed the stem of his pipe through and against his cheeks. "I didn't know . . . until today. Now I suspect I know who it is. Someone can be very embarrassed, of course."

Cosima rose. "All right. I believe I understand you, Mr. Oliver. I don't think we have anything more to discuss."

"Are you prepared to make an offer?"

She shook her head. "I'd been thinking of a small offer—the nuisance value of the claim. Until today. Until now. But not now. Not a goddamned *nickel*, Mr. Oliver. Not a *god . . . damned . . . nickel!*"

Rick pressed the tip of his nose into her navel. Cosima flexed her shoulders and clenched her eyes tight shut. She hoped . . . and he did what she hoped: kissed her belly and then her hips and then the lips between her legs, which he could kiss as he kissed her face because she kept herself shaved. He ran his tongue over her labia, then between them, provoking delightful sensations. "Mmm . . . Gussy," he murmured.

Then the damned phone rang. "Let it ring," she whispered; but Rick was too conscientious to let a telephone ring when he could answer it, and he rolled over and picked it up.

"Jack Putnam," he said, handing her the telephone.

Cosima sighed and took the receiver. "Hi, Jack," she said. "Where are you?"

"California," he said, pronouncing each syllable and holding on almost affectionately to the last one for that extra instant that gave his speech its distinctive slowness. "Hey, Cosima, I hope I haven't called at a bad time. Got a minute?"

"Sure, Jack."

"It *is* a bad time. But you told me I could call this number. Tell the guy I apologize."

"I met with Burton Oliver this afternoon," said Cosima.

"Yeah. The telephone note said you had. Isn't he a *prick?*"

"Well, I'll tell you what he suggested, Jack. He implied that *I* replaced Vanessa Kingston in your affections."

"In my bed, he meant. Jeez, Cosima, that's a *great* idea. Wish I'd thought of it."

"I don't. He's talking about embarrassing somebody. Is there somebody he *could* embarrass? Is that a consideration?"

Jack's smile came across the telephone line, in his voice. "Well, I'm an adult American male. I haven't seen Vanessa for about six months. But nobody's gonna be embarrassed. What the hell? Couple of good friends. You know. Coupla gals didn't want me to be lonely."

"Okay. I have to proceed on the basis of your word, Jack. Now, I told Oliver we wouldn't settle—so he'll do his damnedest. You have a problem with that?"

"Tell you somethin', Cosima. Mr. Burton Oliver is the problem. Originally, Vanessa tried to stick me up for a hundred thousand. I wouldn't have minded giving her something, say twenty-five thousand, for old times sake. Maybe even fifty. When I wasn't quick to come up with it but instead told her, hey, that's too much, it was then that she went to this lawyer, and that's when she started talking about palimony. You know, really, Cosima, she's not a bad girl. I wouldn't have minded doing something for her, but now anything I give her, that lawyer's gonna get half of it. That makes me mad."

Cosima rolled on her back, her head on the pillow, staring at the ceiling; as Jack spoke, she yawned. She smiled lazily at Rick. "How would it be if we gave her something he *couldn't* get half of?" she asked Jack.

"Jeez, Cosima, what do you have in mind?"

"Let me ask you something, Jack. You told me Vanessa is no actress, just a dancer. How bad is she?"

"Well . . . She's a pro, anyway. She's had training. She sets her sights too high. She's always done that. But, I don't know. Maybe . . ."

"How would you like it if we settle this thing so that you're happy, Vanessa's happy and Oliver gets screwed?"

"What's it cost me?"

"Just my retainer. And thanks for the check, by the way."

"That'd be smart lawyering, Cosima. Damned smart lawyering."

"Can't promise anything, Jack. But I'll let you know."

"Okay. Hey, listen, I'm making a run to New York—in on the red-eye, then back, you know—Wednesday and Thursday. Got an hour free? Lunch? Drink?"

"Wish I did, but I'm going down to Washington Wednesday. I'm not sure if I'll be back Wednesday night or have to stay over into Thursday. You can check with my office if you want to."

"I'll do that. What you doing in Washington, Cosima? Getting ready to run for President?"

"Trying to get a bill passed."

"Anything I'm interested in? Any way I can help?"

"Private bill, to confer citizenship on a ballerina."

"Sounds like you, Cosima, like something you'd be interested in. Okay. Listen, tell the guy who answered the phone I'm sorry."

"He's my law partner, Jack," she said, winking at Rick. "We were studying a case."

"Okay. Keep in touch. G'night, Cosima."

She handed the telephone to Rick. She wanted to return to their interrupted interlude of play but judged from Rick's shifting, glittering eyes that his concupiscence had lapsed and would not immediately be restored.

"What are you going to do?" he asked. "How are you going to work this so that Jack will be happy, Vanessa will be happy, you will be happy and only Oliver will be unhappy?"

Cosima sighed. "Well . . . if we're going to do some lawyering, let's do some lawyering. Look up a telephone number for me, while I go to the bathroom. It's not in the book, it's in my little personal book, in my bag. It's not too late to try a little call. Scribble down the number of Lawton Lanier."

She flew to Washington on Wednesday. Tuesday night she received a telephone call from Jerry Patchen. He had called about nothing in particular but only wanted to chat, and in the course of the conversation she said she was going to Washington in the morning.

"My god, Cosima, *I'm* in Washington. Not only that, the gig ends tonight. Tomorrow . . . I got a few days off. Hey! We got to get together! *Got* to!"

"Well, I don't know, Jerry. I'm going to be with my sister Emilie. I'm trying to get a private bill started, to confer citizenship on Lana Terasnova. The Justice Department is trying to deport the kid. Emilie—"

"Cosima . . . No excuses. Tell Emilie you got to see Jer. C'mon."

"Well . . ."

"I'm staying at The Madison. You know, it's the only hotel I've ever stayed in where I have to change out of my stage clothes at the club before I come back to the hotel. They told me when I called for the reservation that I couldn't come in the hotel in my black rubber. How *'bout* that?"

"I guess they're more uptight than most. Look, Jerry, I'll be tied up all day. Where can I call you?"

"I'll be at the bar at The Madison at seven."

That was more definite than she wanted to be. But he wasn't suggesting; he had fixed an appointment and expected her to keep it. "Okay, Jerry," she said. "Seven o'clock."

She flew down on the Eastern shuttle, and by eleven o'clock she was in her sister's office in the Rayburn Building.

Emilie Bernardin McCarthy was Emilie McCarthy in Washington. She represented the Eighteenth District of New Jersey, not the Fourth District of Connecticut; and the pictures and mementos in her office spoke New Jersey. The

160

only suggestion of her family was a small photograph of her mother and father that sat on the credenza beside her telephone. Otherwise, her pictures were of her husband and children and of New Jersey politicians and celebrities— including autographed photos of Governor Kean, Senator Bradley and Congressman Peter Rodino. The handsome, four-foot-long model of an oil tanker displayed in a glass case to the right of her desk was the gift of the shipowners and suggestive of the seaport in her district. A football painted with the score of a Giants-Dallas game rested on her credenza.

"The goddamned ideologues are after that girl's ass, Cosima," she said. "There's no point kidding around. You know, these private bills are normally unanimous-consent kinds of things." She shook her head. "It won't work on this one. When I ask unanimous consent for a bill to grant American citizenship to a ballerina named Svetlana Nikolaievna Terasnova, I'm not going to get it. I can name half a dozen Republicans who are going to jump up and yell no. Then I've got to put the bill through committee and get it *passed*—after which I have to herd it through the Senate. I'm going to have to call in some IOUs, and issue some of my own. I—"

"I'm sorry," Cosima interrupted. "I should have brought Lana with me. If you met her—"

"I don't have to meet her, Cosima. I'd *like* to meet her, but I don't have to. I'll trust your judgment about her."

Cosima sighed and shook her head. "So little . . . so innocent. And talented, I'm told. What possible harm could she do this country?"

Emilie smiled. "Cosima, there are people in Congress who don't think we should have admitted Baryshnikov. Even Solzhenitsyn. My god! They're Roosh-ans, ain't they? So far as the Justice Department is concerned, it's an easy concession to the Bible-Belt lunatic fringe. People who are subject to deportation have no constituency. The lunatics have. It's a small constituency, but it's there. And vocal."

161

"Am I asking too much of you, Emilie?"

Emilie leaned back in her chair. She was dressed in a severe charcoal-gray jacket and tailored skirt, and a white silk blouse with a fat bow at her throat. She looked like one of those women who suppose they can achieve more if they diminish the distracting difference between themselves and men; Cosima knew that Emilie had no such thought, that in reality she had long ago adopted a style she thought compatible with her size and weight. Her cigarette lay burning in a glass ashtray, and she reached for it and drew in smoke.

"No," she said. "No, you're not asking too much. You have to understand, though, that it's going to take *time* to get this bill through—assuming I can get it through. You're going to have to delay the deportation as long as possible. It'll be a touch-and-go thing at best."

"I've got the appeal filed in the Circuit Court. If we lose that, I'll try for a habeas corpus. I can delay her deportation six months, maybe a year. Beyond that . . ."

"I'll need every bit of six months," said Emilie.

"You have to understand," said Cosima, "that she is entirely deportable. She was a member of the youth wing of the Soviet Communist Party. She lied when she entered the United States. In the end, we're going to lose our appeals. I thought maybe the Justice Department would let the case slide when they saw the injustice of it—or saw that someone was going to fight it."

"I've told you why they won't," said Emilie.

"I'll get you all the time I can," said Cosima.

Emilie glanced at her watch. "We're having lunch with four congressmen—one from the Immigration Subcommittee of the Judiciary Committee. Play it very cool with them. We'll talk about what a harmless, talented little girl this Russian is. Don't say anything about what you and I think of the cheap ideological crusade to deport her."

"Understood," Cosima said.

Jerry Patchen was in the bar at the Madison at seven, as he had said he would be. Cosima was late. Ten minutes late. He had finished his first drink and had begun to wonder if she would really appear. He remained confident she would. It was not Cosima's way to be late by accident; she would have planned to be late—by a measured number of minutes.

Planned. That was Cosima: everything to plan. Cosima was like a painting or a sculpture, or for that matter a work of music. He had not reached for a trite cliché; his thought was that Cosima was like something that began as an idea and then was shaped to match the idea. Looking at the Bernardins, though, he couldn't believe any of the family had had the idea. No, probably it had been her own. She had conceived well, then executed well.

Why not? She'd had everything she could possibly need to perfect herself—education and discipline, which together engender confidence and poise, an utterly maniacal competitive spirit, plus plenty of money.

She had inherited money from her grandmother, aggressiveness from her father. Old Leon had fixed a decidedly sickly eye and a weak, artificial smile on him when they met at that cocktail party in Cosima's office. He told Jerry his father had delivered ten cases of a '71 something-or-other only a week before. He had meant the comment to be friendly, maybe, in a condescending way, but the image it brought to Jerry's mind had been of his aged father carrying ten cases of wine—to the back door, of course—of the Bernardin house, in the heat of an August day.

He had scored on Leon Bernardin when he hired Cosima for his lawyer. He didn't have to bed her to score on the old son of a bitch; he had already scored.

The day after he paid Cosima the big retainer that underwrote Bernardin & Loewenstein, Jerry had told his father: "Hey, pop, guess who works for me now? I mean, she's my lawyer. Cosima Bernardin. She works for me."

His father had grinned, showing a set of bad teeth. "I can talk about this, Ruggiero?"

"You tell everybody, Pop."

He had expected a bonus when he retained Cosima Bernardin as his lawyer—not necessarily that sooner or later she would sleep with him, but that word would go around in Greenwich that Leon Bernardin's daughter worked for the son of Basilio Paccinelli. He would never have to say he slept with her. That would be surmised.

It *was* surmised. His father told his buddies in the Cos Cob Rotary Club, they told their buddies in the Byram Rotary Club, and pretty soon every Rotarian in southern Connecticut knew that Cosima Bernardin worked for Ruggiero Paccinelli and assumed the rest. Rotary did not, after all, rigorously exclude females from its uptight ranks for nothing; to the brother Rotarians, a woman was a living, threatening agglomeration of debits against the treasury of grace. They assumed Paccinelli did what they imagined they would do.

Well, tonight he would turn their surmise into fact.

He sat on a small, leather-covered couch in a corner of the bar, facing the door so he could see Cosima when she came in. He was wearing a gray tweed jacket with black slacks, white shirt, dark-red-and-blue striped tie; and no one here, apparently, recognized the handsome man with dark curly hair as the frenetic leader of Bull Dog Fangs. Still, he had attracted attention, especially from one of the waitresses, whose reaction to him was an erotic signal he knew very well, also from three or four other women around the room, whose eyes shifted inquiringly toward him as often as they could without being obvious. He was comfortable with their attention. If Cosima didn't show up—

"Contessa!" he called across the room as soon as he saw Cosima—precisely ten minutes late. He rose and stepped toward her. In the center of the room, he put an arm around her waist and kissed her cheek. "At last! C'mon over. Sit down. You want one of those Bombay gin martinis?"

"Why not? I've had a rough day."

"Where's your bag?" he asked. "Hey, you didn't wear *that* all day. Where'd you change?"

164

"In my room, of course."

"What room? Where?"

"Here. In the Madison."

"*Cosima* . . . What'd you get a separate room for?"

She tilted her head a little, regarded him with a teasing, ambivalent smile. "Insurance," she said.

"Contessa"—he smiled, but this smile, too, was ambivalent—"if you think you're going to get away from me this time . . ." He shook his head. The smile broadened to a grin. "If you wanted to, you shouldn't have come looking so beautiful."

She was wearing a simple dress of turquoise silk with a glittering flowery pattern woven in silver thread. Except for a band of the fabric running front to back over her right shoulder, her arms and shoulders were bare. A knotted silver cord drew the dress in tight around her waist. The skirt ended an inch above her knees. She wore a silver bracelet, no other jewelry.

"Do we have a reservation for dinner?" she asked.

He nodded, smiling almost ingenuously. "Arranged," he said. "When I call. I hope you like trout stuffed with fish mousse. That's what I'm having them do for us. Rabbit paté to start. Also a baked brie. Champagne. Wines. I spent an hour going over it." He grinned boyishly. "Is it gauche to tell you that?"

"But *where*, Jerry?"

"In my suite. I told them we'd begin at eight, probably."

"Trout stuffed with fish mousse . . ."

"With fresh truffles. I told the chef my lawyer demands fresh truffles. I told him you are French-educated and will look at his choice of wines with a very critical eye."

"Critical nose and palate, Jerry," she said quietly.

"Yeah. That, too." He put his hand on hers. "I hope it's okay with you, Contessa," he said. "You're dressed to go out, but—"

"But you wanted to do something special," she said.

He nodded. "Right."

165

He knew she wouldn't think him ingenuous. She would understand full well that his rococo arrangements were meant to make it difficult for her to refuse to go to his suite. The truth was, no arrangements were necessary; he had known from the moment she walked into this bar that she would spend the night with him—she wouldn't have come otherwise. *She* had known earlier than that; she had known when she called the hotel and took a room, rather than leaving a message that she would be unable to keep her appointment to meet him this evening. Obviously, she had decided to let him have his wish. He was not surprised. Cosima Bernardin was no ingénue. She'd made a decision.

The waiter brought her drink. Jerry watched her lift the martini, nod across the glass in the suggestion of a toast, and sip.

"If somebody had told my father that someday I'd be sitting in one of the best hotels in Washington with the daughter of Leon Bernardin, my old man would have made that sign Italians make with the finger—you know?—that says somebody is crazy. *'Pazzo,'* is what he'd have said. *'Matto.'* "

"What would he say now?" she asked.

Jerry laughed. "He'd say, 'My son, the *pazzo musicista,* is keeping company with a rich girl, the daughter of Don Leon Bernardini.' "

"Is that what he calls my father? 'Don Leon?' 'Bernardini?' Really?"

"Don This and Don That is what he calls all the Back-Country people he thinks are rich. He and his friends. Some of them call *me* Don Ruggiero."

"Do they dislike my father? And people like him? I've always wondered."

"Hey, Cosima," he said, "do you remember how once a year, maybe Christmas Eve or Easter, the whole Bernardin clan used to show up at Saint Catherine's and the priests would fawn over you, as if the Holy Family, maybe the second cousins of Jesus, had come to church? Somehow, even to the church itself, the Bernardins were better parishioners than we were."

"Then you *did* resent us!"

"No, not really. But the older people hold men like your father in a certain awe. Not for money and position—rather for what they see as the education and worldly experience that gives people like you a mysterious competence for coping with the world, in a way my father and his Italian friends think they could never do. They think their lives are rigidly hedged by the necessities of family and church, and—"

"Jerry, that's what my father talks about all the time," she interrupted. "Faith and family, family and faith."

"But they don't seem to *burden* a man like him. Family and faith don't circumscribe his imagination. I don't think my father could ever have been anything more than he was. But he wouldn't try, either. His generation lives within the embrace of family and church, and sometimes that embrace is a hard squeeze."

"They tried to squeeze *you*," she said.

"Sure. They don't like what I do. They can't understand how I can make money at it. They know I do, but it somehow seems a little less than respectable. And, of course, I'm not married—"

"You don't have to be of a traditional Italian family to be pressured about that," said Cosima. "My father often says—in my presence—that the baptisms of his grandchildren are his proudest moments. That's a rebuke to me, Jerry. I'm the only one of his children who hasn't given him a proud moment."

Jerry shrugged. He grinned. "You sure your family is French?"

"Of course I'm sure. Sometimes, though, I have to review things I do and say—and wonder if I do and say them because I want to, because I believe them, or out of rebellion. Do you ever think that way, Jerry?"

"I'm more rebellious than you, Cosima. I broke out of

it. Absolutely. Permanently. If my family loves me, they have to take me as I am. No concessions.''

"None?"

"Well . . . very few."

She raised her glass and smiled at him before she took another sip. "Not so easy, is it?" she asked, smile rapidly fading.

The suite was splendid. Yellow silk on the walls. The furniture mostly Federal—though not real antiques. On this mid-October evening when Washington weather was still moderate, a small fire burned quietly in the marble-framed fireplace in the sitting room. A bottle of Dom Perignon was already open and waiting in its silver bucket. In the crushed ice of a silver bowl, big shrimp waited.

As soon as they were inside the door, Jerry reached for Cosima and gently kissed her. It was the first time he had ever kissed her, except in a brotherly, maybe facetious way. He was as she had expected: strong, inescapable, even when he was gentle.

He ran his fingertips across her bare shoulders, around her neck. "Cosima," he said. "I have a little surprise for you. Come in the bedroom a sec."

She let him lead her by the hand into the bedroom, where a king-size bed waited for them. Spread out on the bedspread were two of the black rubber suits that were a trademark of Bull Dog Fangs.

"You've talked about the rubbers," he said. "Two or three times you've asked about them. I thought you'd like to try them. I never thought of you coming dressed like—I mean, so beautiful. Anyway, I thought—"

Cosima drew her breath deep. "Uh, Jerry . . . uh, sure. Going to surprise the hell out of the waiters."

Jerry grinned. "I'll change in the bathroom. You in here. I'll toss you a towel. Your skin has to be absolutely dry to get into the pants. Dust on a little talcum powder. Nothing under them, you know.''

Her skin was dry. She toweled herself a little just the same, also dusted herself lightly with talcum powder as he suggested. She had to stretch the rubber to force her legs into the pants. As she forced the resisting rubber up, pulling, stretching, writhing, she felt it tighten on her ankles, then her calves, then her thighs in a tight grip. Though she tugged at the waistband, the pants reached only to her hips, well below her navel. There were short zippers on each side, and as she pulled them up she felt the rubber tighten on her nates and draw in her abdomen. The rubber vest had no fasteners. The one Adela Drake wore sometimes opened and exposed her little breasts. This one served only to display Cosima's.

''Jerry Patchen, you son of a bitch,'' she muttered as she studied herself in the long bedroom mirror. The tight, shiny rubber conformed itself to every curve of her body. Behind, it had shaped itself to her cheeks, intruding between so her furrow was explicitly defined.

Weird. Well, good. A crackling fire. Champagne. Trout stuffed with fish mousse. Truffles. For a moment she wondered if he hadn't hired gypsy violinists.

''Contessa . . .''

He came from the bathroom, dressed as he dressed for the stage. At close quarters, the effect of his rubber pants was even more startling than it was under stage lights. The rubber clung to his male parts. What was more, it held them in such a tight grip that they were more definitely outlined than they would have been when they hung loose.

''You are *gorgeous!* Oh, *god,* Cosima, you are more than a man can dream!''

She slipped her feet into her shoes—silver and so not wholly incompatible with a black rubber costume. ''Jerry . . . It's not *me,* but it's interesting.''

''It takes away some of that big dignity of yours, Contessa,'' he said.

Cosima tossed her head and ran her hand over her short hair. "Don't believe it, Italiano," she said. The gesture had opened the vest and exposed her breasts. "My dignity is something I *keep,* tits out or whatever."

"The Cosima panache," he said. "C'mon. We've got champagne and shrimps waiting. Then . . . then a lot of good things."

Though she had thought she would, she did not retreat into the bedroom when two very professional waiters served their dinner. She did grip her rubber vest and deny them the sight of her breasts. Manfully, they averted their eyes from her belly and legs, leaving her to wonder what they would say of her when they returned to the kitchen.

The dinner was exquisite—exquisitely chosen, exquisitely prepared, and circumspectly served. With the entrée, dessert was brought and put aside, and the coffee was placed over a burner, so the waiters need not return.

"It's perfect, Jerry," Cosima said. She thought he needed the assurance—and deserved it. "No one could have chosen better."

She said it in spite of the bizarre character of an exquisite dinner served to two people in fetishist costumes. His innocence, which she had been unable to concede in the bar, was manifest here, in the fantasy he had created. It was flattering. He had *demanded* she come here; then he had created an adolescent fantasy of seduction.

A contrast. More—a conflict.

"You're not going back to your own room?" he asked.

"Would you let me?"

"Well . . . I wouldn't keep you here by force."

Cosima smiled. She was serene. She had made herself so, intentionally, by drinking from all his wines: the champagne first, a musty red Bordeaux with their paté, a Chablis, *premier cru,* with the fish—and now a port that sat beside the assorted cheeses provided for their dessert. It was well, she had judged, to dull her inhibitions, for she expected this man's carnal demands to be substantial. That is what she had decided to dare. After all his florid preliminaries, the occasion had to reduce itself in the end to something very simple. She was a little apprehensive, but she was confident, too. Her judgment had not often failed her.

After he poured a little of the port into each of their glasses, he stepped behind her, seized the rubber vest with two hands, and lifted it off. He took her hand and led her from her chair at the table to the couch nearby. He brought the port and the cheese to the low table before the couch.

"I never saw a pair like them," he said, nodding at her breasts. "As beautiful as everything else about you."

Cosima glanced down. "They *are* nice, aren't they?" she agreed. "I'm lucky about that."

He touched the nipple of her left breast with his index finger and forefinger. "Great big marvelous titties," he said.

Cosima reached for her glass and took a tiny sip of the sweet wine. "Not stylish, you know," she said.

"Oh, to hell with stylish. The styles are made by fags." He bent over and kissed her nipples, first one, then the other. "Hey," he said. "Let's get these rubber pants off. Mine are strangling my hard-on."

"Mine are strangling everything they touch," she laughed.

It was not easy to get out of the skintight pants. The struggle set them laughing. In a minute, even so, they were naked and staring at each other with unabashed curiosity. Jerry almost gasped, then grinned, seeing that she was smoothly shaved. His engorged penis had stood at attention as soon as it was freed from the binding rubber: smooth, blue-veined, and of intimidating length and girth.

Jerry reached for her hand, took it, and guided it forcefully to him. First her fingers, then her palm, felt the warm,

171

rigid body of his swollen member, then the loose bulk of his scrotum as he pushed her hand under.

"*Fenomenale,* eh, Contessa," he murmured softly. "*Lo-piace?*" He slipped his fingers between her legs, between her shaven lips. "*Me piace questo,*" he whispered.

She understood enough to know he'd said he liked what he was touching—and before that he'd called his penis phenomenal and asked if she liked it.

She nodded. "I like it," she murmured. "And so do a lot of other girls. Put a rubber on it, Jerry."

"I hate the damned things."

"So do I, but—"

"Awright!"

He trotted in the bedroom and returned with the foil package already torn open. She watched him roll the condom down to his pubic hair: for her a supremely erotic sight. But it turned him impatient, and he dragged her to him, seized his shaft in a firm grip and thrust it between her legs and up. Though they were standing, he was so big he had entered her. He stepped back; holding her so tightly against him that he did not slip out of her, he lowered himself onto the armless chair where he had sat to eat and pulled her onto his lap, astride him, spreading her and affording him deeper penetration.

Cosima clasped him around the neck, gasping as the ecstacy captured her. "*Presto!*" she muttered hoarsely.

When she woke, she had a sense it was late. She could hear rain falling outside. He had tossed a hand towel over the bedside clock, and she could not tell what time it was; she sensed that the weak gray light of a wet autumn morning had not wakened her until long after her usual hour.

Jerry slept on. For hours he had clung to her, reluctant to let her wriggle out of his arms even though he was asleep. It must have been dawn before he rolled away from her and

172

flung himself wide over half the kingsize bed. He snored. He was snoring now.

She touched him. "Jerry . . ."

He started. "Oh, *god!* Cosima . . . Oh, Jesus yes!"

"What time is it, Jerry?" she asked him softly. "Pull the towel off the clock."

"Ummm, uh . . . Nine-twenty." He yawned. "Just nine-twenty. Cuddle up."

"I have to *get* up, Jerry. I have to get back to New York."

"Aww, no. Say, that coffee's still hot. I poured what was left in the thermos carafe."

Cosima rolled off the bed and retrieved the carafe and two cups from the dresser. She handed them to him, and while he poured she stood at the window and looked out at the rain and low clouds that hung over the city like a gray and tattered sheet. She sat down on the bed and accepted a cup of black coffee that was not quite hot enough but that did serve to alleviate the filthy taste of morning-mouth.

"I doubt the shuttle is flying, from the looks of that," Jerry said, nodding toward the window and the weather.

"Then I'll take the Metroliner. I simply *have* to be back in New York sometime this afternoon."

"It's only Thursday," he said. "What the hell good is Friday? Listen, stay through tonight, and I promise I'll get you on the first shuttle in the morning. You'll be in your office just as soon."

"If I catch the eleven o'clock, I can be in my office before two this afternoon," she said.

"Is your business so good already that it's so demanding? Hey, don't forget you're spending your time with a *client.* Call New York. Tell Rick you're with me. Tell him we're discussing business. In fact, I can think of some things we might talk about."

Cosima looked out the window once again. It was possible he was right, that the shuttles were not flying. Anyway, if they were, they'd be delayed. It was unrealistically optimistic to say she'd be in her office by two o'clock. Anyway, she was tired, had eaten too much, drunk too much. "Well . . ." she said.

Jerry handed her the telephone.

Rick was not yet in the office, but Teresa confirmed that the shuttles were not flying that morning, though the forecast was for clearing after noon.

When she put down the telephone, Jerry was grinning, and he had developed an enormous erection. "Hey," he said.

She drew back her shoulders and lifted her chin. "Already? I can't do it all night and all day and all night." Her words were a more lighthearted response than the Italian word that come to her mind: *stallone,* stallion.

He chuckled. "Bet you could. All day, all night. Anyway, there's something I want that I didn't get last night. I bet you give great head, Contessa."

"Uh-uh," she said warily. "I don't do that. I don't like it."

"Aw, *come on!* Sophisticated girl like you . . . You were an angel last night. C'mon." He lifted his shaft in his hand, presenting it to her to accept into her mouth. "C'mon."

Again, a demand. His grin failed to deceive her, and she understood he was making no suggestion, no request; he expected to be given what he wanted. She took her head emphatically. "No, Jerry. No."

"Why not?"

"Because I don't want to. That's reason enough."

He sighed. "Contessa . . . it's important to me. I want you to learn to like it."

Cosima put aside her cup and the dregs of lukewarm coffee. "We don't share the same tastes. About a lot of things."

"I'll make my share of concessions. You make yours."

She frowned. "I hear an assumption, Jerry. I hear an assumption that you and I are going to be together so much that we have to make adjustments for each other. I haven't made that assumption."

He too put his cup aside. His body stiffened. "What do you mean by that?" he asked, a new hard edge on his voice.

"I have not assumed we would be sleeping together on any regular basis," she said crisply.

"I didn't take you for a one-night stand, Contessa."

"What did you take me for, Jerry?"

He stood and walked to the bathroom door. When he turned to face her, he saw that his erection had subsided. "Something special," he said caustically. He nodded. "Yeah. Something special."

"I thought last night *was* something special," said Cosima. "I wouldn't have come if I hadn't thought it was going to be. And it was. It was glorious, every bit of it. And I'm grateful to you. But I didn't understand that it implied anything . . . any commitment. It didn't to me. I don't see how you and I could make a commitment to each other. We don't mesh. We're not the same kind of people, in a whole lot of ways. We had a good time last night. Maybe we can do it again sometime. In fact, I'll stay tonight. But we needn't start making concessions to each other. They won't be necessary."

Jerry leaned against the doorframe. "The daughter of Don Leon Bernardini," he said, speaking with a bitter, mock-Italian accent, "can have no serious relationship with the son of Basilio Paccinelli."

"Oh, cut the crap!" she snapped.

"Is what I got from you last night covered by the retainer I paid you—or do I get a bill?"

Nine

On what was almost certainly his last sailing day of the year, Leon Bernardin found himself more than fortunate. The late-October day was cool, but a white sun glared on the blue water. Though he would have liked to have more crew for the sloop, Susanne and Cosima were capable of handling the sails. As he guided *Lafayette* out of Captain Harbor and onto the open water of Long Island Sound, the wind freshened. It came out of the west. He called for the spinnaker, and the two girls jumped to hoist it. He watched critically. They were not a great crew, but they would get the spinnaker out in their good time, and he would run ahead of this wind, maybe as far as New Haven.

Exhilarated by the wind and spray, feeling the sloop gain speed, Leon sucked in great draughts of the fresh air. His gray hair was covered by a khaki cap with a huge black bill that stood far out above his forehead. He wore a heavy gray yachting sweatshirt, with a hood that could be drawn over his head but now hung down his back, also with a pouch in front where he could warm his hands. His pants were khaki twill, his shoes rubber-soled deck shoes.

Susanne was cranking away on the winch, hauling on the

halyard, raising the spinnaker. Cosima scampered around forward, handling the spinnaker pole and guy. The girls were dressed for boat handling, in sweatshirts like his, in tight, faded blue jeans and white canvas deck shoes. He had made sailors of them, if he hadn't done anything else with these two. They set the spinnaker in acceptable time, it filled, and the sloop surged eastward, passing Greenwich Point three hundred yards south, affording the season's last beach zealots a handsome view. He scanned the length of the short beach with his binoculars—seeing, as he had expected, half a dozen people staring at him through their own.

With the halyard, sheet and guy securely cleated, they could take their ease in the cockpit. Susanne disappeared into the galley to brew a pot of coffee, and Cosima sat down on the seat to the right of the companionway.

Leon pushed his cap forward on his head, to lower the long bill over his eyes and diminish the sky glare. "Lost your client, did you?" he asked.

"I don't know for sure," she said. "I haven't heard from him since I saw him in Washington. Whether I've lost him or not, though, I can't build a law firm on one client."

"He was paying the rent."

"And will continue to pay it for a while," said Cosima. "I have no intention of refunding a dime of his retainer."

"You might be well advised to do so," said Leon. "You might be well advised to return all of it."

"The thought crossed my mind," she said. "What are *your* reasons?"

"However much money he may make," said Leon, "Ruggiero Paccinelli is Ruggiero Paccinelli. His father sells liquor, and Ruggiero sells . . . *dreck.*" He spat on the word. "And why not? What else could he produce?"

"Dad—"

"No. You are well rid of this client. It is inappropriate that the foyer of a law firm should be decorated with posters of men and women clad in rubber suits, with red and green hair."

"I am trying to build a law firm based on a show-business clientele," said Cosima. "I could hardly have had a better start than by representing Bull Dog Fangs."

"Merchants of dreck," he said. He leaned to the left and watched a bit of flotsam—a tangle of boards and chicken wires—bob past *Lafayette*. "Respectable clients—"

"Clients who earn thirty million dollars a year aren't easy to come by," she interrupted. "The old firms have them tied up."

"Maybe by now you understand what you did when you left Hamilton, Schuyler."

"I kept my self-respect," said Cosima tersely.

"That's a question of definition," her father said.

She understood he had dismissed the subject; she could tell from the tone of his voice. But she wasn't willing it should be dismissed. "I have two good men in my office," she said.

"How long can you afford to keep them on a payroll?"

"Well, I certainly don't have Hugh on any payroll. He earns a damned good income."

"In which your firm does not share."

She nodded. "In which Rick and I don't share. My problem right now is to build some business for Rick. I appreciate the work you gave him, but I have to find something more for him."

"I can't make work for him, Cosima, if that's what you're suggesting."

"I don't *want* any more work from you," she said. "I don't want the firm to be dependent on you. We were too dependent on Jerry."

"It seems to me you are losing a lot of money on your independence."

"Not as much as you might think," she said. "Except for the Fang, Incorporated, retainer, I'm letting Rick take all the fees we earn. The retainer is still covering expenses. I—"

"You are earning nothing," said Leon sternly. "You have been without an income since May."

"Since July, actually," she said. "Hamilton, Schuyler settled accounts with me in July. They owed me fourteen thousand and change."

"You've no clients—"

"Actually we do. We're still handling Adela Drake's divorce. I'm working on the Terasnova deportation case, and she's been able to come up with a little money. I handled a matter for Jack Putnam, for which he paid a respectable fee, and now he's talking about some other work, including his taxes."

"A small amount of business to support a suite of offices in the Pan Am Building," said Leon dryly. A gust had pushed the boat off course a few degrees, and he turned the wheel to bring the bow back to where he wanted it. "Have you set some sort of limit for yourself? How long will you allow yourself to be without income?"

"A year," said Cosima. "If I don't have a firm by sometime next summer, then I don't have a firm."

"Do I understand Jack Putnam will be with us for dinner?"

She nodded. "For dinner."

Jack had called last night, saying he was delayed in New York through Tuesday—"And surely, Cosima, surely there's some time when we can . . ." Sometime was not flexible, it turned out. He was free Saturday evening and all day Sunday. She was not free Saturday evening; she was firmly committed to dinner with her family. So, he was coming for dinner. She had promised they could leave early.

She stood on the platform at the Cos Cob station and met the 6:05 from Grand Central. People—complete strangers, almost surely—waved good-bye to Jack Putnam as he left the train. He stepped out on the windswept platform, glancing up and down, unsure she would be there, as every passenger being met always was; then he spotted her, grinned and strode toward her.

"Cosima! *God!* Great to see ya! Jeez!"

She walked into his embrace, and they kissed each other on the cheeks. As they had been that day when they met on Nantucket, they were very similarly dressed. She noticed. It confirmed once again the similarity of their backgrounds. On a cool, windy, late-October day, you wore a silvery fleece-lined ski jacket, maybe with a stripe on the sleeve— his was blue, hers red—with your black or tan corduroys. She still wore her deck shoes from the morning's sailing. He had not been sailing but was wearing the same. He stepped back from her, shook his head as though marvelling and grinned.

"Hey, Cosima, god . . . damn. A thing of beauty and a joy forever."

He was a joy to see—and to hear: that expressive voice, making half-drawled words. She couldn't believe there was anything false about him. Neither could tens of millions who watched him on the screen, which may have explained his appeal. But she knew it was nothing recently contrived. Jack had always been like this.

Always, that is, as long as she had known him. Always, a *man,* yet with a singular kind of maleness: something difficult to define—a man who saw no need to prove he was a man. The contrast between him and . . . well, say . . . Jerry Patchen. Jerry flaunted his manhood, and she had to wonder if that was because he was himself not confident of it. Jack didn't need to accumulate conquests to prove himself. He didn't need trophies: anything from cunts preserved by taxidermists to small animals blown to pieces by big guns. His manhood was more secure than that.

Cosima laughed. "C'mon. You have to *walk* to my place."

"Wha'? You live in the railroad station?"

He picked up his voluminous nylon bag and followed her down the concrete steps from the platform, across the road and into the waterfront complex of condominiums.

"Yeah, a Scotch would be nice," he said before she had closed the door or offered a drink. "Jeez, I thought you'd never ask."

"Put your bag in there," she said, pointing to the door of the second bedroom. "I'll pour."

He was wearing a gray YALE sweatshirt. He leaned into a corner of her couch and stuck his legs out as far as he could. "Y'ever tempted to murder anybody?" he asked, tipping his head to one side and holding his mouth open.

"Every day," she said from the kitchen.

"I want to *direct* a picture. Y' know? How can you stand around a set and see what those guys do without getting the idea, so you can do it yourself? I don't think I've been directed—how should I say?—*optimally*. I haven't been directed optimally. Christ, they're trying to make another John Wayne out of me."

"I hardly think so, Jack," she said as she handed him a heavy Scotch. She splashed brandy into a snifter for herself, sat down on the other end of the couch and leaned back, as he was doing. "John Wayne? Uh uh."

"I don't mean cowboys and marines, anything like that," he said. "I mean I don't want to be a stereotyped character. People go to see, say, Dustin Hoffman on the screen, they never know just what kind of character he's going to be. 'Cause he's an *actor*. Wayne never acted. He never had to. They never gave him a chance. Me neither, lately. Maybe John Wayne could have been a great actor, if he'd had the chance."

"You always wanted to see him play a villain," she said.

"Yeah, villain! A bad guy! Shoots people for no good reason. Jeez, Cosima, there must be big, handsome villains *someplace*."

"So what do you want to play, Mephistopheles?"

Jack twisted his face into a mock-demonic grin. "Yeah!

Mephistopheles. Or Willy Lohman. I played Willy on the stage, you know. Except for little pecks on the cheek, Linda, his wife, never got a kiss—much less a bedroom scene.''

She laughed. ''I've seen your buns on the silver screen.''

He shook his head, turning down the corners of his mouth. ''Not mine. Stand-in. Even *that* I don't get to do.''

''You want to direct yourself in an X-rated picture?''

He shook his head. ''I'm serious. I'm typed, and I don't like it.''

''You've made a lot of money,'' she said. ''You're demanding to direct your own pictures—''

''With script approval,'' he said.

''Well . . . five, six years ago you thought you were lucky to get any kind of screen part at all.''

''Jeez, Cosima! You have a bug planted in these damned meetings I've been in all week? I've heard that line fifteen times.''

''It comes to mind,'' she said.

''You, too— *Et tu, Brute?*''

''Could you fund a film?'' she asked. ''All on your own?''

Jack rose from the couch, walked to the double doors that overlooked Cos Cob Harbor and stared at the gray day, the closing weather. ''I'm thinking about it,'' he said quietly.

''If it doesn't work, you'll make a beggar of yourself,'' she said.

''Beggar . . . ?''

''The money you've been raking in from pictures you don't like makes you an independent talent. You lose it all, everybody'll know it, and you'll beg for roles. You'll never go begging, really, because you're a recognized talent, but if you're living day-to-day off what you make, you'll take what they give you and be glad to get it.''

''Living day-to-day—''

''Also, the industry will have a motive to keep it that way—to keep you on a leash. If you're thinking of financing your own picture, Jack, be damned sure it's a winner.''

He returned to the couch. "I'd go broke on Mephistopheles," he said, tipping his glass back.

"Would you?" she asked. "What do you think?"

He drummed his fingers on her coffee table. "I think it might be a good idea if you were with me when the meetings start again on Monday morning," he said.

Susanne sauntered across the room as if Jack meant nothing to her, but when she spread her arms to enter his embrace, he thrust a hand toward her, took hers and shook it.

"Susanne," he said. "How very nice."

She nodded. "Isn't it?"

He was the only outsider at this family dinner. They gathered in the living room before a muttering fire—Leon Bernardin in blue suit, white shirt and bow tie, an aging, weakening figure to someone like Jack who had not seen him for several years; Elizabeth Fitzgerald Bernardin, diminished by drink and cigarette smoke and still the Boston Irishwoman who persisted in breaking through her brittle façade; her daughter Susanne, also coarse, bibulous, lascivious, and aging at tragic speed; Charles, whether tweedy or just seedy, it was difficult to say, but attached to Sybil, who was so determinedly scruffy that her invitations to this house must have been infrequent. Then, of course, there was Cosima, who seemed to fit the house but not the family. She was the youngest, and perhaps the genes that had produced her elder siblings had been exhausted by the time she was conceived, so that she was something fresh and new. Anyway, she was exquisite. As for himself, Jack had been here before. He knew them all, except Sybil; and, except for Cosima, he could have lived happily without ever seeing one of them again.

Sybil's clothes locked her in a pigeonhole: an ill-fitting coat—Jack supposed it was called a coat, what else could it have been called?—of mud-colored wool she had woven herself, over a plain white T-shirt, with a voluminous dark blue

183

skirt that flopped around her ankles as she walked. Her quick announcement that she and Charles did not own a television set didn't help either. ("On the other hand, maybe she's a great piece of ass," Jack whispered to Cosima.)

"Generally, we don't talk about business at dinnertime," said Leon. They were still at cocktails, but his injunction covered the cocktail hour, too.

"Oh, I'm with *you*, Mr. Bernardin," said Jack. "In fact, sometimes days go by, I don't talk about business at all."

Leon Bernardin apprehended the derision under Jack's words, but he didn't take offense; he raised his eyebrows and flashed his all-purpose smile.

"Anyway," Jack continued as if the little exchange between him and Leon had not occurred, "I'm the beneficiary of a piece of damn smart lawyering, and if any of you don't think she's a fine lawyer, you don't know what fine lawyering is."

"I have never quite comprehended the *relevance* of what lawyers do," said Sybil, biting off and spitting out the word "relevance" like a squirrel ridding himself of a bit of hickory-nut shell.

Jack cast her a scornful smile. "What's relevant?" he asked. "The stars? The bugs? I happen to think it's people. And that's what lawyers deal with."

"So do actors," said Cosima.

"You think so?" asked Sybil.

"Yes," said Cosima. Then she nodded at Jack: a signal to go on with what he was saying. She had long since decided not to debate with Sybil. There would be no honor in making a foil of the poor drab.

"Anyway," said Jack, "y'see, this girl, Vanessa, lived with me for a long time. We played house, you know. And when I decided the game was over, she wanted to play divorce." He shrugged. "So, okay, I was willing to give her alimony. Something. Do what was right. But she gets this lawyer, Burton Oliver, and he comes up with a demand of ten thousand a month for the rest of her life."

184

Diana Grabaldan - Outlander

Ed McBain - Beauty & The Beast

- Jack and the Beanstalk

"And Cosima got you off with . . . ?" Susanne asked.

"With *nothin'*. I don't have to pay a cent. On the other hand, Vanessa's happy. She got something she wanted more, likes better."

"What did you do, Cosima?" her father asked. "A bit of manipulation?"

Cosima sipped from her Bombay gin martini. "I'm not sure it's a good idea to talk about it," she said.

"I'm proud of it, proud of her," said Jack. "What she did was, she contacted Lawton Lanier—the English producer who's been working out of this country since about 1982. Anyway, Cosima suggests to him that he could do her a favor by setting Vanessa up in a part in some picture. Which he does!"

Leon sucked in his cheeks and frowned. "I suspect it was a little more complex than that," he said. "A favor . . ."

"It *was* more complicated," said Cosima, "and some of it is confidential." She spoke directly to Jack. "Some of it is *confidential.*"

Jack grimaced with wry amusement. "Right. Part of the favor is going to be repaid by Cosima and part by me." He grinned at Cosima. "Maybe he'll go for the Mephistopheles."

Cosima laughed. "I doubt it."

"Are you saying," asked Cosima's mother, "that this young woman was given a role she wasn't qualified to play?"

"No," said Jack curtly. "Vanessa's got an exaggerated idea of her talent, but she can handle the part she got very nicely. Lanier will be good for her. He told her her acting was too academic, too much the product of her drama school."

"He told her to be more sloppy," Cosima laughed.

"Maudlin," said Jack.

"And in return for this," said Elizabeth Bernardin, struggling to focus her perception through the fog of all she had drunk during the afternoon and evening, "the young woman withdrew her lawsuit?"

"Hey," said Jack. "Vanessa's happy. She couldn't be happier. She's in London, where they're shooting on location. She called me, said thanks." He mugged. "Called me collect, for god's sake!"

"All neatly settled, I guess," said Susanne, a little sarcastic.

"Very neatly," said Jack with a happy grin. "And that aggressive jackass of a lawyer got nothing."

"Nothing?" asked Leon.

"He was on a contingency fee," said Cosima. "He would have gotten half of any settlement we made with Vanessa."

"No settlement, no fee," laughed Jack.

Leon handed his glass to Susanne to be refilled. "It might have been better, Jack, if you had paid the lawyer a little something." He spoke to Cosima. "You've made an enemy."

Cosima raised her brows high. "It would have been a little difficult to arrange," she said, "I mean, it would have been a little difficult to explain to Mr. Burton Oliver why he was receiving a modest check from Jack. What were we paying for? Besides, the man was a total ass. A shyster."

Sybil shook her head. "Is that what lawyers do?" she asked.

"It's what good ones do," said Jack.

They left the house in Cosima's Porsche about ten. "This is no wild nighttime town," she said. "Singles bars . . . teeny hangouts . . . The problem with having a drink in Greenwich on Saturday night is avoiding the obese, beer-soused louts from some industrial-league softball game— them and yuppies who can't hold their liquor. It's a party town, but you party at home. I didn't have any invitations for tonight. We could go by the country club."

186

"Jeez, Cosima, I—hey, we don't have to go anyplace. I mean, why not go back to *your* place?"

She nodded. She could guess what *that* suggestion implied.

In her living room he asked her if she minded if he took off his necktie. He went in the guest bedroom, and when he came out he had taken off not just the tie but also the shirt and had pulled on a black cashmere sweater over his T-shirt.

"Can we sit out there?" he asked her, pointing at the terrace beyond the glass doors.

"Sure. Scotch?"

"Pourquoi non?"

She changed, too, into soft blue jeans and a worn gray sweatshirt. They sat facing the Sound, savoring a cool, damp breeze laden with saltwater smells. For a long time they were silent. Then Jack spoke:

"Cosima. Let me make something easy. I'm not going to suggest we . . . sleep together. I mean—in case you were worried."

She could not help but laugh, though she did it quietly, since she knew he had spoken quite ingenuously. "I wasn't worried," she said. "I was going to say no, but I would have been flattered by the suggestion."

"Well . . . I thought we might enjoy the rest of the evening more if we got that out of the way."

She turned and faced him across the little round table that stood between their chairs. "You're a thoughtful man, Jack," she said softly. "Thoughtful . . ."

"Hey, it's not that I wouldn't like it. I know I would."

"So would I, probably."

"Yeah, but I don't want anything quick or casual. Not with you. Anyway, you're going to be my lawyer, and I'm not sure the two kinds of relationship fit together."

She nodded. "That's what I tried to tell somebody else."

"Paccinelli?"

"Yes. How'd you guess?"

"He's a prick," said Jack. "Is that a pun? Forgive it."

"He's a real talent, you know."

"Is he?"

"Yes. He's a talented musician," she said. "He really is. More than that, he has a genius for music; he understands the close relationship between music and mathematics. Some of the critics have begun to perceive parallels between Paccinelli and Bach, Paccinelli and Mozart."

"Seriously?"

"Seriously," she said. Then she smiled. "You should read what's been said of him in the *Times* and the *New Yorker*. The serious critics call him 'Paccinelli,' never 'Patchen,' as if they can't quite bring themselves to incorporate into their urbane dissertations a term like 'Jerry Patchen and The Bull Dog Fangs.' Some of them fault him for having sold out his talent for fame and fortune."

"Well . . . has he?"

"I don't know. I don't know how you could say that of a man who has given up his life for what he does. The man eats, drinks, sleeps and copulates only at odd hours when he can snatch a moment for it. Worse than that—he *thinks* only when he can find a moment. Consequently he does things thoughtlessly . . . off-handedly."

"Is there something going between you and him, Cosima?"

She shook her head. "Impossible," she said.

"Ah-hah! Impossible is a word people don't use unless—"

"*Impossible,*" she insisted. "Absolutely impossible. Some of the reasons aren't very pretty. No, I'll put it another way—some of the reasons aren't . . . fashionable."

"I understand," said Jack. "You don't have to say it. Personally, I admire what you're telling me. Maybe not everybody would, but to hell with them."

Cosima lifted her brandy snifter. "To hell with them," she murmured.

Something else good about Jack: he knew when to talk and when to keep quiet. Now he stared out across the

188

Sound, silent as if withdrawn. She was almost sorry for the statement she had earlier welcomed: that he did not expect to sleep with her. He was a success, as Jerry was—yet, his success was dissimilar, with a contrast she could appreciate. And he lived with it differently. He was not possessed by himself. To see that was a privilege. She wanted to be closer to it.

Jack's Monday-morning conference with the producers and backers of the picture he wanted to direct was scheduled for ten-thirty. Cosima arrived at her office at nine, so as to have time to adjust her schedule and make room for Jack's meeting. She found in her mail a letter from Burton Oliver.

The envelope contained two letters, actually: one just a short note saying that the longer letter had been sent by messenger to the office of the Association of the Bar of the City of New York. That longer letter read:

Mr. John F. McGowan
Counsel
Committee on Professional Ethics
Association of the Bar of the City of New York

Dear Mr. McGowan:

My purpose in writing this letter to you is to institute a formal complaint against a lawyer practicing in this city.

About six weeks ago a young woman called at my office and sought my advice and assistance relative to the abrupt termination of a romantic relationship. This young woman, Vanessa Kingston, shared living quarters for approximately six years with the stage and film actor John T. Putnam, better known as Jack Putnam, during which time she sacrificed her own career to assist him in establishing his, on the specific understanding that he would support and assist her with her career and otherwise when he became a success. I advised her that his abrupt and unjustifiable termination of the relationship, coupled with his refusal to assist her in any way, was actionable and advised her to sue.

Putnam retained as his counsel one Cosima Bernardin, who practices law under the name of Bernardin & Loewenstein, with offices at 200 Park Avenue. Miss Bernardin called at my office to discuss the case but was unwilling to make any realistic offer of settlement.

Approximately a week after Miss Bernardin came to see me, my client called at my office and advised me that she wished to drop her claim against Mr. Putnam. When I inquired as to why, she told me she had been offered a role in a motion picture and was no longer interested in the lawsuit. When I pressed her for further explanation, she said she had been contacted by a producer named Lawton Lanier and had signed a contract to play a role in a film that will be shot in Europe. I advised her that need not interfere with her pursuing her rights against Mr. Putnam. She then told me that Mr. Lanier had made it a condition of her employment that she release all her claims against Mr. Putnam—that he had in fact insisted she write and sign a release before he would sign her contract. When I telephoned Mr. Lanier, he refused to discuss the matter with me. Specifically, he refused to tell me how he even knew of the lawsuit Miss Kingston was preparing to file against Mr. Putnam.

It is entirely apparent that Miss Bernardin procured Mr. Lanier to secure a release from Miss Kingston. It is apparent that Miss Bernardin employed Mr. Lanier as her surrogate to obtain a settlement of Miss Kingston's claim against Mr. Putnam. In effect, Miss

Bernardin used Mr. Lanier surreptitiously to negoti-
ate with my client outside my presence and without
my knowledge, for the purpose of procuring a release
that was not in the best interest of my client and that
she would not have signed if she had received proper
counsel from me. Such conduct is a serious violation
of the Standards of Professional Conduct and merits
censure at the very least, if not suspension from the
practice of law.

I spoke yesterday with a representative of Hamilton, Schuyler, Depew & Chase, the firm with which
Miss Bernardin practiced law until she was dismissed
from the firm earlier this year. I am advised that
Hamilton, Schuyler has raised with Miss Bernardin a
complaint that she has solicited the firm's clients and
has in fact taken at least one away from the firm—in
violation of her employment agreement and of course
in violation of the Standards.

I respectfully request the Committee on Professional Ethics to initiate a formal inquiry into this
young woman's conduct as an attorney and counsellor
at law. I will be happy to testify before the Committee
or render it any other assistance it may require.

Sincerely yours,

Burton Oliver

A scowling Hugh Hupp tossed the letter across his desk.
"You beat him out of his fee, Cosima. Can't expect him to
like it."

"Jack Putnam likes it," she said. "Vanessa Kingston
likes it. Lawton Lanier likes it. Oliver is the only one who
doesn't."

"She's really going to get this role?" Hugh asked. "You
mean to say she really *can* act?"

"Well enough," said Cosima. "It's not a terribly demanding part. Lawton didn't have to make any great concession to give her a break."

Hugh smiled cynically. "I can see why you didn't fit the mold at Hamilton, Schuyler. It's an imaginative way to practice law, Cosima, but you can get your ass in a sling this way. In fact, you may have already, in a minor-league way," he said, reaching across his desk and tapping the letter with one finger.

"How should I respond?" she asked. "Or should I?"

"You do nothing until you receive notice from the Bar Association that it is investigating. Then they'll ask you for an interview, probably. And you go and be interviewed. At that interview, you'll be represented by counsel. Me."

"You take it seriously," she said.

He nodded. "You can't ignore these things."

Judge Eleanor MacGruder put her hands delicately to the hinges at the outer corners of her rimless, dewdrop-shaped spectacles and adjusted them to suit her. "Uh . . . Matter of one . . . Svetlana Nikolaievna Terasnova, deportation proceeding," she read from a paper before her on the bench. "The Justice Department is present in the person of Mr. Layman Langley, correct?"

Langley rose. His nod to the judge was almost a bow. "That is correct, Your Honor," he said.

His fixed smile was fixed again this morning, Cosima noted. She wondered what it would take to unfix it this time. Appearing again in a dark blue three-piece suit, he recalled to Cosima's mind the term Hugh Hupp applied to young lawyers like him: "Vestling—a fellow so insecure about his status that he wouldn't take off that ugly, misshapen garment in the office on the hottest day of summer with the air-conditioning not working, for fear somebody might ask him to sharpen a pencil." Vestling. Langley was one, for sure.

"Miss Terasnova is represented by . . . ?"

"Cosima Bernardin, Your Honor. Bernardin & Loewenstein."

Judge Eleanor MacGruder was a Carter appointee to the United States Court of Appeals, Second Circuit. She had labored in the legal department of the Environmental Protection Agency, and someone had suggested that intelligence and faithful service to the government might qualify a woman for a judgeship. Forty-five years old, she was by appearance as mousy a woman as anyone could imagine, but she had built a reputation as a sharp, no-nonsense judge.

"The Justice Department's motion?" she asked Langley.

"To dismiss a frivolous appeal, Your Honor," said Langley, his smile still adhesively fixed.

"Proceed, Mr. Langley."

"On the record, which is not to be controverted," said Langley, "the deportation of Miss Terasnova is not in question. The Justice Department respectfully suggests to Your Honor that the appeal filed in this Court was filed for the sole purpose of delay. The facts are beyond question. They have been, indeed, admitted by Miss Terasnova. The law is clear. There is no issue on which this Court can reverse the findings and order of the District Director. In fact, Your Honor, the Department respectfully submits that the Court is without jurisdiction. The statutes provide—"

"I am familiar with the statutes, Mr. Langley."

"Then may I hope Your Honor will grant our motion?"

Judge MacGruder could not peer over her glasses, they fit too tightly to her face; she lowered her chin almost to her chest and regarded Langley with skepticism that could not have been better expressed if she could have peered over her glasses. "You will not, perhaps, object if I hear what counsel for Miss Terasnova has to say?"

Langley bowed again and sat down.

"Miss Bernardin."

Cosima rose. She wore a charcoal-gray wool jacket and matching skirt. "Your Honor," she said, "my client is a talented young Russian ballerina. The effort on the part of

193

the Department of Justice to deport her is lawful, as Mr. Langley says. It is also unconscionable. He will tell you that I am doing everything I can to delay the case. That is exactly true, Your Honor. A bill has been introduced in the House of Representatives to grant Miss Terasnova American citizenship. I candidly acknowledge that I am doing whatever I can to delay the case until the bill may be passed. If this Court dismisses this appeal, then I will immediately file in the District Court a petition for a writ of habeas corpus. As Your Honor knows, I cannot file a petition for habeas until I have exhausted my client's rights to appeal from the order of the District Director.''

''Am I to understand, then, Miss Bernardin, that you do not oppose Mr. Langley's motion to dismiss the appeal?''

Cosima glanced at Langley, whose smile had not yet been erased. ''Your Honor, the law is as Mr. Langley has characterized it. We cannot bring new evidence before this Court. This Court is compelled to assume that the findings of fact issued by the Director are true. I filed the appeal pro forma, because I had to file it to establish jurisdiction for the District Court to hear our petition for habeas corpus. Before *that* court, in *that* proceeding, I will be able to introduce new evidence.''

''Which will be futile,'' said Langley. ''She will file the petition only for delay, as she's just admitted.''

''Actually,'' said Judge MacGruder, ''different questions arise in a habeas corpus proceeding.''

''If Your Honor please,'' said Cosima, ''I might point out that if it is unseemly for me to try to delay this case, it is just as unseemly for Mr. Langley to continue his obsessive attempts to accelerate it. We filed this appeal only a month ago, and yet here we are already with a motion to dismiss—which Mr. Langley has somehow managed to have set forward on the calendar. This country cannot possibly be harmed by the presence of a tiny ballerina, and I entertain strong suspicions of the motives behind the anxiety of the Department of Justice to deport her.''

"Miss Terasnova lied to get into this country," Langley said, "and she—"

"I've read the record, Mr. Langley," said the judge. She paused, shrugged. "So, counsel. Do you want to submit the case and your statements on the record?"

"I have a question, Your Honor," said Langley. "Where is Miss Terasnova?"

A faint smile deepened the tiny wrinkles in the corners of the judge's mouth. "I'm sure I have no idea," she said.

Once more Langley bobbed his head, that half-bow. "I think Miss Bernardin should tell us where her client is."

"Why?" asked Cosima.

Langley shrugged. The smile broke at last as he blew out breath and his lips fluttered. "The—The Department is entitled to know," he said.

"Your Honor," said Cosima, "I think I understand why he wants to know. The Department of Justice will seek to arrest Miss Terasnova as soon as your order of dismissal is docketed. On the day this appeal was filed, they refused to allow her to remain free for the three hours it took us to arrange her bail. Instead, they held her in jail for three hours. I have no intention of telling him where she is. Once we've filed our petition for habeas corpus and bail is fixed and posted, then Mr. Langley can know where Miss Terasnova is."

Langley's smile returned. "You see the problem, Your Honor?"

Judge MacGruder shook her head. "Not exactly," she said. "Are you asking me to *order* Miss Bernardin to tell you where Miss Terasnova is?"

"That might be appropriate, Your Honor."

"You can file a motion for such an order, supported by a memorandum of law. In the meanwhile, the Court will take the motion for dismissal under advisement," said the judge.

"Uh . . . the Department had hoped Your Honor might rule today. Particularly in view of the fact that the issues

195

are crystal clear, as Miss Bernardin has admitted. The motion before you is only one to dismiss a frivolous appeal. A very simple matter.''

"I don't want to be precipitate, Mr. Langley. I'll review the file. You will be notified.''

Cosima watched the Langley smile disintegrate. He shot a hard glance at her. She ignored him and watched respectfully as Judge MacGruder picked up her file and left the courtroom.

"I think a federal judge has just done you one hell of a big favor,'' was Hugh Hupp's reaction when Cosima returned to the office that Thursday afternoon, 29 October. "Langley was right in thinking she'd rule from the bench.''

"I'm going to have to keep close watch,'' said Cosima. "The day she decides and puts an order on the journal, we have to get the petition for habeas corpus filed.''

"I suppose Rick has it ready,'' said Hugh.

"Has had it ready since we were notified that Justice was moving for dismissal of the appeal.''

"She could sit on that motion for another six weeks,'' said Hugh. "I have a feeling that when the Department got the hearing set forward on the docket, they never guessed what judge would be assigned to hear it.''

"I wish you could have been there,'' said Cosima. "It worked out great, but you know my courtroom experience is limited.''

Hugh shrugged. "That's how you get it. Plunge in. You were lucky the water was warm this time.''

"Oh, Hughie!'' She laughed, and in an effusion of euphoria she rushed behind his desk, threw her arms around him and kissed him on the forehead.

"Uh . . . am I interrupting something?'' Rick had stepped into the door of Hugh's office. "I can come back.''

Still laughing, Cosima hurried to him and kissed him on the cheek. "Judge MacGruder took Lana's case 'under advisement,' " she told him. "Delay! Two weeks, four weeks, six weeks, a dollar!"

Rick grinned. "Hey, great! And I've got something curious that may be great, too," he said. He looked past her, at Hugh. "Hey, Hugh. Afternoon mail. A letter from— guess who?"

"Ronald Reagan," scoffed Hugh.

"Who?" asked Cosima, still exuberant.

Rick kept his left arm around her, gently patting her on the backside. "An eight-page letter, would you believe it? Single-spaced. Seriously concerned about the possible tax consequences of an offer he has received from Gold Medal Records, Incorporated. Proposed contract being mailed directly to us from Gold Medal. Please review for tax consequences, ask Cosima to review for other aspects, et cetera, et cetera, et cetera. Signed in his absence by his secretary . . . Ruggiero Paccinelli!"

Cosima stiffened with sucked-in breath. "So," she said coldly. "Are we to understand we are still his lawyers?"

Rick laughed, but it was a nervous laugh. "It would appear so," he said. "At least for the time being."

"Are we supposed to show our gratitude in some way, I wonder?" she asked.

"Play it by ear, Cosima," said Hugh firmly.

She nodded. "Try to keep him as your client, Rick," she said. "It's going to be a little difficult for me to talk to him. I didn't tell you half of what happened in Washington."

"How close is he to running through the retainer he paid you?" Hugh asked.

"That money will cover a lot more legal services than he's received so far," said Rick.

"Retainers are not just advance payments against services, Rick," said Cosima. "He *retained* us. That means he paid us to become his lawyers, to be available to him, not to take other clients whose interests might conflict with his. You don't have to bill a retainer out at so much an hour."

"If you kids want a suggestion," said Hugh, "I suggest

you send Brother Paccinelli a bill when you've finished the work outlined in this letter. If he pays it—"

"If he pays it, we have a client," said Cosima. "If he doesn't, he is just trying to get us to work out his retainer—and that, by god, I do not propose to do."

"Anyway, we may have some expenses," said Rick. "He's talking, too, about our looking at a new pension-fund arrangement. We may need help from a specialist."

Cosima's grim expression softened. "No kidding," she said. "That gives me one hell of an idea."

"Cosima . . ." said Rick quietly, cautioning.

"Joan Salomon," said Cosima, lofting her chin, letting a smile develop and turn to a grin. "Joan asked me to call her, to be sure to call her. Okay. Now is the time to call her."

Ten

"You like sushi?" Cosima asked Joan Salomon.

Joan shrugged. "It's always a risk," she said. "Half the time I eat it, it gives me the trots. Which says something, doesn't it? If it makes me sick, why do I eat it? Because I like it! Hey, you got a sushi place in mind?"

"Right. And Rick will join us."

Joan looked all around Cosima's office. "God!" she said. "The blessings of having your own firm! What would it take you at Webster, Kent to have an office like this? Twenty years? No. Because there aren't any offices like this at 80 Pine Street. Anyway, if you wanted to furnish and decorate an office like this, somebody would frown and cluck and tell you it 'isn't quite appropriate.' "

"Hey," said Cosima. "There are some *nice* offices at 80 Pine, as there are at 120 Broadway. The buildings aren't the problem. I wouldn't mind being downtown, really. In the Wall Street area. But this space was available. Sublease. We may have to leave someday."

Joan snapped her lighter and lit a fresh cigarette. She smoked heavily. Cosima wished she didn't, but she would never say anything to her about it. She'd told other friends their smoking was offensive. She would not say it to Joan.

A compact Jewish woman whose body tended to produce loose flesh, Joan somehow managed to remain solid: with a little more flesh than she should have carried around, maybe, but not flab. Her carelessly cut light brown hair fell over her forehead and over her eyebrows. The skin of her cheeks was roughened by her compulsive smoking, and maybe by her drinking, but her brown eyes peered out intently from behind the wisps of hair that fell over them, suggesting—and not fancifully—a keen intelligence. She dressed thoughtlessly, generally in loose sweaters and skirts that had this year become unstylishly long. She needed pockets: that was one of the objectives of the way she dressed. She could not carry a purse around everywhere for her cigarettes and lighter, so she managed always to wear something that had pockets for these necessities.

Webster, Kent determinedly kept Joan Salomon in the back rooms. What she did for the firm's clients was presented to them by vestlings. But they paid her. They appreciated what she did, and they paid her.

They sat down at twelve-thirty at a table in a Japanese restaurant on 44th Street. It was clean and bright. On their way from the captain's desk to their table upstairs they passed by the sushi bar, where half a dozen Japanese wielded threatening knives and sliced raw fish and all the other components of sushi into the circles of fish, rice and spices that would appear on the plates. Japanese businessmen from the offices in the Pan Am Building sat on stools at the bar. Cosima and Rick had noticed them there and decided to eat where the New York executives of companies like Mitsubishi took their lunch.

"I don't exactly see, Joan," said Rick cautiously, "how you could have any part in setting up a pension plan for Fang, Incorporated."

"Two ways," she interrupted him. "I *lie* to Webster,

200

Kent so they don't know what I'm doing—which doesn't bother me in the least—or I *quit.*"

"Joan—"

Cosima had begun to laugh, which interrupted him. She was looking at the tray of drinks the Japanese waitress was about to put on their table—a hot flask of sake for Rick, vodka on the rocks for Joan, a martini for Cosima. Her short laugh was for the martini. Half a dozen times she had told waitresses here she wanted an olive in her martini, and half a dozen times she had received a martini with a lemon twist. It had become a joke.

Not for Rick. He could not curb his irritation. "Miss," he said curtly. "This has happened once too often."

"Rick. Let it go."

"No. There is no reason why you should pay the price of a drink in this place, week after week, and never get what you order. I'm going to have this straight, once and for all." He looked up at the waitress, who was by now bewildered. "Miss. Martini. Okay? No twist of lemon. *Olive.* Okay? You understand olive? Tell the bartender the lady wants an *olive* in her drink, no twist. Okay?"

"Ahr-riv," the waitress repeated. "Ahr . . . riv."

"Olive. You got it?"

The Japanese girl smiled, nodded and hurried away, carrying back the tray with the martini.

"Great, Rick. Now, god knows when I get a drink."

"I get tired of this, time after time," he said. "They pretend they don't understand English. It's just an excuse for sloppy service."

"Yeah," said Joan with a satirical smile. "Who won the goddamned war, anyway?"

"Jesus," muttered Cosima. "All I wanted was a goddamn *martini*."

"Yeah. Well . . . Jerry Paccinelli wants a pension plan," said Rick. "It's going to have to be something sophisticated, and it will have to comply with ERISA and all the rest of it. You're a pension-plan specialist, Joan, and I'd sure like to have you work on it, but I don't see how we can arrange it."

Joan put her cigarette aside and picked up her vodka. "Speaking seriously," she said, "I'm not sure we can either, unless I do something radical."

"You can't lie to Webster, Kent," he said. "I know you won't, but even if you wanted to, we couldn't agree to it."

"Which means," she said, "we have met to talk about my joining Bernardin & Loewenstein." She switched drink and cigarette. "Right?"

"I think it's worth talking about," said Cosima. "I guess the question is, can you bring any business with you? Right now, Fang is the only client we have that requires your special skills. There's a pretty good fee in setting up a plan for Fang, but where would we go from there?"

Joan shook her head. "I can't bring any business from Webster, Kent," she said.

"We understand that," said Cosima.

For some reason, Joan kept her left hand in her lap and continued to shift between cigarette and vodka with her right only—putting the cigarette in the ashtray, picking up the drink, sipping, putting down the drink, picking up the cigarette again, then repeating the whole sequence. "I'd like to leave Webster, Kent," she said. "I can't tell you how much I admire you two, for having had the courage to walk out of Hamilton, Schuyler."

"It's a question of business," said Rick. "Clients. Neither of us is making half of what we were making before we left."

"It comes down to this, Joan," said Cosima. "We'd like to have you with us. We've talked about it. Hugh Hupp agrees. To make room for you in the office, we'll have to rent some additional square footage, which fortunately is available. We can sublet another room. We've also got good luck about walls and doors. We can simply unlock one door and lock another one—we don't have to tear any walls down. The additional rent and telephone and so on will run about fifteen hundred a month. Teresa can handle a little more secretarial work, but not far down the line we're going to have to have a second secretary. We're looking at two thousand a month, minimum—before you can take a dollar out of the office. Actually, of course, we can carry it a little while—"

"Cosima means *she* can," said Rick. "Out of personal funds. She carried me for a while. I owe her my share of the costs for that time, and pretty soon I'm going to start paying her back."

"I can carry myself," said Joan. "I have some money. Two thousand a month for the privilege of joining your firm, then how do we divide the fees?"

"For the present," said Cosima, "Rick takes whatever fees are attributed to his work, even if the client is mine. We can do the same for you, for a while. Sooner or later we'll have to write a partnership agreement, with the usual division of fees, based on bringing in business as well as on work done."

"Would I be coming in as an employee or—"

"A partner," said Cosima. "Rick and I are partners. Hugh is 'of counsel.' If you want to come in, and we can agree on a deal, we'll change the name of the firm. Bernardin, Loewenstein & Salomon. Has a good ring to it, hmm?"

With quickness that could only have originated in a nervous reaction, Joan switched cigarette and glass again. "Sounds like a dream," she said. "To escape Webster, Kent . . . If I were talking to anybody but you two, I'd say you wouldn't believe what I have to put up with in that firm. But you two know." She sipped vodka. "I've paid my goddam dues, I'll tell you that."

"You can go broke with us, Joan," said Rick. "Don't overlook the risk."

"There's a risk for you, too," said Joan. "Ah—here's your new martini, Cosima."

The little Japanese waitress, with a broad innocent smile, put a fresh martini on the table in front of Cosima. There was no twist of lemon peel—but no olive, either. Instead, floating on the gin and vermouth, lay a twist of *orange* peel.

"Ahr-iv," said the girl, wide-eyed, as Rick flushed and Joan covered her laugh with a quick hand.

Cosima pointed a cautioning finger at Rick. "Well, thank you," she said to the waitress. "Very good. Very good. Thank you."

The waitress smiled, bowed, and departed.

Now Joan could laugh. "Every martini served in this place for the next *week* will have a twist of orange in it!"

"Damn!" snorted Rick.

Cosima sipped the martini with the orange peel. "Not bad," she said. "On the whole, I think I prefer that to a lemon twist. Of course . . . I have always been an iconoclast. Do we start drafting an agreement, Joan?"

Joan frowned. "Not unless we have a completely open understanding," she said. "Cards on the table. Okay?"

"Whatever you have in mind," said Cosima.

Joan lifted her glass and drank the remaining vodka. The waitress was two tables away, and she showed her the glass to indicate she wanted another drink. "Do you two sleep together?" she asked bluntly.

"It's been known to happen," said Cosima. "Not regularly. Not an element of the partnership."

"Forgive the personal question, and thanks for the frank answer," said Joan. "Now from my side. You may have figured this out, Cosima. I think they suspect it at Webster, Kent, though nobody's ever mentioned it. Anyway . . . *I* sleep with somebody. And I love her." She nodded. "I love her, and if anybody at Webster, Kent—or anybody at Bernardin & Loewenstein—doesn't like it, tough shit; I won't give her up for a place in a law firm. Can you live with that?"

"I don't have to live with it," said Cosima. "Who I sleep with is none of your business, and who you sleep with is none of mine." She grinned. "So long as it's not with a client or a judge."

"It's no secret," said Joan.

"I do have one requirement in that respect," said Cosima. "I don't go around wearing a big metal button reading HETEROSEXUAL. I don't want a partner who goes around with one reading HOMOSEXUAL. If you're a gay-rights activist, then I guess we've got a problem. I promise you I won't appear on TV screaming 'Straight!' I don't want to see a partner of mine yelling 'Gay!' "

Joan nodded. "Deal," she said.

"You're not likely to embarrass us," said Cosima. "We may embarrass you, though. You have to understand that I am being investigated by the bar association, on a charge of unethical conduct."

"I've never had that opportunity," said Joan wryly. "What'd you do, swipe a client from the old boys?"

"It's a little more complicated than that," said Rick.

Joan tipped her glass and sipped the last drops of vodka and water from the melted ice. Then she lifted the glass. "What the hell?" she asked. "You can take my being queer, I can take your being unethical."

Cosima and Rick met Max Wilmot for a drink in the bar at Charlie Brown's, in the Pan Am Building, just off the escalators from Grand Central, at six that evening. They told him Joan Salomon was almost certainly going to join their firm.

"What firm you going to raid next?" he asked as he wiped beer foam out of his mustache. "Webster, Kent . . ." He shook his head. "They're not going to like it, kids. They had plans for Joan Salomon."

"Don't give a damn what they like," said Cosima. "They don't *own* her. We're talking about lawyers, not athletes. You can't purchase lawyers and force them to stay with you till you've worn them out."

Max stared curiously at her. Could Cosima have had too much to drink? She and Rick had been here when he came in, sitting at one of the round tables in the little cubicles that separated a few tables from the crowd. She had been drinking a Bombay gin martini when he sat down and had ordered another one since. It wasn't just what she said—"don't give a damn" was unlike her, in his experience and judgment—but the odd smile with which she said it. Besides, she was in some sort of brittle mood; he could see it in her eyes, which darted from him to Rick and back again as if she expected a challenge from one of them. He decided to go on with what he'd meant to say:

"Joan Salomon is a comer. Her name is around. Webster, Kent is going to resent her leaving. They're going to figure you recruited her."

"Recruited . . ." said Cosima. She shook her head. "No. She's *unhappy* at—"

Rick sighed loudly. "What the hell, Max," he said. "Why should *anyone* practice law in firms like Hamilton, Schuyler or Webster, Kent?"

Rick too? Max laughed, then grinned. "Hell, man, you know perfectly well why. *Insecurity.* In-se-by-god-curity. No one with sufficient confidence in his own talents would put up with rhinocerosism, whether in a law firm or a corporation; but the world is short of people who are sure they can make it on their own, out in the cold, cruel world. So they crawl under organizational security blankets and suck off the top dogs. That's how the world goes round. So, big deal. The only part that's disgusting is how they insist it's all so very wonderful."

Cosima grinned. "I like Max's philosophy," she said.

"Then you don't like your father's," said Rick.

Rick surprised Max, who knew that criticizing Leon Bernardin usually generated cold anger in Cosima. Bernardin was a controversial figure on Wall Street, with uncritical admirers and militant enemies in about equal proportions. Max was not sure Cosima had any sense of the antagonism her father evoked.

He wondered if she had read the article he had read, a

year or so ago in the *Wall Street Journal*: a profile of Leon Bernardin. It said he had inherited too much to be called a self-made man—which was probably the only cliché about the rich that did not apply to him. "He is smart and tough," the article said. ". . . indefatigable, dogged and consistently better informed than his competitors."

The general theme of the article had been how Bernardin Frères gathered and used information.

Like the Rothschilds, Bernardin Frères operated a worldwide intelligence-gathering network, the article said. The writer told the story of an Austrian businessman who applied to the Zurich office of Bernardin Frères for a loan of thirty million dollars. The Zurich office approved the loan, but since the amount exceeded its loan authority it forwarded the documents to the New York office. The Austrian came to New York to promote his loan—only to be turned down by Leon Bernardin himself, who reminded him that at least four of his past business ventures had failed, one because of undercapitalization, one because of inadequate market research, and two because of unskillful control of cash flow. The Austrian at first furiously denied all of this, then accused Bernardin Frères of having planted spies inside his companies. Leon Bernardin, as the writer described it, calmly handed the man a file of computer printouts of articles from European financial papers and wire services in three languages. Each of the man's business misadventures had been the subject of published reports over the years, some of them in sources virtually unknown to American bankers—but thoroughly well known to Bernardin.

The smooth Austrian almost effortlessly persuaded another New York bank to grant the loan, which went into default within twelve months.

What was more, Bernardin had kept away from mortgage-investment pools—as *Forbes* had reported. Bank of America lost a billion dollars on them. Many other big banks took major losses on mortgage-investment pools. But not Bernardin Frères. Leon Bernardin would not invest in them.

When the crunch came in 1985, Bernardin Frères wasn't crunched. A reputation that had already been strong was reinforced. The old bastard was something of a genius. A cynical genius, but a genius.

"I *don't* like my father's philosophy," Cosima agreed with Rick. "No one else in the family does, either—except maybe Pierre."

"To which, I am sure," said Rick, "your father's response is that all of you can afford the luxury of your individualistic philosophies because none of you have ever really had to make a living."

"Isn't this getting a little personal?" Max asked.

Cosima showed Rick a twisted smile. "Which of our rooms do you have bugged?" she asked with a soft laugh.

"I'll tell you something else your father is going to say," said Rick. "He's going to say something like—'Another Jew? You mean you're taking another Jew into your partnership?'"

Cosima reached for her martini. "I think this *is* getting a little personal," she said to Max.

"He said that about *me,* didn't he?" Rick persisted.

Cosima glared at him. *"Yes!* . . . and I don't give a damn."

Rick nodded. "Yeah. Problem is, you *do.*"

Cosima shrugged at Max. "Why do I have to hear this? If Rick was a failure and wanted to rationalize it by pleading he's a victim of anti-Semitism, that's one thing. But he's *not* a failure. Goddammit, Rick, maybe my father doesn't like you. Does *everybody* have to like you? If ten thousand people like and respect you, is it soured because *one* doesn't? Talk about in-se-goddam-curity!"

Rick shook his head, lowered his eyes, and reached for his Scotch. "I've said too much," he said.

"Maybe you haven't said enough."

A moment of silence followed, in which Cosima and Rick avoided each other's eyes and Max sipped his beer thoughtfully and tried not to show them how distasteful to him the conversation had become. He broke the silence.

"Tell you what, folks. I'm going home and cook up some din-din. I'm one hell of a chef, in case you didn't know. Welcome to join me. I can always feed two more."

"I'd like that, Max," said Cosima. "Another time."

Max nodded and drained the last swallow of beer from his mug. "Well, then," he said. "You going down to the station?"

Cosima glanced at Rick. "I don't know," she said. "Probably not. Maybe I'll stay in town tonight. Maybe I'll go down to Rick's place and try to repair the relationship."

She kept a few personal things in Rick's apartment—comb and brush, toothbrush, cosmetics, underwear, a pair of jeans, a sweatshirt. This evening she had rejected his suggestion that they stop by some little restaurant in the neighborhood; and while he puttered in the kitchen, trying to put a meal together, she took a shower.

When she came out, barefoot and comfortable in the jeans and sweatshirt, he was heating something in the microwave, and two large beef patties were sputtering and smoking in a skillet. He stood back, trying to avoid flying drops of grease that would have stained his suit or necktie.

"Go change," she said. "I'll finish that for you."

After an amused moment of self-analysis, she decided the artificial euphoria of the martinis was wearing off too much and needed augmentation. After three at lunch, followed by a short time in the office and two more in Charlie Brown's, she had been drinking them with conscious purpose. She had four, all told, in Charlie's and was pleasantly wobbly. She poured herself another, from the bottle of Bombay gin that Rick now kept in his kitchen. Rick would probably remark on it when he returned. She didn't give a damn. Sometimes . . . Attitude adjustment. A euphemism. Some-

209

times—what the hell?—attitude could use a little adjustment.

He returned, having made a quick change into tan corduroys and a maroon sweater. The space between the counter and cabinets in the kitchen was so narrow he had to squeeze past her to get to the refrigerator, pressing hips to her bottom. He put his arms around her, cupped her breasts in his hands, and nuzzled her on the neck.

"You're having another drink?" he asked.

"Yes. So have one yourself, you uptight Hebrew asshole."

She could feel him laughing. "Hey, you *have* had—"

"Want to see the real me come out?" she asked. She turned to face him. "That's allowed sometimes, isn't it?"

"Sure. I guess so," he said. But he was doubtful. She could hear his uncertainty. Then she felt him draw breath. "Yes, sure," he said with more conviction. He reached past her and pushed the skillet off the burner. "Of course," he said, and he kissed her.

Cosima grabbed her martini from the counter and walked out of the kitchen to the living room. She went to his couch and sat down. "The real me," she said, taking a swallow from her glass. "Hardly ever seen in this life. Uptight switched off. For five minutes. A little of the veneer peeled away."

"If you had enough hair to let down—"

"I couldn't let it down. Somebody'd point out that my hair was down."

She could see he was sensitive to the crisp stress in her voice.

"I thought you were happy, Cosima," he said—and she could hear in the way his voice trailed off that he knew in an instant it was the wrong thing to say.

Still, she didn't restrain herself. She looked up and spoke sarcastically. "Sure. Like everyone is always telling me, I've got everything everybody wants."

Rick tried to lighten the dialogue. "Including a scorched

hamburger and some rubbery Chinese vegetables in a plastic pouch.''

Cosima lifted and flexed her shoulders, rotated her head, rubbed her chin on her chest, her cheeks on her upper arms. She closed her eyes tight. "Happy . . ." she whispered hoarsely. She opened her eyes. "Happiness is an intermittent condition. You're happy for a moment now and then, miserable a moment later, and most of the time . . . well, most of the time you don't think about it. How many moments do any of us have when we're consciously happy? More when we're consciously miserable, I can tell you.''

"We try," Rick suggested weaky—a cliché that afflicted him with conspicuous apprehension of inadequacy.

"Which is fatal," she said. " 'The pursuit of happiness.' What a crock! Pursuing it is the surest way not to find it.''

"Found at all, it's found under the umbrellas, I'm afraid," said Rick. "Religion—''

"Crutches," she interjected. "Not umbrellas, crutches. Alcohol, substances, psychiatry, religion . . . whatever people make themselves dependent on. Remember the old phrase 'fat, dumb, and happy'? Do you have to be dumb and crutch-dependent to be happy? To hell with that. Happy— happy, if at all, on my own fuckin' terms . . .''

Rick sat down beside her. He tried to draw her into his arms, but she remained rigid. She allowed herself to be pulled closer to him, but she did not relax.

"Anyway," she said. "Are they dumb happy? Just because they look like they are? Is that what you have to look like, to be happy?''

"Cosima," said Rick. "Why don't we go out to a little place where we can have something tasty and a decent wine?''

She sighed and tipped back her martini. "Okay," she said. "I'm boring you. Let's do. Let's go out.''

As she stirred to rise from the couch, he stood and offered her his hand. "You're not boring me," he said. "One thing you are not, ever, is boring.''

"Sure."

She realized as she walked toward the bedroom, where she would run a brush through her hair and pick up her billfold, that the martini she had just finished had been one too many. She had to make a resolute effort to walk steady. But she set her feet down deliberately, fixed her eyes on the bureau and walked with the overstated gravity her condition induced. As she brushed her hair, she remembered she had no underwear beneath her jeans and sweatshirt and wondered if she shouldn't put on a bra and panties. Then she decided, what the hell, a compulsion to be underweared was another part of uptight. She pushed her feet into a pair of Topsiders that lay on the floor of the closet.

Rick was there. He had come into the bedroom. He came toward her as she ran her hands down over her sweatshirt, smoothing it; he put one arm around her and ran the other hand across her head and down over the back of her neck.

"Cosima . . ."

She met his eyes with hers, sure of what he was going to say and wishing somehow she could signal him not to.

"Cosima, I love you."

She could not turn her face away from him. She could not lower her eyes. She had no option, but to stand with her chin uptilted just a little, to meet his eyes with hers, to confront the challenge in his quiet, honest words.

"You don't love *me*, of course," he said.

"Why'm I not allowed to say for myself?"

"Do you?"

"I'm not *in love* with you."

"You wouldn't consider marrying me."

"Rick . . . I wouldn't consider marrying *anybody* right now."

He nodded. "Yeah. I shouldn't have told you."

"You didn't have to."

"I'm not subtle."

"I should hope not, about a thing like that."

He drew her closer to him, which she let him do. He

caressed the back of her neck. "It could be so perfect," he whispered. "I would worship you."

Cosima sighed. "Maybe I would disappoint you."

"I don't want to be just a friend."

"You're more than that."

"But it won't work. It won't happen."

She broke away from him and retreated to the living room. As he came from the bedroom, following her, she raised a hand to stop him short of enfolding her in another embrace.

"It isn't impossible, Rick," she said. She stopped, drew a breath. "Unlikely, maybe. Not impossible." She grabbed for her glass and drank the last dregs of the martini, with the water from the melted ice.

He sat down on the couch. "Yes, impossible," he said.

"Not for any reason you think," she declared.

"Sure."

"No, by god!"

"Okay . . . listen, there's a Hungarian place two blocks from here. Hungarian food, Romanian wine. 'Kay?"

"Okay, Rick. Hungarian food, Romanian wine. And maybe a little less significance. From both of us. Agreed?"

He nodded solemnly. "Agreed."

He rose and gave her his hand to help her up. She stood, but she stumbled against him.

"Cosima—"

"Don't feel so good, Rick," she said. "Hungarian . . ." She shook her head. "Let's just go to bed. Take me to bed, Rick. Sorry. Bathroom . . . bed."

Eleven

Adela Drake could not appear on the street without a team of security men surrounding her to fend off the mob. Except in the middle of a squad of bodyguards, she could not enter the courthouse for the final hearing on her divorce from John Woody. She understood this better than Cosima and asked Cosima to meet her at the Waldorf the morning of the hearing. They would be picked up and driven to the courthouse in a limousine that would be followed by a second car filled with her guards.

Cosima went up to her suite.

"Rick sends his best, also his apologies," said Cosima. "He would have gone to court with you this morning, but he's in a meeting with a pair of IRS auditors. The meeting was supposed to end yesterday, but it looks like it's going to last the rest of the week."

Adela sat on a couch facing a marble-top coffee table, her back to a window overlooking the east side of Manhattan, the river and the broad, anonymous expanse of city beyond.

In chairs facing her, awed by the suite and the city, and awed now by Cosima as well, sat two apprehensive young women. Adela rose and introduced them: two friends from North Carolina who would be her witnesses. Cosima had told her she wouldn't need to bring in witnesses from out of town, that members of the band or any other friends would do; but Adela had brought these two shy, drab girls anyway, maybe for moral support.

It was obvious to Cosima that Adela had dressed with anxious attention, conscious of an incongruity between her style as a rock musician and the dignity she expected to find in the courtroom. She wore a navy blue blazer and gray skirt, a white blouse with a high collar closed by a small floppy tie. She wore a little pink lipstick and had darkened her brows and lashes a little. It was all very modest, very discreet—but of course her head remained shaved except for the bristly narrow hedge of red and green hair that ran from her forehead to the nape of her neck.

"I tried on a wig," she said to Cosima. "But it looks ridiculous."

"No need. Look, this isn't going to be a big deal. I know it is for you personally, of course, but . . . the courtroom procedure isn't going to amount to anything. It'll be over in five minutes."

"John might show up," said Adela.

Cosima shook her head. "Even if he does, it's too late now."

"Be an awful scene," said Adela.

"On the basis of what I read in his letters, I judge your John's a blusterer and not much else," said Cosima. "I don't think he'll show his face in New York. To be perfectly frank with you, I think he's too much a coward to venture into this city."

One of the witnesses shook her head. "John's a strong man," she said.

"Maybe he is, out where his swaggering and his loud mouth count for something," said Cosima.

Rick had received a letter from him:

Okay NY lawyer smartass what kind of a man are you what kind of a lawyer

My wife says you tole her my lean aint no good well
I got a lawyer here says it is also lots of folks that
knows more than some Jew lawyer boy from NY
One thing—that NY court got no say in a marriage
of N Car people so you go ahead and put some kind
of court order on up there and you or her come down
here with it we shove it up your ass
What I want to know is if marriage is marriage or if
in NY you got some kind of Jew marriage that dont
count
I come up there and give you a nuckle sanwich
You shut off that divorce stuff right now or I make
you wish you had

"Almost feel sorry for him," said the other witness.
"I can't feel sorry for a man who repeatedly threatens to
do his wife physical harm," said Cosima.
"I know, but he's up against more than he can handle.
I mean, look—" The witness spread her arms and indicated
the luxurious suite, the city beyond the wide window. "And
you, Miss Bernardin. Smart, beautiful New York lawyer.
And all the money Adela's got to fight him." She shook her
head. "Besides, what the New York newspapers said about
him was picked up and run back home . . . His letters he
wrote to Adela were run in the papers. And the TV . . .
That one show made him out to be an idiot. All Johnny can
do is get mad. It's all he can do."
"Bonny . . ." said Adela quietly. "I have to do this."
Bonny nodded. "Oh, sure."
Adela asked them to pray with her before they left for the
hearing. Cosima stood with her eyes down, but she was
looking out the window while Adela asked for forgiveness
and help and understanding. The two witnesses joined in
her fervent "Amen," and Adela picked up the telephone
and called for her security men.

* * *

Reporters and photographers pursued them to the door of the courtroom, yelling questions and demands. Shrieking fans jostled with the media men and women. Cosima saw one girl knocked to her knees. The four burly plainclothes guards could hardly keep the horde back, and inside the courthouse they were joined by uniformed policemen who shoved and yelled and opened a path.

Their entry into the courtroom caused a disturbance that interrupted the proceedings already in hearing. The judge banged his gavel. A bailiff rushed toward the door, shouting stridently that there were no more seats inside.

"Parties and lawyers only! Parties and lawyers! No seats. Press seats full! Close the doors."

Even the four security men were excluded. They formed a threatening human barricade before the double doors, and the bailiff was able to pull them shut.

In the well of the courtroom, beyond the rail and below the bench, an obese and sweating woman stood open-mouthed and staring at the spectacle in the back of the room. She was the plaintiff in the case being heard. Beside her was her lawyer, a tall, well dressed, somewhat haughty black man. Two other fat women were her witnesses. A thinner woman was her interpreter. Before the interruption, she had been stating her case in Spanish.

The judge—The Honorable Roy A. Lindsay, according to the sign on the bench—had closed his eyes as a sign of his impatience. He opened them now and pointed at a row of seats reserved for the parties, lawyers and witnesses. Judge Lindsay, too, was a black: a glossy, chocolate-colored man, bald, with a fringe of wooly black hair above his ears, wearing a set of half-glasses; he was a man whose patience was tried every hour of every day. He grimaced at Adela and Cosima and waited until they were seated in the row behind the rail. When the clamor in the courtroom was low enough to let him hear, he nodded at the group in front of him, and the lawyer prompted the Hispanic woman to resume her testimony.

The room was small and squalid. It had been furnished in the twenties; except for the judge's high-back chair the furniture and fixtures of the twenties remained, worn and scarred. The windows behind the judge were covered by ripped and faded old green blinds. The light fixtures were bulbs burning inside milk glass globes that served as sarcophagi for six decades' accumulation of the desiccated remains of insects that had been unfortunate to wander in from the top and die before they could find their way out. The chairs squeaked. Though red-and-white signs said NO SMOKING, some still did, and the air was foul.

Reporters in the rows of seats behind Adela leaned forward and began to whisper questions. Judge Lindsay glanced irritably at them, then shrugged and made no effort to silence them.

Neither did he try to quiet the excited litigants and lawyers in the front rows, who grinned and nodded and waved at Adela. Someone passed along a scrap of paper to be autographed. It had to be passed by a lawyer—a flushed old man in a checked sport coat—who might have been asleep but for the attention he had to give to keeping his cigar ashes from falling on his slacks.

The case in progress ended abruptly. The judge handed the lawyer a sheet of paper, and the lawyer smiled a businesslike smile and led his client and her party out of the well.

"I suppose," said Judge Lindsay, glaring at Adela, "I have the privilege of seeing Mrs. John Woody, also known as Adela Drake."

Cosima stood. "Yes, Your Honor. Cosima Bernardin, her counsel."

The judge sighed. "Well, I've got several cases ahead of you. But to restore some semblance of sanity to this courtroom, I'm going to take your case up next. Step forward!"

Cosima led Angela and her witnesses through the gap in the rail and into the well before the bench.

The bailiff hurried to encounter them. "Plaintiff?" he

asked, pointing at Adela. "Witnesses? Right hands." He raised his right hand, to show them what to do. In his left he held a Bible. He shoved it among them, and the three women put their hands on it.

"D'you-sol'mly-swear-t'-tell-truth-whole-truth-nothin'-but-th'-truth-in-perceedins-now-at-hearin'-s'help-y'God?"

"Miss Bernardin," said the judge, without waiting to see if the three young women swore. "Don't think I've seen you here before. It will be easier and more efficient if you let *me* do this."

Cosima was surprised, but she nodded and murmured, "Certainly, Your Honor."

The judge stared for a moment at the papers in his file, then looked over his half-glasses and spoke to Adela. "Mrs. Woody, you've sworn in this petition that your husband did this, that, and the other. Is it the truth?"

Adela glanced at Cosima, who nodded, and she answered, "Yes, Your Honor," in a strained whisper.

The judge tapped the file with his finger. "And the rest of what you've said in here, about when and where you were married, that you've got no children, and you're a resident of this state and county—all that's the truth?"

Adela nodded.

"Could you ask her to speak up, Judge?" a reporter called from behind the rail. "And, as far as that's concerned, could *you?* Can't hear back here."

The judge smiled tolerantly and shook his head. He looked at the two witnesses. "Now, you two are her witnesses, right? Has Mrs. Woody told the truth?"

They stammered an affirmative.

"Both of you know her?"

They nodded.

"She have a good reputation, that is, for telling the truth, being a good person?"

"Yes . . ."

"Yes, absolutely."

The judge now lowered his head and regarded Cosima over his glasses. "Miss Bernardin. Anything to add?"

"Not a thing, Your Honor," said Cosima solemnly, trying to suppress a smile.

He nodded. "You are a lady and a scholar. I hope I'll have the privilege of seeing you here again. You do relieve a dull day." As he spoke he was signing the decree. "Here's your divorce, Miss Drake. Pleasure to see you, too."

"One quick request, Your Honor," said Cosima. "Could you let Miss Drake's bodyguards in now? Unfortunately, I have a feeling we're going to need them."

"How would you have handled this if there had been some hitch in the case?" Cosima asked Jerry Patchen. She glanced around the conference room in the Hyatt Regency, where he had invited a hundred reporters and cameramen for a one o'clock reception, cocktail hour, and buffet, to afford them an opportunity to meet with Adela Drake and ask their questions. For once, Jerry was not the center of attention, even though he was a striking figure in a bright red velvet Dior warm-up suit, with gold chains glistening in the curly black hair in the deep V of the half-unzipped jacket.

Adela had changed her clothes. She was meeting the news media in the rubber clothes she wore on stage, except that she was wearing a pair of flesh-colored leotards under them, so that her breasts were not exposed when the loose vest opened. She had also wiped off the demure pink lipstick she had worn for the hearing and had replaced it, not with black, but with a vivid and very deep red. She stood on a little platform at one end of the room—guarded by three of the four men who had taken her in and out of the courtroom—answering questions, smiling for cameras, speaking into microphones that were shoved toward her face.

Adela was a professional, Cosima observed. Not just as a musician—more importantly, in containing her dread of yammering crowds, suppressing her emotions from the morning and adroitly affecting the persona expected and wanted. She was smart, too. Her witnesses were in her suite at the Waldorf, not here; she was taking them to a performance of *Les Miserables* that evening, and the media would never see them.

"I had complete confidence in you, Contessa," said Jerry.

Cosima saluted him with her glass. "I bet you did," she said.

He shrugged. "What else? I'm glad you handled it, incidentally, rather than Loewenstein. You're already on the noon news shows—my gal Adela looking like a scared puppy, my lawyer Cosima looking like she has everything one hundred percent under control. I mean, *Contessa.* . . *!*"

Like Adela, she had made a small change between courtroom and press conference. She still wore the sleek, tailored, charcoal-gray skirt and light gray knit turtleneck she had worn in the courtroom, but she had replaced the gray blazer with a loose, mid-thigh-length, red-and-gold-plaid coat; and she had added an item of jewelry, a diamond-and-gold bracelet.

"Rick did the legal work, Jerry," she said. "If Adela tells you there was nothing to it, the fact is there was nothing to this morning's appearance. The judge had in front of him a file that had all the facts, all the law. Rick had taken care of it."

Jerry grinned and glanced around. "Legal work, my butt, Contessa," he said in a low voice. "You—"

He stopped because a reporter had intruded between them. "Hey," the dark-haired young woman said to Jerry. "Was this divorce to make room for you?" she asked bluntly. "Hi, Cosima."

"Jerry," said Cosima. "Say hello to Della Rosario of the New York *Post*. She's been following Adela's case ever since the morning when I showed her Woody's letter where he threatened to give Adela a 'nuckle sanwich.' "

"I noticed your byline," said Jerry. He squeezed the

221

hand of the stocky, dark-haired reporter. "No, the divorce was not for my benefit. In fact, I don't think it was for anybody except Adela herself. I don't think there's anybody waiting in the wings."

"That would be my opinion, too," said Cosima. She nodded toward Adela. "What you see there is what you get."

"Not exactly," said Della Rosario. "What you saw in court this morning is what you get. Timid girl. Except for . . . except for you, Jerry, she'd be like her two witnesses."

"Okay," said Jerry. "Little born-againer from the South. Yeah, okay." He grinned and spread his hands. "Hey. Your question was, *me?* The answer is no. For sure."

"You don't have a drink, Della," said Jerry. "Let me—"

"Generally, I don't do it at noon," she said.

"Generally you don't get exclusive stories at noon," he laughed. "How 'bout a headline—ADELA AND ME? NO, SAYS JERRY!"

"Well, a glass of white wine."

He snapped his fingers at a waiter with a tray. "White wine for the lady. *Pronto.*" Then he smiled at Della Rosario and said, "I appreciate your coverage of Adela's story. I suspect it made everything a whole lot easier."

The reporter smiled knowingly. "A little cooperation between lawyers and reporters can accomplish good things sometimes."

"Adela and I are fortunate," said Jerry. "Our counsel knows how to use the power of the press."

"God, Jerry!" Cosima laughed. "Don't suggest I *used* the media. What I did was *cooperate.*"

"As you said yourself, an uncontested divorce doesn't take much lawyering. On the other hand, maybe it was the news coverage that discouraged that loudmouthed little redneck from contesting. I think the PR work may have been better than the law work, in this case."

"We had no worthy antagonist," said Cosima. "I don't know how it would work if we did."

"I can promise you it wouldn't have worked," said Della, "if the subject hadn't been Adela Drake of Bull Dog Fangs."

Cosima cocked her head at Della and asked, "How about a pretty young Russian ballerina threatened with deportation?"

Back in the office, Cosima found a copy of the New York *Post* on her desk. It lay open to the story of the divorce hearing. Above a photograph the headline read:

FANG KEYBOARDER, GLAMOROUS LAWYER STUN DIVORCE COURT!

The picture was of Adela and Cosima, with the two witnesses, fighting their way out of the courthouse through a pressing mob of shrieking fans.

The dingy old precincts of Manhattan Domestic Relations Court may never be the same after this morning's hectic appearance by Bull Dog Fangs keyboarder Adela Drake and her society-girl attorney Cosima Bernardin.

In and out fast for a quickie divorce, the fabulous rock star was subdued, even bashful. Except for her red-and-green Mohawk hairdo, she might have been the lawyer and her lawyer might have been the client. Probably she would not have been allowed in the courtroom in the fetishist rubber clothes she wears on stage. But for her court appearance she elected to appear downright mousy.

Ms. Bernardin, on the other hand, showed a cool, sexy style that no one failed to notice. A tight, sleek skirt, ending exactly at her knees, clung like Saran wrap to her legs . . .

Cosima turned back to the front-page photograph. They had chosen a picture that showed her taking a long stride, and the skirt *was* clinging to her legs.

Tall, busty, stylish—and oh, so aloof and in charge—Cosima Bernardin showed why a staid firm like Hamilton, Schuyler found it necessary to do without her, as well as why a growing number of the rich and famous are turning to her as their lawyer.

"What rich? What famous?" her father asked as he tossed the newspaper aside.

"Newspaper hyperbole," said Cosima lightly.

They were riding from Lower Manhattan to Connecticut in his chauffered Mercedes. She had taken a cab to his office. He said it added half an hour to his trip for the driver to have to come by the Pan Am Building to pick her up—or to let her off there in the morning—so she had to use cabs for part of the trips she took with him. This evening he had telephoned and asked her if she wanted a ride. He wanted to talk to her, he had said.

"Even so, what rich and famous could they be talking about?"

Cosima tipped her head and turned to face him across the wide seat of the big car. "Bull Dog Fangs," she said. "Jerry Patchen and Bull Dog Fangs. No one in this country is more famous than Jerry Patchen right now. You may not like it, and it may not last, but he is one of the most recognized faces in the world."

"And he makes a lot of money," said Leon Bernardin wryly.

"So does Adela Drake. And she's nearly as famous."

"Notoriety," he said. "Not fame."

"A distinction the news media do not make," said Cosima, putting her finger on the *Post* that lay between them.

"So I see." Someone, he had told her, had brought the copy of the paper to him; on his own account, he never looked at it. "Rich and famous."

"Then there's Jack Putnam. Famous. Not rich like Jerry, but doing very well, thank you. Also, Watson Waugh was in the office Monday. He asked us to review his will. It's an estate-planning problem that Rick will handle. We—"

"Who is Watson Waugh?"

"The Broadway producer! One of the most successful."

"Ahh. And your ballerina, in whose case you've involved your sister."

"And my ballerina," said Cosima. "Her case may be the best thing I'm doing."

"Indeed? Now, what about this Joan . . . Joan Salomon, I believe her name is. What about her?"

"She's joining the firm. As a partner. She is an expert on pension plans—one of the most highly regarded in the city."

"So regarded by Webster, Kent, Harriman & McCoy, where she was expected to attain senior partnership," said Leon. "I may tell you frankly that Robert McCoy telephoned me and asked me if I could exert my proper influence to discourage you from raiding his firm."

"And what did you tell him?"

"I told him I had no influence in the matter." Almost imperceptibly—yet perceptible to Cosima, who had a special intuition for it—Leon Bernardin smiled. "No influence at all."

"I didn't raid Webster, Kent," said Cosima. "Joan is leaving because she doesn't like the firm."

"They liked her, apparently. They expected to promote her to a senior partnership."

"Yes, if she was willing to wait quietly in line, climbing the hierarchical ladder slowly, and never putting her hand on too high a rung, for fear someone above would step on it. She has too much talent for that."

Leon sighed. "Bernardin, Loewenstein & Salomon," he said, nodding skeptically. "A partnership of malcontents. Plus Hupp—an eccentric."

"I am proud of them," she said defiantly.

"This Salomon girl," he said. "She's another Jew, of course."

"I believe so," said Cosima, as if she were uncertain.

"Yes. Yes, she is. Your office has a decidedly Jewish character."

Cosima shrugged. "My secretary is Hispanic."

"Cosima, I will not have it suggested or implied that I am anti-Semitic. Anyone who knows me knows I am not. It is folly, just the same, to overlook the objective fact that Jews do tend to display certain idiosyncratic traits, and if you are not on guard they will build their distinctive characteristics into your firm. They will make it, in short, a Jewish firm, and once it is so identified, it will be by definition unacceptable to some clients."

"I'm not an expert on social attitudes, anti-Semitism or others," said Cosima, "but I can't help think you're talking about something from fifty years ago, something that has all but disappeared, particularly in this part of the country, particularly among the kind of clients I'm looking for."

"The entertainment industry is a part of the corporate world," said Leon. "As is publishing. As is communication. A law firm that is not attractive in a corporate board room—"

She shook her head. "I can't believe it."

"Your friend Loewenstein believes it," said Leon tersely.

Cosima frowned. "A telling point," she said quietly.

Her father opened his briefcase and took out a file. He was terminating the conversation.

"If you're not black, you can't guess the dimensions of racism," said Cosima. "If you're not a Jew—"

"Perhaps," said Leon as he opened a file and glanced at

a prospectus. "But let me remind you—you are one of three partners. What prevents the other two—your two Jews—from squeezing you out?"

Cosima grinned. "Is the daughter of Leon Bernardin going to be squeezed out of the firm she established and funded?" she asked. *"Dad* . . . I'm not a dummy. We don't have a full, formal partnership agreement yet, but Rick and Joan have signed a letter of understanding. They are called partners, but my vote on partnership questions counts for more than both of theirs combined. And Hugh, of course, doesn't have a vote. That's the way it is, and that's the way it's going to be. It's *my* firm, and it's always going to be my firm."

Leon Bernardin glanced up from his prospectus and smiled as before: invisibly to someone not experienced in recognizing these evanescent concessions of amiability. "Ah," he said thoughtfully. "So."

"Hey, Contessa. No demands. No plans. If something happens, something happens. If it doesn't . . . well, it doesn't. We'll live. We *did* have a good time, didn't we? Didn't *you?* Hey. Casual. Okay?"

"Jerry . . . I'm not afraid of you. I'm not putting you off. But I have an obligation tonight."

"Dinner *en famille* at Casa Bernardin?"

"As a matter of fact, no."

"A date with Rick?"

Cosima laughed. She was in her condominium, sitting on her couch, naked. She had been drying her hair with a blower when the telephone rang. She had played indoor tennis with Susanne—always a taxing, frustrating experience—and had come home sweaty and bruised from a fall on the court. She had showered, then mixed a martini to sip while she dried her hair.

"Guy Savoy, Contessa. That's where I'll take you for dinner—Guy Savoy. Can't beat that offer, not in Greenwich. Hey, listen, *my* obligation, if I can't find another one, is to sit down over a platter of pasta and a gallon of dago red, with mom and pop and my fat sister. Help!''

"Sister," said Cosima. "That's my obligation—dinner with my sister and her husband and another couple. You know, they're fixing something special. I can't just call and tell them I'm not coming, that I got a better deal.''

"You the odd woman at this party, Contessa? You got no date?''

"Jerry . . .''

"Best behavior, Contessa. I won't come in a rubber suit—or bring one for you. I won't rip off a great Italian fart at the dinner table. Hey, not only do I got to eat with my slob sister, I also hear some of the old man's fuckin' Rotary brothers are coming, with wives. Can you imagine the quality of the conversation I'm gonna have to listen to?''

"Jerry . . . Be here at seven. The people you're going to meet are Bill and Priscilla Craig. Back country. New money, new Greenwichers. They're sharp people, no Babbitts . . . no Rotarians. He's a futures trader and damn good at it. He's made a lot of money, both for his clients and himself. She's devoted to him, and they've got a couple of kids. So hands off Priscilla. Absolutely hands off.''

"Marching orders," he said. "Yes, ma'am. I always obey the orders of my superiors. And how about the contessa? Hands off her, too?''

"What was it you said, Jerry? No demands. No plans. If something happens, it happens. If it doesn't, no hard feelings. Deal?''

"Deal, Contessa. Seven.''

"I have to admit, every bit of that's a mystery to me," said Jerry to Bill Craig. He had asked Bill to explain what he did on Wall Street and had listened with conspicuous patience to a brief explanation. "I've never looked into it.''

Bill's self-confidence remained complete, unshaken by his unexpected guest. "Well, I'll tell you, Jerry," he said. "I've heard your name, but I have to confess I've never come to one of your performances or heard a recording of one. We're in the same situation—we haven't the remotest notion of how each other can make a living in such peculiar ways. I will say, I think you could learn my business if you applied yourself to it, but I could never learn yours."

"Jerry's requires *talent,*" said Susanne.

"Bill's requires talent," said Cosima. "Ask his clients. They came through October 19 . . . well . . . not exactly unscathed, but—How would you put it, Bill?"

"There are degrees of unhappy," said Bill. "I've got some mighty miserable clients, but people who lost six or eight percent of their net worth aren't nearly as unhappy as people who lost *twenty*-six or eight."

"You survived, then?" asked Jerry.

"Damn right he did," said Cosima. "My father was impressed."

They sat around the fireplace in the Craigs' living room: Cosima, Jerry and Susanne on the couch that faced the hearth, Bill and Priscilla on chairs drawn near. The fire breathed; a low drone of air moved in through the firescreen and up the chimney, picking up in its passage an occasional spark but generally a thin, wavering curtain of yellow-blue flame.

The two men were dressed alike in blue blazers with gray slacks. Cosima wore a ginger cardigan over a matching turtleneck, with a comfortable soft ankle-length tweed skirt: countryish, Novemberish, comfortable. Her sister, who wore nothing as well as Cosima wore it, had chosen a long-sleeved black velvet miniskirt. Her skirt had crept back halfway between her knees and crotch as she sat facing the fire, nibbling nuts and sipping Stolichnaya. Priscilla, too, was in style, with a thigh-length skirt and dark stockings. Her belted, knit dress was bright red.

The children were in the north wing of the house, in the

keeping of an au pair. They had been allowed to make an appearance, then had been banished.

"Is there such a thing as talent, really?" asked Susanne. "I wonder—"

"Was Winston Churchill a great man?" said Cosima.

"Meaning—?"

"Meaning, is there such a thing as a great man? Or talent? Or is what we call talent just good luck—the good luck to be in the right place at the right time?"

"No way," said Bill firmly. "I've had no luck. None at all. What I've achieved—"

"Could you have achieved it fifty years ago, with the same skills?" Cosima asked. "Or have you been lucky enough to possess a talent that is the talent for our time?"

The telephone rang. Priscilla reached for it, then handed it to Susanne. Susanne listened for a moment, then hung up and shook her head.

"Bert. No Bert tonight. It seems Colonel Qaddafi has agreed to an exclusive interview, and Bert's trying to set it up for Walter Cronkite to fly to Libya.

"I analyzed the time and what's called the demographics," said Jerry. "What I do is what I judged the people will pay for right now. Cold, calculated market analysis. I can do something else, if that's what the market wants. And one of these days I'll have to, because this fad won't last."

"Try wearing one glove," said Priscilla.

"I wish I could figure a way to introduce a condom into the act," said Jerry with a grin. "That seems to be the symbol of our time."

"If I could have figured a way to introduce one into *my* act, I'd have one child less," said Susanne.

"Why, Miz Wilkinson," said Bill, "y'all don't practice *birth control?*"

"If I didn't, I'd have a baker's dozen by now."

"My fat sister doesn't," said Jerry. "She and Dominic have done it six times and have six loud brats. They are *blessed,* my father says."

"You think your parents got you by doing it once?" Susanne asked.

"Did it once, waited to see if she was pregnant, and if she wasn't, tried again," said Jerry. "Exactly how the Pope says to do it."

"I have always been grateful that I need take no notice of anything the Pope says," said Priscilla.

"You catch the Oklahoma football game?" Bill asked.

The au pair came to the kitchen to help Priscilla serve dinner. Bill and Jerry sat before the fire, finishing their drinks. Cosima stepped outside to the deck overlooking the pool to escape the warmth of the house for a minute or two. She was followed immediately by Susanne, who stepped to the rail of the deck beside her.

"Where's Rick?"

"I don't have a thing going with Rick," said Cosima. "There's no significance in a weekend without seeing him— or a week without seeing him, for that matter."

"How bout Ruggiero Paccinelli?"

"Him either."

"He got a schlong on him?"

"*Susanne* . . . Dammit."

"Oh, *you* wouldn't know," Susanne laughed.

"If you want to find out, be my guest," said Cosima coldly. "*I* won't tell Bert."

Susanne kept laughing as she walked back into the house.

Cosima remained on the deck, staring at the night sky, the stars, and the weak glow of the town on the low clouds. She had been wondering lately if she should not sell the condominium on the harbor and buy into something in the city. She had been trying to decide if she was bound to Greenwich by any valid tie, if there were any reason, really, for her to live twenty-five miles from her office instead of twenty-five blocks. How much was it all worth, the plastic

231

bucolic that suburbanites created for themselves? How much of it would she miss?

Tonight smelled good. She could smell woods: wet oak leaves on the ground, the pungent smells of nut pods cracked by squirrels, the aroma of wood smoke from chimneys and in the distance the cool, briny odor of ocean water.

The door opened and Priscilla came out from the kitchen.

"Am I holding things up?" Cosima asked.

"Not at all. The potatoes need ten more minutes in the microwave. The more of them you put in, the more time they take, you know. It's hard to guess them. Almost impossible."

"Didn't know that," said Cosima.

"I'm a treasury of housewifely minutia," said Priscilla. "You wouldn't believe what I can cope with—what I *have* to cope with in a town that can't distinguish quaint from grubby."

"You loved California," said Cosima.

Priscilla shrugged. "Bill will net a million dollars this year, market collapse or no market collapse. Sunbelt or no Sunbelt, New York is where it's *at*, and within commuting distance of New York is where we're going to live."

"I love the city," said Cosima.

"So do I. But I'm not *in* the city. I'm stuck in fuckin' *Greenwich*. It's a great place for people who sleep here, I suppose. But I don't leave at 6:48 A.M. and get back at 7:23 P.M.. I'm here all day—I have to *function* here—which is a pain in the ass. I'm sorry. I've had a tough week."

Cosima laughed. "Another idyllic myth all shot to hell," she said.

Priscilla reached for her hand. "C'mon," she said. "Time for one more drink before those goddamned potatoes are done."

In the house, they found Susanne and Jerry together by the fireplace: Susanne unable to conceal her irritation with the gushing au pair, who had just discovered who Jerry was.

232

"Ooh," she said, "in Belgium you are just as popular as you are here."

"Monique," said Priscilla. "Please."

The girl reluctantly returned to the kitchen and, with Priscilla, finished putting dinner on the table. Bill asked Cosima to pass on the wine he had already opened and engaged her in a brief discussion of vintage years. From the buffet in the dining room, Cosima saw Susanne grinning and nodding at something Jerry had said, and she saw her rub her hip against his as they left the fireplace and came to the dining room.

As she had done at Café Le Bec Fin, Susanne changed the seating arrangements suggested by Priscilla to suit herself and sat beside Jerry. Cosima sat alone on the opposite side of the table, where Bert would have sat. Susanne was renewed: ruddy cheeks gleaming, and eyes sparkling, she fairly effervesced.

Cosima knew why and didn't care. Her only interest was in how they would work it.

Priscilla fussed too much over her dinner. Bill apologized for the wine. There was nothing wrong with either the dinner or the wine, except their want of confidence. Cosima ate with pleasure, a thick slice of rare roast beef, and enjoyed the wine, a respectable St. Emilion.

Jerry encouraged Susanne to tell stories from the tennis tournaments and about her championship. Susanne told it all again gratefully: she was happy to be allowed to reminisce about her fifteen-year-old triumph, the most important thing that had ever happened to her.

Encouraged by Bill, Jerry spoke of his work. He had to earn his life-time's income in a few years, he said. Popularity was fleeting anyway, the physical and emotional strain would destroy him if he tried to go on longer.

"It's like that in the markets," Bill said. "You have to make your killing and get out. There's the emotional strain, just like you have, Jerry, plus a factor that's the equivalent of your popularity—that is, a man's ideas wear out, you can't go on being the bright young fellow who figured the way to beat the system. In fact, I can see another parallel. You have imitators. Well, so do I. Anyone can see what we do—we have no secrets—and what we can do, somebody else can do, maybe just as well, once we've shown them how. Maybe in your case, it will be understood that nobody's as good as the original—"

"Somebody will be better," said Jerry, shaking his head.

"So I make eight hundred thousand this year," said Bill. "And maybe next year anyway. Next year—" He shrugged. "Yeah, next year. But after that, I don't know. We get a lot of newspaper stories about how much we make. But we're like professional athletes—those big numbers may represent all we'll ever make."

"Maybe you'll have to get a job," said Susanne, half scornfully.

Bill flashed with anger. *"No way,"* he said. "Never. You're sitting at this table, Susanne, with people—Jerry, Cosima, me—who will *never* have jobs."

Susanne smiled at Priscilla. "What was that political term they had in England a hundred years and more ago? 'The ministry of all the talents.' Here we sit, Priscilla. In the company of all the talents. Jesus! God, I hope *you* have talent. I know I don't. Not anymore."

Halfhearted attempts to repair what Cosima saw no reason to repair took the next two or three minutes, after which everyone self-consciously addressed the food on the table.

The coffee maker, operated by a timer, began to brew, filling the dining room with the aroma of freshly ground coffee. Priscilla rose to clear away a few dishes—a service one did not usually ask of an au pair—and Cosima rose to help her.

"I . . ." Susanne frowned. "Hey, guys, I'm sorry, but I feel sort of weird."

Priscilla, in the kitchen, stiffened; Cosima nudged her and whispered, "Just wait for the next line."

"Well uh, look, you got your car, haven't you, Su-

234

sanne," said Jerry. "I'll drive you over to Round Hill. Maybe you got a little flu bug comin' on. Get you over there and let your mother and father put you to bed."

"Well . . ."

"Yeah. That's what we better do. Hey folks, I'll be back in—what'll it take me, twenty minutes? I'll be back in half an hour. Hey, don't hold up coffee and dessert. Just go ahead. I'll be back as soon as I can."

Jerry led Susanne to the door, supporting her with an arm around her as she murmured apologies to Priscilla and Bill.

Bill followed them to the door and returned to the dining room with a troubled look.

Cosima sat down at the table. "Don't be upset, folks," she said. "My sister's getting laid. Jerry won't be back. All I ask you is, don't tell Bert. He wouldn't be surprised, but why tell him?"

Priscilla sat down, somewhat liquidly. "With that swaggering guinea greaseball?" she muttered.

"Hey, *Priscilla,*" Bill interjected. "C'mon."

"Ruggiero Paccinelli," said Priscilla with firm, quiet emphasis, "is a predatory macho Italian who holds women in utter contempt. Mediterranean machismo. *God* but it's contemptible!"

"Well . . . It's Susanne's business," said Bill weakly. "If she wants to—"

"He'd have propositioned *me* if Susanne hadn't climbed his leg first," Priscilla sniffed.

"Hey, Hon!" Bill protested. "Susanne is Cosima's *sister!* Jerry's her friend."

Priscilla sighed and slumped. "I hope I haven't offended you," she said to Cosima.

"Susanne collects trophies," said Cosima with a shrug. "So does Jerry. They'll enjoy adding each other to their respective collections. And Jerry's being Italian had nothing—well, almost nothing—to do with it. What I suggest *we* do is forget about it. Why should it be more significant to us than it is to them?''

Bill Craig leaned back in his chair, clasped his hands behind his head and grinned. ''Flying weather tomorrow,'' he said. ''The islands are pretty much buttoned up for the winter, but we were thinking of the ski areas up in Vermont and New Hampshire. Lunch in some country inn. Like to go?''

''I'd like to,'' Cosima said.

When Jerry called Sunday morning he got her telephone recorder.

In her office on Monday morning, a letter waited for her:

ASSOCIATION OF THE BAR
OF THE CITY OF NEW YORK

Cosima Bernardin
Attorney at Law
200 Park Avenue
New York, NY

Dear Miss Bernardin,

You are hereby advised that a complaint has been brought against you by a certain member of the Bar who alleges that you have been guilty of conduct in violation of the Standards of Professional Ethics. A preliminary and informal investigation by this office has produced sufficient evidence to suggest that a subcommittee of the Committee on Professional Conduct should conduct a more thorough investigation. You are advised that such a committee has been appointed and charged with the duty of determining whether or not any conduct of yours requires professional discipline.

The conduct complained of involves your representation of one John T. Putnam in a dispute with one Vanessa Kingston.

The procedures followed by such subcommittee are as follows: First, the subcommittee will evaluate the complaint and the facts assembled by this office. If it determines the complaint may be valid, you will be notified of the exact nature of such complaint and the evidence supporting it. Second, a hearing will then be held, at which hearing you will have ample opportunity to produce evidence of your own and rebut the charge. Third, if the subcommittee is satisfied there is valid reason to do so, the charge will be reported to the full Committee, before which you will again have opportunity to appear and present your view of the case. Fourth, if the full Committee elects to proceed against you, it will prosecute you before the judges of the Appellate Division. As I am sure you know, the judges may impose penalties varying from a private reprimand through permanent disbarment.

Be assured that at this stage, all proceedings remain entirely confidential.

If you wish to be represented by counsel other than yourself, please advise me, and I will place such counsel on the list to receive all notices, etc. issued in the matter.

You should anticipate that the subcommittee will require approximately two months to determine whether or not the complaint against you requires a hearing. I will notify you immediately if such a determination is made.

Very truly yours,

John F. McGowan
Association Counsel

Twelve

Leon Bernardin remained in the foyer to greet his guests. Dressed in a black tuxedo with a black silk waistcoat, he held a glass of champagne in his left hand. He shook the hand of every man who arrived, kissed the cheek of every woman and hugged every grandchild. That was what he considered proper. It was also a tradition. Not everyone who came would be greeted by the hostess, not everyone might be greeted by his children, but every guest would be greeted by Leon Bernardin. Elizabeth wandered away into the party somewhere, he didn't know where; the rest of the family were everywhere; but he remained near the door until he was satisfied no more guests were coming.

It was a tradition that all the family came for Christmas, at least to this party if not on Christmas Eve and Christmas Day. He expected them to be here, almost demanded that they come. His neighbors were here as well; some of them he didn't even know, but it was part of the tradition that they should be invited.

The decorations were resplendent. The driveway was lined with candles burning inside hurricane globes. The trees were strung with tiny lights, the big spruce to the left of the door with old-fashioned colored lights. On the door a huge wreath of pine circled a shiny brass hunting horn adorned with a red velvet ribbon. In the foyer a pine was strung with popcorn and hung with scores of candy canes. In the living room another tree reached the ceiling and was decorated with glittering glass balls and blinking lights. Pine roping was strung everywhere.

(Another Bernardin tradition: The elegant Christmas decorations throughout the house would all be taken down and put away tomorrow or Sunday. They were for the party, for the public, so to speak. For the family's Christmas they would be replaced with simpler, more personal trimmings—ornaments remembered from childhood and treasured and not to be put on display before party-comers who would not know how to appreciate them.)

A string quartet played carols in a corner of the living room. The fireplace roared and crackled. Four uniformed maids carried trays of champagne and hors d'oeuvres. In the game room a lavish buffet covered the pool table. The array of food was dominated by an immense cheese from which anyone could carve, and trays were kept mounded high with big shrimp.

When finally he left the foyer and walked into the middle of his Christmas party, Leon, as always, was amused by the diversity of his guests and by the fact that not one of them knew who all the others were. In fact, he didn't himself. But they were his family, his neighbors and a few of his associates in business, plus an odd assortment of people his children had invited.

Oddest of all, maybe, was Adela Drake, the newly divorced member of the Paccinelli band. He had invited Hugh Hupp, wanting a good look at him and not being sure Cosima would invite him, and Hupp had called a few days ago and asked if Mr. Bernardin would mind if he brought Adela Drake. By then Leon had understood that Susanne had invited Ruggiero Paccinelli, so one could hardly object to the strange little girl who played the electric piano. So she was here. She was very modestly dressed and could have been

239

inconspicuous except for the naked scalp and bristly hedge of red and green hair.

Inconspicuous now but perhaps to be conspicuous later was the little Russian ballerina Cosima was defending against deportation. It had been Elizabeth's idea—or maybe Emilie's, since Emilie was sponsoring a bill to grant her citizenship—to invite Svetlana Terasnova. It was Elizabeth's idea, in any event, that later in the evening she would play the piano and the ballerina would dance. If he guessed right, her skirt would come off, as would a pair of sleeves that didn't seem attached to what he now supposed was a black leotard, and all she would need do to perform would be don her toe shoes. She had arrived this afternoon, and she had rehearsed with Elizabeth, who had gushed that she was ''in love with Lana.''

Cosima—Well, Cosima could never be inconspicuous. She was wearing a black silk evening dress—he presumed it was called an evening dress—as simple as a dress could be, except that it scooped very low in back and the skirt ended halfway between her hips and her knees and was trimmed around the hem with a rich edging of mink. She wore dark stockings and simple black silk, high-heeled shoes. She was the most striking woman there—as she was always the most striking woman everywhere she went—a fact she accepted serenely, as though it were inevitable—and there was nothing she could do about it.

''Explain to me again,'' he said quietly to her, ''who this man Wilmot is.''

''An editor, writer,'' Cosima whispered. ''New York *Law Journal. The National Law Journal.* A good friend!''

''Ah. Well, see to it that someone talks with him. He seems to have a little trouble finding a common ground for conversation in this crowd.''

''I'll ask Joan to take care of that,'' said Cosima.

''Yes. And who is Joan's friend, Patricia?''

''Her sister,'' said Cosima. ''Patricia LaRouche. In from Chicago. She can't just walk away and leave her.''

240

Leon nodded, but he was skeptical of the explanation. He stared for a moment at Cosima's new Jewish lawyer, but he hadn't time to stare at her for more than a moment. He had other guests to see to.

Max was glad when Cosima guided Joan and Patricia toward him. He had in fact found it difficult to make conversation with most of the people at this party. He had been glad to meet Bill Craig, whose name he had heard, but before he could talk with Craig and his wife for more than a moment, a man rushed up, edged in, introduced himself as Pierre Bernardin and engaged Craig in what seemed to be an urgent dialogue about some aspect of futures trading.

Susanne wore a dramatically low-cut evening dress: a black velvet top with separate black velvet sleeves, and a lemon yellow, silver-thread-embroidered silk skirt that barely covered her hips. A lush fringe of fluffy yellow ostrich feathers was attached at the hem and fluttered around her legs.

"Where's Rick?" she asked Cosima. "The rest of your firm is here. Wasn't he invited?"

"He was invited," said Cosima.

"Aha. So."

"Is Jerry a friend of yours now?" Cosima asked Susanne. "Dad says you're the one who asked him."

Susanne smiled coquettishly. "I did ask him."

"Did he tell you what his father's friends call Dad?"

Susanne lifted her chin. "Uh . . . What?"

"They call him Don Leon Bernardini, and it isn't a compliment. *I* wouldn't have asked him here. He's my client, worth a quarter of a million in fees next year, and I wouldn't have asked him."

"Does Dad know you slept with him?" Susanne challenged.

"Does he know *you* did?"

Susanne tossed her head and laughed. "Well . . . Jerry's like one of the family, isn't he?"

"No," said Cosima.

Elizabeth Bernardin was truly fascinated with the tiny Russian ballerina and was determined that the girl should not be left alone in the company of so many formidable strangers. She guided her from room to room, introducing her to some of the guests but never abandoning her to them. She knew that Emilie had introduced the citizenship bill, and she took the first opportunity to introduce Lana to her.

"I am very grateful to you," Lana said to Emilie: her first words to the big woman she probably found it difficult to believe was Cosima's sister.

Emilie had clothed her generous figure in a voluminous coat of black silk embroidered with leaves and flowers in gold thread, which she wore with a floor-length black skirt. "Be grateful," she said gently, "when we succeed. I know Cosima has told you it is going to be difficult to get your bill passed in time."

Lana's face darkened. "Yes," she said. "I understand."

"This is my husband," Emilie said, putting her hand on the arm of Thomas McCarthy and pressing him forward to shake Lana's hand.

McCarthy was always reluctant to shake hands. He suffered a lifelong skin disease that was not communicable and not disfiguring but roughened the palms of his hands. He was an amiable man, anxious to be liked; and, though he was by no means handsome, his open, innocent face was appealing, and his conversation was bland, so that he made friends easily.

"I was in your country—your former country—for a few days once," he said to Lana. "I was a naval officer, just a young fellow doing my reserve obligation on a destroyer, and we paid a call at the port of Vladivostok."

"I am sure you were treated hospitably," said Lana soberly, yet with a hint of irony.

"In fact, we were—except we were not allowed to venture outside the area of the port," he asked.

Lana nodded solemnly, still with the spark of a smile in her eyes.

Tom McCarthy saw the smile and was confused. "Emilie," he said. "We've got to do everything we can for this young woman."

Emilie nodded. "Yes, that's what we are doing. Uh—Cosima." She beckoned to Cosima, who was standing near, talking to Hugh Hupp and Adela Drake. "We're doing everything we can, aren't we? About Lana."

"Everything we can," Cosima agreed. "I've arranged an interview for her. I think we'll work up a little public relations for her."

"Where's the court case?" asked Emilie.

"Judge MacGruder is still sitting on the Justice Department's motion to dismiss our appeal from the order of the Immigration Service," said Cosima. "Seven weeks. I can't believe it."

"Well, seven weeks is seven weeks. I'd like seven months. I'd think we have a chance to get the bill through then. If you're going to do a public relations campaign, get going."

"All of this is very distressing," said Elizabeth, who had been frowning and shaking her head. "What *possible* reason could anyone have for deporting Lana?"

"No valid reason," said Emilie. "It's a right-wing crusade. But ask some of my congressional colleagues from places like Utah and Texas. They'll give you reasons."

"When I present Lana, to dance, shall I tell the people she is under threat of deportation?"

Cosima and Emilie exchanged glances, and Cosima replied, "Why not?"

At the buffet table, with glasses of champagne in their left hands and shrimp skewered on toothpicks in their right, Jerry Patchen and Jack Putnam stood talking.

"Jeez, am I ever glad to see short skirts come back," said Jack. He popped his shrimp in his mouth. Chewing it, he went on, *"Look* at those two sisters. God! Cosima—Hey, she told me one time that you call her Contessa. What would you call Susanne?"

"Paladina," said Jerry. "That's what I call her."

" 'Paladina' . . . Wha's that mean?"

"Champion," said Jerry.

"Tennis champion," said Jack.

Jerry grinned and shrugged.

"Oh-ho! Well . . . Me, too. Long time ago. In fact—I used to be invited to these parties. Years ago. The invitation this year was out of a clear blue sky."

"Cosima," said Jerry.

"No. From the *paterfamilias*. Cosima says she didn't have anything to do with it."

Jerry popped his shrimp into his mouth. "Umm," he grunted.

"Hey— Isn't this party a hell of a note?" asked Jack. "You and I'd go broke if the rest of the country was like this. I mean, nobody's asked for an autograph. Nobody. You notice? I'm an unknown here. Nobody in this crowd goes to the movies. Even the kids."

"It's Greenwich," said Jerry as he reached for another shrimp. "When the Duke and Duchess of York—Andrew and Fergie, you know—came here for a polo match a couple of months ago, a certain little class of people went nuts, absolutely surrendered their dignity in a scramble to get close. And ninety-five percent of the town couldn't have cared less. It's a humbling damned place for celebrities."

"Hell . . ." Jack drawled. "I'm not staying around. I'm not tired of being famous yet."

Charles Bernardin and Sybil had come to the buffet while Jack and Jerry were talking. A word of hers stopped them. *"Cholesterol,"* she hissed at her husband.

With an exchange of wry glances, Jack and Jerry moved away—not without grabbing another shrimp before abandoning the constantly replenished mounds.

Leon came in. Sybil stood scowling at the food laid out on the covered pool table. Charles had managed a rented tuxedo for the party, though his black shoes were run-down and looked as if they might have been the last ones his father bought for him before his marriage. Sybil was wearing a long skirt; otherwise, she was dressed in home-woven.

"I'm sorry the children aren't with you," said Leon. "I'd looked forward to seeing them."

"Our children don't fit into this kind of thing," said Sybil, "—as last year demonstrated."

"Since then," said Leon coldly, "you have had a year to amend their manners. I should think you'd have found it incumbent on you to do so."

She smiled sourly. "Our children are being reared for something rather different."

"Yes. Genteel academic poverty. Intellectual squalor. Very stylish. But of course you wouldn't know—you've never experienced it."

"Dad—"

Leon stared down his son and went on. "You've never lived on a faculty salary. How many of your colleagues know that the fund I manage for you generates twice the income of a tenured professor with an endowed chair? If your children *choose* academic poverty, fine; I shall love them just as much. In the meanwhile, I suggest you rear them so they can make a choice, not so ill-mannered and uncultured that they cannot appear in polite company."

"Dad—"

Leon Bernardin spun on his heel and walked back into the living room.

Susie, Susanne's daughter, was sixteen: a stunning slender blonde. Dressed by her mother, she wore a black velvet minidress with the skirt augmented by piled bows of rose-colored silk. It was her first year to be svelte, dress svelte, and her uncertain happiness in it had been sanctioned by her grandfather's gallant compliment. She wore her hair tightly bound behind her head, her accustomed pony tail gathered and held by a jewelled clasp. She was talking before the fireplace with her cousin Leona, Pierre's elder daughter, also sixteen years old but still carrying her little-girl fat and demurely dressed in frilly white.

245

"It *is* Jerry Patchen. Go speak to him if you don't believe me," said Susie.

Leona shook her head.

"And the other one is Jack Putnam. Put a hairpiece on him, you'll recognize him easily enough."

Leona frowned and stared. "Why would they be here?"

Susie glanced around. "Jack Putnam diddles Aunt Cosima," she whispered. "And—this is a *big* secret—Jerry Patchen diddles my mother."

"Susie!"

"Well, it's true."

"It isn't true! Anyway, if it was, how would *you* know?"

Susie drew back her shoulders, thrusting out her little breasts. She glanced around the room again; then, satisfied that no one could hear, she confided in her cousin. "I saw a letter Jerry Patchen wrote to my mother."

"Really? What'd he *say?*"

"He calls her 'paladina,' which means 'champion.' He thanked her for a great night, said she gave wonderful head."

"Susie!"

"Well, that's what he said."

"That's *crazy*, to write a letter like that. Crazier to leave it lying around."

"It wasn't exactly lying around," said Susie. "And it's not lying around anymore. I tore it up and flushed it down."

"Ohh . . . I guess so. I'm sorry, Susie."

Susie shrugged. "I'm not sorry. Jerry Patchen, for god's sake! Friend of the family now." She grinned wickedly. "Maybe *I'll* get a chance sometime."

Elizabeth sat down at the piano and began to play. At first she received only casual, polite attention; then, as it became clear that she was playing forcefully, people began to gather around the piano. She rose after a few minutes and told them they were privileged this evening to see a brief performance by an exceptionally talented dancer, a Russian ballerina who had defected to the United States from the Soviet Union and who was "threatened with deportation by the philistines who have for the time being seized political power in this country." She swept her arm toward the door, and Svetlana Terasnova made a dramatic entry. Elizabeth gestured for the crowd to make room around the piano, where the rugs had already been taken away. She sat down and began to play, and Lana began to dance.

Cosima had not seen her perform before. She was no connoisseur of the dance, and she realized that the tiny ballerina was performing in a restricted space that imposed a severe limitation; nevertheless, even an observer with but small discrimination could see that Lana possessed an exceptional talent. To say she was lithe was insufficient. She had total command of her body. At such close range, her audience could see how she retreated within herself, absorbed the music and moved as though she were dancing on the piano keyboard and making the music. They were enthralled.

"That's *beautiful*, Cosima," Jack said to her when he could speak over the applause for Lana. "She's a major talent."

Cosima turned. She had not realized Jack had slipped up behind her. "If I can prevent them from sending her back to Moscow—"

He shook his head. "The problem is," he said, "you're dealing with exactly the same kind of people in the Justice Department that she'd have to deal with in Moscow. Same mind-set. The one talks communism, the other capitalism, but in the end they have the same mentality—small and righteous and arbitrary. Teach 'em to speak each other's languages, and they could take each other's places."

"Yes," said Cosima. "Yes, that's true."

"Anyway . . ." He glanced around and bent over her to whisper in her ear. "Can a man get a *drink* around here? Champagne gives me a headache."

She shook her head. "Not at the Christmas party. No martinis. No Scotch. No cognac. A tradition."

247

"Jeez, Cosima. I guess I can have ginger ale. That's the alternative, isn't it? Can you and I slip away and have a *drink* after the party?"

"Sure."

"Need to talk to you sometime. That contract—"

"I received a new draft in yesterday's mail," she said. "Haven't had time to review it."

"Got another offer," he said. "Gonna have to decide what to do—do another picture or direct a picture."

"Depends on the script, doesn't it?" she said.

"Yeah. Piece of crap. I'll show you."

"I'm no judge of scripts."

He shrugged. "Why not? I'd like your opinion. I won't rely on it, but I'd like to have it."

Joan and Patricia had remained close to Max ever since they were introduced to him. Like Jack, he did not favor champagne; it soured on his stomach. Joan Salomon was uncomfortable too because she could not have a cigarette. She had noticed that no one in the house was smoking, in fact that there were no ashtrays, and she had acquiesced to what was apparently the Bernardin canon.

"The money represented in this house tonight could buy New Zealand," she remarked to Patricia and Max.

Patricia LaRouche glanced around. She was a tall, gawky young woman, narrow-shouldered, with long thin arms and hands, and dishwater-blond hair as unkempt as a kitchen mop. She wore a pink sweater adorned with a large rhinestone snowflake pin and a multicolored quilted skirt. She was the owner of a small advertising agency of three people—herself, an artist, and a secretary—and she had no contact with people whose money could buy New Zealand. Their money and status overwhelmed her.

"Bankers," said Max. "I recognize two vice presidents of Bernardin Frères."

"Never mind the bankers," Joan said. "It's the goddamned *neighbors* that represent big bucks in this crowd. I mean, these are commuters who don't commute on the trains; they commute in limos. The bald fellow over there doesn't commute to the City; he commutes to Armonk—meaning IBM. The fellow he's talking to is Davis—I mean, *the* Davis, the one that raids corporations. Personal worth estimated in excess of three billion. And what do you want to bet Leon Bernardin didn't pick them out as people he wanted to invite—they just live around him, they're just his neighbors."

"I've been looking at the jewels," said Patricia. "What a place for a robbery."

Max shook his head. "Not in Leon Bernardin's house. I've got an eye for this kind of thing, and I bet you I can identify four private detectives in the crowd."

Cosima approached, with Jack. "Hey, kids. You meeting everybody? Like Jack here—Jack Putnam."

"Jack *Putnam?*" Patricia murmured to Joan. "Oh, my *god!*"

Jack overheard and said to Cosima out of the corner of his mouth, "That's more like it. Makes me feel like I'm *somebody.*"

"Mr. Putnam," said Patricia. "I don't think you've made a picture I haven't seen."

Emilie and Tom McCarthy had brought their son, Tom, and his wife, Margaret, also their daughter Vicky. Tom Jr. was twenty-five, a new architect, and Margaret was seven months pregnant with their second child. Vicky was twenty-one, a student at Smith, studying to become a lawyer like her Aunt Cosima. The two young women were much alike. Except for her pregnancy, Margaret would have been as slender as Vicky. Both were blondes. Vicky wore a navy blue evening sweater and a long, slim, wool skirt in the Black Watch tartan. Margaret wore a voluminous red satin maternity jacket and a matching skirt.

"So that's the famous Svetlana Terasnova," Tom Jr. said to his wife and sister. "Talented, I suppose—though I'm no judge."

"What's she going to cost us?" Vicky asked.

"Hmm?"

"What's it going to cost Mother, politically speaking, to have stuck her neck out for this Russian?" asked Vicky. She lifted her champagne flute and sipped delicately. "And where's the trade-off? What good does it do her?"

"I suspect she just thinks it's right," said Margaret. "Your mother sometimes does things just because she thinks they're right."

"This one because *Cosima* thinks it's right," said Vicky. "It's another one of Cosima's obsessions."

"Cosima—" Tom began.

"Is a *manipulator*," Vicky interjected. "Of all our aunts and uncles, she's the most like grandfather. Too smart for other people's good. She uses people, just like he does."

"It would be a tragedy to deport that ballerina," said Margaret.

Vicky shrugged. "I don't know. The Justice Department thinks she should be deported. They don't come to decisions like that without a great deal of thought."

"The *Justice* Department?" Tom sneered. "You think those hard-line conservatives give anything a 'great deal of thought'?"

"Oh shit, Tom," shrilled Vicky. "It's okay to be Democrats and liberals, but we don't have to be idiots about it. What's wrong, really, with the Justice Department? Maybe it's about time Americans gave a little thought to what's good for America, rather than what's good for some Russian ballet dancer. Anyway, Mother's going to lose votes over this one, I bet you anything—and just for some new fixation of Cosima's."

Leon suggested to Hugh Hupp that he cut off a piece of the cheese and try it. "And you, too, Miss Drake," he said. "This wheel is imported from Denmark for the party every year. To be altogether frank with you"—he paused to smile—"I hope there will not be too much left over. I've found myself finishing it on the Fourth of July."

Adela reached in and cut herself a generous slice. She

was hungry but had been reluctant to eat. She was conscious of the curious stares she attracted, and she feared she would do something clumsy and make Hugh sorry he had brought her. What was more, she was afraid she would drop shrimp sauce on her clothes. The cheese, though, seemed undemanding and unlikely to cause a gaffe; she held it in her hand and began to nibble on it.

"I've a question for you," Leon said to Hugh.

Hugh had partaken blithely of the champagne and was in a gentle, eyebrows-up, philosophical mood. "Sure," he said.

"Is Cosima in danger of disbarment?"

Jarred by the question, Hupp changed his mood. "No," he said. "Not a chance. On the other hand, she is probably in some danger of a reprimand, maybe even a suspension. I doubt the suspension, frankly. Private reprimand. Public reprimand. More likely private. And, frankly, what bothers me most is how she'll react to it. Cosima's proud. Cosima'll tell 'em to go to hell and—"

"She has never liked," said Leon with forceful precision, "to be questioned—for anything she's done. Since she was a child."

"There is a degree of"—Hugh searched for a word—"*piety* in this business. It may be something like the trial of Galileo—men knowing they're wrong, still pressing their case."

"Men . . ." said Adela.

"Maybe women," said Hugh. "The subcommittee may include women. But the kind of women who get on committees like that are . . . How can I put it? Anyway, often they're tougher on women than men would be."

"Is there anything we can do?" Leon asked.

Hugh turned down the corners of his mouth. "Like what?"

Leon shrugged, smiled. "A bit of . . . *proper* influence."

Hugh shook his head. "I'm not sure there's any way to exert 'proper' influence."

251

Jerry Patchen was bored. He'd tried to talk with Cosima, and Cosima had talked with him cordially enough; but Cosima was busy, circulating among the guests, playing junior hostess. He had tried to talk with Priscilla Craig, but for some reason she had been cool and had interrupted the conversation at the first opportunity to separate herself from him. Susanne was here with her husband and children, so there was no chance to slip upstairs or out on the lawn with her. Adela . . . Adela, for god's sake, was sharing a room at the local Hyatt Regency with that three-times-her-age lawyer, Hugh Hupp. Joan Salomon . . . It took about five minutes to figure out that one. And Lana Terasnova . . . Cosima, that bitch—or maybe someone else—had warned the cute little ballerina to keep her distance from the leader of Bull Dog Fangs.

And the rest of the crowd. Many had no notion who he might be, or knew and were only mildly curious about him, as they might have been about an extraordinarily long snake displayed under glass. Even the kids—What kind of kids *were* these? Jesus!

"You're Max, right? Cosima's friend Max Wilmot. Right?" He extended his hand. "Jerry Patchen."

"Oh, sure. Nice to meet you."

"Uh . . . ?"

"Joan Salomon and Patricia LaRouche."

"Joan, you're setting up a proposal for a retirement plan for me, aren't you?"

Joan was intensely uncomfortable by now for want of a cigarette, but she focused on this man. Cosima was for some reason apprehensive about him; Rick detested him. He was not very handsome, in her judgment. There was something coarse about him that she found repugnant, maybe because he was aware of it and flaunted it insolently as something people just had to accept from him, whether they liked it or not. Though he had, for the moment, the adoration of millions of fickle zealots, to whom he was a demigod, he might be forgotten tomorrow.

"I think we'll be able to achieve a very substantial tax saving for you," she said.

"I understand you're doing something for Adela, too."

"Right. Setting up a tax-sheltered retirement plan."

"Independent of what she'll participate in as a member of my group?"

"Coordinated," said Joan.

"I'd like to know how that works. How it coordinates, I mean."

"It will coordinate in such a way as to have no impact on the Fang, Incorporated plan."

"How much will she put in?"

Joan smiled. "You'll have to ask her."

"I'm asking you."

"And I can't answer. I can't discuss your business with other clients, and I can't discuss other clients' business with you."

Jerry darkened. "Adela wouldn't have a nickel except for me."

"Maybe so," said Joan calmly. "But as a matter of legal ethics I can't and won't discuss her business with *anyone*."

He glanced across the room, to where Adela stood close to Hugh Hupp, engaged in conversation with him and Tom McCarthy. "I'll be damned," he said. "Excuse me."

As he headed toward Adela and Hupp, he noticed that the ballerina was almost alone—alone, that is, except for a pimply teenager who was engaged in earnest talk with her. He turned and walked up to the pair.

"I enjoyed your dancing immensely," he said, interjecting himself forcefully into their conversation.

The tiny Russian dancer looked up into his face. "Thank you," she said, puzzled and not entirely welcoming the intrusion.

"Jerry Patchen," he said.

"Oh, yes . . . I have heard the name."

"And I have heard the name Svetlana Terasnova," he said. "Always mentioned with admiration."

253

He had won her attention. The pimply boy was forgotten. Jerry dismissed him with one hard glance, and he retreated.

"Have you ever considered working in a ballet written in the rock idiom?" Jerry asked Lana.

"Yes. Yes, I would think it very interesting."

"I'd like to talk with you about it sometime," he said. "We might be able to agree on something very good, something good for both our careers. I mean, we could discuss it. If it didn't work, we would keep it to ourselves and never show it to the world."

He sensed that behind her façade of solemn innocence, Svetlana Terasnova was disciplined and tough. You didn't become what she was by being a pushover. In fact, he imagined he could sense cautious appraisal in the calm dark eyes she fixed on his face. If his imagination did not carry him too far, maybe he also saw interest.

Any maybe Cosima saw it, too, from across the room. She broke away from her brother Charles and bore down on them. "You two have met," she said blandly. "Good. Lana, my mother was looking for you a moment ago. She's with someone she wants to introduce you to."

Lana glanced around and spotted Elizabeth. She looked up into Jerry's eyes. "I am pleased to have met you," she said simply. Then she hurried away.

"Hey, I think I'm gonna leave now," Jerry said to Cosima. "Thanks for the invite. Uh . . . I'll say my thanks to your mother and father. Look, I'm going back into the City, I guess. Unless you and I could, uh—"

She shook her head. "Not tonight, Jerry," she said solemnly. "You're also invited, you know, to breakfast at the Hyatt Regency in the morning. No one wants to drive back tonight. Some of us may do a little nightcap partying, too, after we leave here."

"Yeah . . . ?"

"Joan and Patricia are staying at the Hyatt. Hugh and Adela. Max. Jack. Bill and Priscilla will be coming. Susanne and Bert. Maybe some others. Just whoever is in the hotel, plus a few who aren't."

"Well, how about lending me the key to your place? Hell, I'll even sleep in the guest room."

"I *have* a guest for the guest room."

"Oh, really?"

"Lana."

He grinned. "Well, I'm sure we could figure out something."

Cosima shook her head. "Jerry . . ."

"*Okay.* I'm going back to the City. And, listen, you tell Adela if she's keeping secrets from me, I might have to get a new keyboard for Fangs."

"I think that's the kind of thing you have to tell her yourself, Jerry."

"Fine," he snapped. "I'm going. Thank the don for me."

He was purposeful again in recrossing the room. He nodded crisply to Adela and Hugh, then strode into the foyer.

"So that is the famous Jerry Patchen," said Sybil. "Uncouth, isn't he?"

"He's a very rich man with a very great talent," said Cosima.

Lana was surrounded by people assembled around her by Elizabeth. "You are very kind," she said repeatedly. She sipped champagne and blushed. "You are all very kind."

Cosima spoke to her mother. "I think I'd better take her home now. It's after eleven, and—"

"What else can we do for that enormously talented child?" asked Elizabeth Bernardin.

"We might have to hide her in the cellar, eventually," said Cosima.

Edging through the small knot of people around Lana, Cosima reached her, touched her on the arm and whispered in her ear that they could leave whenever she wanted. Lana nodded. She was tired. Cosima apologized to the people around her and led her toward the door. Jack was waiting in the foyer. They left together, though he would drive his rented car to the condominium on the harbor.

"Are you really very tired?" Cosima asked Lana as she drove her down Greenwich Avenue.

"Yes, very."

"Well, Jack Putnam will be joining us, and he and I may go out for a while. You needn't worry about the telephone. If it rings, the machine will answer it."

Lana nodded.

Cosima glanced at the tiny girl, her delicate profile outlined by the dimmed lights of the stores on The Avenue. "If Jack is there in the morning, you won't mind, will you?"

Lana kept her eyes on the street ahead, but she smiled. "If he is not using his room at the hotel, I can go there," she said.

Cosima laughed. "He may need it for himself," she said. "We've made no deal."

They urged Lana to stay in the living room long enough to have a cup of coffee with them. She did. She poured cream in her coffee, then stirred in two heaping spoons of sugar. Jack put aside the jacket of his tuxedo and pulled off his tie. Cosima slipped off her shoes.

"I knew only one," she said in response to Jack's question as to what the Soviet authorities did to returned defectors. "She was a good dancer. She was naive and tried to defect in Prague. People hid her, but the Czech government found her and returned her. She was not imprisoned. She was sent to Kostroma—not far from Moscow in kilometers but as far as the moon in every other way. She had to work to eat. They arranged for her a job. For two years from trucks she unloaded bags of potatoes. You know what this does to the body? She will never dance again."

"You know what they did to the pianist Vladimir Feltsman?" Cosima asked. "He didn't try to defect, he only applied for permission to emigrate. For two years he was not allowed to play in public. For six years after that he was allowed to play only a few concerts, always in provincial towns."

"Jeez, girls," said Jack. "Can't let it happen."

After Lana went to bed, Cosima and Jack sat silently for a few minutes, absorbed in thought. She mused on how she would react if he asked her to make love with him. She guessed it was on his mind.

"Want a drink?" she asked.

"Pourquoi non?"

She poured Scotch for him and cognac for herself, and after she handed him his drink she walked to the window, parted the curtains a bit and looked out over the Sound.

"Know something?" he said quietly. He waited until she glanced back over her shoulder at him. "You're a god-damned *vision*, is what you are. That dress . . . lot of leg showing, and those dark stockings . . . you raise a man's enthusiasm, you know that?"

She turned. "Yes, I suppose so," she said. "I seem to have gotten that reaction all evening."

He sighed. "I said it wrong," he mumbled. He got up and walked to her. He put his hand on her arm. "I meant it right. I mean— Hell, Cosima, you *are* sexy. That's for sure. But . . . you're unique." He nodded. "Unique . . ."

Cosima traced the line of his lapel with her finger. "So are you, Jack," she said soberly.

He leaned forward and kissed her lightly. "What'd I say the last time I was here?—that I didn't want anything quick or casual between you and me. Well . . . if something happens this time, it wouldn't be quick or casual. I've thought about you a lot, for two months."

She frowned, but she did not back away from him. "This is getting a bit serious, Jack," she said quietly.

"And do you remember what you told me two months ago?—that if I'd asked you'd have said no."

Cosima nodded.

"Is it no tonight?"

She paused, not sure how she wanted to answer. "How meaningful would it be?" she asked.

"Meaningful, Cosima," he declared earnestly, in that half-drawl that so often characterized him. "Meaningful."

She nodded. "It would be for me," she said.

He lowered his chin, and he smiled, looking up at her roguishly from beneath his brows. "I can't tell you I've never done it meaningfully before," he said. "But, more often than not, it's been—Well, you know."

"I haven't been saving myself for my someday husband, either," she said.

Jack put his arms around Cosima and held her gently. He put his mouth to her neck, just below her ear. "I want you very much," he whispered.

"Not just tonight?" she murmured against his shoulder.

"Not just tonight," he said.

He wanted to see her. Undressing was simple. She was wearing nothing under the short, fur-trimmed black dress—nothing except dark panty hose—and when she lifted the dress over her head she was all but naked. He asked her to stop, not to take off any more; he led her to the couch, where he drew her down beside him and began to kiss her: first on her mouth and eyes, cheeks and neck, then on her breasts.

"There's no hurry, is there?" he said. "I want to savor you."

"No hurry," she whispered.

They remained on the couch, lying in each other's arms, caressing, fondling, exploring, learning. She helped him to undress. Impatient to see his member, she jerked his sling-shot underpants down to expose it and lifted it gently between her hands. He was uncircumcised, but his strained foreskin did not contain his red, wet glans; it thrust forward into the air and light, with a glistening drop of his fluid standing on it. She touched that drop with her finger and transferred it to the tip of her tongue. She smiled impishly, yet the boldness of the gesture brought the blood high in her cheeks. He kissed her fervidly, pressing his tongue between her lips as if to recapture the drop of fluid she had taken.

"Not just tonight, Cosima," he whispered. "No way. This has gotta be for good."

She nodded. Her head was tipped back to expose her throat to his lips and tongue, and her eyes were closed. "For good, Jack . . ."

Thirteen

For many people the last two weeks of December are an oppressive nightmare. They long for the third or fourth of January, when the pressures abate and they can return to undemanding, nonthreatening humdrum. For a few only is the season a fairyland, and for the fairylanders, usually something besides the season engenders its anomalous euphoria. Like family. Like children. Like a new love affair.

Cosima spent Christmas at the house on Round Hill, in the bosom of her family; the following Monday she met Jack at Kennedy Airport, and they flew to Paris for New Year's. They stayed at Hotel George V, and for a week they enjoyed winter in Paris—walks along the Seine, where autumn leaves were still a wind-stirred litter; excursions through the stores and galleries, where Cosima bought nothing but a small luminous painting by Symbari, which she told Jack she wanted for her bedroom; half a day in the Musée d'Orsay; superb dinners in celebrated restaurants; some shows . . .

Before they left the States, Cosima had telephoned her Passy roommate, Madeleine Milhaud, now Madeleine Deschanel. When they arrived at the George V they found flowers and champagne waiting for them, compliments of M. et

Mme. Deschanel—together with a note saying that they were to be the guests of Madeleine and Olivier at Tour d'Argent for dinner on Wednesday evening.

"Do you know why we called her Perle?" Madeleine asked Jack as they sipped apéritifs and scanned the menu at a table near the bar. When Jack acknowledged he had not even known Cosima had a nickname of any sort, Madeleine laughed and told the story of the priest the girls called Père Lubricité. "So—we call him also Père Lu, and from that comes Perle—Cosima."

Madeleine was still the fun-loving girl she had been fifteen years ago. She had filled out, was stouter than she had been, and she had allowed a hairdresser to strip the color from her light brown hair, so that she was a platinum blonde. She was stylish, with a Parisian flair. She admired Cosima's dress, the same fur-trimmed black one Cosima had worn to the big party; hers was a red and gold brocade, tightly fitted to her generous form, with a skirt a bit longer than Cosima's but still well above the knee. Olivier Deschanel, a solemn Frenchman in rimless glasses, struggled to understand and speak English and to affect a jocund personality, which probably was unnatural to him. He was co-owner of a company that manufactured surgical instruments, and he said he planned to visit the States in the spring, in an effort to introduce his company's instruments to American surgeons.

"You should have Cosima as your American lawyer, then," Jack drawled.

"This would be very good," said Olivier.

The restaurant overlooked Notre Dame, anchoring its island in the middle of the Seine, serenely magnificent in the subdued glow of floodlights. *"La ville lumière,"* Jack mused. His French did not extend much beyond that.

"Well . . . You two. Hmm?" Madeleine asked. With Gallic gestures she underscored her meaning. She grinned. "Hmm?"

Cosima reached for Jack's hand. "Probably," she said.

"This trip is an experiment." She looked up into Jack's eyes. "And so far, we haven't had an explosion."

Olivier Deschanel was mystified. "This is, I think, an American idiom," he said. *"Comment s'appelle ceci en français?"*

"N'importe," said Madeleine. *"Ils sont amoureux."*

"Ahh . . ."

Madeleine grinned at Cosima, then at Jack. "And how does Papa like this?"

Jack laughed. "All too well," he said.

"This I understand," said Madeleine.

Olivier shook his head.

"My father," said Cosima to Olivier, "is pleased that I am travelling with Jack—and not with my Jewish law partner or a certain Italian musician who is a friend of mine."

"Ahh," said Olivier with a broad smile.

"You are, then, of course a good Catholic," said Madeleine to Jack.

"As a matter of fact, no," said Jack. "My family has been Protestant since the day Luther nailed up the ninety-five theses."

"Aie! Pas possible!" laughed Madeleine.

"It's the alternatives, you see," said Jack, mock-seriously. "Having seen the alternatives, Leon outright sponsors me. I mean, he makes occasions for us. He invited me to his Christmas party, when Cosima didn't. He—"

"My father invited Olivier to spend a week with our family at our beach home at Hyères," said Madeleine.

"Yes," said Olivier soberly. "Monsieur Milhaud was very kind to me."

"If I hadn't married Olivier," said Madeleine, "my father would have put me out on the street."

"We have a good marriage," said Olivier.

"Yes," she agreed. "Very good."

"I'm happy for you," said Cosima.

"If it's good, what you have, never mind that Papa wants it too much," said Madeleine. "I remember him, when he came to Passy. What a strong man! You were afraid of him, Cosima. But you're not now. Are you?"

Cosima shook her head. "I love him," she said quietly. "But I'm not afraid of him anymore."

Jack tipped his head to one side and regarded her with a satirical smile. "By god, I am," he said.

Their return flight would arrive at Kennedy in midafternoon; and Jack would then transfer directly to a flight to Los Angeles. His appearance at the Bernardin Christmas party had been made possible only by a seventeen-day holiday interruption in the shooting of a picture. He had gone to New Haven to be with his family, had come down to Greenwich for the party and had returned to New Haven. On the day he and Cosima flew to Paris he had been scheduled to return to Los Angeles. Shooting on the picture resumed on Monday, January 4, which was the day they were recrossing the Atlantic; and he would be a day late on the set.

He slept most of the way across the Atlantic. She read and looked out the window; sometimes she just sat and looked at him. It would be weeks before they saw each other again. Maybe months. Good. There'd been a certain . . . precipitousness about the last two weeks—also a sense that they had been pushed from behind. She wondered if they hadn't deliberately avoided definitive words. They kept using the words from their first night: that they wanted something continuing and meaningful, but what the hell *was* continuing and meaningful? Love and marriage? Two words they had not used, even when prompted by Madeleine at the Tour d'Argent? Maybe that in itself was meaningful.

On the other hand . . . Did anyone have weeks and months to throw away? And what *was* impetuous, anyway? She had fallen in love prudently once . . . and disaster. Impetuous? Yes, anything with Jack was that. One memorable night, then six nights in Paris—but that didn't count because the nights in Paris had been fairytale nights. Unforgettable. With *this man*. He was ten years older than she was, and ten years more experienced—of this he was absurdly conscious. He was *wise*—he thought. The grinning character who drawled "Jeez, Cosima" was the persona he had created for stage and screen; behind this contrived façade there was a brisk, trenchant mind: astute and effective. In his wisdom he was reasonably self-content. In her judgment he had cause to be.

(His discontent with his physical self was amusing. He carried a little too much weight—but what man didn't? What was funny, though, was how his penis embarrassed him. It was small—at least in her experience it was—and when at rest it retreated inside his foreskin like a turtle pulling its head back inside its shell. It rose to its occasions and performed its office manfully, as she insisted—which he took for a wry joke—but he was tormented by a fixation of inadequacy. To encourage him, and maybe also because it wasn't as gross as some, she had done with it what she had always refused to do with others.)

She closed her eyes and dozed. The Atlantic below, seen through occasional breaks in the cloud cover, was monotonously blue-green, peppered with chunks of white ice. She had lost interest in the book she had bought in a bookshop on the Seine yesterday, specifically to read on this flight. It was late afternoon in Paris, but she was already half-attuned to New York time and knew she had gotten up at two in the morning—enough to make anyone sleepy. A waking dream seized her senses, and she mumbled something in annoyance, dreaming that her bags—only they were great wooden crates—were riding around the carrousel at Kennedy and she could not press through the crowd to get to them.

"Cosima . . ."

She started. Jack held her hand. He was looking at her, quietly concerned.

"Sorry . . ." she muttered. "Dumb dream."

He leaned over and kissed her cheek. "Whatever—it's okay, baby."

She glanced at her watch. "Two hours . . ." she said. "Another two hours to Kennedy."

He took her hand between both of his. "It's been a wonderful week, honey," he said.

She nodded. "I enjoyed every minute of it. I'm sorry it's over."

"When are you coming to California?"

"Well, I—"

"You know, like a weekend. If business is pressing. Out Friday night. Red-eye back on Sunday, if you have to. Hey, next week! Well . . . I'll have to check the shooting schedule. But . . . Hey, Cosima, you've *gotta* come."

"I guess—"

He squeezed her hand between his. "Cosima . . . I, uh, haven't said it in so many words, but I know you understand I love you. I do. I, uh . . . *I love you.* Simple. Uncomplicated. I love you."

She nodded. "I love you, too, Jack," she whispered.

Rick closed the door behind him. He sat down facing Cosima across her desk. "How was Paris?" he asked.

She heard an unsubtle crispness in his voice and understood its origin—it was the same tone she had heard when she first told him she was spending a week in Paris with Jack Putnam. She chose to answer affably. "Not like this," she said, glancing at the wet snow falling past the window and settling into a slippery brown slush on the streets.

"It's a fine time to come back to New York," he said. "When the city is at its best."

"We never cease to love it," she said, peering out at the thickening snowfall.

"I have something to tell you," said Rick.

"It sounds ominous—*you* sound ominous."

"I don't think you're going to hear this from anyone else. But I think you have to know it."

"It *is* ominous."

"It's a problem with Hugh," said Rick. He sighed. "Where to start . . . ? Okay. For some thirteen years Hugh has done the copyright work for NATINCO. When he started, their copyright problems were few, and the firm that represented them didn't have a copyright specialist, so Hugh got the work. Then NATINCO started acquiring more licenses, and the copyright problems proliferated. It's probably Hugh's best client, generates more fees than any other, certainly. Now—"

"Somebody's taking it away from him," Cosima interrupted.

"You got it."

She shook her head. "Well . . . It can happen."

"It didn't just happen," said Rick. "There's more to it."

"I was afraid of that. Fill me in first. NATINCO is. . . ?"

"North American Technological Information Network Company. It's an on-line distributor of technological journals and monographs, plus newsletters, industry magazines, and so on. If you've got a desktop computer with a phone connection and a printer, and pay the fee, you can call up articles from several hundred sources, all on technological subjects, for just about any industry. NATINCO publishes nothing. It only distributes what others publish, by means of highly sophisticated computer and communication techniques. Anyway, it's a growing company in a growing business, and Hugh's been its copyright counsel almost from the beginning."

"Complicated copyright problems, I suppose," said Cosima.

"Absolutely. Some of the NATINCO sources are digests of articles published by journals that haven't given a license to NATINCO. Some of the journals don't hold copyright in what they publish. A lot of what NATINCO offers on-

266

line is government publications, but some of the government publications have been supplemented with editorial features from private publishers. All kinds of problems."

"So who's trying to take the client away from Hugh? And why?"

"We can't prove it," said Rick, "and there'd be no point in trying, but the problem almost certainly originates with Dan Nash."

"Nash? What the hell's *he* have to do with it? And how do you know?"

"How do we know? Well, NATINCO leaks—like any other company. And Hugh has friends there. If anyone who talked to him were found out, it would jeopardize their jobs, so they won't confirm what they told Hugh, not in any forum. Besides, Hugh doesn't want to get them in trouble. But the story is pretty clear, from two or three sources."

"Old story, hmm?" said Cosima. She leaned back in her chair and clasped her hands behind her head. "Nash. If you lift enough rocks, you'll find an ugly insect crawling around. Nash."

Rick shrugged. "For general purposes, NATINCO is represented by Deveboise, Plimpton—which, incidentally, is absolutely innocent in this. They've represented the company since about 1981. Because Hugh had done NATINCO's copyright work from the beginning, the board of directors decided to leave it with him, and apparently Deveboise, Plimpton had no objection. And they still don't. But Emile Logan, the new president of NATINCO, does object, strenuously, and convinced his board that the copyright work should be turned over to Deveboise."

"They're competent to handle it," said Cosima dryly.

"Logan seems to have been turned against Hugh over a lunch at the Harvard Club," said Rick. "One of the men at the table told Hugh what was said. Your name was mentioned. So was mine. Even Joan's."

"Nash?"

"Yes. He told Logan you were kicked out of Hamilton,

Schuyler for mishandling a client and for insubordination. He described you as having become hysterical when you were confronted with it. He told Logan you are under investigation by the Association of the Bar for unethical conduct and may possibly be suspended from the practice. You are a petulant little rich girl, he said, whose father staked you to an office in the Pan Am Building so you can play at being a lawyer.''

"Defamation," she grunted.

"Forget it," he said. "The man will never testify. Anyway, that's not all of it. Nash told Logan you wanted a tax lawyer, so you used what he delicately called 'feminine wiles' to lure me away from Hamilton, Schuyler. Of course, I wasn't very bright, so I fell for it.''

"I'm afraid to guess what he said about Joan. You *did* say he used her name, too?''

"Joan left Webster, Kent a week before she would have had to confront a partners' meeting on the subject of her dalliance with a secretary. His term for her: 'an aggressive bull dyke.''

"Goddamit! But— This Logan must be an *ass,* to believe—"

"He wanted to believe it," said Rick. "He shot himself in the foot on a licensing agreement five years ago. It was Hugh who caught the error, and Logan has never forgiven him.''

"And the directors? What kind of idiot directors . . . ?''

"None of it was presented to the board," said Rick. "Not a word of it. Logan got a vice president named Bennett—a gofer—to move that Hugh be dropped and to argue the motion. This Bennett said Hugh had essentially retired but instead of definitively retiring had established an office with a controversial new firm—very new, six months new, that had already established a reputation for stealing clients from what he called 'real' firms, and for aggressive practices. That association—he called it an 'unfortunate' association—would become very costly for NATINCO in any negotiations or litigation over licenses. Any 'respectable' New York firm, as he put it, would resent the connection between Hugh Hupp and Bernardin, Loewenstein & Salomon, would suspect our firm's tactics and motives, and would harden against us."

"How very nice," said Cosima, containing her anger.

Rick raised his hands. "Hugh told me," he said. "I promised not to tell you. He is afraid of your reaction, that you might do something . . . well—"

"Reckless," she said icily.

"Cosima . . ." He stopped, sighed noisily. "There is nothing we can do."

"There's nothing the two of *you* can do," she said. "Don't be so sure *I* won't find a way to do something."

"Not through what I've told you," said Rick. "Hugh won't give either you or me the name of the man who told him what Nash said. And if he did, the man would deny it."

"Nash . . ." she muttered. "I'd like to castrate that son of a bitch."

"Cosima—" She braced herself for another sober platitude, but suddenly the old Loewenstein smile returned. "Cosima, you can't do that. Nash has been castrated already. In fact, I'd guess he's castrated every day."

She smiled, but her smile quickly turned sour. "Maybe so, but he's one up on us," she said. "And he can do it again."

"Hugh's not hurting," said Rick. "I mean financially. He can stand the loss. It's a blow to him in another sense, though. He was proud of NATINCO, proud of the part he played in making it a success. And he thought he had friends there."

Cosima sniffed. "I suppose you and I thought we had friends at Hamilton, Schuyler."

Rick shook his head. "If we did, we were fools—we mistook cordiality for friendship. In business you can't afford to extend friendship. It's far too costly."

"Hugh . . ." she said with a sigh. "Does he blame us? At all?"

"No."

"Is he angry, or—"

"Angry. Disappointed. He feels betrayed. And frustated. *He'd* like to castrate Nash—and Logan, too."

"I love that guy," said Cosima quietly. "Goddamit! Those bastards got at him through us."

"No," said Rick. "Hamilton, Schuyler got at *us* through *him*. It's war. And we're overmatched."

Thursday afternoon. Tuesday's snow was now just dirty water standing along the curbs. At five it was dark, and the lights of the city gleamed on the wet pavements. Cosima stood at her office window, unable to shake Hupp in his office about his loss of NATINCO. He had shrugged it off, but she knew it had affected him more than he wanted to admit. When she had asked him if he wanted to terminate the association with her firm she had been encouraged to see his face harden and his eyes flash anger as he declared it would take more than "a pair of little pricks like Nash and Logan" to drive him away from a deal he liked.

She was thinking of staying in the city for the night. The forecast was for another snowfall overnight, and coming in in the morning might be nasty. She didn't need a change of clothes. She was wearing a wool jacket and trousers in gray check, with a turtleneck black sweater, and in her closet was a tailored skirt that matched the jacket and trousers. She could—

"Cosima." It was Teresa, her secretary. "Judge MacGruder is on line one."

"Uh-oh. I know what this means." She picked up the telephone. "Cosima Bernardin."

"Miss Bernardin, I'm calling to tell you I will dismiss the Svetlana Terasnova appeal tomorrow morning. If you're going for habeas corpus, you should be ready to file by ten o'clock. I'll put the order on at ten."

"I appreciate your call very much, Judge MacGruder."

"You understand I have to telephone your opposing counsel now. Of course . . . he being a Justice Department lawyer, and it being after five o'clock, he may not be there."

"I wouldn't be surprised," said Cosima.

"What progress on getting your private bill passed?"

"Well, now that Congress is back in session, I think we may be able to move it. It will be a fight."

"Yes, I imagine it will be.

As soon as she hung up, Cosima stepped out to speak to Teresa. "A little overtime tonight, if you can," she said. "It won't take long, but we've got to prepare a petition for habeas corpus in the Terasnova case."

Teresa glanced at her watch and nodded. She was a delicately beautiful Hispanic, twenty-eight years old, the divorced mother of two. Cosima avoided asking her to work late because she knew Teresa was always anxious to get home to her children, who lived with their grandmother in Queens. Teresa never complained about being asked because she regarded herself as fortunate to have this job.

Cosima had anticipated the necessity of filing this petition, and her file contained a Xerox of a petition for habeas corpus that she had obtained from the files in the clerk's office of the United States District Court. It had been filed by an immigration specialist she respected, and all she had to do to adapt it to Lana's case was change the names, dates and case number.

"I am learning a little about the law," said Teresa. "But would you mind telling me why habeas corpus? And why now?"

Cosima looked up from pencilling changes on the copy. "Habeas corpus is a writ for securing release from unlawful custody," she said. "Technically speaking, Lana was not in the custody of the Immigration and Naturalization Service until her appeal from their order was denied. That's

271

technical, but that's how the law looks at it. Once her appeal is denied, she is in the custody of the INS, which will deport her immediately if they are not prevented. So—habeas corpus. And even that's a technical step. The whole point is to delay deportation until my sister can get a private bill through the Congress.''

Teresa drew a deep breath, filling her chest and thrusting her firm little breasts forward. ''If an officer would drive me through my neighborhood in a car with windows covered so I couldn't be seen, in ten minutes I could point out twenty illegal aliens, some of them dealing in drugs, some in other things. *Them* they don't trouble to pick up and deport.''

''They're not communists,'' said Cosima.

She sat in her office while Teresa typed the petition and accompanying papers—still half dejected, conscious of the increased movement in the city, people hurrying home. The strings of red taillights stretched away up Park Avenue as far as she could see, paralleled by a brighter string of white headlights inching south. She placed a call to Emilie in Washington, but Emilie was not in her office; her aide thought she might have left for her apartment. She could not telephone Lana; she was on a tour; if Cosima remembered right she was dancing in Cleveland tonight.

''Gussy . . .'' It was Rick—who else ever called her that? He stood in the door, tipping his head toward Teresa and the clacking typewriter. ''The habeas corpus, huh?''

Cosima nodded. ''Judge MacGruder called a few minutes ago.''

Rick came to stand beside her at the window. ''It's what we expected, of course. Judge MacGruder did us a hell of a favor to hold it up this long.''

She glanced at him. ''True,'' she said.

''When do you have to file the petition?''

''In the morning. The dismissal order will be docketed at ten.''

''You'd better stay in town,'' he said.

''I've been thinking about it.''

He stepped away from her and sat down. "You're welcome at my place. Just like always." He thought for a second and frowned. "Well . . . not like always. Anyway, you're welcome to stay. There's only one bathroom, but the couch folds out."

She turned her back to the window. "We can have dinner anyway," she said.

"Yes, that would be all right."

"*Rick* . . ." She disliked what she heard in his voice. "C'mon. Really. You and I— What are we going to do, break up the firm?"

He glanced toward the door. The typewriter clattered on; even so, he lowered his voice. "A *Methodist* wouldn't do, the way I heard it."

Her voiced hardened. "If you persist in assuming I am anti-Semitic because I didn't fall in love with you and resisted the idea of marrying you, then let's break up the firm—there's no way we can associate in this office, or any other way, as long as you think I hate Jews."

"You don't hate Jews, Gussy," he said gently. "But you couldn't marry one."

"*The hell I wouldn't.* I could marry a Buddhist, I could marry a Moslem—if I loved him. I'll tell you what I don't think I could marry, though—a *believer*—a man who lets his creed screw up his life."

"You're a Catholic—"

"*When . . . it . . . is . . . convenient . . . Rick.*"

"Which is no faith at all."

"Which is why you and I could never make it together," she said. "Because in the end, whatever you may say, you *believe*. In part of it, anyway. Jerry doesn't. Jack doesn't. Nor my father. And sure as hell not me."

"Something to cling to."

"Like a crutch, you mean?"

The typewriter stopped, whether because Teresa had heard them and paused, or because she needed to insert a new sheet of paper in the machine, they could not tell. Then the clacking began again.

"In my life," said Rick quietly, "I've told two women I loved them—Lydia and you. I didn't lie to either."

Cosima walked to his chair and put her hand on his shoulder. "I didn't think you were lying," she said softly.

Rick stood. "The couch unfolds," he said.

"And we can have a nice dinner somewhere," she said.

"You assure me, Miss Bernardin, that the Attorney General was informed?"

Cosima stood before Judge Ralph Waldo Emerson Hawthorne, United States District Court for the Southern District of New York. He stared down at her, his face flushed, his blue eyes bulging, veins throbbing at the sides of his head as if he were suffering hypertension. His pursed lips were tight and wrinkled.

"I can only repeat what I told you, Your Honor," she said. "Judge MacGruder informed me of her action by telephone and stated to me during the brief conversation that she was placing a call immediately to Mr. Langley at the Justice Department, so that he would know what she was telling me."

"And you assure me that the Circuit order dismissing the appeal was put on the journal of the Court at ten this morning?"

"Once again, Your Honor, that is what Judge Mac-Gruder told me."

"And you are petitioning for a writ of habeas corpus and want your client free on bond pending disposition of the action. Where is your client now?"

"I believe she is in Cleveland, Your Honor. She is touring with the New York Ballet."

"It would have been appropriate for her to be here, Miss Bernardin."

"We had no way, Your Honor, to guess the date when

the Circuit Court would dismiss the appeal. In fact, I haven't been able to reach my client. She doesn't know the appeal has been dismissed."

Judge Hawthorne was probably older than he looked. He looked perhaps fifty. His dark brown hair, clipped short, was gray only at the temples. Inside his black robe, he was small; his shoulders were rounded and his hands were petite and delicate. He flipped through the papers Cosima had filed only half an hour before.

"On first impression, Miss Bernardin," he said, "I don't see that this court has jurisdiction to grant a writ of habeas corpus. I am sure you are aware that Paragraph 9(c) of Section 1105a(c) provides that no petition for habeas corpus will be entertained if the validity of the deportation order has been determined in any prior judicial proceeding. You had your appeal. The Circuit Court dismissed. There's your prior judicial proceeding."

"Respectfully, Your Honor, I would argue to the contrary," said Cosima. She and Rick had rehearsed this last night, over dinner, then in his apartment. She knew the argument she was about to make was weak, but she had to make it; in any event, she would learn something from the judge's reaction to it. "The section Your Honor has just cited also provides"—she flipped over a sheet in her file—"that the administrative order and the Attorney General's findings of fact shall be conclusive only if—and I quote—'supported by reasonable, substantial and probative evidence on the record.' The Attorney General moved to dismiss the appeal on the ground that it was frivolous. The Attorney General's motion to dismiss and his supporting memorandum are attached to the petition, Your Honor. The Assistant Attorney General pressed hard for dismissal. He had the case advanced on the docket of the Circuit Court, and he urged Judge MacGruder to dismiss it from the bench on the day the motion was orally argued. And, the appeal *was* dismissed—on the ground that it was frivolous. We were never afforded an opportunity to show that

275

the order and findings were *not* supported by 'reasonable, substantial and probative evidence.' "

The judge seemed to have withdrawn within himself and to be ignoring her as he turned the pages of a maroon volume of the Untied States Code. Cosima looked over her shoulder at Rick, who sat behind the rail, frowning, apprehensive.

"Did you press that point, Miss Bernardin?" asked Judge Hawthorne.

"We never had a chance, Your Honor."

Again the judge stared somberly at a page in the Code. Cosima stood waiting at the lectern. Besides Rick, the only other people in the courtroom were three attorneys waiting to present other matters. She overheard a hoarse whisper— "Look at the *behind* on her! Jesus!" The judge heard it and glanced gravely at the embarrassed lawyer, who had not realized how his whisper would carry. Then he, too, ran his eyes up and down over Cosima, critically as if he saw something unpleasant.

Judge Hawthorne sighed loudly. "Is this the only basis for your petition, Miss Bernardin?" he asked.

"No, Your Honor," said Cosima. "Paragraph 9(c), which you cited to me earlier, also provides that a person under threat of deportation may raise in habeas corpus proceedings any grounds for reversal of the deportation order which could not have been presented in prior proceedings. Miss Terasnova is the subject of a private bill that has been introduced in the House of Representatives, a bill to grant her citizenship. It would be cruel and futile to deport her a matter of weeks or months before she receives citizenship at the hands of Congress. When we filed our petition for review in the Circuit Court—indeed, when we argued the matter before that court—no such bill had been introduced. The fact that the bill is pending raises a new issue we could not have raised in the prior proceeding."

Turning his head to one side and looking at Cosima from the corner of his eyes, Judge Hawthorne nodded knowingly.

"All right, Miss Bernardin. Now I understand. If I issue the writ, then obviously the Attorney General is going to appear and oppose your client's release. Then you are going to want a full evidentiary hearing. And, considering the state of this Court's trial docket, you know the case could not be heard for months—during which time you expect your bill may be passed."

Cosima nodded. "I hope I can prevent my client's deportation to the Soviet Union until the bill can be passed, Your Honor. That is correct."

"So you want to use the processes of this Court for the purpose of delay."

"For the purpose of justice, Your Honor," said Cosima.

"In my experience, Miss Bernardin, justice is almost invariably the last-resort argument of an attorney with a weak case. Let's leave justice out of it, shall we?"

"I should hope justice would never be left out in Your Honor's courtroom," she said crisply.

Two of the lawyers laughed.

Once more, the judge pursed his lips, and he drew his breath in through the round opening. He shook his head. "And if I refuse the writ, you will go back to the Circuit Court of Appeals."

"I will, Your Honor."

"Justice delayed is justice denied, Miss Bernardin, and I have to be concerned about justice for the people of the United States. I seem to have little choice but to issue the writ, ordering the Immigration and Naturalization Service to show cause why your client should not be released from technical custody. And *that* is going to result in months of delay. Your definition of justice seems to be anything that will delay the deportation of your client."

Cosima understood that this was a time to stand silent. She struggled to effect a bland expression.

"I seem to have little choice," Judge Hawthorne continued. "Now, so far as bond is concerned, I suppose if I don't grant it and remand your client to the immigration detention center pending the outcome of these proceedings, you will take that to the Circuit Court."

"Yes, Your Honor."

"Very well, Miss Bernardin. The writ issues. Bond is fixed at twenty-five thousand dollars. The writ will be returnable on . . . Tuesday. That is, Tuesday, January 12. I expect your client to be present in this Court on that day."

"She will be present, Your Honor. She will have to interrupt a tour, but she will be here."

"Perhaps these proceedings are more important than a dance tour, Miss Bernardin."

She waded in slush from the Cos Cob station to her condominium. She had come out on the train, late in the afternoon but not late enough to ride with her father. Anyway, she hadn't wanted conversation with her father this Friday afternoon. Inside, she poured herself a splash of cognac and stood at the window, looking at snow falling on the Sound. Then, after a minute, she flung the drapes shut and closed out the whole gray, snowy, slushy world.

She showered. Every winter the cold penetrated her clothes, and when she laid a hand on her hips or bottom, even on her breasts, she felt cold flesh. She stood under the hot water and let it warm every inch of her. She dried herself, wrapped the big terry bath sheet around her and went back to the living room to start a fire in her fireplace. Happily she had a woodbox in the kitchen, and one of the twice-weekly maid's duties was to see that the box was always full, with a few pieces of wood laid in the fireplace, too. She had a Nantucket firelighter: a ceramic ball on a wrought-iron rod, like a hard drumstick, which stood in a pot of lamp oil. To light a fire, all she had to do was put the oil-soaked drumstick under the wood in the fireplace, light it with a match, and the hot fire from the soaked-up oil would continue long enough to light the wood. She squatted and started the fire, and in a moment she could feel its heat.

Her couch faced the fireplace, and she stretched out. She picked up Woodward's *Veil* and began to read; in a few minutes she was asleep.

For a few minutes. Then the telephone began to ring.

—Susanne: Was she having dinner at Round Hill tonight? Answer: no.

—Jerry, calling from Atlanta: Did she have any interest in a couple of days in Palm Beach—sleeping apart? Answer: no.

—Her mother: Was she having dinner at Round Hill tonight? Answer: no.

—A solicitor. Would she like to hear about a new strategic mutual fund? Answer: no.

She went in her den and switched on the answering machine. In the living room, she unplugged the telephone so it would not ring. Wide awake, she made herself a sandwich from some week-old pickle loaf with lettuce and mayonnaise. She poured a Diet Coke. She sat with the sandwich and Coke and read again, until again she went to sleep.

When she woke and checked the recorder she found a call from Jack. She returned the call. It was 5:30 P.M. in Los Angeles, and he was still at the studio.

"Jeez, honey, I miss you! God, I miss you. I called you last night. Where were you?"

"Had to stay in town. Unexpected. I didn't leave the answering machine on here. Hey, I miss you, too."

"I wanted you to catch a flight out tonight."

"Couldn't have done it, Jack. I had to be in court this morning. Have to be in court Tuesday morning. Lana's case."

"Oh, gawd . . . They on that again?"

"Now and forever," said Cosima.

"Anything else? Any other news?"

"Yeah, they're going to disbar me."

"Wha . . . ?"

"I got the notice this afternoon. The bar subcommittee finds 'reasonable cause'—as they put it—to think I may

279

have violated the rules in the Vanessa business. They're going to hold a hearing on it."

"You need me? I mean, for a witness?"

"I don't think so. I'm going to tell them to go fuck themselves."

"No, honey. Don't do that. You *won't* do that. 'Course, if you do . . . Hey, you can come out here and—I mean, you know . . . we can get married. Jeez, wha'd I just say? What a hell of a way to propose. Anyway, you don't *need* that shit. If you want it, that's somethin' different. But you don't need it. I got a whole different life waiting for you."

Her voice stuck. "Jack . . ." She sobbed. "Yours is the only positive, friendly voice I've heard today."

"Well, I love you," he said very quietly. "I wish I could be there, hold you."

"You'd like it," she said, taking control of her voice. She tossed aside her towel. "I'm starkers."

"Lucky you. I'm made up to be a friggin' steelworker, smeared with genuine dirt, in clothes I've genuinely sweated in."

"I love you, too, Jack."

"Hang in there, baby," he said. "I'm sorry things are rough for you. In another way, though, I'm glad. Shows you can need me."

"I *do* need you, Jack."

"Well, I need you, too. Next weekend?"

"Oh, god, I doubt it," she said. "Everything's . . . Well, never mind how everything is. As soon as possible, darling."

"I can't get away. It's gotta be out here."

"As soon as *I* can get away. The first free days I have. For sure. For . . . *sure.*"

Fourteen

"Miss Bernardin, you told me Mr. Langley had been informed of Judge MacGruder's dismissal of the appeal."

"No, Your Honor," said Cosima emphatically. "I told you that Judge MacGruder told me she would call the Justice Department immediately after her conversation with me."

"Well, you knew what action Judge MacGruder was taking *eighteen hours* before Mr. Langley was informed."

"Judge Hawthorne . . . Judge MacGruder telephoned me about five o'clock on Thursday. She told me she would docket the order at ten o'clock Friday morning—which, incidentally, she did. She then said she was going to call the Justice Department as soon as she hung up from her call with me, so Mr. Langley would know exactly what I knew. I gather that Mr. Langley was no longer in his office at five or ten minutes after five."

"She said she would call—"

"I can obtain her statement to that effect, if Your Honor wants it."

Judge Ralph W. E. Hawthorne spoke directly to Layman Langley. "When did *you* hear from Judge MacGruder?"

"When I arrived at my office on Friday morning, there

was a note that she had called. I called her. She told me she would docket the dismissal at ten o'clock."

The judge shook his head scornfully, as if he had just heard of an enormous irregularity.

"May I ask Mr. Langley a question, Your Honor?" Cosima asked. Judge Hawthorne shrugged.

"Mr. Langley . . . Your telephone note. Did it say when Judge MacGruder had called? If so, when had she called? And did she tell you on the telephone that she had tried to reach you Thursday afternoon?"

Layman Langley, wearing his usual three-piece suit, this one gray, stood behind his table and impatiently tapped his file with two fingers. For some reason, this morning his customary shallow smile had been replaced with a cloudy frown.

Lana sat at the table beside Cosima. She had flown back from Chicago to attend this hearing, and she was apprehensive. In spite of Cosima's assurances, she was afraid she would be held. Also, this judge frightened her.

Della Rosario, the reporter from the *Post,* watched from a seat behind the rail. Cosima had called her.

"Dilatory tactics, Your Honor," said Langley resentfully. "We are simply looking at dilatory tactics."

"Miss Bernardin doesn't even deny that, Mr. Langley," said Judge Hawthorne. "So we know it. You know it. I know it. The question is, what can we *do* about it?"

Langley stabbed his file with the same two fingers. "Section 1105, Your Honor—'No petition for habeas corpus shall be entertained if the validity of the deportation order has been previously determined in any civil or criminal proceeding.' Miss Terasnova *had* her appeal. It was *dismissed.*"

Cosima shook her head and smiled. "No, Your Honor. Mr. Langley obtained dismissal of the appeal on procedural grounds. Judge MacGruder never considered the validity of the deportation order. We have her order of dismissal before us. It reads—'On motion of the Attorney General this appeal is dismissed as a frivolous appeal. The Court has not

282

considered and does not rule on any substantive issue.' Section 1105 also provides that this Court shall entertain a petition for habeas corpus if the prior judicial proceedings were ineffective to test the validity of the deportation order.'' She shrugged. ''The validity of the order was not tested.''

Judge Hawthorne glowered at Langley. ''It might have been better, Mr. Langley, if you had not been so quick to move for dismissal.''

''Your Honor,'' said Cosima with a broadening smile. ''In his impatience to dispose of this case without full hearing, Mr. Langley shot himself in the foot.''

Judge Hawthorne sighed loudly. ''So I suppose you want—''

''An evidentiary hearing on the merits, Your Honor,'' she said. ''This moves us over to Chapter 28 of the Code, where Section 2244 provides for an evidentiary hearing on the merits of material factual issues.''

''What *factual* issues?'' Langley demanded.

''We will start with the nature of the organization of which Miss Terasnova was a member,'' said Cosima. ''We will continue with the circumstances in which she joined. I have reviewed the file in the office of the Immigration and Naturalization Service. All this and a great deal more was glossed over in the administrative hearings, and—''

''*Your Honor!* Nothing was glossed over. Miss Terasnova has never denied she was a member of Komsomol. The circumstances of her joining are irrelevant. What is more, she lied—tried to conceal her membership—''

''Not really,'' said Cosima. ''The evidence will show that when she applied for her visa she was a frightened little girl, a defector from a Soviet ballet company, and did not understand what she was being asked.''

''*Your Honor!* All this was reviewed at the administrative level!''

''And we are entitled to *judicial* review,'' said Cosima.

Judge Hawthorne rapped his gavel. ''*All right.* All right. Faced with an admission that this proceeding is for purposes of delay and for no other purpose, I am nevertheless faced too with the reality that Miss Bernardin will appeal any adverse order—which could result in even longer delay. We will therefore set the case for an evidentiary hearing at the earliest possible date."

"I remind Your Honor," said Langley, "that the Attorney General has the right to move for advancement on the Court's trial docket."

"And you may be assured, Mr. Langley, that the case will be slotted into the first opening."

Langley, who had remained standing, dropped heavily to his chair. "Thank you, Your Honor," he muttered.

Judge Hawthorne glared at Cosima. "Miss Bernardin," he grumbled. "This is your second appearance before this court. I will ask you to review the question of appropriate attire for an attorney appearing as an officer of the court. I think I hardly need be more specific."

Cosima flushed. "I'll keep it in mind, Your Honor," she said.

As soon as the judge left the courtroom, Layman Langley stepped over to Cosima's table. "Personally," he said, "I find your outfit *very* attractive. It's always a pleasure to be opposed by a beautiful young woman."

Cosima tipped her head and regarded him obliquely. "I find *your* outfit attractive, Mr. Langley," she said. "And it's a pleasure to appear against a handsome young man."

Langley stiffened. "You won't get your private bill through, you know," he said. "Even if you do, the President will veto it."

"I'll cross that bridge when I come to it."

"Do you think you can hold this case up until the next Administration comes into office?" he asked, nervously, as if the idea had just occurred to him.

She smiled. "Let's hope that's not necessary," she said.

* * *

They rode uptown in a cab—Cosima, Lana and Della Rosario. Cosima had anticipated the attitudes she would encounter in the courtroom, and she had wanted Della at the hearing, to see how it went, before they went to 21 for lunch with Hugh and an extended interview with Lana.

"What'd the old bastard expect you to be wearing?" Della asked.

"Something mannish," said Cosima. "White blouse buttoned up to the throat. Necktie or floppy bow. Jacket, skirt—gray, dark blue, or black. Low-heeled shoes."

"Skirt below the knee," said Della. "I remember one of my first assignments as a reporter. I went to a legislative hearing in Trenton. That was in '72, the first time around for miniskirts, and mine was pretty mini, I guess. Anyway, they wouldn't let me in the hearing room. I was *humiliated*. Worse than that, I was afraid I'd lose my job, because I'd been kept out of the hearing. Hey, kid, that—" She gestured toward Cosima's gray-and-green-checked skirt, maybe two inches above her knee when she was standing, her dark green jacket, and her cream white knit blouse with a wide, loose collar and a deep V above the first button. "Hey, that's . . . *modest!*"

"I suspect Judge Hawthorne would rather not see female lawyers at all," said Cosima.

"Hey," said Della. "Suppose we have a photog come up after lunch? I might be able to get a story in—IS THIS IM-MODEST? JUDGE SCORES LADY LAWYER'S DRESS!"

"I'd like to have the picture taken and put in your file, Della," said Cosima. "It may come in handy sometime. For right now, I'd rather you didn't run the story. You know the old lawyer cliché? 'If your case is weak on law, attack on the facts. If it's weak on the facts, attack on the law. If it's weak on *both* law and facts, attack the judge.' Although I've got a hostile judge, it would be a mistake to attack him just yet."

Hugh was at his table at 21, his first drink in front of him. "Well, young lady," he said to Lana, "since you're here and not in jail, I assume the hearing went reasonably well."

"It could have been worse," said Cosima. "You've met Della."

"Sure," he said, patting her shoulder as she sat down. "Last time I saw her, she asked me a highly personal question."

Della grinned. "I asked him what was the relationship between him and Adela Drake," she said to Cosima. "And I don't think he told me the truth."

Hugh faced Della with a scowl she would have taken as genuine if she had not known him. "It has been my lifelong custom to lie to reporters," he said gruffly. "Only way to handle 'em."

"Well, I'd rather you lie than not talk to me," Della laughed.

"Used to be the way, not to talk," he said. "Time was, lawyers thought it was beneath their dignity to talk to the news media. Besides, it was unethical to release news stories."

"Time was, I couldn't get past the reception desk at a Wall Street firm," said Della. "Still can't some places."

"I remember a lawyer in Chicago, as late as, oh, 1980, giving me a lecture over dinner on how to handle the news media," said Hugh. "He was defending a rather prominent man, whose name I forget, against a felony charge, and they were mobbed by reporters every time they left the courtroom. And he told me with great pride how he handled them. 'No comment,' he'd say. 'No comment. No comment.' Even if he happened to encounter a reporter by chance somewhere and the reporter asked him nothing more than 'Aren't you Attorney So-and-so?' his answer was 'No comment.' He was *proud* of how he handled reporters, thought he'd found the secret, thought he was a master at it. I'll never forget how smug he was."

"The old attitude," said Cosima.

Hugh nodded. "He was a member of one of the biggest

firms in Chicago. Two or three years later there was a horrible scandal in the firm, involving one of the senior partners—something to do with money and sex. They were so upset with this man that they locked him out of their offices. He came back from vacation and couldn't get in. They were absolutely *desperate* to keep the story quiet, but this partner went straight to the Chicago newspapers. Editors and reporters who'd been stung by the old 'no comment' act gave the story front-page coverage—joyfully, I imagine. The firm was damn near ruined. It split. The partner who'd gotten his side of the story published and had made himself look wronged took some of the firm's best clients."

"Well . . ." said Della. "To good media relations." She raised the glass of white wine that had just been put before her.

Cosima sipped from her martini and with amusement watched Lana toss back a double shot of vodka and swallow it at a gulp. She nodded at the waiter, who still stood by, astonished, and handed him her glass to be refilled.

"And incidentally," Della added, "you can congratulate me. The *Post* and I are parting company. Starting next week, I work for New York *Newsday.*"

"Congratulations, indeed," said Cosima. "I hope you'll still be assigned to Lana and me."

"I expect to cover the continuing saga," said Della.

"So," said Hugh. "Did Ralphie Hawthorne give you a hard time?"

"He's hostile," said Cosima. "No question about it."

"Shouldn't surprise you," said Hugh.

"He's a new judge, right?" asked Della. "His name wasn't familiar to me."

"Two years," said Hugh. "Appointed to be a conservative in the District Court. He was a partner at Perkins, Hubbard. Did ROTC when he was in college, served as a lieutenant in Korea. Won the Silver Star. The experience ruined his life. It rendered him piously patriotic and infallible. He is reputed to have smiled once, around 1963, but no one can confirm it."

"What I can't understand," said Della, "is Langley. What's he got up his ass?"

"He's a Mormon," said Hugh. "Need I explain further?"

"Yes, you damned well do," said Cosima. "I've got a Mormon friend in Connecticut who's a lovely man—bright, human, even liberal."

"Layman Langley," said Hugh, "is a professional believer. He believes in whatever is shoved at him—church, flag and apple pie—and the problem with him is, whatever he believes is by definition *right,* and whoever doubts it is *wrong*—which means he just tolerates you and me, just tolerates us and congratulates himself for doing it."

"In the Soviet Union," said Lana, "the same problem. Those who believe run the country—believe in Marx, Lenin, Mother Russia. It gives them a certain strength, that. All the many people who doubt . . . they are powerless. I think doubt is healthy."

Della made a note of what the ballerina had said. Her interview had begun without her asking a question.

"Langley says the President will veto our bill," said Cosima.

"He's got an in," said Hugh. "He'll have the Presidential ear."

"He asked me if I meant to delay the case until a new President takes office."

"Don't count on a new President being any improvement," said Della. "Five years from now we may look back on the present one as a rational moderate."

"I figure we make it politically expensive," said Cosima. "A public relations campaign. Nasty old men want to deport beautiful ballerina. Della?"

Della shrugged. "I'll do what I can for you," she said, speaking to Lana. Then she turned to Cosima. "But it will take more than I can do. You've got to get the *Times* at least. The Washington *Post*. Others . . . like the Miami *Herald*, Boston *Globe*, Los Angeles *Times* . . . A hell of a big PR campaign."

"It may be the key," said Cosima. "You could start it, Della. We can key on you and go on to other papers from there."

"I thought I knew something about how to practice law," said Rick. He held a copy of the New York *Post*. "I think this is going to drive your judge into a frenzy."

"I can't worry too much about the judge," said Cosima. "He hates the case. We're going to lose with him. For sure. I have to go a different way."

Della Rosario had done a job. The front page of the *Post* displayed a picture of Lana Terasnova, dancing on stage in a white tutu. The headline, in big black letters:

THREAT TO NATION'S SECURITY?
IMMIGRATION OFFICIALS WANT TO DEPORT BALLERINA!

The story, under Della Rosario's byline read, in part:

Because she would have been otherwise denied the opportunity to take ballet training, Svetlana Terasnova enrolled in Komsomol, the youth organ of the Soviet Communist Party. At first opportunity, she defected to the West. When she came through U.S. immigration she was asked if she was a member of any "totalitarian organization." Not having read the turgid language of certain sections of the U.S. Code, she answered no. Now she finds herself the target of a crusade by the Justice Department to deport her back to the Soviet Union.

On any given day, anyone with brains can identify ten thousand illegal aliens on the streets of New York alone, dealing in cocaine, crack, heroin—or, for that matter, in arms for various totalitarian regimes—and the Immigration Service and Justice Department seem to live with it. If one fragile young ballerina is maybe, just maybe, a Red—Horrors! The country is in danger, and we must deport her.

It is a shabby crusade, by narrow-minded men. Why did Svetlana come here? Because she wants to dance, unfettered by the Soviet limits on artistic freedom. She didn't come to sell narcotics, or to deal in arms. She came to dance, just to dance. What origin, this obscene campaign to deport her?

Inside the paper, where the story was continued, a photograph showed "Harassed ballerina, with her attorney, Cosima Bernardin."

Rick put the paper on Cosima's desk. "The Justice Department is not influenced by New York tabloid newspapers," he said.

"I'm taking Lana to Washington," said Cosima.

Congressman Jim Bob Pryor pursed his lips around a stubby black cigar, pulled it out, and allowed a thick blob of smoke to float up over his rimless, octagonal eyeglasses, and into his yellow-gray hair. The Representative from the Seventh District of Mississippi was thin and wrinkled and pale, and his watery light blue eyes swam behind his lenses. He was the chairman of the Immigration, Citizenship and International Law Subcommittee of the House Judiciary Committee.

They sat at a conference table: Cosima, Lana and Emilie McCarthy, Pryor and Thomas Diggins, ranking Republican on the subcommittee.

"Back home," said Pryor, "we don't hardly ever see any ballet dancin'. I guess folks'd call it toe dancin'." He smiled

290

and let another mouthful of smoke issue from between his lips. "Always admired it, personally, though I never saw it much."

"I wish you could see a performance by Miss Terasnova," said Cosima.

"I'd enjoy it, I'm sure," he said.

"You've been in this country four years, isn't that correct, Miss Terasnova?" asked Diggins.

"Almost five years," said Lana. "I walked away from a Soviet ballet troupe in Toronto in 1983. The Canadians let me stay. Then I came to New York."

"And when you entered the United States, you were asked if you had been a member of any Communist organization, and you answered no. Isn't that right?"

Lana nodded. She regarded Diggins, the Representative from the Seventh District of Arizona, without apprehension. He was a bland-faced man, about forty years old, who asked his questions unemotionally, with no implication of hostility. He had before him the memorandum Cosima had prepared for the subcommittee, and he had made notes on it. He made more now.

"And that wasn't true, and you knew it wasn't true," said Diggins. Even these words he could say amicably. "Why, Miss Terasnova? Why did you lie to enter the United States?"

"I did not understand," she said, "that it was wrong to answer that way. I mean, I did not know I would later be told to leave because I had said this."

"You knew you wouldn't be allowed to enter the country if you answered truthfully," said Diggins.

"I didn't know," she said. "But I thought it might be so."

"So you didn't tell the truth."

She nodded gravely. "I didn't."

Cosima had dressed Lana for her day in Washington in a cream white wool dress, covered by a matching loose coat. Lana never wore makeup. Her wide, intent, innocent blue eyes were her most appealing feature, and she faced these two men with her direct gaze, conspicuously absorbing every nuance in their questions.

Diggins held his yellow pencil between two hands. "Let's suppose something, Miss Terasnova," he said. "Suppose—and god forbid it should happen, but suppose—the United States and the Soviet Union went to war. And suppose you were called on to serve in the armed forces of the United States: not to shoot at anybody, but to do work that would contribute to the American war effort and so indirectly to the killing of Russians. Would you do it? Could you do it?"

"It would be very difficult," she said solemnly. She shook her head, glanced at Cosima then at Emilie. "Difficult—" Then her chin rose. "But just as difficult, if I were back in the Soviet Union, to have any part in anything that would kill Americans."

Diggins wrote studiously. "So," he said. "You have a family in Russia, don't you?"

Lana nodded. "My mother. My brother."

"Do you hear from them?"

"Hear . . . ?"

"Do they write you letters, call you on the telephone?"

"Yes. My mother writes me letters. I have spoken with her on the telephone three times since I left the Soviet Union."

"Would she like to come here?"

Lana shrugged. "My mother is a biochemist. She cannot come. She does not want to come."

"Your brother?"

"My brother is an electronics engineer. I have not heard from him since I left the Soviet Union. He thinks I am a traitor. At first he thought I had been drugged and kidnapped."

"Then I suppose he does not want to leave the Soviet Union."

"No. Our family are beneficiaries of the Soviet system. We live better than other people. The difference between me and my mother and brother is that I was not allowed to perform as I wished. My art was made subservient to government purposes. My mother's work and my brother's are also subservient—but to them that was of little moment. There is a difference between art and technology."

"You haven't mentioned your father, Miss Terasnova."

"My mother divorced my father not long after I was born—when she learned that his grandfather was an officer in the White Russian army, was executed in fact when the Red Army was victorious."

"You mean she divorced him for political reasons?" Diggins asked incredulously.

"For very practical reasons," said Lana. "This taint in my father's family would have prevented us from attaining what we achieved. If my brother and I had remained the legal descendants of a notorious counterrevolutionary, we could not have become an engineer and a dancer. My father is a car cleaner in the Moscow subway."

"And that's the system you wanted to escape," suggested Congressman Pryor.

"Yes," said Lana. "A government of bitter old men."

"You think things have changed since you left?"

She turned down the corners of her mouth. "They talked of change before. Nothing changes, in the end."

Pryor rotated his cigar between his lips, sucked on it, then rolled out another almost-liquid blob of smoke. "Tawm," he said to Congressman Thomas Diggins. "I'm ready to report this bill favorably to the full committee. I'll get my Democrats to sign the report. You agree? Can you get your members?"

"I'll sign a favorable report," said Diggins. "I can get one more signature. I'll also have a dissenter."

"Well . . . Figured that," said Pryor. "But we'll report it to the Judiciary Committee, Emilie. And we can get it out of there. You won't get unanimous consent on the floor."

"Will you join me on the bill, either of you?" asked Emilie.

Congressman Jim Bob Pryor smiled. "Don' believe I'll go that far," he said. "I'll vote for you. I'll vote for you in committee and on the floor."

Diggins nodded. "So will I."

Emilie stood, and Cosima and Lana followed her cue. "We appreciate it, gentlemen," said Emilie.

Rain was falling when Cosima and Lana finished their round of appointments in Washington and caught a cab for National Airport and the shuttle. Snow was falling again in New York. Hugh Hupp looked down from his office window and grimaced. Slippery sidewalks were more threatening to him than they were to men with two good legs.

Adela Drake sat in his office, drinking a cup of coffee. She had arrived on a flight from Miami only two hours ago, had checked in at the Waldorf and had come directly to Hugh's office. Since there was almost nowhere in New York where she could sit down for a quiet dinner without being badgered by requests for autographs—or at the very least stared at for the hedge of green and red hair on her bald head—they would have dinner together in her suite.

They had planned to walk the short distance from the Pan Am Building to the Waldorf, but the snow had moved Hugh to call for a car.

"Jerry was annoyed when I left," she said.

He turned his back on the window. "What's he got in his craw?"

"He wanted me to travel with the band."

"He wanted to sleep with you."

"Probably," she said. "The idea comes on him when there's nobody else available."

"Nice fellow, Jerry."

"I'm going to have to have lots of legal advice," she said. "I'm thinking of leaving Fangs."

"Your contract expires . . . ?"

"March 1."

"What do you want to do, Red?" he asked. Red was his nickname for her; it referred to her red-dyed hair and also to her southern background—he sometimes called her a redneck. "Give up showbiz?"

"No way," said Adela. "But I want to do my own thing. I can do my own vocals. I can work alone, or I'll pick up a couple of sidemen to work with me. I can get enough bookings to finish out the year. I can get them right now."

"No great legal problems," said Hugh.

"Question is, how much will I have to change my act? I mean, if I go onstage with my hair like this, in a black rubber suit, couldn't Jerry claim I was stealing the image he created and made into a multimillion-dollar trademark?"

"You can't use his music," said Hugh. "You'll have to do something different."

"I can get good music. There are a lot of composers. But— The image . . ."

"Well, what do you have in mind? Anything?"

Adela drew a deep breath and sighed. "I think as many people come to look at Fangs as come to hear them. You know, we don't do terribly well with records. We do extremely well with concerts and very well with posters. Records sell respectably but not in proportion to the other two. I think I've got to keep the image somehow . . . but change it."

"Change it how?"

"I've got a designer working on it," she said. "She's talking to me about shaving off the rest of my hair. Then something— Well . . . Something more revealing. She's got several ideas."

"Sounds different enough," said Hugh. "I—"

His telephone buzzed. He picked it up, shrugged an apology to Adela and took the call. It was from Lawton Lanier.

"I appreciate your returning my call," he said. "I'm afraid I'm going to have to ask you to appear as a witness in a matter. No. Only one day. Only part of one day. It's

295

a disciplinary hearing before a subcommittee of the bar association. Right, out of that business with Jack Putnam and Vanessa Kingston. That's right. That's how I feel. Okay. What I'd like to do is sit down with you for half an hour, probably not more, and discuss your testimony. Can we set an appointment for that? Well, the hearing is in two weeks—Tuesday, February 2. Okay, thanks. No, I'll come to your office. Ten? That'll be fine."

For a moment after he put down the phone, Hugh sat looking at Adela, not seeing her, with his lower lip drawn back between his teeth. Then his focus shifted abruptly, and he said, "Something more revealing . . . What's become of you and Jesus?"

Her father: "I can't help but think your obligations argue persuasively against your leaving the city this weekend."

Rick: "The shit's hit the fan, Cosima. Is this thing that serious?"

Joan: "Go, for god's sake. The world won't fall apart."

She flew to L.A. from Kennedy on Friday afternoon, knowing Jack would not be back from a location shoot until nearly midnight. He had hidden the key to his apartment and told her on the telephone where to find it. A taxi dropped her in Malibu, about six. She found the key.

His apartment overlooked the beach from across a busy highway, and it had a view of the Pacific. The sun had set, but the sky remained dull red. She explored the rooms, looking for something she could fix for him to eat when he came home. It would have to be sandwiches; he didn't seem to keep much food on hand. She checked his liquor. There was plenty.

In his bedroom closet, with his clothes, she found a negligee and a pair of light blue feathered slippers. They weren't new, not bought for her visit. She didn't pretend to think he was celibate, and she was amused that—either carelessly, or quite honestly—he had left these things for her to see.

She supposed, really, that he would have hidden or disposed of anything he didn't want her to see, and she was entirely bold in exploring the apartment.

He had a piano in his living room, and apparently he played. She hadn't realized that. Extensive shelves were filled with books, with a gap only where he displayed a family photograph: his parents and his grandfather. Two framed playbills for Off-Broadway shows hung above the piano—featuring his name as star. At least twenty of his books were tomes on the crafts of acting and directing. Among his records was a Bull Dog Fangs album, a recent one, purchased out of curiosity, she had no doubt.

She mixed herself a martini, using his Beefeater gin. She took it to his bedroom, where she sipped it as she undressed. She decided to take a nap, since he would not be home until late. She sat his alarm clock for ten, and when she had finished her drink she stretched out on the bed.

She loved him. She could think of reasons why she shouldn't, but she did. His self-esteem was healthy and real—and not an obsession with him. He didn't have to pretend. He didn't have to exaggerate. He was as scornful of machismo as she was. He felt no obligation to prove his manhood. It was there, it was a fact, and he was comfortable with it. And she wanted to see him. Needed to see him. This was something new in her adult womanhood: a new vulnerability. Unexpected. Disturbing.

The alarm woke her. She showered, then dressed in the intimate things she had bought for this trip—a sheer black nightgown that blurred the lines and colors of her body only by its score of narrow vertical pleats, except at the tight-fitting bodice, where a wide strip of fine black net exhibited her breasts. Across her hips she wore a black silk G-string. Black silk high-heeled shoes completed the costume.

She had a sense of its proposterousness, yet an appreciation that it would titillate—which was its purpose. *He* would love it. For that reason, *she* would wear it.

"Aw Jeez, *Cosima!*"

They were the words she had expected. And he drew her into his arms and squeezed her, kissing her fervently, pressing their hips together so she could feel his erection.

"A goddamn *angel* is what you are! An *angel.*"

He had said he was playing a steelworker. He looked like a steelworker, smelled like what she imagined a steelworker must smell like: sweat and dirt. He was unshaven. His hair was wildly unkempt. And she felt in him the fatigue of a man who had put in a hard day. For a moment it was a vignette from a life neither of them had ever known, maybe the source of a glimmer of understanding.

"Hey!" he said. "Cosima . . ." He shook his head. "I *love* you, honey baby!"

She kissed his throat, his cheeks, his eyes, finally his mouth. "I didn't *want* to love you like this, Jack," she told him in a husky whisper. "I didn't need this. And all that doesn't make any difference. I *love* you! *I love you, Jack!*"

"For a month I've been remembering that . . . that velvety tongue—all around, all up and down, all over. You'll do that for me, won't you, baby?"

Cosima lifted her chin, twisted her neck, thrust out her breasts. "I'm good at that, aren't I? Tell me I'm the best you ever knew."

"The *best!* The goddamned best, Cosima."

"Then I'll do it. If I'm the best, I'll do it."

Fifteen

The subcommittee of the Association of the Bar assembled around a conference table in a drab, dusty, walnut-panelled room. The maroon carpet was threadbare. The thick, dark varnish of the paneling was checked from age and dryness. Bulbs burning orange inside milky white globes lighted the room meagerly and cheerlessly.

The five members and their counsel sat together at one end of the table, with their chairman at the head. Burton Oliver sat at the right side of the table, more than halfway down: the complainant. Cosima and Hugh Hupp, her counsel, sat opposite him. At the foot of the table a reporter took the record on a Stenograph.

Burton Oliver settled a moment's hard stare on Cosima, lowering his chin a bit so he would see her through the upper half of his rimless bifocals; then he pinched his lips even tighter on his pipe and turned his attention to the chairman.

The chairman of the subcommittee was Robert L. Blocker, a senior partner from Gardner, Finley, Levin & Ferris—a trim, handsome, gray-haired man, also wearing rimless glasses. He had made a point of circulating, speaking to everyone, and he opened the meeting precisely on the hour by introducing the members of the subcommittee to Cosima and Hugh. Besides himself, the members were P. D. (for Paul Donald) Dougherty of Quarles & McGrath; William Tate of Johnson, McNamara, Cohen & Bauman; Robert Blyleven of Maxwell, Donovan, Margolin & Stanley; and James Reardon of Reardon & Smith. Also at the table was John McGowan, committee counsel.

"The matter before the subcommittee is an unfortunate one," Blocker said in a dry, almost raspy voice. "It involves a complaint by one member of the bar, Mr. Burton Oliver, against another, Miss Cosima Bernardin. "Let the record show that Miss Bernardin is present and represented by her counsel, Mr. Hugh Hupp. Mr. Oliver is present. I understand there are some witnesses waiting outside. Mr. Oliver, as complainant, do you have any preliminary motion you wish to make before we proceed?"

Oliver pulled his pipe from his mouth. He shook his head. "No."

"Miss Bernardin?"

Hugh Hupp shook his head, but Cosima spoke. "I have a request, Mr. Chairman," she said. "Since this room does not seem to be very well ventilated, I think we would all be better served if no one smoked."

Besides Oliver with his pipe, two members of the subcommittee were smoking cigarettes. James Reardon smiled and crushed out his cigarette. P. D. Dougherty glared at Cosima and shook his head, then dropped his cigarette in the ashtray where it lay in a litter of old butts and smoldered. Oliver knocked his pipe on his ashtray and tucked it in his jacket pocket.

The chairman turned over sheets in his file. "Mr. Oliver," he said, "has brought to the attention of the Association a certain complaint relative to interference in—"

"*Alleged* interference," said Hugh.

Blocker nodded. "—alleged interference," he continued without changing his tone or pace, "in Mr. Oliver's representation of his client, one Vanessa Kingston. If the facts

300

alleged by Mr. Oliver are true, they would constitute misconduct by Miss Bernardin in violation of the Standards of Professional Conduct. The subcommittee has heard Mr. Oliver before, but he has not been heard formally or in the presence of Miss Bernardin or her counsel. So, we will hear him again. Mr. Oliver.''

Hugh interrupted. ''Mr. Chairman, is this going to be sworn testimony, or an unsworn statement?''

Blocker shrugged lightly. ''Which would you prefer, Mr. Hupp?''

''The accusation made against Miss Bernardin,'' said Hugh, ''is based solely on the complaint of Mr. Oliver. I doubt there is any evidence whatever of the facts he alleges. Indeed, there couldn't be, because what he alleges isn't true. Now, if this subcommittee is going to proceed simply on his naked statements, without any testimony or other evidence, then I'm going to move the subcommittee drop the matter and forget it.''

''I'd be glad to be sworn, Mr. Chairman,'' said Oliver. ''In fact, I'd prefer it.''

''Very well,'' said Blocker. ''Raise your right hand, please.''

Cosima was in a defiant, impatient mood. She never liked to be questioned, and to be at the mercy of this subcommittee was outrageous. Who were these men? Only one of them—Reardon—practiced in a small firm. The rest were partners in big firms. Dougherty and Tate were older than the chairman; Blyleven and Reardon looked like junior partners, under forty.

John McGowan, their counsel, was a little man with piercing dark brown eyes in a tiny, tanned face. He was as bald as Oliver, but his head was tanned and not liver-spotted. If she judged him right, he was valued by the Association for thoroughness and precision, for presenting facts and never offering an opinion.

''Do you solemnly swear that the evidence you are about to give in these proceedings will be the truth, the whole

301

truth, and nothing but the truth, as you shall answer to God?"

"I do."

On this cold, formidable January morning, she had elected to wear her gray checked coat and trousers with her black cashmere turtleneck. It was a measure of disdain, maybe—and so at least one member of the committee took it, if she understood the glance he had given her when she came in.

Oliver began his statement—

"In August of last year I was retained by a young woman named Vanessa Kingston. She is an actress. For some six years she had been the companion of the actor John Putnam, known as Jack Putnam. Mr. Putnam had abruptly terminated the relationship, and Miss Kingston believed she had a claim against him, based on an explicit agreement between them that she would help support him as he built his career, in return for which he would offer her help and support in the event he became successful. He did, of course, become successful, and shortly after that he dismissed Miss Kingston."

"According to her," said Hugh.

Oliver nodded. "According to what she told me in my office in August. So . . . I contacted Mr. Putnam and advised him of Miss Kingston's claim. Essentially, he ignored it. He spoke to Miss Kingston on the telephone once or twice, but he would not return my calls or letters. I notified him of our intention to sue.

"Shortly I received a call from Miss Bernardin, notifying me that she was Mr. Putnam's attorney. And a little later Miss Bernardin came to my office to discuss the possibility of settlement. She became rather angry during our discussion and told me her client would not pay a cent. I was surprised at this, because he had made an offer of settlement—one that was entirely inadequate, but an offer just the same. She told me to go ahead and sue, she wouldn't talk to me any more."

Oliver took his cold pipe from his pocket and turned it over and over in his hands as he spoke. "Approximately a week after I met with Miss Bernardin, my client came to my office and told me she wanted to drop her claim against Jack Putnam. When I asked why, she said she'd been offered a role in a motion picture which was to be shot in Europe and that she would not be available for depositions, for a trial, for anything. I said we could work the schedule around her employment commitment, but she insisted she wanted to drop the claim. When I pressed her for more explanation, she told me she had already signed a release of any rights she had against Jack Putnam, that signing such a release had been an element of her employment contract.

"The contract was with a producer named Lawton Lanier. I inquired around as to who he might be and learned he is an English producer, recently come to New York, and I learned that he is a personal friend of Miss Cosima Bernardin. It was perfectly obvious what had happened. Miss Bernardin asked Mr. Lanier for a favor—and she got it."

Oliver paused, looking uptight and dissatisfied. Cosima stared at him contemptuously. He *should* have been dissatisfied, she thought—his statement was weak, incomplete.

"Mr. Oliver," the chairman prompted him, "please state for the record and for the benefit of Miss Bernardin and her counsel just how Miss Bernardin's alleged arrangement with Mr. Lanier violates the Standards of Conduct."

Oliver sighed, tightened his lips over his teeth and said, "Miss Kingston's claim against Mr. Putnam was bona fide. It might not have prevailed in court, but it was a real claim, which she was entitled to press, even to litigate. I so advised her. She was represented by her own counsel, and so long as I represented Miss Kingston it was a violation of the canons of ethics for another attorney to contact my client, directly or through a surrogate, out of my presence and without my knowledge, and obtain from her a release she was ill-advised to sign. Such conduct constitutes an interference in the lawyer-client relationship. I can cite you many cases that so hold."

Oliver paused again, and the chairman asked if he was finished. He said he had a witness. "Before we hear your witness," said the chairman, "we will let Mr. Hupp ask such questions as he may want to ask. Mr. Hupp?"

Hugh rubbed his hands together before his chin and blew on them. "Your complaint, Mr. Oliver," he said slowly, "is one hundred percent *surmise*. You *suppose* Mr. Lanier acted at the behest of Miss Bernardin. Do you have any evidence of what you suppose? Is that what we are going to hear from the witness you are going to call?"

"Do you suggest, Mr. Hupp," asked Oliver, "it is a *coincidence* that within a week after a rather unpleasant confrontation between me and Miss Bernardin, Miss Kingston came to me and told me she had been offered a lucrative movie contract by a friend of Miss Bernardin's and had signed a release that friend demanded of her? Is it a coincidence that she was offered a movie role that week, when she had tried for years to get one and could never get it before?"

"*I'm* interested in the answer to *that* question," said P. D. Dougherty, the man who had scowled when asked to put out his cigarette. "I understand from the prior statement Mr. Oliver made that this man Lanier has refused to talk to Mr. Oliver. Is that right, Mr. Oliver? For the record."

"That is correct, Mr. Dougherty," said Oliver, nodding.

"The sequence of events," said Dougherty, "is rather persuasive circumstantial evidence—in my estimation."

"Mr. Hupp? Further questions?"

Hugh shrugged. "What for? He's *guessing* about what happened. That's all he's doing—guessing."

"For the record, Mr. Oliver," said the chairman, "tell us about your efforts to get a statement from Miss Kingston."

"Unavailing," said Oliver.

"Other questions? Anyone? Then do you want to call your witness, Mr. Oliver?"

Oliver licked his lips. The absence of his pipe stem between them caused a set of nervous tics: licking, biting, flexing. "I would like to call Mr. Daniel Nash," he said.

"Son of a bitch," Cosima muttered quietly in Hugh's ear.

"I like it," Hugh whispered. "He's about to step on his cock."

McGowan went out to bring in Nash. Nash walked in, smiling, nodding to each of the members of the subcommittee. He had just put aside one of his little cigars, and the smoke still trickled from the corners of his mouth. He remained standing while the chairman swore him to tell the truth. When he sat down his eyes still had not met Cosima's.

"Mr. Nash," said Oliver. "Please tell the subcommittee your firm affiliation."

Nash nodded and smiled. "I am a partner with Hamilton, Schuyler, Depew & Chase."

"And Miss Bernardin was once a partner there. Is that correct?"

"That is correct."

"Describe for the committee the circumstances in which Miss Bernardin was discharged from the firm."

"*Objection,*" Hugh growled. "The circumstances that led Miss Bernardin to *resign* from Hamilton, Schuyler, Depew & Chase are wholly irrelevant to the allegations Mr. Oliver has made." He grabbed a sheet of paper from his file and tossed it in the center of the table. "Mr. McGowan's letter to Miss Bernardin, stating the nature of the allegations she would face in this proceeding, explicitly limits the scope of this hearing to the matter of Mr. Oliver's representation of Miss Kingston and Miss Bernardin's representation of Mr. Putnam."

"I understand," said Dougherty, "that Mr. Nash can

offer some insights into Miss Bernardin's overall character."

"Miss Bernardin's character is not in question," snapped Hugh. "Mr. Oliver has alleged that she committed a specific unethical act—of which of course he's presented no evidence. That is *all* this hearing is about. That is what we were *notified* it's about. If you wander off to any other subject, the whole proceeding is a nullity. Due process objections."

"I suppose," the chairman mused, as if he were voicing thoughts not fully formed, "that a predilection toward unethical conduct, if it were displayed during Miss Bernardin's tenure at—"

Hugh interrupted, slapping his hand on the table. "Mr. Chairman," he declared, "if Mr. Nash is allowed to testify in this proceeding—that is, about events at Hamilton, Schuyler—the proceeding becomes nugatory. But I may tell you something further. If Mr. Nash testifies, then I will have the right to impeach him as a witness. And I will insist on that right, and I *will* impeach him."

"Seems to me," said Dougherty, *"that* would be going far afield. What do you mean, impeach him?"

Hugh planted a hand on the arm of his chair and pushed himself more erect. "When a witness testifies, his veracity is a relevant issue. Hornbook law."

"Do you mean," asked William Tate, "you question Mr. Nash's *veracity?*"

Hugh leaned back. "I certainly do, Mr. Chairman," he said. "I will be glad of the opportunity to question him under oath." He nodded. "Glad of it. Been looking forward to the chance. Didn't imagine I'd get it here today."

"I'm not sure we can permit that kind of cross-examination," said the chairman uneasily.

"Then so rule, Mr. Chairman," said Hugh scornfully. "Then we will have on the record, first, your ruling that opens this hearing to issues never raised in our notice, and, second, your ruling denying me the right to the most basic cross-examination of a hostile witness. Rule that way, Mr. Chairman, and we can all push back our chairs and go home—this whole business will have become futile."

During this exchange, Oliver and Nash had been whispering urgently. Now Oliver turned to the chairman. "Mr. Chairman," he said in a strained voice. "In order to spare Mr. Nash from embarrassment, I'm excusing him as a witness."

"Bob," said Dougherty to the chairman. "Do you share my feelings that we've lost control of this hearing?"

The chairman removed his glasses and rubbed his eyes. "The thought has occurred to me," he said wryly. He turned to Nash to excuse him, but Nash was already on his way to the door: his anger apparent in his stride and the set of his shoulders. "Mr. Hupp," said Blocker. "Since you appear to have seized control here, what do you want to do now?"

"I want to move that the charge be dismissed," said Hugh. "But before I do that, we do have a witness. I'm not sure why we bother, but since Mr. Dougherty seems to think there might be circumstantial evidence of misconduct by Miss Bernardin, maybe we had better hear from him. Mr. Lanier is waiting outside."

Lawton Lanier was sworn in and sat down comfortably. He was a man of distinguished appearance: yellowish white hair carefully combed across his long head, ruddy cheeks, penetrating gray-blue eyes, a cleft chin—altogether a rather handsome man, looking perhaps a little older than his fifty-five years. His speech was Oxonian; he had picked up almost no Americanisms. He wore a gray flannel suit and a cream yellow tattersall vest.

"Miss Bernardin herself will question Mr. Lanier," said Hugh.

Cosima took a moment to face Lanier with a quizzical little smile, as she ran an index finger lightly across her chin. "You and I are friends, aren't we Lawton?"

"I am pleased to number you among my friends," said Lanier.

"And if I asked you for a favor, you'd probably do it."

"If 'twas in my power," said Lanier.

"So did you do me one with respect to Vanessa Kingston?"

Lanier tipped his head to one side and shook it calmly. "No. Did her one, perhaps. Did myself one, perhaps. Didn't do a favor for you, Cosima."

"Did I ask you to give Vanessa Kingston a contract?"

"No."

"Did I ask you to secure from her a release for Jack Putnam?"

"No."

Cosima turned to the chairman, smiled and shrugged.

"Mr. Oliver?" said the chairman.

Oliver shook his head.

"Well, *I* have a question or two," said Dougherty. "Mr. Lanier, why did you refuse to talk to Mr. Oliver?"

Lanier regarded Dougherty curiously, as if he wondered who this intrusive man might be. "I saw no reason why I should," he said blandly. "Miss Kingston's description of him didn't make him seem like the sort of chap I'd care to know."

"You felt no obligation to talk to him?"

"What possible obligation had I?"

P. D. Dougherty was a senior partner in the corporation-law department at Quarles & McGrath. His straight, thick hair was white, but his brows were black. His forehead was long, his jaw was long and his pale blue eyes were all but hidden by his drooping lids. "None, I suppose," he said sarcastically to Lanier. "But, tell me, how did you come to call on Miss Kingston to audition for you at that particular time?"

"I didn't," said Lanier. "That is, precisely said, I didn't call her in to read for me. I'd heard her read. I suppose she answered every casting call for five years. She—"

"And never got a part," said Dougherty.

"Not a-tawl," said Lanier. "She'd had parts. I knew her name and had formed a judgment of her talent. When I had a role that suited her, it was quite natural I should think of her."

"So it *was* a coincidence that you found a role for Vanessa Kingston a week after Miss Bernardin met Mr. Oliver?"

Lanier shrugged. "Something like that," he said insouciantly.

"How did you know Miss Kingston was threatening to sue Jack Putnam?"

"Miss Kingston told me, of course."

"And why, then, did you ask her to sign a paper releasing Putnam from her claim?"

"Chiefly because I didn't want her getting the kind of public notice that would come from such a lawsuit. 'Twas bound to be negative. Anyway, her talent wasn't so great that she could work with a big emotional distraction. I simply told her—I've an opportunity for you, but I want you free of all such complications."

"And it is your sworn testimony that Miss Bernardin did not suggest to you that you obtain this release?"

Lawton Lanier settled a bold, steady gaze on P. D. Dougherty. "It is," he said quietly.

"They are not stupid," said Hugh over their pre-lunch drinks at 21. "Oliver is stupid. Nash is stupid. But"—he shook his head emphatically—"the five members of that subcommittee are not stupid."

"All they have to work with," said Cosima, "is what's on the record."

Hugh nodded. "Which is nothing. But they know what's behind the record. They can't do a thing about it, but they won't forget it."

"Not very nice fellows, I thought," said Lawton Lanier.

He sipped from his glass of Glenfiddich, neat. "The little fellow who waited outside with me. Uh . . ."

"Nash," said Cosima.

"Yes. He came storming out, glared at me as though *I* had done something evil to him, grabbed his coat and stalked off."

"I think they'd have dismissed after Oliver made such a weak case and I ran Nash out of the room," said Hugh. "I think we engaged in a bit of overkill—which may come back to haunt us."

"I enjoyed it," said Lanier.

Walking out of Association headquarters and up the street, Cosima had been moved by two sentiments: exultation over a satisfying victory, certainly, but also uneasiness over how the victory had been won. Burton Oliver had never been a worthy antagonist. (She had in fact said to Jack that a fly swatter would be enough armament to dispose of him.) Still, he had subjected her to a humiliating process, had compelled her to defend herself before a kangaroo court; she had hoped to *annihilate* him in this morning's hearing. Those men—they were his *cronies*: contemptuous of women lawyers, especially young women lawyers, every one of them. She . . .

But maybe Hugh was right. Maybe she had overreacted. And, of course, she *had* explained the whole problem to Lawton Lanier and asked for his help. She had not specifically asked him to give Vanessa a role, but of course it was not a coincidence that he had. She had not asked Lanier to perjure himself; yet, she couldn't deny she had thought he might. It was an unfortunate way to launch a new career in the law.

"How is Vanessa doing?" she asked Lanier, anxious to change the subject.

He raised his glass again. "When I engaged her for her role," he said, "my hope was that the film would play in theaters. Now I have begun to think it will run as a two-hour television special. That is bad news for Vanessa—and maybe good, at the same time. Because of the editing for television, her part may be cut short. On the other hand, it is an essential role, so she may have a continuing part in the series that will develop from the pilot.''

"Nothing is ever easy, is it?" Cosima asked. "Nothing is ever conclusive, nothing ever simple. It never just happens, huh?" she asked Hugh.

"Today," he said, "we won the Battle of Austerlitz. Will we face a Waterloo?" He shrugged. "Look at it another way. The soldiers who won at Antietam also won at Gettysburg. Victories are always an advantage. We wear our laurels. Let somebody try to knock them off."

Cosima sighed heavily. "I am grateful to both of you," she said. "Some people tried to knock my laurels off today. And instead we knocked them off their pins. For today. For . . . today."

Svetlana Terasnova scampered off the Lincoln Center stage: breathless, flushed, beaming to the applause of the other dancers who stood in the wings. The applause from the audience continued: a sustained roar of approval and enthusiasm.

"Once more!" yelled the stage manager.

Lana trotted out again. She stood for another quarter minute, letting the applause envelop her like a great warm blanket; then, with a refined sense of timing, detecting the least ebbing, she scampered off again.

"Bravo!" It was her manager, Aleksandr Khvostov. "Beautiful, Lana! Lovely!"

"Thank you, Shondor," she said. She started toward her dressing room. She had been aware that he was not alone, that another man had been standing with Shondor in the dim backstage light; but she had paid no attention, until now when she realized that the other man was walking beside Shondor as he followed her toward the dressing rooms.

Her room was small, but it had space for a chaise lounge

311

and a chair, besides the chair in front of the mirror. It was brightly lighted, and when Shondor led the man into the room, she recognized him.

"You have met Mr. Paccinelli, I believe," said Shondor.

"Yes," she said uncertainly. She had of course met him, at the Bernardin Christmas party. She had been impressed, but she remembered what Cosima had said of him: that he was an aggressive man, in whose presence she should be cautious.

"At the party in Greenwich," said Jerry. "You danced beautifully that night—almost as beautifully as you did tonight. And my congratulations, incidentally, on a marvelous performance."

Lana nodded. "Thank you," she said quietly.

Paccinelli. He performed in obscenely tight rubber clothes, under garish strobe lights. She had seen his poster in Cosima's office. Tonight he was most conservatively dressed, in a dark blue suit.

"You are exquisitely beautiful, too," said Jerry.

She nodded again. She was wearing a costume of black fishnet over a flesh-colored body stocking, for the role of Death in the Martha Graham ballet they were performing tonight. Although striking, dramatic—even erotic—on stage, the costume was not flattering up close and in flat light; there it lost all its magic and looked contrived, even shoddy: she would have preferred Shondor and Mr. Paccinelli had stayed away from her dressing room until after she joined the company for their final bows and could put on street clothes. She was self-conscious, too, for her stage makeup; it was for the stage, not for personal contact.

"Mr. Paccinelli," said Shondor, "is thinking of writing and sponsoring a ballet."

Jerry nodded affirmation. "You remember," he said. "I mentioned the idea at the party. It may not be apparent in most of what we do, but the kind of music I write and perform has its discipline, not alien to the discipline of the ballet. I think the two disciplines can be merged. Indeed,

312

they *have* been merged. I think it is possible to stage something"—he stopped, and for a moment she was unsure of why; she suspected it was for dramatic effect, not likely because he was moved by what he was saying . . . yet, could she be sure?—"artistically valid," he said, astonishing her by the conclusion his sentence had reached.

"Mr. Paccinelli," said Shondor, "is thinking of funding this project."

Lana turned to the mirror, to see if her perspiration had streaked her makeup.

"He has provided us with copies of reviews of his music," said Shondor. "He is highly respected, by famous critics."

Cosima had said as much: that Ruggiero Paccinelli was an esteemed composer, one whose reputation was minor yet solid. His talent was conceded only grudgingly, she had said, by critics who despised what he did on stage but could not deny his genius, however much they wanted to. She turned away from her mirror, to look more intently on this man she had, at Cosima's suggestion, all but ignored.

He was quintessentially male. He exuded it. Shondor was a man, an uncompromising masculine figure with none of the ambivalence that so disgusted her in too many men in the theater; but next to Ruggiero Paccinelli—Jerry Patchen—he was an anemic incarnation of basal virility. The man flaunted it.

"Mr. Paccinelli," said Shondor, "would like to discuss with us the possibility of a ballet in his unique idiom."

And this was how Lana found herself in a luxurious suite in the Hyatt Regency Hotel on Forty-second Street, as midnight approached, sipping champagne and facing an elegant dinner ordered by Jerry and served by obsequious waiters. He was not only a paradigm of masculinity; he was a dominating man who had skillfully put Shondor aside and brought her here alone—for a purpose neither she nor Shondor had for a moment misunderstood.

He spoke frankly of the show he wanted to produce. He

talked about the music he would write, about the songs and dance that would intrigue the American audience and earn a thousand fortunes.

"Nothing that would damage your reputation or career, you understand," he said. "I want to write a *ballet*, not a rock musical—a ballet combined with a dramatic play with music."

"What would *your* role be?" she asked.

"Maybe none," he said. "Probably none. I will write. And produce, maybe direct. I don't think I should appear on stage. That would be a distraction. Also a risk. I mean, the critics would likely address what they anticipated, not what they saw. Frankly, Lana, I have little or no talent for performance. I *created* Bull Dog Fangs. Someone else could perform it."

She watched him fillet the two trout left by the waiters. They had offered to do it, but Jerry preferred to do it himself—and did it deftly.

"Perhaps I should not be surprised by your modesty," she said. "But I am."

"Honesty," he said. "Not modesty. I am not modest. But when I watch you perform, I know you are doing something I could never do."

Lana ran her hands down her legs, over the rough denim of the jeans she had put on in her dressing room. She had expected to go home to her apartment afterward, not to come to a sumptuous dinner in an opulent suite. She was self-conscious of the faded blue jeans and black sweatshirt.

She was conscious too of why she was here, of his expectation. She was realistic about that. She would not have come here if she had felt unable to deal with it. He was going to ask her to let him—What was the American word?—fuck her. So . . . Why not? Wasn't she a woman? She wanted to do that sometimes. She needed to do it. Why not with a handsome, virile, personable man—one with also a boyish artlessness. He would be grateful. He could be a good friend.

"Lana . . ."

So. He spoke softly. He was about to make the proposition.

"After dinner," he said, "I can take you home. I'll go with you in a cab and make sure you're safely home. I'd hoped, though, that you might stay."

Lana lowered her eyes and nodded. "I expected this," she said quietly.

He reached across the table and put his hand on hers. "Only if you want to," he said.

She looked up into his eyes. Her solemn little face softened with the intimation of a smile. "I do not mind," she said.

Jerry grinned. "Don't mind," he laughed. "I think I may just have been very adeptly put down."

Lana looked at him with sober, puzzled curiosity. "What I mean is, I would not dislike fucking with you."

He laughed again. "You would not dislike it. All right. But do you think you might *like* it?"

She nodded. "Maybe . . . Probably."

"Then . . . ?"

She turned her head from side to side, looking at the array of food spread before them on the room-service tables. "After dinner?" she asked solemnly.

Jerry tried to choke back his laugh, for fear of offending her, ruining her complaisant mood. "Yes," he hurried to say. "Yes, after dinner. We have all night."

"Yes."

"Lana . . . Would you take off your clothes? I know you are very beautiful. I would like to be able to look at you while we eat."

Should she indulge him? She asked herself, then answered, why not? Tonight she felt like being a little reckless.

Stripping took only a moment. She exposed to him the trained and constantly exercised body of a dancer: hard little breasts, flat belly, taut bottom, sleekly muscled arms and legs. He was intrigued by how nonchalantly she stripped for

315

him and with what unruffled poise she sat there nude and sipped from her glass of champagne.

"You're a goddess, Lana," he said; and that didn't stir her either. He wondered if he'd be able to arouse her in bed.

Her penetrating eyes were fixed on him. "You have done this with Cosima too?" she asked.

"Let's don't talk about Cosima," he said. "In fact . . . Lana, it would be better if we don't tell Cosima about tonight. Or even about the show we might do. Not yet."

Lana nodded.

Sixteen

"So far, so good," said Emilie on the telephone. "The vote was twenty-three to five. So we've got a recommendation from Judiciary. Now I've got to get it out of Rules and onto the floor of the House—and that won't be so easy."

"The Rules Committee—"

"Opposition won't be the problem. The problem will be scheduling."

"The five who voted no . . . What did they say?" asked Cosima.

"Nothing. Just voted no. Pryor offered the report of the Subcommittee and moved to report the bill. Diggins seconded. There was no discussion. But five voted no. Their reason was very clear—they knew who Svetlana Terasnova is and why we're going for a private bill. Someone had talked to them."

"Our friends from the Justice Department," said Cosima.

"I would assume so."

"Who were the five? Right-wing ideologues?"

"Four Republicans, one Democrat," said Emilie.

"They didn't argue the case in committee because they

knew you had the votes to get the bill out," said Cosima. "That means, I suppose, that they are looking for somewhere else to take their stand. On the floor . . . ?"

"I don't know," said Emilie. "But now is the time to start your public relations campaign. Get me news stories. Get me editorials. I'm going to need clippings."

"I've got some lined up," said Cosima. "I'll call for those and get to work on arranging others."

"The more the better, kid," said Emilie.

Cosima had taken this call at her parents' house on Round Hill, where Emilie had telephoned on Friday evening after the recorder had answered a call to Cosima's apartment. When she put the phone down, Cosima returned to the living room, where her father was sipping the second of his pre-dinner martinis, her mother was staring distractedly into a glass empty but for ice cubes, Susanne was pouring Stolichnaya over ice and Bert sat on the couch before the fire, warming himself and drinking a double martini.

They were comfortable: Cosima and Susanne in soft jeans and sweatshirts, Bert in corduroys and a sweater. Leon, from lifelong habit, was comfortable in his three-piece darkblue suit.

"That was important, I take it," her father said, a little reproachful that Cosima should have left the room to take a telephone call at this hour, even from Emilie.

"The House Judiciary Committee reported out Lana's bill," said Cosima. "She wants me to put the PR campaign in high gear now."

Bert turned and spoke to her over the back of the couch. "I can run your spot on 'What's News?' any time you want it."

"I'm grateful for that, Bert, and I do want it," said Cosima, retrieving her martini from a side table.

"I should like to inquire of something," said Leon. "It would appear to me that a great deal of money is going into this campaign of yours to save the Terasnova girl from deportation. Is she paying it? Or any part of it? Where is the money coming from?''

Cosima frowned at her martini, where the ice had melted while she was on the telephone. She stepped to the bar, picked up another glass, put in ice, poured herself a fresh drink. "Lana has very little," she said. "It's *my* project for now."

"So the case you describe as the most important that you are handling isn't earning you any fees?"

Cosima nodded. "Essentially."

Elizabeth carried her empty glass to the bar and poured in a big drink of Scotch. She glanced around, then abruptly left the room.

"I have another question," said Leon. "Have you heard further from the committee that was investigating you?"

Cosima drank from her glass as she sat down beside Bert. "As a matter of fact, I have," she said. "A messenger brought a letter this afternoon, from John McGowan, the lawyer for the association. The subcommittee has recommended to the full committee that the Oliver complaint be dropped."

"What was the vote?"

"The letter didn't say. I doubt I could find out. It's probably a secret."

"Then is the matter finished?"

"The subcommittee found," she said, "that the Oliver charge was not supported by 'any probative evidence' but only by 'circumstantial evidence and speculation.' " She shrugged. "And that does, indeed, finish the matter."

"Have you called Jack?"

"No. I only got the letter this afternoon. He's out on location. I don't know if I could reach him."

"You should try," said Leon. "I'm sure he's concerned. It was, after all, his legal problem that—"

"I don't think I can reach him before Sunday."

"Ahh . . . Sunday." Her father nodded thoughtfully.

319

"Jack has been worried about this, you know. He told me he was."

"I know."

"You should relieve his anxiety, Cosima."

"I will."

"If *you* don't, *he* will," Susanne sneered.

"I could maybe get the boys at 'Sixty Minutes' to take a look at the Svetlana case," said Bert to Cosima. His thoughts had not shifted to the subject of her hearing—or maybe he had heard his wife provoking her father and wanted to cut her short. "Maybe I could."

"Anything you can do, Bert."

"Did it ever occur to either of you," Susanne asked, "that getting the girl a lot of public attention might be the worst thing you can do for her? Did you ever think of maybe just trying to slip the thing through?"

Cosima shook her head. "Can't be done. Lana is already a cause célèbre at the Justice Department."

"And you stand no chance of winning in court?" asked Leon.

"None whatever. The way the law reads, she is one hundred percent deportable. All we can try to do is delay deportation until the bill is passed."

"Is there no alternative to her being sent back to the Soviet Union?" Leon asked.

"Another element of the problem," said Cosima. "I've also got to try to find another country that will take her, if it comes to that. I'm hoping the public relations campaign will help with this, too."

"What word from the redoubtable Ruggiero Paccinelli?" asked Susanne.

"He's talking about doing a videotape," said Cosima.

"It would be hard to get Fangs on the air," said Bert. "They're a little too raunchy for the networks."

"Too raunchy for cable, even," said Cosima. "At least that's the reaction so far, except from the Playboy channel.

Anyway, Jerry doesn't really care. He thinks there's more money in selling the tape than in having it broadcast.''

"What's *your* part in this?" Leon asked.

"The contracts," said Cosima. "We're negotiating a complex deal. This will be a copy-proof videotape. A new technology. Everybody who wants the tape will have to buy his own.''

"Of course, if you broadcast it—"

"Right. It could be taped off the air or off cable. That's another reason why Jerry isn't particularly interested in broadcasting.''

"Well . . ." said Leon. "If your mother returns, we can go in to dinner." He tipped his glass and drank the last of his martini. "If your mother returns . . .''

Elizabeth did return shortly. She handed Cosima a check for fifteen thousand dollars. "For Lana Terasnova," she said. "For her fees and other costs. That's a beginning. There'll be a lot more.''

"Mother, I—I can't accept—"

"I made two phone calls," said Elizabeth. "That produced twelve thousand. I added three from my own account—which I'm sure your father will match. You can count on a hundred thousand. I'm sure I can raise it, here and in Boston. I want you to set up an account, Leon, that Cosima can draw on. As checks come in, I'll deposit them, and she can use the money to meet the expenses of saving that girl from deportation.''

Susanne and Bert were returning to the City after dinner, on the 11:06 from Cos Cob. Since they left the house on Round Hill before ten, Cosima suggested they come to her condo for a drink; they could walk over to the station from there.

Bert went to the bathroom. Susanne opened the drapes and stood looking at the Sound.

"It's gotten serious between you and Jack, I understand."

"You could say that."

"How serious?"

"Very serious."

Susanne grinned. "You're a good girl, Cosima."

"What prompts that comment?"

Susanne took a swallow of her Stolichnaya. "You've dutifully fallen in love with the man the parents picked for you."

"Susanne . . . Damn it!"

"It's true. The man they really wanted you to marry was Bill Kemper. They—"

"Susanne. That's cruel."

"I just want to remind you what a baneful influence the parents can be. Kemper was handsome. Kemper had money. Kemper was a good Catholic. The fact that he was an egomaniacal little prick didn't bother them—he was still the perfect match, just what they wanted for their beautiful new-lawyer daughter. They *pushed* him at you, Cosima. You were damned lucky he *was* an egomaniacal little prick. Otherwise you probably would have married him—and would probably be divorced from him by now."

Cosima sighed. "I was in love with him, don't forget, *before* Mother and Dad started pushing him."

"They could see what he was, and they pushed him anyway. They would have been happy to see you marry a prick, because it would have been a 'suitable' marriage."

"I'm in love with Jack," said Cosima.

"Are you? Or do you think you're *supposed* to be?"

"It's all right with Jack and me. It'll be okay."

Susanne glanced toward the guest room door, beyond which Bert remained in the bathroom. "Charles is the only one of us whose marriage partner wasn't nominated by Mother or Dad," she said. "They arranged Pierre and Lucy, Emilie and Tom—"

"Bert?" Cosima asked. "I thought—"

322

"They didn't pick him for me, but once they met him they pushed him, too. They'd been afraid I'd marry a tennis bum. They didn't like the looks of Bert, but he was such an improvement over what they thought I'd hook onto that they got behind him and pushed. And that's what they're doing to you now, pushing Jack between you and Rick, you and Jerry—both of whom scare the hell out of them."

"Jerry? They don't know I—"

"The hell they don't. Half the goddamned *town* knows it, Cosima. Knows that *I* did it, too. Anyway, you might be surprised at how much Dad knows. It's his business to know things, and when it comes to his family, he—"

"Spies on us," Cosima conceded.

"Ever since Bill Kemper, they've been scared to death of who you might pick for a husband."

"Well, they didn't pick Jack for me. They just didn't."

" 'Be sure to call Jack, Cosima. Be sure to call him. Relieve his anxiety,' " Susanne mocked.

"All *right*, Susanne!"

"Just thinkin' of *you*, kid sister. Just tryin' to hit you with a little reality. Just don't want you pushed into something you really don't want. So, if you *do* want it . . ." She shrugged. "And you're going to have to forget that—"

"I'm *going* to forget it. I've *already* forgotten it."

"I can't, though," Susanne said pensively. "It's been a long time. I was just nineteen. I'd done it before, but he was the one who made me love it and want it. I'll never forget."

"Try," said Cosima.

A native New Yorker, Rick Loewenstein rode the subways daily and without misgivings. He was only half conscious of the dim, flickering lighting, the dirt, the graffiti, the noise, the swaying, the crowding and the predominance of Spanish in the conversations going on around him. He had a New Yorker's practiced skill at keeping a bland face and never meeting anyone's eyes with his own. Even if he saw someone he knew, he was unlikely to speak. The subway was not a place for camaraderie or conversation.

He was surprised, then, when someone said, "Loewenstein, right?"

He glanced at the man who had spoken and was startled to find almost a mirror image of himself; physically alike, but more than that, dressed much the same, carrying a briefcase as he was, almost certainly another lawyer. He could not place him.

"Bob Blyleven," the man said. "Maxwell, Donovan. We met when we were working on the Cambridge case."

Rick was grateful for the reminder. Without it he would not have remembered the man. "Right," he said. "Nice to see you."

He recalled the Cambridge negotiations. Blyleven had been there as an assistant to a more senior member of his firm, just as Rick had been, and the two of them had developed briefly the empathy that sometimes happens between two strangers who find themselves in the same not-very-comfortable situation: in this case, gofers.

"Tough goddamned day," said Blyleven. He glanced at his watch. "Dammit. Wife'll be . . . gone out, time I get home."

Blyleven had been drinking, Rick decided. Nothing unusual. Out of the office at six-thirty or seven. Stop at a Lower Manhattan watering hole for half an hour of attitude adjustment before going home and imposing the day's frustrations on the family. Stand around in the sawdust and peanut shells, maybe alone, confronting your life in clichés, speculating maybe on what it might be like to initiate an affair with that tight-butt little associate in the jolly group at the bar . . . Lawyers. Brokers. Bankers. Most of them would be half-sloshed before they set their shoulders and walked out to face the commute.

"Interesting affiliation you got," said Blyleven. "Cosima

324

Bernardin." He shook his head melodramatically. "God
. . . a'mighty! What a bitch!"

"You know her?" Rick asked coldly.

"I was on the subcommittee that heard the ethics complaint against her two weeks ago. Jesus, man, did she ever
come on."

"Cosima's a powerful personality," said Rick dryly.

"She ever make you wish you were back at Hamilton,
Schuyler?"

"No. Never."

For a minute or so Blyleven was silent, swaying with the
train, as seasoned in oblivion as was Rick. Then, as the
train pulled into the Grand Central stop he said, "You getting off here? Me, too. My place is on East Forty-sixth. Uh
. . . Hey, how about a quick one in Charlie's? Like to ask
you a question or two about your partner."

They were lucky in Charlie Brown's. They found two
seats together, on the stools that face the window and the
crowd rushing for the down-escalators to Grand Central or
emerging from the up-escalators and trotting through the
Pan Am Building lobby for the street. Rick picked up drinks
from the bar while Blyleven held their places.

"You married, Loewenstein?"

"Divorced."

"Then you and Cosima Bernardin . . . ? Forgive me, I
shouldn't have asked that."

"The answer's no," said Rick. "Unofficially, she's engaged to Jack Putnam, the movie star."

"Jack . . . Jesus Christ! She's something, isn't she?"

Rick nodded.

Blyleven turned serious. "Do you know what she and
Hupp did in our hearing?"

"I heard it described," said Rick.

Blyleven sighed and drank from his Scotch. "Burton Oliver is nothing but a goddamned schmuck. We'd have had
to dismiss his complaint. She didn't have to toss a grenade
at him."

"Do you know why she did?" Rick asked. "Did it come out, why she was furious with him?"

Blyleven shook his head.

"He suggested to her that the reason Jack Putnam broke up with Vanessa Kingston was that he wanted to sleep with Cosima."

"Well . . . You can see how he might think so. I mean, Putnam *did* break up with Vanessa, and now you say he's engaged to Cosima."

"I can testify," said Rick firmly, "that Jack Putnam did not break up with Vanessa Kingston to start an affair with Cosima Bernardin. When he became Cosima's client, there was nothing between them. I don't believe they even *thought* of it. I can tell you for sure that when Oliver suggested what he did, it simply was not true; the man was just being nasty; and it made Cosima very, very angry."

"Well anyway, it was overkill," said Blyleven. "Oliver just didn't have a case."

"Then why was there a hearing?" asked Rick bluntly.

"I'm not supposed to talk about it."

"But you *are* talking about it. If there was no case, why was there a hearing?"

"A couple of members of the subcommittee wanted it. Two did, two didn't. The Chairman, Bob Blocker, said what the hell, we'll have a hearing, then we'll dismiss, and everybody will be satisfied."

"Why did two members want a hearing if it was clear there was no case?"

Blyleven shook his head. "I don't know."

"Yes, you do," said Rick caustically. "It's the same reason why Oliver tried to bring in Nash to testify to god-knows-what. Somebody at Hamilton, Schuyler got to somebody on the subcommittee. Now tell me I'm wrong."

"I don't know if you're right or wrong. There was some talk about what a brassy bitch she is. She's offended some people. She offended some at the hearing, you may have heard. When she told P.D. Dougherty not to smoke—

Jesus Christ, Loewenstein! The man's a *senior* at Quarles & McGrath!''

"Which entitles him to be rude and blow his smoke in people's faces?"

"I would guess that P.D. Dougherty blows his smoke wherever he pleases."

"Not in Cosima's face," said Rick. "Not in mine, either. That's why we left Hamilton, Schuyler—so senior partners can't blow smoke in our faces."

"Yes, and they hate you for it."

"Precisely. Which brings us back to the subject. Someone at Hamilton, Schuyler— How about *you*, Blyleven?"

Blyleven stopped his glass short of his lips. He grinned. "Christ, you gotta be kidding!''

"Okay," said Rick curtly. "Forgive me for asking."

"You know why?" said Blyleven just as he took a sip of Scotch.

"Why what?"

"Why I would have voted to dismiss the complaint, no matter what the goddamned evidence was?"

Rick glanced around. The conversation had taken such a turn that he wanted to be absolutely certain no one was listening. He leaned closer to Blyleven. "Tell me," he said.

Blyleven, too, looked around. He sighed heavily, raised his drink, and said, "Loose-juice. Loose-tongue potion. Forget it."

"Not now, my friend," said Rick firmly. "Let's hear it."

"You're saying you don't know."

"I don't know."

Blyleven sighed again. For a moment he covered his mouth with his hand, while he pondered whether to say anything, and if he did, how to say it. He bit his lower lip. "Loewenstein," he said. "Certain facts are facts. You don't have to hear them from me. Knightley International funded the whole damned string—I mean, all their hotels—on loans from Bernardin Frères. They're in default. That gives Leon Bernardin the right to name three directors, which he has

327

done. He can still foreclose or put the company in bankruptcy, but right now he has three of the seven directors in his pocket—and the others are scared of him. Knightley also owes our firm more than a million and a quarter in unpaid fees, and until we are paid—*unless* we are paid—certain partners' bonuses are going to be pretty anemic. Besides which, the board might elect to appoint a different firm as corporate counsel. You got it? Need I say more?"

"Yes, you need say more," Rick prodded him. "You damn well do need to say more."

"What more?" shrugged Blyleven. "It's obvious, isn't it?"

"The essential point is not obvious," Rick insisted. "What you've told me is, your firm dictated your vote. What I want to know is, did the firm do it because Leon Bernardin called and *demanded* something—or because the firm was afraid of how he *might* react?"

"I honestly don't know," said Blyleven. "Nobody told me."

The telephone rang in Rick's apartment after midnight. It was Blyleven.

"Hey, Loewenstein, listen. What I said this evening was straight out of the Scotch bottle. There wasn't a word of truth in it. I mean . . . I mean, really, man."

Rick blinked. The telephone had wakened him. "Understood," he said. "Look . . . Get a good night's sleep. Like you said, facts are facts, and I didn't have to get them from you. I won't mention your name. Not to anybody. I didn't see you this evening, okay? If I know anything, it's because I figured it out for myself. Don't worry about it."

"I appreciate that," said the thin voice on the telephone. Rick guessed he had gotten up to call after his wife was asleep. "It's damned good of you, Loewenstein. Damned good of you."

328

"Jerry . . . Jerry . . . Jerry, what the hell are you doing here?" Cosima asked. She ran the back of her hand down her left cheek. "Can't you see— How'd you know we were taping?"

They were in the CBS studio where Cosima and Lana were about to videotape the interview for the Svetlana Terasnova segment of the March 7 broadcast of "What's News?" Both had spent fifteen minutes in the makeup room, being colored and dusted for their appearance under the lights. Two technicians were wiring them with tiny microphones and FM transmitters when Jerry Patchen walked in.

Jerry nodded at Lana. "She needs me," he said. "I've been coaching her a little on how to speak, how to hold herself on camera."

Cosima glanced at Lana, and with one glance she understood. She shoved herself between Lana and Jerry, so the girl could not hear. *"Lana?* You've— You . . . guinea son of a *bitch!"*

"Cool it, Cosima," he said. "You don't own her."

"Ah . . . But *you do.* You've *had* her!"

He shrugged. "I'll pay her legal fees," he said. "Just add them to my bill."

"They're paid," Cosima snapped. "She's not your pet."

"Cosima . . . I'm doing something *good* for Lana. I—"

"Do you know what's at stake? Do you know what happens if I can't stave off her deportation until Emilie can get the bill through? Do you know what happens if the ideologues pressure the old man in the White House into vetoing it? Do you have any idea what it will do to her image—and her chances—if it gets around that she's been fucking Jerry Patchen? Do you— Or do you give a damn?"

Jerry glanced at Lana, who was trying to look past the woman still attaching her microphone, trying to hear the angry words. "Cosima, for Christ's sake," he whispered.

329

"Nobody knows, and nobody will if you don't make a scene. And I'm gonna *help*."

"You want to help? Turn around, wave good-bye and walk out. And don't come near her until we get her citizenship."

"I'm not a fuckin' pariah," he said.

"Ha! You said it just right. A *fuckin'* pariah is what you are—one that fucks everything in sight. Me. Susanne. Adela. Lana. And that's just in the last six months. And just the ones I know."

Jerry looked again at Lana. "I'm not walking out, Contessa," he said. "I've got a stake in this girl, too."

"Well, that just about does it. What you gonna do, take her to Argentina after she's deported? Just what the hell are you going to do for her, Jerry? You—my god, you haven't got her pregnant, have you?"

"I've only . . . it's only been two weeks. Anyway, I won't get her pregnant."

"Oh no, of course not. Not you, you predatory stud."

"Don't try to come between me and Lana," he said. "She won't accept that, Cosima. Neither will I. I may be a Cos Cob guinea to you, but I'm nothing like that to her. And I'm going to help her. I'm going to, and there's nothing you can do about it."

Two minutes later Bert brought Larry Sullivan to meet Cosima and Lana, and Jerry was still with them. Sullivan was courteous enough to Cosima and Lana, and plainly his attention was focused on them, but plainly too he was intrigued with the famous rock star. When Jerry said he wanted to do anything he could to help Lana, Sullivan asked if he would be willing to tape a short interview about her, which could perhaps be made a part of the show. Jerry said he would be glad to, and Cosima's urgent signals to Bert did not prevent the taping of a Jerry Patchen interview.

* * *

"I had no influence over it. Bert had no influence over it. Once Jerry showed up at the taping, Sullivan went crazy for it. He all but forgot what the goddamned show was *for.*"

Cosima had phoned Emilie from the living room of her condominium. Jack had extended a weekend trip to New Haven to spend the night with her here. They had been putting out food, so they could watch "What's News?" at eight, when Bert called and told Cosima that the Patchen interview had been incorporated into the show and there was nothing he could do about it. She had called Emilie immediately.

"I'm taping the show here," said Cosima to Emilie. "If we want to show it to senators and representatives, we can cut the Jerry Patchen part out. I know what you're saying— that identification with a stud rock musician won't do Lana's image a bit of good. I tried to prevent it. I did every damned thing I could to prevent it."

While Emilie responded, Cosima turned to Jack, smiled and shook her head. She had to drive him to Kennedy in the morning, for an early flight to L.A., and this evening and night was all the time they had—all they'd had in five weeks. When the telephone rang she had begun to change for him—from jeans and red sweatshirt into a white silk teddy she'd thought he'd like—and she'd been interrupted and stood at the end of a stretched telephone cord, still in the sweatshirt, but without the jeans, showing her legs and a pair of white panties.

"It's a setback, Emilie. I can't help it. No, don't call me when it's over. Jack's here, just for tonight. I'll talk to you tomorrow."

Jack had switched on the television set. "Lucky the show's not preempted for basketball," he said.

"I don't know if it's lucky or not."

"Couldn't keep his hands off her, huh?"

"Another goddamned *challenge* to him. Another goddamned trophy to add to his collection."

331

"We're in some kinda luck," said Jack. "Your part is the first segment."

"After four commercials and three minutes of Larry Sullivan explaining to us what we're going to see. I can't *stand* network television. So damned condescending . . ."

Sullivan was a professional mouth, not a journalist. Bert had told Cosima how everything on "What's News?" was written for him, how he had to be briefed about every segment to be sure he understood it before he was turned loose before the cameras. He was rarely allowed to appear live; his gaffes had been memorable. He was, on the other hand, a handsome man: lots of well-coiffed dark hair, a cleft chin, dark whiskers that the makeup crew allowed to show as a faint bluish shadow under his skin and—most of all—intent, unblinking blue eyes that evinced a penetrating intelligence and subtle skepticism.

The Svetlana Terasnova segment began with a one-minute view of her performing in a Martha Graham ballet. The performance was well chosen: a ballet in which she appeared as a rural American girl, dancing in a bucolic setting. The short fragment showed something of her talent and also showed her as a strong, vibrant performer, displaying vigor and personality.

Then Larry Sullivan described her problem in sympathetic terms, very much the way Cosima had outlined it to him. He interviewed Lana alone, then Cosima alone, then the two of them together. He let Lana say that she had defected to the United States to find freedom. Cosima's assertion that the Justice Department was engaged in an obsessive crusade against Lana Terasnova had not been edited out. Cosima spoke of the private bill. The main points they had wanted to make remained intact on the tape.

Then there was to have been another fragment of dance, but this had been cut out to make time for the Jerry Patchen interview.

Sullivan faced the camera. "When we met with Svetlana Terasnova and her attorney to tape this segment, we were surprised to learn that a celebrity had come to our studio with Miss Terasnova. We asked him to give us *his* impressions of the effort by the United States government to deport this talented young woman—which he consented to do. Ladies and gentlemen, Mr. Jerry Patchen!''

The camera swung to follow Sullivan as he walked into a set where Jerry sat in a Danish chair facing a small round table. Two cups sat on the table. Sullivan sat down in the second chair.

''Mr. Patchen, you are a friend of Miss Terasnova's. How did a famous rock star chance to meet a Russian ballerina?''

Jerry was dressed in blue blazer and gray slacks, white shirt and striped tie. ''Actually, it wasn't by chance, and it's not surprising,'' he said. ''My real name, you know, is Ruggiero Paccinelli, and as Ruggiero Paccinelli I have a graduate degree in music and am very much interested in what are called the more serious forms of music, certainly including opera and ballet. I saw Miss Terasnova perform. I learned she was threatened with deportation. I offered to help her in any way I could. It would be a tragedy if a talent of her stature was deported from the United States. It would be a loss to our country.''

''I understand,'' said Sullivan, ''that you are thinking of writing a show for Miss Terasnova.''

''Not exactly,'' said Jerry. ''I am writing a musical show. It is in the rock idiom, but it will bear almost no resemblance to what you see and hear at a performance of Bull Dog Fangs. It will have a strong ballet component, and I would be very fortunate if I could secure Svetlana Terasnova as my lead dancer. *Very* fortunate.''

The camera moved in on the face of Larry Sullivan. ''So there you are. A beautiful and talented dancer. But one with unfortunate elements in her background, which threaten to exclude her from the United States. What's news? Svetlana Terasnova is news, and we will be watching the development of the legal entanglement surrounding her right to stay in this country. That, too, will be news.''

As the show broke for commercials, Cosima picked up the remote control and switched off the television set. She sighed and shook her head. "That, uh . . . it could have been worse.''

"Much worse," said Jack. "If you don't mind my saying so, I think Paccinelli did one hell of a job. Is he serious about that show he's writing?''

Cosima nodded. "Lana told me he's writing a show for her. I figured it was how he seduced her.''

"How'd I seduce you, baby?" Jack asked, his focus having abruptly changed. He reached for her sweatshirt, tugged up on it, and she raised her arms and let him pull it off. He leaned over and kissed her nipples, first one and then the other. "Was it easy? On a scale of one to ten, did you let me do it easy, or—''

"I thought I seduced you," she said.

She pulled down the white panties, lay back on the couch and received him. She could see he wanted her now. There would be time for other things later. And he would want other things. He always did.

She had learned in Paris, again in Los Angeles, that he was an eager, vigorous lover, and one with certain expectations. She had learned that he would not demand, but he gave without reservation and expected her to reciprocate. So she had learned the taste of his member: nothing unpleasant when he had washed, and the taste of his ejaculate, surprisingly bland. With her tongue she had learned the interesting difference in the textures of the stretched skin of his erect organ and the wrinkled and hairy skin of the great bulging sac beneath. As she sucked and nibbled on his foreskin, she learned that unique and delicious sensations resided in it. He writhed and moaned when she caressed that circle of excited flesh with her tongue. Her dexterous, intelligent tongue and lips could manipulate that better than could her lower parts, receptive though they were; and she delighted in the erotic power she had never guessed she had. She had learned to give what she had never thought she could, and to find profound satisfaction in it.

"Let yourself down on me, Jack," she whispered to him when he had exhausted himself and hung panting above her, holding his weight off her with his knees and hands. "It's okay."

He settled down gently. He was heavy, but his weight was welcome, somehow comforting.

"I love you, Jack," she said. "It makes a world of difference, doesn't it? I mean . . . I never guessed how much better it would be with a man I really love."

His breath was still coming hard. He closed his eyes, licked his lips and nodded.

Seventeen

When Cosima and Rick established insurance and retirement programs for Bernardin, Loewenstein & Salomon, Hugh Hupp elected not to participate, which was his right since technically he was only sharing office space with the firm and was not a member. For this reason, none of the partners had seen any document that listed Hugh's birthday; and when the day came, on March 17, and he said he had been invited by some friends to join them for lunch at the Yale Club, Cosima and Rick accepted his explanation that it was to celebrate Saint Patrick's Day. When he sat down with three old friends and they raised their glasses to toast him, he was feeling a little smug about how he had kept the occasion hidden from people who might have made the kind of fuss he did not want to have to endure.

These were *old* friends: men of his own generation, three lawyers who had practiced much as he had, alone or in small firms, for forty years.

Alfred Ireland, who was two years older than Hugh, had been a sergeant in the platoon commanded by Lieutenant Hugh Hupp, and he had seen him hit, heard him scream, had seen him fall on D-Day. He spent six more months in combat before he himself was wounded, in Belgium, in December 1944. He had caught up with Hugh in a bar on Third Avenue in 1948: a joyful reunion. He was a small, gray man and wore a defiant yellowish gray guardsman's mustache.

Jim Nelson had been told that in his late years he looked something like Franklin D. Roosevelt. It was true. He even had some of the mannerisms, though no one could be sure he hadn't consciously adopted them *after* people began remarking on the physical similarity. He had the strong chin, the ready smile showing uneven teeth, the smooth, sometimes flushed cheeks, and he wore small rimless glasses—though not the FDR pince-nez. He had met Hugh Hupp at the University of Michigan, to which he had returned after serving as a naval officer in the Pacific. Toward the end of the war, he had held the rank of lieutenant commander and was the commander of a submarine that operated in the Sea of Japan during the final months before the surrender.

Hugh's third friend, Joe Begg, was a fleshy man who looked older than the others, though he was in fact the youngest. He rarely took the pipe from his mouth, and over the years his lower lip had conformed to it, hanging out and down, creased by its weight. He carried a kit with him: three GBD pipes which he smoked alternately, never letting one get too hot too long, a supply of his special tobacco mixture, a blowtorch lighter and an assortment of cleaning and scraping devices, all in a zippered pouch of fine pigskin. He was from Boston, was a Brahmin and talked like one, and he had served as a fighter pilot for a few months in '42 and '43—after which he spent twenty-eight months in a prisoner-of-war camp.

Of these four men, not one wore anything green on Saint Patrick's Day. To them—to Begg especially—the Irish, the American Irish in particular, were a mob of semibarbaric boobs who pretended to be proud of being Irish because they had nothing else to be proud of. Just after they sat down at their table they had shared jokes about the fact that

337

half the green-clad revelers on the streets of New York were black or Hispanic.

"Well, Uncle Hughie," said Al Ireland when they had finished their first drinks and were looking for the waiter, "I believe you are entitled to congratulations above and beyond those that go with attaining the age of sixty-seven . . ." Uncle Hughie was the name he'd been given in the infantry company forty-five years ago; and it had stuck. He had been a second lieutenant when he was first given it, probably because he was a year or two older than other lieutenants—and at that age it had seemed a significant difference. You could go and talk to Uncle Hughie, the word had been; he was older and knew how to listen. "If you know what I mean."

Hugh had retained from those long-ago years a facility for returning a sardonic comment with a silent but pregnantly meaningful stare: heavy eyes blasé under formidable black brows, waiting, letting the challenger struggle to fortify his challenge. Now he regarded Ireland silently with just such a stare and waited.

Al Ireland had known him too long to be intimidated. "I refer," he said, "to your teenage girlfriend, the one with no hair."

Hugh was not so modest as to be unflattered. He conceded a little smile.

"The third Mrs. Hugh Hupp?" asked Joe Begg in his sandy Boston accent. "Aunt Adela?"

"Uncle Hughie," said Jim Nelson, tipping his head back in a conscious or unconscious emulation of FDR. "Is this true? Al says congratulations. My god, I'd be inclined to proclaim a *miracle!*"

Hugh had caught the eye of the waiter. With a circular motion of his hand over the table he showed him they would have another round. "Have you gentlemen ordered me a birthday cake?" he asked innocently.

"That's what we want to know about," said Al, ". . . your goddamned *birthday cake!*"

Hugh picked up the menu and pretended to become absorbed in it. "To begin with," he said, "she is not a teenager. She is twenty-nine years old."

"Thanks for correcting me on that," said Al. "Are there any other errors in our suppositions?"

Hugh looked up from the menu. "Infinite errors, gentlemen," he said. "Infinite errors."

"She is, to my mind," said Joe, "considerably less interesting than the group with which you have elected to practice law. And I am far more interested in them than I am in Miss Adela Drake."

"Well, I must say, we all envy Uncle Hughie," said Al. "Twenty-nine years old . . ." He grinned and shook his head. "And Cosima Bernardin—"

"Cosima Bernardin *and* Joan Salomon," Joe interrupted.

"Right," said Al. "A bizarre trio of girls. Cosima, Adela and Joan—money, honey and funny."

"Bizarre comment," grunted Hugh. "And maybe a little personal, if you don't mind."

"Adela Drake is a client of yours, I believe," said Joe.

"A pretty good one, too," said Hugh. "She makes a lot of money. She needs legal advice and help. I've lost a couple of corporate clients lately. I'm glad to have Adela for a client."

"It's money and funny who've *cost* you clients," said Al.

"I doubt you know what you're talking about," said Hugh.

"*Don't* doubt it," said Al. "Cosima Bernardin was tossed out of Hamilton, Schuyler only ten months ago, and already she's been hauled before an ethics subcommittee. The four of us sitting around this table represent a hundred and sixty years of law practice, and none of us has ever been threatened with disbarment. What's more, Hugh, the word is around that . . . Well, I don't know how much you know about this, so I've gotta be careful how I put it. But the word is she shot down the subcommittee by bringing in a witness who lied for her."

339

" 'The word is . . .' " Hugh mused. " 'The word is . . .'
What word? *Whose* word?"

"The *word,* Hugh. It's around."

"I have no doubt of it," said Hugh sullenly. "But who
put it around? And why?"

Jim Nelson glanced around the dining room, especially
at nearby tables where the intensity of this conversation had
been noticed. He leaned across the table toward Hugh and
spoke quietly. "I've been a friend of yours more than forty
years, Hugh. So I guess I can ask, if anybody can. Was
Lawton Lanier lying through his teeth at that hearing?"

"For a procedure that was supposed to have been confidential—"

"Even so . . ." Jim persisted.

Hugh shrugged. "Who knows? When I went to interview
him, he said exactly what he said in the hearing. Was it the
truth?" He shrugged again. "Which of you vouches personally for the veracity of every witness you offer?"

"It's said also," said Joe, "that you launched a vitriolic
personal attack on Daniel Nash of Hamilton, Schuyler."

"I did, with relish. He's a lying little scum."

The waiter arrived with their round of drinks, and when
they were on the table Joe Begg raised his glass.

"While we get older, Uncle Hughie gets younger. While
we grow fat and placid, he gets more pugnacious. I don't
know about you gentlemen, but at my age I can hardly get
it up—while Uncle Hughie, who's a year older than I am,
is servicing a twenty-nine-year-old girl. Is it the Scotch,
Hugh? Or is there another secret?"

Hugh, who had turned saturnine moments earlier, now
grinned. "Remember the cliché," he said. "What counts
is not how old you are but how you are old."

Al Ireland saluted Hugh with his martini. "You'll forgive
my being pushy, I hope," he said. "You've always fascinated me. I'll never forget—" He stopped, caught by emotion.

Hugh shook his head. "Never mind, Al," he said. He

340

knew what Al would never forget: the sight of his friend hit and falling in sand already stained with the blood of men who had fallen there before him. He had tried many times to express what he had felt. "To old times," said Hugh, holding up his glass.

"And new times," whispered Al.

"And better times," added Joe.

They had given this toast many times over the years. It had a capacity to interrupt, to turn them quietly thoughtful. Its meaning had changed in forty years, but it had not lost its evocative power. They had talked, years ago, about forming a last-man club—putting maybe a case of wine or even a fund of money aside to become the possession of the survivor—but had decided against it, dreading the dark feelings that would have to accompany claiming the prize. So far, they all survived, but they faced their birthday and anniversary gatherings with apprehension.

Hugh understood their intrusion. He would not have accepted it from anyone else.

"Do I see in the paper that your girl is giving a concert on her own, minus Bull Dog Fangs?" Joe asked.

Hugh nodded. "Tomorrow night. Her contract with Jerry Patchen expired the first of the month, and she decided to take off on her own."

"How did Patchen accept that?"

"We're finding out tomorrow morning. He's coming in for a meeting about it."

"Seriously said, Hugh—"

"Seriously said," Hugh interrupted, "the answer is no. Which doesn't say it might not happen."

Al laughed. "You bastard."

"Okay," said Hugh. "We've talked about money and honey. What do you hear about funny? You say Joan Salomon has cost me clients. Why?"

"She was fired from Webster, Kent, Harriman & McCoy—"

"*No!*" Hugh barked. "Joan Salomon was *not* fired. Cosima Bernardin was not fired. Rick Loewenstein was not fired. Each one of them walked out of a big firm for the kind of reasons none of us ever joined one."

"Malcontents," said Joe. "Obsessively independent."

"Well, how can any of *us* be contemptuous of *that?*" Hugh asked. "When the son-of-a-bitchin' war was over—when I was released from that goddamned hospital and finally got that ruptured duck—I knew I would never again in this life call any man 'sir.' And I never have, and I never will. There's *no* son of a bitch is 'sir' to *me!*"

"We've heard that of you, Uncle Hughie," Al chuckled.

Hugh smiled sardonically. "Yeah. Well, neither is anybody 'sir' to Cosima Bernardin. Or to Rick Loewenstein or Joan Salomon. I like that in those kids."

"The story they tell of Joan Salomon," said Al soberly, "is that she eats pussy. Not only that—she goes hunting it."

"Bullshit," said Hugh. "She has nothing to hunt for. She's married, as you might say."

The three other men stared pensively at their drinks, Joe pulling smoke from his pipe and releasing a thick white billow. They were all brimming with thoughts yet reluctant to speak. Al Ireland, who had always been the boldest, sighed and spoke—

"The story from Webster, Kent is that Joan Salomon was dismissed because she tried to seduce a receptionist." He shrugged. "How could they say that, Hugh, if there's nothing behind it?"

"How could a policeman arrest a man if he's not guilty of a crime?" asked Hugh sarcastically. "How could a newspaper publish a story that's not true? C'mon, Al!"

"You've still got the Reischauer Group. Haven't you?"

Hugh nodded, abruptly apprehensive that Al was about to say something portentous.

"I was talking to Blake Summers day before yesterday," said Al. "Harvard Club. He, uh . . . asked me what's going on with you. Wanted to know why you'd associated

342

yourself with such a disreputable group of lawyers. I'd suggest you talk to him, Hugh. When the general counsel for Reischauer wants to know—"

"What the hell am I supposed to say to him? 'Hey, fella, I'm sorry I'm sharing office space with a poor little rich girl and a notorious dyke. I hope you won't think ill of me.' "

Al shook his head. "I don't know what to tell you. I reminded him that you are only sharing space, are not a member of the firm, and that anyway he might want to remember that Cosima is the daughter of Leon Bernardin. Frankly, that carried a little weight. But I think you might want to do some fence-mending with Blake, if you want to be sure of keeping Reischauer. It's an honest concern, Hugh," Al said, tapping the tablecloth with his finger. "The man is not prejudiced. He just wants to know what's going on."

Jerry Patchen arrived an hour late. Cosima had no doubt as to why. Well, two could play the game. She let him sit in the outer office for fifteen minutes. Rick and Joan fidgeted; Hugh was amused. Then she called Joan into her office—she alone—and sent out word that they were ready to see Mr. Paccinelli. Unhappy Rick remained behind the closed door of his office, under a strict prohibition from Cosima to join the meeting for at least fifteen minutes.

"Well, Contessa—" Jerry said irritably as he sat down in one of the chairs facing her desk. "What the hell's so important this morning?"

"Everything we do here is important, Jerry," she said.

They were not in fact busy. Rick was no longer the only one worried by the state of the firm's business. He had pointed out to Cosima that she was devoting most of her time to the matter of Svetlana Terasnova; although the hundred thousand dollars her mother had promised had been donated, and more, much of that was going to expenses. In any event, the future of the law firm was uncertain, since

Cosima was not performing her chief obligation: to find more business. Today, Rick could not bill for more than an hour's work. Neither could Joan. No law firm could survive on that.

It was essential, Rick had reminded her forcefully while she kept Jerry Patchen waiting, that Bernardin, Loewenstein & Salomon not lose Fang, Incorporated, as a client—and Hugh's odd personal relationship with Adela Drake jeopardized the Fang account.

Jerry raised the question immediately. "What I want to know," he said, "is who you represent—Adela or me?"

"Mutually exclusive, Jerry?" Cosima asked, austerely calm.

He lifted his chin and stared at her. Cosima had come to the office this morning in a thigh-hugging tailored red wool skirt, worn with a long red cashmere cardigan sweater opened to show her white silk blouse. Through the glass of her desk he could see her crossed legs, her dark sheer stockings.

"There's a conflict of interest there, don't you think, Contessa?" he asked. "Adela had a contract with me."

"Which expired the first of the month," said Cosima. "No one here represented her in anything contrary to her obligations to you."

"I'm not sure she wasn't getting advice from Hugh Hupp," said Jerry. "They, uh—"

"In the first place," Cosima interrupted him, "Hugh is not a member of this firm. We share this office suite. He—"

"Bullshit, Contessa."

"In the second place, I assure you that no one here—Hugh or anybody else—advised Adela not to renew her contract with you. That would have been a conflict of interest, and we didn't do it."

"I bet—"

"In the third place, Adela didn't terminate her contract with you. *You* terminated it."

"Her demands were . . . unreasonable."

"And you wrote her a letter telling her you wouldn't meet them and the contract would be allowed to expire. *After* it expired, she brought some of her new propositions to us and asked us to review her contracts."

"You handled her divorce. You handled her poster deals."

"Under her contract with you, she was allowed her independent poster deals. We have not violated your trust, Jerry."

Jerry swung around and looked out at the gray skies over the city. "She's an ungrateful bitch," he said.

"Grateful," muttered Cosima, nodding. "You can't bank gratitude, Jerry. She might argue, and I guess she does, that you aren't grateful for her contribution to Fangs."

"Shit . . ."

Joan sat to one side, drab compared to Cosima, in a nubby wool suit of mixed dark colors. Jerry turned to her—

"What about *you*, lady? Weren't you handling work for Adela before her contract expired?"

"With respect to her own money," said Joan quietly.

For a moment Jerry's eyes lingered on Joan's plain, rough face, as though he thought he glimpsed something behind her impassive eyes. Then he jerked his head around toward Cosima.

"She gonna make a lot of money?" he asked.

Cosima nodded. "I'd judge she's going to do all right. We'll see tonight, huh?"

"I'm working tonight," he said.

"Give me a call, late. I'll tell you how it was."

"Let me ask you something, Contessa. What if I tell you I don't like your representing both me and Adela?"

"You mean you want me to choose?"

"Suppose I did?"

"I'd like to be able to choose you, Jerry," she said. "But if you backed me into that corner, I'd choose Adela. Neither you nor anybody else is going to tell me which clients I can

345

represent. If you were right about any part of it—conflict of interest and all that—it'd be different. But you're not."

He dropped his arm over the back of his chair and crossed his legs. "So here's something else half a million dollars a year doesn't get me," he said with the hint of a wry smile.

"You can't screw me, Jerry—not figuratively or literally—for half a million, a whole million, or two or three million." She paused and grinned. "Now, uh . . . . offer me five million and I might reconsider."

"You've got some balls, lady," he sneered.

"Thank you, Jerry," she said. "I like to think so."

For her first performance independent of Bull Dog Fangs, Adela appeared in a small club on Prince Street, called The Black Prince. It was a small, smoky bar with a stage and two dozen tables—one of those places that, for reasons no one can explain, becomes briefly fashionable, for a while is the place all trendy people think they must go, then is abruptly forgotten. For now the Black Prince fad was at its peak, and its owners hoped to be able to keep it there by booking the most famous performers they could afford. For The Black Prince, the availability of Adela Drake was great good fortune, while for Adela being able to introduce her new act there was good luck, too.

Cosima, Hugh and Rick were able to get inside only because Adela had insisted a table must be reserved for them. Every chair at every table was taken, every stool at the bar; fifty or more people stood around the walls. They were the kind of people who inhabited these places—hyper: eyes too bright, speech too quick and brittle, haunted with self-consciousness, tormented with anxiety to be noticed. "Nibelungen," Hugh grunted, and only Cosima laughed, because only she understood his reference to the wealthy subterranean dwarfs of Teutonic legend and Wagnerian opera, carried over into the fairy tale Snow White.

Adela had taken on a new name—The Infinite Adela—

346

and everywhere her name appeared, on posters outside and inside, and on little programs the management had distributed, it appeared as a logo consisting of her name and the mathematical symbol for infinity—

∞ ADELA ∞

Cosima overheard chatter at a nearby table, where two couples were laughing over the speculation that the symbol was a minimalist drawing of a penis and scrotum.

It was difficult to believe the crowd would shift its attention from itself to any performer, but when the room was darkened and the lights came up on the stage, the room went silent, a few gasped, and the performers had rapt attention.

The stage was white—white walls, white equipment, even a white floor. It seemed almost afire in the overpowering glare of a battery of lights whose beams seemed all but solid above the crowd. The light was cold blue-white; every hint of warmth had been filtered out of it; it looked like moonlight gone mad. Adela's sidemen were on stage: a guitarist and a percussionist, both dressed in coldly gleaming white satin, playing white instruments, and wearing the white makeup of mimes. Adela's electronic keyboard had been refinished in white, and it was fixed to a gleaming steel stand that held it up and tipped at an odd angle—obviously she meant to play standing, without the keyboard intruding between her and her audience.

The percussionist set up a beat. The guitarist joined him, shortly imposing the suggestion of a musical theme behind the beat. Both of them were, of course, loudly amplified.

"LADIES AND GENTLEMEN! THE BLACK PRINCE . . . IS PROUD TO PRESENT . . . THE . . . INFINITE . . . *ADELA!*"

Adela strode to the middle of the stage, bowed to her audience, turned and nodded to her sidemen and grabbed a microphone from a stand. With her left hand she reached to her keyboard and added an amplified few chords of counterpoint to the theme the guitar had established. Then she began to sing.

Her crowd was enthralled before she picked up the microphone, before she touched the keyboard, before she sang a note. She had shaved off the hedge of dyed hair and was completely bald. She was dramatically pallid. Maybe she had applied a trace of the white mime makeup her sidemen wore, or maybe she had dusted herself with white powder; anyway, she wore black. Maybe she or her designer knew something of what the Marquis de Sade wrote of the erotic effect of black on white, or maybe they had achieved it by chance; anyway, the blatant black-and-white contrast was spectacular.

It began with the startling black makeup that had long been something of a signature with Adela: the black lipstick in particular but also the treatment of her eyes with charcoal black mascara and eyeshadow. Her costume for the stage was a very simple, very short black silk slip, loose, low cut, and held up with spaghetti strings. From under the slip, narrow black ribbons from her garter belt lay as stripes down her white thighs, to her sheer black stockings. Her spike-heeled shoes were black patent leather.

Whether or not Adela could sing or not was immaterial—and in Cosima's judgment, fortified by the opinion of Hugh, who nudged her, leaned over and expressed himself forcefully, she could not. She didn't have to. She sang as well as Jerry Patchen. The point was, she was putting on a show; her singing was good enough to carry it off.

Her performance was erotic, which was a necessary element of this kind of show, and she had that under control. It reached for the hypnotic, which, if she could achieve it, was the key to success.

The music— Hugh had handled the copyright implications of her purchases, without any attempt to judge what she was buying. He knew full well he had no basis for judgment. As Cosima listened, she knew she hadn't either; but

348

she formed some ideas of what she heard. In fact, she heard what she guessed was the secret of Jerry Patchen's success: that this music, which Adela had bought from respected and successful composers, lacked the direct forcefulness of the rock music written and performed by Jerry Patchen. What she heard now was vibrant, and it engaged the attention of the crowd, but it lacked the mathematical power of the music performed by Bull Dog Fangs. It was too complex. What was more, it lacked the subtlety of Jerry's structures. Above all, it was not memorable. This crowd might walk away tonight trying to hum or whistle something of what they had heard, and they might succeed, but serious musicians would pay it no attention.

If she understood— She shrugged. Maybe she didn't.

Anyway, she wished Adela well. She wanted Adela to succeed.

She looked at Hugh. *My God!* My god, Hugh was in love with Adela. It manifested itself in an odd—or maybe not so odd—way. He disliked her show. He didn't like to see her on display: bald, suggestively dressed, now rolling her hips like a stripteaser, now slinking across the stage like a cat, whipping her microphone cord after her, now leaning over the edge of the stage, mugging maniacally at her cheering crowd, and always shrieking the ribald lyrics of her songs.

It was, regardless, a professional performance. It was in fact a tour de force. Adela totally won the audience during her first number. Cosima had to wonder how in the world Adela had learned to play an electronic keyboard mounted on a stand and tilted at such a wild angle, so she could face her audience, sing, dance, mug and still force music out of the box, sometimes with just her left hand, sometimes with both, pounding the keyboard as she moved. She must have practiced at this— God knew when and how much!

The show was styled beyond the music, of course—out of Adela's experience with Jerry's crowds. She abandoned the keyboard entirely and prowled across the front of the stage, grinning at her crowd as she belted out the earthy lyrics of the songs she and her manager had revised to suit the image they meant to create for her. On Jerry's stage she had let her vest fall open and had exposed her breasts. Here that never happened. It was obvious that she wore no brassiere, and what this crowd saw of her breasts was just their weight swinging around inside the loose black silk of her slip—which was even more erotic. As she postured, the slip crept up her hips until the crowd could see that, though her garter belt was black, her panties were white.

(This had an odd origin, which came out in one of her publicity releases. "Elvis," she was quoted as saying, "always liked girls to wear simple white panties. I guess we can do that for his memory." It was pure cynicism, pure hype. Adela's name for Presley was "the greaseball junkie.")

"There's something we all have to concede about her, Hugh," Cosima said through hands cupped around his ear. "She's a *performer*. There's *contact* between her and this crowd. I wasn't at all sure it would be there. But it is."

Hugh nodded.

Rick leaned over to join the conversation. "Where's the born-again?" he asked.

Cosima only grinned, but Hugh frowned at Rick and said, "She's grown up."

Leon Bernardin slapped at the newspaper he had shoved across the breakfast table toward Cosima. "I don't buy this rag," he said—it was the *Daily News*—"but I was alerted to have this one delivered."

The paper was folded open to the page where one of two big stories was the account of an interview with Vanessa Kingston. It was headed by a large photograph of her—a tall, slender young woman fashionably dressed in a ribbed-knit short dress. Her severely plucked eyebrows arched in thin lines over big, dark, solemn eyes. Her dark hair was bound tightly behind her head. The story read:

Arriving at Kennedy Airport on a British Air flight from London, where she played a featured role in the upcoming TV pilot "Rosie's," actress-dancer Vanessa Kingston declared she was only changing planes in New York, that she was on her way to L.A., where she will lay claim to her old flame, movie star Jack Putnam.

Jack has been a busy fellow during her absence, squiring glamorous rich-girl lawyer Cosima Bernardin. Reminded of this, Vanessa grinned, waved two fingers and said, "Jack and I have always been like this." She held the two fingers very close together.

"And that's how it's going to be," she added.

"Is that how it's going to be?" Leon asked when he could see that Cosima had finished reading the story.

Cosima shrugged. "I don't think so."

"You don't *think* so? Do you *know?* What are you going to do about it?"

"I'm not going to do anything about it. I don't have to do anything about it."

"You're that confident?" he asked.

"If I can't be, then to hell with it," said Cosima.

Even so, when she reached her office she decided to telephone Jack. Probably he hadn't seen the story. He should know. It was only 6:30 in L.A., about the time he would be leaving for the studio. Maybe she could catch him before he left.

Sitting at her desk, looking out on the glaring sunshine of a spring-promising March day, she punched in his number and listened as the telephone rang.

"Hello . . . ?"

It was a woman's voice, a sleepy woman's voice. Cosima hung up.

Teresa stood in the open door of the office, ready with some kind of message, unaware of what call Cosima had just completed. "Uh, excuse me," she said. "There's a call from the clerk's office, Federal District Court. The judge in the Terasnova case is calling in the lawyers for some sort of hearing. They want you to call tout de suite."

Eighteen

Judge Ralph Waldo Emerson Hawthorne drew in the corners of his mouth and glared at Cosima, who stood before his bench.

"Miss Bernardin, you have achieved two months' delay already. If you and your sister can't get the bill passed—"

"The wheels of the Congress grind slowly, Your Honor," she said.

"Yes, slow for sure," said the judge.

"Anyway, I am going to set this case for hearing in May—which gives you almost two more months. You can't complain."

"I don't complain, Your Honor."

"I should think not. Now—I am looking at Monday, May 23. And what I want from you—and from Mr. Langley—is your assurance that the case will not occupy more than three days' time on the trial docket of this court."

Cosima glanced at Langley, who stood beside her, placidly contemplating the exchange between her and the judge. "I don't see how I can give you that assurance, Your Honor," she said. "Let me put it this way. I *do* assure you that my case in chief will not occupy more than three days. Indeed, it will not occupy two days. I cannot, though, guess how long Mr. Langley may require to cross-examine my witnesses, and I have no idea what witnesses he will want to present and how much I may have to cross-examine them. You have my commitment, Your Honor, that I will complete my case in *two* days—subject to the limitations I have just suggested.''

"Well I require you, Miss Bernardin, to sit down with Mr. Langley and reach a sensible agreement, limiting the issues to be presented and the number of witnesses to be called. I want a commitment from the two of you that this case will not occupy more than three days of this court's time. If you two cannot reach an agreement, then I will set the limits myself.''

"I will discuss the matter rationally with Mr. Langley, Your Honor; and if he is able to talk rationally, I am sure we can come to an agreement that will meet your requirements.''

Once again the judge drew in the corners of his mouth, and he fixed his sober, bulging eyes on her. "Mr. Langley has an established record for reasonableness, Miss Bernardin.''

"I shall be happy to see evidence of that, Your Honor.''

Langley agreed to come to her office for their discussion, and he appeared there that afternoon. When she came out to greet him in the reception area she found him standing mesmerized before the Bull Dog Fangs poster.

"Mr. Langley.''

"Ah. Miss Bernardin. Uh . . . Your client, huh?''

"Yes. Fang, Incorporated is an important client for our firm. We specialize in legal matters relating to the arts and show business.''

"That explains your special interest in Svetlana Terasnova,'' he said as he followed her into her office.

"Well . . . Not necessarily. As far as I'm concerned, Mr. Langley, the Terasnova case is a matter of simple justice.''

354

"Umm," he said. He was sucking on a cough drop—she could smell eucalyptus. "That depends on how you define justice."

"You and I define it differently," she said.

He shook his head. "Not necessarily. We represent different clients."

She let the comment stand while he opened his briefcase and removed a yellow legal pad. Though his signature smile remained constant, she noticed that he frowned deeply as he bent over the briefcase. The creases that came just above the bridge of his nose looked painful. His face was more than usually flushed. For a moment he closed his eyes.

"You'll have to forgive me," he said. "I'm subject to migraines." With a finger he pulled down on his right cheek, distorting his eye. "Also, I've got a speck behind my lens, I guess. Do you wear contacts? I fight mine constantly."

"Do you have a migraine now?" she asked sympathetically.

"Yes."

"Well . . . Would you like to postpone—"

"Oh, no. I have appointments—" He repeated the frown. "Excruciating sometimes . . ."

It was strange to hear a man talk about an excruciating headache and a painful speck behind his contact lens, while he continued to suck a cough drop and maintain a glued-on smile. She had long since learned the smile was meaningless—maybe nothing but a tic—but it was incongruous with the conversation.

"We really can reschedule, you know," she said.

He shook his head. "Would you think it odd of me if I stretched out on your couch while we talk?"

"Uh . . . of course not. Not at all."

He glanced at the yellow legal pad on which apparently he had intended to make notes; he dropped it in his briefcase and lay down. Though there were two pillows on the couch—Cosima herself sometimes briefly napped there—he put those aside and lay flat on his back, his suit jacket and

355

his vest still in place, still buttoned. His feet extended beyond the arm of the couch, but he seemed not to mind that. He closed his eyes.

"My secretary has some Advil or something," she said.

"Ah, thank you no," said Langley. "Nothing helps." The smile was a little less distinct, but it was still there, more incongruous than ever. "Now. We can talk. I won't sleep, of course. I just need to be on my back with my eyes closed."

"All right," she said. "What of the trial?"

"Well . . ." He crunched the remainder of his cough drop between his teeth and swallowed it noisily. "Miss Bernardin, would you mind if I call you Cosima. I'm uh . . . called Bud."

"Fine," she said.

"Cosima . . ." He opened his eyes, then closed them again. "Have you explored the possibility of Miss Terasnova's deportation to a country other than the Soviet Union? Suppose she were deported back to Canada, which is where she defected in the first place. Suppose she were deported to the U.K., or to France."

"Why should they think she's less a threat to their countries than the Attorney General seems to think she is to ours?"

"Well—"

"Even supposing it could be arranged," said Cosima, "then we would never see her dance in this country again. She would never get a visa to return to the United States to perform. There's a principle involved here, Bud."

"Yes, there is," he said. "The principle that you can't violate the laws of the United States and expect to escape all punishment. It's a matter of right and wrong."

"It's also a matter of depriving this country of a major ballet talent," said Cosima. "For political reasons."

"Why should a deportable ballet dancer be treated differently from a deportable sailor who jumped a Polish ship? If he enters illegally and lies to conceal his affiliation with a

Communist political organization. Cosima . . . Really, you can't assure me, absolutely and of personal knowledge, that Svetlana Terasnova is not a KGB agent."

Cosima laughed. "C'mon, Bud, for Christ's sake!"

He opened his eyes and turned his head to look at her. After a moment he closed them. "It was only a rhetorical statement—as I know you understand."

"Are you going to oppose my introducing evidence at the hearing?"

"Of course. I have no choice. And you know you are going to lose. I imagine by now you've *memorized* Section 1105a, and I suppose you've read *Toma v. Turnage.*"

"I've read fifty cases," she said. "I don't find the law so very clear."

"It is clear," said Langley. "In these cases, the courts are limited to considering the evidence adduced before the administrator. What's more, eventually the hearing you had in the Court of Appeals will be held to have been the hearing you are entitled to under 1105a, and the habeas proceedings will be ruled a nullity."

"You're confident of that?"

"I'm confident of it," he said.

"In the meantime, maybe the private bill—"

"The President will veto it," Langley said flatly.

"Why?"

"Because he's committed to firm enforcement of the laws. Because he's committed to protecting this country's borders against intrusion by people excluded by the immigration laws of the United States."

"On a first-name basis—which is what you asked for—and off the record, let's drop the cant, Bud, and talk about the *real* reason why the administration is obsessed with deporting one beautiful, talented little girl. Don't give me this bullshit about what the President's committed to. Off the record— *Why?*"

"An important element of the President's constituency believes that *no* Russian, no matter who or why, should be

357

admitted to the United States as an immigrant," said Langley without opening his eyes, lying flat on his back in his dark brown suit, his face toward the ceiling as if he were staring at it. "If you add to that the fact that Miss Terasnova was a member of Komsomol . . . Cosima, it just isn't possible to ignore."

"Solzhenitsyn . . ." said Cosima. "Baryshnikov . . ."

"No difference."

"Solzhenitsyn writes books your 'important element of the President's constituency' can't understand," said Cosima. "Baryshnikov represents an art they don't understand. And they hate what they don't understand."

"You come rather easily to such conclusions, Cosima," said Langley in a voice that was becoming torpid as he lay there.

"If you are certain the President will veto the bill," she said, "then it becomes essential that I win the case in the courts."

"It's futile," he said languidly. "You're checkmated."

"Not yet," said Cosima. "In spite of your obsession."

He opened his eyes and regarded her as if he had never seen her before. "You're on the wrong side of the case, that's all. It's nothing personal. I wish you could see that it's not personal."

She turned toward the window and stretched her legs out in front of her. "You like working for the Justice Department?" she asked.

He had closed his eyes again and spoke toward the ceiling. "We're overworked," he said. "We're underpaid. We're underappreciated. But we are compensated in another way—in the knowledge that we're doing something to restore *values* in this country. I'd work for nothing—for a while, anyway—for that."

"There's no possibility of compromise between us, is there, Bud?"

He shook his head weakly. "I can't compromise with you, Cosima. There is no way this case can be settled. It

358

may be unfortunate for this one small dancer, but the principles involved cannot be compromised.''

" 'Principles,' " Emilie mused.

Cosima nodded. "Principles."

They were sitting in Emilie's office in Washington. The sun had set, and through the windows they could see the harsh lights of traffic moving through a cold, rainy evening.

"Everything we've done—"

"Don't be too quick to assume it's been for naught," said Emilie. "Langley threatens a veto, but Langley may not know. Anyway, there can be a lot of horse trading when the time comes. I may be a New Jersey Democrat, but my vote in the House is just as good as the vote of a Republican from Vermont—and the White House calls and asks for it from time to time. Maybe I'll give it to them"—she paused to grin—"on some bill where I was going to vote their way anyhow."

"Seriously, Emilie, I came down here to suggest that maybe you should drop the bill. If it's going to be vetoed, if you have to horse-trade to try to save it, it may be too costly for you politically. I can't ask you to go that far. After all, it means nothing to your constituents."

"It *does* mean something to my constituents," said Emilie. "We love the arts in the Eighteenth District of New Jersey. Anyway, Edmund Burke told his constituents he had to think of the interests of the nation, not just *their* interests—which is an argument I pull out from time to time."

"You have the option, though," said Cosima. "I want you to understand that I won't object if you decide you have to drop the bill."

Emilie smiled. "Anyway, it's too late. The Rules Committee has put it on the calendar for Friday morning. There'll be a brief debate, then it will pass. I've got to get a Senate sponsor. I've spoken to Moynihan. I think he'll let us put his name on it."

"Jesus . . ." Cosima murmured.

"You're *down*, little sister. What's the matter?"

Cosima closed her eyes for a moment. She sighed, nodded, "I . . . I'll be all right. This thing's had me discouraged. Then . . . Dad's called me every day this week about Jack. And I haven't heard from him. He's not on location. Vanessa is back from Europe. She's in California. Worse than that, I think she's living with him again."

"You love the guy, little sister?"

Cosima nodded.

"If you'll take my advice, you'll get on a plane and fly out there."

Cosima shook her head. "No way. By now he knows about the *Daily News* story, for sure. It ran a week ago. If he doesn't want to call and reassure me—"

"Then to hell with him," Emilie interrupted. "Too easy, Cosima. I mean, this is soap-opera stuff. If you want to know what's going on with Jack, you go see him. At least you call him."

"The hell I do," said Cosima. She tossed her chin indignantly.

"Then it's my judgment, Cosima, that you don't really love him. If you did, you'd make a fool of yourself for him."

"I won't beg," said Cosima grimly. "I won't crawl after him."

In the house on Round Hill, Greenwich, Connecticut, Leon Bernardin closed the door to his study and picked up the telephone that was his exclusively: his private line that could be picked up on no extension in the house. He was dressed in a maroon silk robe over white pajamas. Elizabeth was away at some musicale, and the house was quiet. He had a splash of Napoleon brandy in a snifter, and he put it down on his leather-topped desk.

The number he wanted to call was in a small notebook

360

he had brought home from the office that afternoon. He checked it and punched in the number.

"Yeah—" said an impatient voice on the other end of the line.

"Jack?"

"Yeah. Who's 'is?"

"Leon Bernardin, Jack."

"Mr. Bernardin! Hey, is anything wrong? Cosima—"

"She's all right, I think. A little worried that she hasn't heard from you."

"Oh right, I should've called Cosima this weekend. I had to go down to Tijuana over the weekend to look at the places where we might shoot a really horrible film somebody wants me to do; and, hell, I didn't get back here until almost midnight last night—like, you know, three in the morning, your time."

"I understand, Jack," said Leon with rehearsed smoothness. "What Cosima's worried about is the *Daily News* story."

"*Daily News?* Oh my god, yes. Somebody sent— Hey, Cosima doesn't think . . . ? Jeez—Maybe I better call her. Soon as we get off the line."

"She's in Washington, Jack. Something about the Terasnova matter."

"You know where she's staying?"

"At the Madison Hotel, I imagine—though I don't know."

"I'll try it. I'll call there and see if I can reach her. I'll, uh . . . Was there something else you were calling about?"

"Oh . . . no. No, I just want to be sure everything is all right between you and Cosima. I was sitting here alone, knowing she's in Washington, and I got to thinking— Well, you understand."

"I sure do, Mr. Bernardin. So thanks for callin'."

She was indeed in the Madison Hotel. She remembered it favorably from the night she had spent there with Jerry

Patchen—and the memory of an unpleasant morning had not diminished her appreciation of the hotel. When the telephone rang at midnight, she was asleep in her room. She had eaten and drunk well, and she had fallen asleep comfortably, obliterating for a few hours a great many things she did not want to think about.

"Cosima? Jack. I expect I woke you."

She looked at the clock by the bed. It was only a little after nine in Los Angeles. "Yeah . . ." she murmured. "I went to bed early."

"I tried earlier," he said. "Then I had to go out a while."

"How'd you know where to call?"

A little laugh came over the telephone line. "I keep track of you, Cosima. Jeez— I mean, wouldn't a guy keep track if he was in love with a girl like you?"

"I suppose so," she said. "Something like that." She was not yet entirely awake. "Where are you, anyway?"

"I'm at home," he said. "I was in Mexico over the weekend. Couldn't call you."

"Oh. Well, I wondered."

"Listen, Hon. Somebody in New York sent me a copy of that *Daily News* story. Hey, you . . . You don't take that seriously, do you?"

"I suppose you're saying I shouldn't."

"No, you shouldn't. That kind of stuff— That kind of stories. It just goes with the business I'm in. Ought to see what they say about me in the *Enquirer*."

"Okay," said Cosima, calm reserve in her voice.

"She came out here. I mean, Vanessa's here. But it's nothing, okay?"

"If you say so."

"I say so. Listen, I've *seen* her. She did what she said in the story—came to me and said let's pick up where we left off. And I said no. Hey, I told her I'm in love with you. Which is true."

"I'm in love with you, too, Jack," said Cosima. She

desperately wished he would tell her why Vanessa had answered his telephone at six in the morning. "More than I want to be, really."

"I know, Cosima. I know, and I'm grateful. Listen, you gotta come out here. It's kinda tough for me to get away right now, but this weekend—"

"Is impossible, Jack. The House votes on Lana's bill Friday. I'm setting up a news conference. I'm trying to get her on one of the Sunday newsmaker shows. The judge has set the final hearing on her habeas corpus for May twenty-third. We're going to lose for damned sure. I've got to try to get the bill passed."

"Maybe next week," he said. "I'll try to get to New York. Anyway, I want you to take a look at the contracts some guys are drawing up for a deal where I'll coproduce and direct a picture. That's what I was doing in Mexico."

"Will, uh . . . will Vanessa be in this picture?"

"You kiddin'? Forget that. Besides, 'Rosie's' is just a pilot. She's committed to a series if they make it."

Still he didn't tell her why Vanessa—it had been Vanessa, hadn't it?—answered his apartment telephone at six in the morning. "Okay, Jack. I'm glad you called."

"Well, I'm glad I did, too. I kinda thought I'd find a message from you on my recorder."

My call wasn't on your recorder because your phone was answered, she thought; but she said, "Well . . . I thought I'd have one from you on *my* recorder."

He laughed. "Musical phones. Anyway, I really am glad I called. I'm glad I found you."

"Seriously Jack—how did you know where to find me?"

"I guess I gotta tell you, Cosima. Your dad called me. Ya know? Your dad."

"When?"

"Early this evening, Pacific time."

"What did he say," she asked.

"Well, he said you were a little upset, 'cause of the *Daily News* article, then 'cause you hadn't heard from me."

"Goddamnit!"

"Yeah, Hon. That was my reaction, too."

Representative Emilie McCarthy rose somewhat heavily on the floor of the House of Representatives. (It would have been a little difficult for Emilie to rise any other way but somewhat heavily.)

"Mr. Speaker!"

"The Chair recognizes the lady from New Jersey, Mrs. McCarthy."

"Mr. Speaker, the Judiciary Committee has reported favorably on the private bill to grant United States citizenship to Svetlana Terasnova. I ask unanimous consent."

"Hearing no objection—"

"Mr. Speaker!"

Speaker Wright glanced at Emilie McCarthy, then nodded at the representative who had risen to object. "The Chair recognizes the gentleman from South Carolina, Mr. Bennett."

The gentleman was John P. Bennett, eighth-term Representative from the Fourteenth District of South Carolina: a small, pale, bald man who, as he rose to speak, consulted his notes through the bottom half of his bifocals. Then he seized them with both hands and settled them more firmly on his nose.

"Mr. Speaker, I have, uh . . . great respect and high personal regard for my distinguished colleague, the able Congresswoman from N' Jersey, and it is because of my respect and regard for her that I rise most reluctantly to speak in opposition to a bill for which she has asked unanimous consent. I cannot, however, believe that my distinguished colleague is aware of all the facts about the young woman she seeks to grant United States citizenship through the extraordinary procedure of a private bill."

Cosima sat in the gallery, listening. Svetlana was beside

her, apprehensive and mystified as always by the procedures of the United States government.

On the floor, no more than a dozen members of the House listened to the Representative from South Carolina. Some were reading, others were scribbling on paper, and still others—a score of them—strolled around the floor, greeting fellow members and chatting. The Speaker himself was deeply absorbed in a conference with members who had gathered around him. Members and pages entered the chamber and left in a constant stream.

"When Miss Terasnova was interviewed at the United States Embassy in Ottawa, Mr. Speaker, she was specifically asked if she was a member of any *Communist* organization. She said no, Mr. Speaker. She said no."

Bennett said nothing Cosima had not anticipated. His speech was the ideological litany the House had learned to expect of him—which was one reason why so few of the members listened when he spoke. He never surprised them. To him, most issues were questions of right and wrong, and he never doubted his ability to identify the right and eschew the wrong. Some of his colleagues referred to him as the most *certain* man in the House.

His certainty appealed to his constituents; it appealed, in fact, to an extended constituency beyond the boundaries of South Carolina, for whom he was a valued spokesman. John Bennett, they said, spoke for what was right. He spoke for decency and honorable values. He spoke for America. So, of course, he was ridiculed by the sophisticates of the big newspapers and television networks, who caricatured him as a redneck hick.

If his neck was not red, his face was—pink, anyway. He spoke almost in a monotone, without stress, reading soberly from his notes, his only emphasis an occasional nod.

"A simple matter," he said. "She lied. She broke our law. She faces deportation. She asks the Congress to *excuse* her, to exempt her from the law, to give her citizenship she has not earned and does not merit."

Bennett used ten minutes, no more. When he had finished, Emilie McCarthy rose to speak. She used only five; but while she was speaking, members returned to the floor.

"She did not speak long for me," Lana whispered to Cosima.

"She doesn't need to," Cosima whispered. "She has the votes."

Bennett demanded a roll call. Several members joined in his demand, so the Speaker ordered a roll call vote.

"The question being—Shall the bill pass? The House will proceed to vote."

It was done by machine. Members pressed buttons on their desks, recording their votes. The vote remained open for five minutes, while members rushed in to vote, then hurried back to committee meetings and other business off the floor.

Prompted by the Speaker, the clerk announced the vote— "Two hundred twenty-four members voted 'Aye,' sixty-one members 'Nay.' "

"The bill passes," said the Speaker laconically.

Layman Langley stared forlornly at the soggy sandwich in the box before him on the conference-room table. He was profoundly uncomfortable with every element of this meeting: that it was being held on a Saturday when he would rather have been at home with his family, that he was expected to content himself with a box lunch from a neighborhood deli, that everyone in the room but him was cheerfully quaffing beer and wine and even hard liquor, and most of all—by far most of all—that a federal judge was here to talk about a case that was pending before him, in the presence of counsel for one side and the absence of counsel for the other, a flagrant violation of basic principles of judicial ethics.

He was distressed, too, by the conspiratorial nature of the meeting. The case against Svetlana Terasnova was strong enough. He did not understand why anyone thought it necessary to assemble a collusive meeting to chew on it.

Anyway, last evening he had received a call from Washington. A meeting at noon, in a conference room at Hamilton, Schuyler, Depew & Chase, 120 Broadway. Totally confidential. Be there. Represent the Attorney General. Listen and report.

Judge Hawthorne sat at the head of the table, as if he were presiding—though he wasn't. He crunched chips and drank Scotch. If he was conscious of the impropriety of his being here, he didn't show it.

Across the table from Langley was Daniel Nash, a partner in the firm whose conference room they were using. Nash was the kind of man Langley found it difficult to like: narrow-eyed, serenely self-confident, thoughtless of the stench from his little black cigar. He had ordered and paid for the deli food, and he had ordered a secretary to wheel in a bar cart. Langley did not understand the connection. Why were they meeting at Hamilton, Schuyler? What did Nash have to do with what they were here to discuss?

The fourth man at the table was Claude Graves, representing Americans for the Preservation of American Values. It was he, apparently, who had called the meeting.

Claude Graves wore a coarse, grizzly beard, a polka-dot bow tie, a tweed jacket and dark gray slacks. He was a heavy man—muscular, generating an aura of power. Langley knew who he was: a Viet Nam veteran, a former public relations agent for defense contractors, a defeated candidate for Congress from Pennsylvania, now the well-paid executive director of an organization he had created for himself. APAV raised money effectively and spent it lavishly, applying the old Gompers principle of helping friends and punishing enemies. Graves had access to the Attorney General whenever he wanted it, to the President if he did not ask too often.

He made the opening statement: that the House—controlled of course by the Democrats—had yesterday passed the private bill to grant American citizenship to Svetlana Terasnova. Only sixty-one members of the House had voted against the bill, which of course meant that a very substantial number did not understand the issue involved. APAV and other organizations would do all they could to spread the word, but it was likely the Democrat-liberal coalition would have the votes to pass it in the Senate. In that case, the President's veto was the only defense left.

"We are damned lucky to have in the White House a President whose commitment is real. We can count on him. But we must not go to the well too often. A veto here"—Graves paused—"is not politically viable."

"The word from the Justice Department is that he *will* veto," Langley said. He did not add that he had told Cosima Bernardin the President would veto her bill.

Graves turned down the corners of his mouth and shook his head. Bud Langley felt the first pangs of a migraine.

"The point," said Graves, "is to avoid having to ask the President for a veto. It's currency we don't want to spend."

"The key," said Dan Nash, "is to discredit both this Russian dancer and her lawyer." He blew a thin stream of the bitter smoke from his tiny cigar. It curled around the boxes and cups on the table. "The one is a liar at best; a Communist maybe. The other is an amoral egomaniac."

"I don't want our motives mixed," said Graves. "Or confused. Our purpose is to prevent this alumna of Komsomol from getting permanent residence in the United States. And to prevent the Justice Department from looking like a gang of idiots." He glanced at Langley. "Right now this Bernardin woman seems to have the government lawyers tied in knots."

"That's temporary," said Langley defensively. "She knows her law, and for a while she had the benefit of a liberal-oriented judge, but the law will defeat her."

"She knows more than the law," said Graves. He, too, smoked short, strong cigars, and he shook one from a pack and lit it with a match. "She knows how to use the media, and that fat little sister of hers knows her way around the halls of Congress.''

''It would be a mistake,'' said Nash, ''to overlook anything where Cosima Bernardin is vulnerable—and, I assure you, she *is* vulnerable.''

''I'd like to see it,'' said Judge Hawthorne. ''She's a sharp little bitch. Strike 'little.' She's a sharp, abrasive bitch. Where is this vulnerability?''

Nash let heavy smoke dribble over his lips as he grinned. ''She sleeps around,'' he said.

''Oh, forget that,'' interjected Judge Hawthorne. ''You ever commit adultery, Nash? I have, and I enjoyed every minute of it. What the hell? I haven't reached the age yet when I'm unable to appreciate an outstanding piece of tail when I see it—and Cosima Bernardin is an *outstanding* piece of tail. Any man among us should be so lucky as to get to lift that skirt.''

Langley was astonished. He had never imagined that the unsmiling Judge Ralph W. E. Hawthorne entertained such attitudes, much less expressed them in such crude words.

''You tell us she's vulnerable,'' Graves said to Nash. ''How? Tell us something more than that she sleeps around.''

Nash put his little cigar aside in a glass ashtray. ''I can't prove what I'm about to tell you,'' he said. ''The evidence is out there somewhere, if we can find it. A couple of months ago a subcommittee of the bar association met to consider charges of unethical conduct against Cosima Bernardin. There was a hearing, in which she literally defied the bar association to discipline her. She all but told the subcommittee to go to hell. And when the vote was taken''—he paused, shrugged—''it was perfectly obvious that one or more members of the subcommittee had been . . . *influenced.*''

Graves reached across the table to the big glass ashtray and stubbed out his cigar, blowing the last of his smoke from the corner of his mouth. "Fine," he muttered. "Wonderful. All we have to do is get the evidence."

"Let me point out a little coincidence," said Nash with a faint smile of self-satisfaction. "One of the members of the subcommittee was Robert Blyleven, a junior partner at Maxwell, Donovan, Margolin & Stanley. The firm represents Knightley International, the hotel chain. Knightley is in deep financial trouble and owes Maxwell, Donovan more than a million dollars in unpaid fees—an amount the firm just can't afford to lose. And guess who else Knightley owes? Bernardin Frères. Right now, Leon Bernardin holds Knightley under his thumb. If he forecloses, he will take the assets, leaving nothing from which to pay Maxwell, Donovan. What's more, when Knightley defaulted, Bernardin Frères exercised its right under the loan agreement to appoint three members of the board. That puts Maxwell, Donovan under his thumb, too—because he can dictate to Knightley that it obtain different counsel."

Judge Hawthorne frowned and shook his head. "You are suggesting," he said sternly, "that Maxwell, Donovan ordered its junior partner to vote to dismiss the charges against Cosima Bernardin. Do you have any evidence at all?"

Nash turned up the palms of his hands. "Why didn't Blyleven decline to serve on the subcommittee? Wouldn't that have been the correct thing to do?"

"Maybe he didn't know the circumstances," suggested Graves.

"*Everybody* at Maxwell, Donovan knows the circumstances," said Nash flatly. "The mailroom boys know the circumstances."

Graves rose from the table and stepped to the bar cart to pour himself a second splash of Seagram's Seven. "Suppose . . . Suppose," he said thoughtfully, "you could establish interference in the subcommittee inquiry as a fact. What difference?" He shook his head. "I'm not interested in Cosima Bernardin. I'm interested in Svetlana Terasnova. Correction—I'm not even interested in Svetlana Terasnova; I'm interested in the Democrat-liberals who've stuck out their necks for her. I understand she sleeps with Jerry Patchen. What's *he* into? Drugs? Kinky sex? As it stands right now, the media are portraying this ballerina as a naive little girl, a sort of Soviet Snow White. She—"

"Not a big issue, Dan."

There it was again, Langley observed: a conflict among these people. They did not share a common purpose. He could guess why. The relationship between Judge Hawthorne and Claude Graves was not hard to imagine—Grave's Americans to Preserve America had helped the judge secure his appointment. But what was the relationship between Graves and Nash?

"I disagree with you," said Nash to Graves. "It *is* a big issue. If we can prove Leon Bernardin used his financial clout to corrupt an investigation of his daughter's professional ethics—"

"The fallout lands on Emilie McCarthy," said Graves, conceding a grudging enthusiasm. "And on her Democrat-liberal friends."

Nash grinned. "Something like that."

"So how do you prove—" said Hawthorne.

"Through Blyleven," said Nash.

Nineteen

Without his prosthesis, which stood in a corner inside the closet in his bedroom, Hugh swung around his apartment on crutches. His leg had been gone for more than forty years, yet still his missing foot itched, still he felt at day's end a weariness in calf muscles that were not there.

His stump required washing and massage and a clean stump sock at least twice a day. Before Adela he had never met a woman who did not cringe at the sight of it. His first wife in fact had never seen it; his second had seen it only once. Neither of them had been able to conceal her abhorrence. They had loved him, at least at first; he had never doubted that with either of them; but it had been in spite of his stump, and each of them had accepted him in bed only when the sock was in place and even the sock covered by pajamas. They had obsessively avoided touching the hideous stub of the leg that had been taken away by German shellfire.

Not Adela. She washed his stump, rubbed it, dusted it with talcum powder and pulled the clean sock up over it. On her knees before him, with no apparent sign of revulsion, she cared for him as no one but the doctors and nurses ever had. Oddly, she seemed to do it as something perfectly natural, as a simple act of caring; if it was difficult for her, she disguised her feelings skillfully or by determination. He was constantly surprised, constantly grateful.

She was performing in New York, thank god. Soon she would go on tour, but for now she was performing in New York, and she had moved in with him. When he came home, she helped him to take off his prosthesis and care for his stump; every other day he shaved her head; and then, sometimes they made love. She couldn't boil water—or wouldn't, more likely. When they didn't eat out, they had food brought in, sometimes at two or three in the morning, when she returned from doing a show. He slept several hours before she came home, then stayed up with her until almost dawn; after he left for the office, she slept most of the day. They shared a joke: that they were a bizarre couple, utterly bizarre.

He was sixty-seven years old and in love with a bald-headed girl of twenty-nine. She was twenty-nine and in love with a one-legged man of sixty-seven.

She said she had been singularly blessed to find him. "I owe it to Jesus," she said. "To my blessed Lord and Savior."

Hugh shook his head and grinned. "I don't think Jesus arranged this one, honey."

"Of course He did. He does everything."

"What would Jesus think of your living with a man you're not married to? And of the way you make love?"

Adela smiled happily. "Jesus *is* love," she said. "I only do what He wants me to do."

She was an innocent: in her stock of ideas, in her music (as he had learned), and in her passions. Perhaps it was her innocence that made it possible for her to confront his stump. To her it was just a fact and nothing more. She was not impatient with complexity; she just didn't recognize it and so reduced nearly everything to simplicity. He wondered if her elemental innocence did not derive from her

373

background in the rural South, where people lived closer to the rudiments.

"I don't feel like eating," she said.

He was sipping Scotch and had just asked her if she wanted to go out for something to eat before she went downtown for her evening performance, or if she wanted him to order something that they could share when she returned. "Chinese?" he asked. "A pizza?"

"Kentucky Fried Chicken," she said. "We can warm it up in the microwave. But promise me you'll get some sleep while I'm out."

"Damn right," he said. "The old man's not used to these hours."

"Well . . . I want a horny man when I get back, not a sleepy one. You want to shave me before I go out?"

He sat on the closed lid of the toilet. She squatted on the floor with her back to him. He covered her head with shaving foam and caressed her cheeks with his left hand as with a razor in his right he scraped off the foam and the fine growth of dark stubble that had grown in two days. He had come to enjoy this queer ritual. It was an act of love, performed with tenderness.

And this time the damned telephone interfered.

A sensible man, Hugh kept an extension in the bathroom. He reached for the instrument on the wall between the toilet and tub.

"Hupp."

"Hugh . . . Rick. I'd like to talk to you for a little while this evening. Your schedule . . . ?"

"Anytime after eight," said Hugh. "What you got in mind?"

"Just as soon not do it on the phone. What'd be most convenient? Me come to your place?"

Hugh looked down at Adela, staring curiously up at him, her head still half white with shave foam. "I'll be alone after eight, Rick," he said.

* * *

Rick had never seen Hugh without his prosthesis. Hugh was wearing a white terry-cloth robe and dark-blue knit pajamas. One pajama leg dangled empty, almost to the floor. Hugh swung confidently into his kitchen, shoved his crutches aside and balanced easily on one leg as he poured himself a Scotch and offered one to Rick. He made a little hop to the refrigerator to get ice, then hopped back to the counter. Rick knew better than to offer help.

Hugh did let Rick carry the drinks to the living room, while he carried a bowl of Spanish peanuts that he clutched with the same fingers that were wrapped around his crutch.

"A question, Hugh," said Rick when they were comfortable and had sipped from their drinks. "A dammed tough question. Do you think there's a possibility, any possibility at all, that Leon Bernardin exerted an improper influence over that subcommittee that investigated Cosima's confrontation with Burton Oliver?"

Hugh reached into the bowl of peanuts and took out a handful. The gesture gave him a moment to ponder the origin of the question. Rick wouldn't ask without reason. . .

"He might have done it without telling Cosima," Rick added.

"I can't think he'd be that stupid," said Hugh. "Obviously, though, you think he did, or you wouldn't be here in the middle of the evening with the question. So talk."

Rick nodded disconsolately. "One of the members of the subcommittee was Robert Blyleven, a partner at Maxwell, Donovan, Margolin, & Stanley. One night about two weeks after the meeting I ran into him downtown. We knew each other. I'd done some business with him in years past. He was about half loaded, and he asked me to stop into Charlie Brown's and have a drink with him. I did. Pretty soon he's telling me his firm had ordered him to vote to vindicate Cosima, no matter what the evidence was. Maxwell, Donovan represents Knightley International; Knightley owes

Maxwell, Donovan a million or so but is insolvent; whether or not Maxwell, Donovan ever gets paid depends pretty much on what the major secured creditor does—and the major secured creditor is Bernardin Frères. Blyleven couldn't say for sure Bernardin had leaned on the firm. He said he didn't know. But he thought it had happened. Anyway, his vote was not free and honest.''

"Shit!"

"Yeah. Hugh—I can't believe Cosima knew.''

"You don't *want* to believe Cosima knew.''

"Which means *you* believe she did.''

Hugh shook his head. "I don't say that. In fact, I don't give a damn what you believe, or what I believe, or what anybody believes. Belief is shit. Only what we *know* counts. And you came here tonight because you know something. I mean you know something more than that this Blyleven character got in his cups and told you a fairy tale. You—''

"Okay," said Rick. "Something more immediate. Blyleven called me this afternoon. He'd had a call from P. D. Dougherty, who was also on the subcommittee, the one who was offended when Cosima asked them not to smoke. Dougherty wants Blyleven to meet him for lunch at the Harvard Club. He wants to talk to him about— Well. About the pregnant topic.''

"Drank too much and talked too much,'' said Hugh.

"He swore he didn't. He swears Dougherty found out just by taking note of the relationship between Bernardin Frères and Knightley International. Dougherty asked him on the telephone why, in view of that relationship, he hadn't declined to serve on the subcommittee. He has Blyleven shaking, I can tell you.''

Hugh tipped his glass and finished his Scotch at a gulp. "Want another one?'' he asked.

Rick checked his glass. "I'm okay for the moment.''

"Then get your own when you want it. Me, I want one now.''

"Can I get it for you?''

That was a mistake. Hugh glared at him, then pushed himself up with one muscular leg, grabbed his crutches and swung gracefully and rapidly into the kitchen.

Rick nibbled at a couple of peanuts, took a small sip of Scotch and glanced around the apartment. He knew Adela lived here too, for the time being; but he could see no sign of her. These were the living quarters of a long-time single man, furnished to his taste. The couch on which they had been sitting was upholstered in brown leather; it had the deep sweet smell of well-cared-for rich leather. The walls were lined with floor-to-ceiling bookcases, filled with maybe two thousand volumes, chiefly of history and biography, concentrating on World War II, but also with hundreds of good novels, representing the best contemporary authors, and scores of oversized art books. Standing in one corner was an old-fashioned grocer's claw, the long-handled tool grocers had once clamped around cans on high shelves, to bring them down for customers. It was handy for a man who did not want to climb on a stool to reach books on his top shelves. This was the only evidence visible in the apartment of Hugh's forty-year handicap.

He had an elaborate and—to Rick—painfully expensive audio system. His television and VCR occupied lesser space, as though the whole concept of video were an afterthought. A spinet piano sat at one end of the room.

"Do you play?" Rick asked when Hugh returned.

"Yeah," said Hugh casually. "Only when Red's not here." He still called Adela Red, though the hedge of dyed hair that had inspired it was gone. "I'd be embarrassed to let her hear my amateurish pounding."

"You have a handsome apartment," said Rick.

Hugh nodded an acknowledgement of the compliment. "So, is Blyleven going to meet with Dougherty?"

"He put him off for a little while. Said his schedule was full this week and next. Dougherty was not discouraged. He asked him to set a date for their meeting. Blyleven didn't set one, but he expects he'll have to see him. He doesn't see how he can refuse."

"Has he told his partners at Maxwell, Donovan?" Hugh asked.

"He didn't say. I got the impression that maybe he hasn't."

"Why'd he call you? What's he expect you to do about it?"

"I don't know."

"He thinks somebody's about to immerse him in deep shit," said Hugh. "So what would you do? You'd want some clout on your side. The only clout available to him is what the Bernardins have. Did he ask you to talk to Cosima?"

"Well, he said he'd like to have her reaction."

"You haven't talked to her?"

Rick shook his head. "I think what Blyleven would like is an assurance from Leon that he did not muscle Maxwell, Donovan. If he can count on Leon Bernardin to say that—in the forceful manner the old boy is capable of—then he can confront P. D. Dougherty and bristle. I mean, indignantly deny everything."

"Well. Maybe you should call Leon."

Rick smiled and shook his head. "He doesn't like me. To tell you the truth, I'm scared to death of him."

"So you want me to call him?"

"If you think it's a good idea."

Hugh leaned back into the corner of the couch. "I don't know, Rick. I don't know. I'll have to think about that one."

"What about Cosima then? Should we talk to her?"

" 'We'? You afraid of her, too? Or—"

"No, I'm not afraid of her."

"You're in love with her, though. Aren't you?"

Rick shrugged. "I suppose I am. For all the good it will ever do."

"Have you considered leaving the firm?"

"Have you? You're the one the affiliation seems to have damaged."

Hugh interlaced his fingers and turned down the corners of his mouth. "I'm sixty-seven, Rick. I came to the big city to make my fortune, as they used to say in fairy tales, and I made it. They can't hurt me. But you—"

"The Reischauer Group?" Rick asked.

"Blake Summers was in the office a week ago. Didn't you recognize him? No, I guess you wouldn't. I told him if his loyalty to me wasn't strong enough to overcome whatever objections he had to my sharing offices with Cosima Bernardin and Joan Salomon, then he could go to hell."

"And?"

Hugh chuckled. "I got a pious little sermon on how much our long friendship meant to him, on how much the company appreciates me. Anyway, I still have the client, at least for this year. I told him I wouldn't want it for more than another couple of years, anyway."

Rick rose and went into the kitchen to refresh his drink. "I was stupid to develop a personal relationship with Cosima," he said back through the door. "Just stupid. I never had a chance to . . . Well, you know. Independent as she thinks she is, she's still dominated by her family, by her father mostly. I—"

"You rationalize," said Hugh curtly. "But if it's difficult for you to stay with the firm—"

"She's brought in every client we've got. Every one. It's less than a year, and we're beginning to make a profit. Of, course, Cosima has never taken a cent from the firm. She lives off her independent income. Even Joan has been very modest about her partner's draw. She has some other money. I'm the only member of the firm who actually lives off it. But . . . Unless we get hurt badly by something like this Blyleven thing, the firm could be a real winner in another year or two."

Hugh had half-withdrawn his attention from what Rick was saying—as his next words made clear. "Let me ask you," he said, "if you see any shadow of the fine hand of Hamilton, Schuyler behind P. D. Dougherty?"

"I . . . don't see it," said Rick.

"What do you want to bet it's there? Son of a bitch!"

"Anyway, do we tell Cosima?"

Hugh shook his head. "Not for the moment. If she decides to make war, she could hurt herself badly. Let's let the thing develop a little."

Cosima's mind was on something else that evening. Sitting at a table at Lutèce, she listened as Watson Waugh described the musical show he hoped to produce.

"Masquerade will open in London," he said. "Because it costs less to open a show there, also because I already have nearly enough money to open in London. But we won't wait six months or a year to open in New York. Unless the show falls on its face in London, we will open here three months after the London opening. Indeed, I have enough confidence to open simultaneously, but a three-month wait does give our American partners a shield—if the show fails in London, we can back out here and save a major part of the investment."

The other woman in their party seemed to be paying little attention to Watson Waugh. She was reading the wine list, her lips moving, curling around the French and German names. Her coppery red hair was cut short around her ears and neck but was abundant on top, where it was held in place with a diamond-studded strand and several diamond pins. Her face was freckled, and her smile—as Cosima had observed—was ready and genuine. She wore a light-blue wool jacket over matching sweater, with a short black skirt. Lucinda Duskin was thirty-five, the second wife of Marshal Duskin. Her husband was in his sixties, a jovial bullet-headed man who wore a double-breasted khaki suit that was unhappily conspicuous in the intimate dining room of Lutèce.

380

"I am an *investor,* you understand, Mr. Waugh, Miss Bernardin," said Duskin. "I'm not an angel, and I'm not a patron of the arts—not to the extent of the amount of money we're talking about here. I'm prepared to take a reasonable risk, or even an unreasonable one, but I do want to believe I stand a chance of recovering on my investment."

Lucinda Duskin looked up from the wine list. "Seven out of ten Broadway shows lose money," she said.

"Not Watson Waugh's shows," said Cosima.

Waugh smiled and bowed slightly toward her. He was a round, cherubic man: bald, stocky, lively of expression and gesture. "Thank you," he said dryly. "I've staged my share of bombs, though, as well as my share of hits."

"Specifically," said Cosima, "if you had invested in *Beautiful Enemy,* you would already have recovered one-third of your investment—and the show has only been open six months."

"We enjoyed that show," said Lucinda.

"Yes," said Marshal Duskin. "Wish I had invested in that."

"Well . . . You listened to the tape I sent you—I mean the tape of the music for *Masquerade.* How did you like it?"

"Pretty songs," said Marshal. Then he shrugged. "Of course, I'm a musical illiterate. Lucy liked it. That's better authority."

"You are talking about seven and a half million dollars," said Lucinda. "An expensive production."

"It will be expensive," said Waugh. "That's why Bernardin, Loewenstein & Salomon have set up a special kind of financing arrangement for me. I'll ask Cosima to explain that to you."

Cosima had come to the office that morning in a checked, vicuna-colored suit of jacket and trousers, worn over a black cashmere turtleneck; before she left for dinner she had substituted the matching skirt for the trousers. She had been

381

sipping on a martini while they talked, and now she pushed it away from her.

"The financing arrangement is not very complicated," she said to the Duskins. "Masquerade Associates is a limited partnership, which will sell one hundred investment units in the production, for $75,000 per unit, and each investor must purchase a minimum of two units. Each purchaser must be an accredited investor under the rules of the Securities and Exchange Commission. There can be no more than fifty investors—in fact, there can't be that many, because some are buying more than the minimum two units. We're expecting some corporate investors and some individuals."

"This isn't the first time I've heard the term 'accredited investor,' " said Lucinda, "but I'm not sure anyone has ever defined it for me." She looked at her husband. "I guess we're accredited investors, aren't we? How did we get this accreditation?"

Marshal nodded to Cosima, and she explained. "Under the SEC rule, to be an accredited investor a person—or a husband and wife together—must have a combined net worth of more than one million dollars, not including their home, and a combined annual income of at least $200,000. The SEC is willing to assume that people with that much in assets and income are sophisticated about investments and so don't need all the protection of the securities laws. Specifically, we don't have to file all the disclosure documents the securities laws require when investments are offered to the public generally."

Lucinda smiled at Marshall. "I guess we do qualify," she said playfully.

"Barely," he responded. With his fingernail he drew a line down the tablecloth beside his glass. "How many units have you sold?" he asked Waugh.

"Twenty-six, as of this afternoon."

"You say some people are buying more than two units?"

Cosima answered. "Watson has bought eight units him-

382

self. The Knickerbocker Theatre Company has bought four units. It's of course in its interest to have a show like *Masquerade* moving into its theatre. The rest of the investors so far have bought the minimum two units."

"Including Cosima herself," said Waugh.

"But—" Cosima continued. "We are talking to one corporate investor who is seriously thinking twenty units. In fact, I spoke with them on the phone just before I left my office this evening, and the deal is all but concluded. The units have only been on the market for two weeks, and we're approaching fifty percent sold."

"If we bought four units, could we sell two of them?" Marshal asked.

"You can sell two units, not one," said Cosima. "And the buyer must be an accredited investor."

Marshal Duskin nodded, pursing his lips. "Sophisticated way of raising funds for a show, isn't it?"

"It's relatively new," said Cosima, "but it's been done before."

"With today's production costs, the old way of raising money, with so-called angels, is no longer effective," said Waugh. "We've had to look for new ways. Fortunately, Cosima is well acquainted with some of the more sophisticated modern methods of raising capital. As you may know, she is a daughter of Leon Bernardin, so she has a specialized knowledge of the field."

"Is your father's bank investing in *Masquerade?*" Lucinda asked Cosima.

"No."

"What does he think of the investment?" asked Marshal.

"He has no opinion. I've never discussed it with him."

Marshal Duskin glanced at his wife and smiled: a significant little smile of amused skepticism. "I suppose we could risk the price of four units," he said. "I think I know where I can unload two of them."

* * *

"Essentially, I suppose, we have two problems with her," said D. Douglas Miller to P. D. Dougherty. "When she left here, she took a client with her, an egregious violation of her agreement with this firm. It was a client who had paid us well over a quarter of a million dollars in fees in the preceding year. She stole it from us—there is no other word that describes what she did. Our second problem is that she is an unethical lawyer, utterly without respect for anyone or anything, and she has been stealing clients from other firms as well."

P. D. Dougherty nodded. Miller and Nash had come to his fifty-first-floor corner office, which he occupied as senior corporation-law partner at Quarles & McGrath. His cheeks collapsed as he sucked hard on a cigarette, drawing smoke through the resisting filter; it made his face longer, thinner, and more sepulchral than ever. "The impudent bitch told me not to smoke," he said. "At the subcommittee hearing. Can you imagine? She told all of us not to smoke."

"Well, there is of course the personality problem," said Miller. He spoke as he always did: in a soft monotone, allowing no hint of feeling to escape from under the colorless mask of his face. His heavy-lidded pale blue eyes communicated nothing more than sustained patience. "She's not an easy young woman to like."

"She shut *you* off pretty damned fast," Dougherty said to Dan Nash. "She doesn't like you, plain enough."

Nash compressed his thin lips and nodded. "She has displayed a decided antipathy for me," he said, adjusting his glasses by seizing their round, caramel-colored frames between his thumb and index finger and, while lifting them, extending his pinkie like a DAR tea drinker. "It's an honor, of sorts."

"Well . . ." said Dougherty. "I did what you asked me to do. I looked into her background as fully as I could—that is, as fully as I could without her finding out what I was doing—before the subcommittee meeting. As I told you

384

at the time, Dan, nothing turned up that we could have used at the hearing. On the other hand—"

"On the other hand," Miller interrupted forcefully but quietly, "she got Lawton Lanier to lie for her. The charges brought by that stupid little scrivener Oliver were nothing as compared to a charge of securing perjured testimony at her disciplinary hearing."

"That he was lying was obvious to everyone," said Dougherty. "He wasn't even a skillful liar, just a defiant one—which he could afford to be because he knew we couldn't *prove* he was lying."

"We can prove it now," said Nash with a smug little grin he could not suppress.

P. D. Dougherty's formidable black eyebrows rose skeptically. "Indeed," he muttered.

"Yes," said Nash. "We've taken a sworn statement from Vanessa Kingston. She's back in this country, you know."

"And has her own reasons for antipathy to Cosima Bernardin," said Dougherty dryly.

"I suppose so," said Nash.

Dougherty glanced at Miller, then settled his eyes back on Nash. Speaking of antipathies, he felt a strong one for Douglas Miller's weasely little partner. Dougherty, in his sixties, was a bit weary of the law, of the incessant confrontations, and he particularly disliked many of the junior partners now entering the ranks of seniors. Too many of them were like Nash: obsequious, pusillanimous, grasping, and, with it all, self-righteous.

Nash had reached into his attaché case and was pulling out some papers. "I've marked the cogent passages," he said. "This"—handing over a sheaf—"is part of the transcript of the subcommittee hearing. It is when you were cross-examining Lawton Lanier. And this"—some more papers—"is the sworn statement of Vanessa Kingston, with marks where she addresses the same questions."

Dougherty scanned the papers. The exchange between him and Lanier was marked in transparent yellow:

MR. DOUGHERTY: So it was a coincidence that you found a role for Vanessa Kingston a week after Miss Bernardin met Mr. Oliver?

MR. LANIER: Something like that.

MR. DOUGHERTY: How did you know Miss Kingston was threatening to sue Jack Putman?

MR. LANIER: Miss Kingston told me, of course.

Nash had marked the corresponding part of Vanessa Kingston's affidavit:

After Mr. Lanier described the part and actually offered it to me, he stated there was a problem. He stated that he understood I was involved in a dispute with Jack Putnam and had retained a lawyer to sue Jack. Mr. Lanier then stated that he would not hire me unless I gave him a signed release which he could give to Jack. I objected to this, but he said it was a condition of my employment. He then dictated a release, which I wrote out in my own handwriting. After I signed it, he told me he would have a contract delivered to my agent that afternoon. He also told me that this part of our conversation was confidential, that I should not tell anyone why I signed a release.

I did not volunteer to Mr. Lanier the information that I was involved in a dispute with Jack Putnam and had retained a lawyer to sue him. Mr. Lanier already knew that and was the first to mention it.

P. D. Dougherty handed the papers back to Nash. "So?" he asked.

"She contradicts him," said Nash eagerly.

Dougherty shrugged. "So we have a contradiction between the testimony of an aspiring but not very successful actress and a poised, successful, confident West End and Broadway producer. I notice she doesn't even mention the essential point, which is whether or not Cosima Bernardin

386

prompted Lanier to demand the release. She doesn't mention it because she doesn't know. She can't testify to that point."

"True," Miller admitted.

"Lanier lied," Nash insisted. "The coincidence—"

"There was no coincidence," Dougherty said. "He didn't just *happen* to demand a release. He lied. You know that. I know that. Cosima Bernardin knows that. And she knows something else, too—that we can't prove it. We *can't* prove it. Vanessa Kingston can't prove it, even if her testimony is accepted as better than his—which it won't be."

"The circumstantial evidence, plus the testimony—"

Dougherty interrupted Nash once again. "Are not sufficient to support suspension or disbarment of a lawyer. We can't reconvene the subcommittee, you know. That's the other point."

"Because . . . ?" Miller asked cautiously.

"Because at least one member—and I suspect more than one—wouldn't vote to discipline Leon Bernardin's daughter, no matter what the evidence."

"You called Blyleven?" Nash asked.

Dougherty nodded. "Of course. *There's* the key."

"Not really," said Miller. "Suppose—with unrealistic optimism, suppose—that Blyleven gave us a statement to the effect that he was improperly influenced with respect to his vote in the subcommittee. He's not going to do it, because he would have to name the partner who gave him his orders; but suppose he did. That still doesn't nail Leon Bernardin, because the partner may have acted out of fear of Bernardin, not because Bernardin called him. And finally, if you nail Leon, you still haven't nailed Cosima, because the old man may have acted on his own, without telling her."

Miller did something unusual for him: he smiled faintly. He ran his hand over the wisps of hair on his nearly bald head. "And beyond that, I'm going to tell you something else. *She did it.* She recruited Lanier to get the release for

Jack Putnam. And she used her father's influence to corrupt the subcommittee. I believe it. I know her. I know that much about her. I also know she's smart enough to build layers of protection for herself. We can get her, gentlemen. But it won't be easy."

"I intend to lean on Blyleven," said Dougherty. "He's still at that level in his firm where he is intimidated by senior partners—something Cosima Bernardin apparently never was."

"Never was," said Nash.

"Maybe we'll test her nerve, sooner or later," said Dougherty. "We're building a case against her. She's not so damned brave and smart that she can't be unnerved. Let her make one little mistake . . ."

"Set your hatchet man on her," said Miller.

"Hmm?"

"Graves," said Miller. "A two-dollar whore if I ever saw one. Let him see what he can find out. I am sure you know about deniability. I'm not sure you can deny him, Paul, but I sure as hell can—and will. In the meantime . . . Our own little buck-stopper."

"What surprises me," said Dougherty, "is that you guys have a lot more interest in screwing this girl than I have, and you look to me to do your dirty work."

"One hand washes the other, Paul," said Miller. "When you put yourself on the Cosima Bernardin subcommittee, you were returning a favor. Now we're even, and you're doing a favor, and we'll owe you one. I wouldn't be surprised if you find some way to call in your chits."

"You better believe it," grumbled Dougherty.

"Ruggiero, you dickin that girl?"

Jerry grinned at his sister. The bones that God had designed to carry a five-foot-four woman had to carry two hundred pounds of flesh, and they were strained. She had been strained by carrying five children to term. At thirty-five, she favored black dresses, flat shoes, dark stockings; she had taken on, almost, the look of a sedentary nun.

"An indelicate question, Clara."

"Ha!" she laughed. "A Russian. A ballerina yet. They gonna deport her? A convenient way to get rid of her."

Jerry shook his head. "Svetlana . . . No, they're not going to deport her."

"Don Leon's daughter is going to save her?"

"Two of his daughters are working on it. And so am I."

Clara chuckled, which sent ripples down her body. "Good luck, then, Ruggiero. You're gonna need it."

Across the room, Svetlana stood with her head cocked to one side, looking curiously into the dark red depths of a glass of wine. "My grandfather makes this wine," a young man said to her—and so compelled her to reassess her judgement that the wine was not very good.

"It is very good," she said.

"Do they make wine in Russia?" he asked.

"Yes . . ." she said tentatively. She considered it a curious question and was uncertain as to why he would ask.

"What would they call a wine like this in Russia?" he asked.

"Uh . . . vino," she said.

"I mean this *kind* of wine, a dry red dinner wine. Is there a name?"

"Red . . . Uh, *Saperavi* maybe. *Mukuzani*. Very good."

"Do your people drink much wine? I mean, besides vodka?"

She nodded. "Much wine. And *champagni*. Yes."

He beamed. "Ah. You know what they say—'A meal without wine is like a day without sunshine.' "

"Who says this?" Svetlana asked.

Jerry had come to her rescue. "These paisans," he laughed. "They swill that poison and tell each other it's good." He reached for her glass, which she surrendered gratefully. "C'mon. I know where we can find something better."

He led her through the crowd of laughing people toward the kitchen. Italians, he had told her: all people of Italian descent. They made her think of home. The Russians were like this: stocky peasants with red cheeks and noses, warm, familial, friendly, filling themselves with the red wine and with other things, too, and readying for what seemed likely to be a generous feast. The house was overheated, and the air was heavy with smells that made her saliva run: meat and tomatoes cooking with ample measures of savory spices. Many women worked in the large kitchen. Besides Jerry, the men did not come in the kitchen.

"Mama," he said. He leaned toward her. "The vodka?" He pronounced it "wod-kah."

The heavy old woman turned and settled benevolent eyes on Svetlana. "Ah, she'd rather drink that than the wine. Where you told me to put it, Ruggiero. In the freezer."

He opened the small freezer, the upright one that was part of the refrigerator, and the bottle of Stolichnaya was there. The vodka was all but frozen; it oozed out of the bottle like heavy oil into the small glasses he had pulled from the cabinet. He had pulled three.

"Mama," he said. "Wod-kah."

His mother accepted the glass and raised it as Jerry and Svetlana raised theirs. The kitchen fell silent, and women looked away from the steaming pots of pasta and sauces to watch Beatrice Paccinelli sample vodka. They laughed as she winced as the cold substance passed between her lips and again as it turned to a volatile liquid in her mouth.

"Ruggiero," she said. "See to it that your father tastes this."

Three hours later Svetlana danced nude for him, in their suite at the Hyatt Regency in Greenwich. An hour after that, when they were in bed, he told her he loved her.

Twenty

"It's not a cause with me," Joan Salomon said to Cosima. "It's a preference, but I never thought of it as a philosophy of life or a cause."

"What do you expect me to say?" Cosima asked.

Joan stood with her back to Cosima, looking out the window, watching the planes taking off from LaGuardia Airport. "Say, 'Don't do it,' if that's how you feel. Say it will hurt Svetlana's case."

"I don't know," said Cosima. "It could do that. There's no way you could put it off for a few weeks, maybe a couple of months?"

Joan sighed. " 'Justice delayed is justice denied.' Seriously, if I don't take the case and run with it, she's going to get somebody else—which either one of us would do in the circumstances. You can't blame her."

"No. No, of course not."

Cosima leaned back in her chair and swung her feet up onto her desk, a posture she almost never assumed. She reached down and rubbed her thighs, then leaned forward and rubbed her calves. She had walked up to 21 for lunch, then back to the office, not enough of a walk to tire the muscles in her legs, but they were tired just the same. She was just plain tired.

Joan had come in to discuss a client she wanted to take on: a young woman who had been dismissed from a job from a brokerage firm on Wall Street because she had admitted on inquiry that she was a lesbian. There was a community of them, of course, and word had circulated that this young woman needed a good lawyer.

"It is very unlikely," said Joan, "that Hobson, Tillman will listen to reason and settle. If I have to file a civil-rights complaint or a lawsuit—" She shook her head. "Media attention. What's more, I have to tell you the sisters *want* media attention, all they can get."

"What kind of woman is your client?" Cosima asked.

"She's not my client yet. I haven't taken her on. She's pretty. Not like me. She—"

"Joan—"

"Not like me," Joan insisted. "I know what words they use for me. They think women like me all look alike. But they never suggest it of Victoria. She's pretty. She doesn't fit the stereotype."

"I wouldn't have guessed *you,*" said Cosima dryly. "Except that you seem to want to wear it like a badge."

"No. I just don't conceal it."

"Well . . . That's immaterial. How do you plan to handle this, Joan? Employment-rights cases aren't your specialty. Or anybody else's in this office. Are you really sure you are the best lawyer for Victoria Edsel?"

"Yes, because I have the sympathy."

"She is going to need more than sympathy."

"Other lawyers have already turned her down. They don't want to touch a case like hers."

"She just hasn't talked to the right one," said Cosima.

"Maybe she has," said Joan.

Cosima nodded. "Okay. Maybe she has. So, I come back to the question. What do you want to hear from me?"

Joan had turned away from her view of the traffic at

LaGuardia and stood with her back to the window. Now she sat down. "If it weren't for your problems with Svetlana, I'd take the case, no question, no doubt. But—" She threw out her hands. "Frankly said, Cosima, would you rather I didn't?"

"Frankly said, I'd like to take on my enemies one at a time," said Cosima. Weary already of propping her feet on her desk, she dropped them to the floor and smoothed her skirt. "If we had some kind of settlement with Lana's case, I'd tell you to take the case and do your damnedest. As it is . . . Well, hell. Dammit!"

"What's more," said Joan, "she can't afford much legal service. I don't know . . . I guess the sisters will contribute."

"In return for which they'll want to tell you how to handle the case. Plus which, a conflict may arise between what is in Victoria's best interests and what is in theirs. That happens when you represent public-interest clients, you know. I mean, look, Joan—I'll settle for any resolution of Lana's case that allows her to remain in the United States, whether we set a useful precedent for future cases or not. As far as I'm concerned, my obligation is to my client, not to other deportable aliens. You've got to think about that."

Joan smiled tartly. "You have a highly practical turn of mind," she said.

"I reject everything my opposition represents and stands for, philosophically and personally. I'd love to make war on them and rub their noses in— In you know what. But Lana doesn't need that. My first obligation is to what Lana needs. Yours will be to what Victoria needs."

"Cosima . . . Do you want me to tell Vicky Edsel I won't represent her?"

"You're damned right I do . . . from a selfish point of view. But—But, no, I don't want you to tell her that. In the first place, it's your judgment to make, not mine. In the second place, there's a goddamned question of principle here, as you well know.''

Joan nodded. "And not just for me."

"Right. Not just for you. I do suggest you don't accept any money from the sisterhood. Or from anyone else. Keep control of the case. You and your client. Absolute control."

"Thanks. I'll keep control."

"Hello, Cosima. Lawton Lanier here. Are you engaged for lunch? Shall I drop by your office at twelve-thirty? Good. See you then."

He appeared on time, accompanied by a young man she had never met, whom he introduced as Bill Gallon. "He'll be with us for lunch if you don't mind," said Lanier. "We've something to discuss."

A surprise. She received another one when they emerged from the Pan Am Building on the west side. A car was waiting for them. It was not a limousine, just a car, driven by another sober young man in a dark three-piece suit. Lanier opened the rear door for Cosima, she got in and Gallon joined the driver in the front. They drove away, off the ramp and down onto Park Avenue South.

"Forgive us if this is a bit conspiratorial, Cosima," Lanier said. "Why it is will be apparent in a moment. Bill— Do you want to show her why?"

Gallon, who was turned to face her, nodded. "I've brought along two pieces of equipment, Miss Bernardin," he said. "I—"

"What kind of equipment?" she asked.

"Let me show you," he said. "First, here is a simple tape player. Let me play you a tape."

He pressed down a key, and the tape rolled:

The sound of a telephone ringing.

"Bernardin, Loewenstein & Salomon."

"Yes. This is Lawton Lanier calling for Miss Bernardin, please."

"One moment, sir."

394

"Yes?"

"Hello, Cosima. Lawton Lanier here. Are you engaged for lunch?"

"As a matter of fact, no. Am I to have the pleasure of lunching with you, Lawton?"

"Shall I drop by your office at twelve-thirty?"

"Twelve-thirty. I'll be looking for you."

"Good. See you then."

"So you're recording your phone calls now," Cosima said to Lanier.

"No," said Lanier, and he pointed to Gallon.

The blond young man with the prominent Adam's apple had already put the recorder aside and was showing her something else. It looked like the big old portable radio that used to sit on a table in her father's den at home—filled with a score of flashlight batteries and almost too heavy for a little girl to lift. This one had a luggage handle on top, just as her father's radio had had, but it was not a simple old-style portable radio. It was some kind of electronic device, with an oscilloscope screen on the front, and a dozen knobs and an array of indicator lights.

"This," said Bill Gallon, "is an electronic countermeasures receiver, ECR 1. Something like fourteen thousand dollars worth of electronics, incidentally. It detects bugs. What's more—and better—it intercepts the signals they are transmitting, so we can listen to them."

"The point is," said Lanier, "my office is bugged. Everything I say there is picked up by a tiny transmitter and sent to a receiver somewhere."

"How long has this been going on," she asked.

"Only a few days," said Gallon. "We first picked up the signal on Monday."

"You have your office swept for bugs every week?" Cosima asked.

"Actually, Miss Bernardin," said Gallon. "Mr. Lanier never had his office swept before. We were working for another businessman, on another floor in the building. His business is highly confidential, and we sweep for him twice a week. On Monday we were working in his office and began to pick up a strange signal. The conversation being transmitted made it plain that the signal was not coming from the office we were sweeping. We worked on it until we found out where it was coming from, and then we went to see Mr. Lanier. There is a microphone in his office and a bug on his telephone line. I would guess they were installed last weekend."

Cosima frowned at Lanier. "I suppose you should be flattered," she said.

"Perhaps," said Lanier blandly. "I've met with several people this week—I mean, people with whom I've had . . . confidential transactions. I've warned them. Actually, I can't imagine why anyone would want to bug my office. Unless—"

"Unless it's someone still trying to find out if I asked you to hire Vanessa Kingston," said Cosima.

"Do you think that's possible?" asked Lanier.

Cosima nodded. "I think it's entirely possible."

She glanced at Bill Gallon, and he read her glance and said, "You may want to defer discussion of anything confidential until you and Mr. Lanier are alone. On the other hand, I may tell you that Mr. Lanier has employed my firm to work on this matter, and he may want to assure you that we are entirely capable of keeping our clients' secrets."

He handed her his business card—

WILLIAM A. GALLON & ASSOCIATES
Security Consultants

William A. Gallon
President

An odd card, she thought. No address, no telephone number.

"I can provide references," said Gallon. "Corporations. Law firms. Brokerage firms."

Lanier spoke. "Bill and I have discussed this thing, Cosima. He's made some pretty good suggestions."

"Okay," said Cosima. "We doing lunch?"

During the conversation they had been going south, and shortly the driver pulled the car to the curb in front of a restaurant in Chelsea. It was in fact called Chelsea Place. They sat in the car for a few minutes while Gallon switched on the ECR-1 and checked for signals that might be emanating from the restaurant. Only when he was satisfied that nothing was being transmitted from the restaurant itself did they go in. And the driver remained in the car, keeping the ECR-1 alive, listening for a transmitter that might be activated only after they entered.

"I feel like I'm going to lunch with a CIA agent," said Cosima.

"They're not as good as we are," said Gallon humorlessly.

The building was decidedly unprepossessing, as was the entrance through what looked like an antique shop, but when they had descended a flight of stairs in the rear they found themselves in a bright, small, pleasant Italian restaurant. They ordered drinks before they resumed their discussion.

"My first suggestion to you, Miss Bernardin, would be that you let us sweep your office. Mr. Lanier tells me you have some controversial law business, and it is very possible that someone has bugged you."

"All right," she said.

"I'll send someone this afternoon," he said. "Now, I will make another suggestion, the same one I made to Mr. Lanier. I suggest you leave the bugs in place, if we find any. If we disable or remove them, that tells whoever planted them that we've found them. If they are determined, they'll try again; and the next set of bugs may be more difficult to detect. What's more important, their presence can be used to give you a very great advantage in whatever controversy you're involved in."

"I get you," she said. "We know they're there. Whoever planted them doesn't know we know. So we can feed them—"

"Disinformation," said Gallon.

Cosima smiled. "Disinformation," she repeated. Her smile widened.

"To do it effectively, you have to know who planted the bugs," said Lanier.

"Not really," said Gallon. "You can create disinformation pertinent to more than one controversy. What you must do, though, is create your disinformation skillfully. Do it crudely, your opposition won't buy it."

"You-sure you're not with the CIA?" Cosima asked with a grin.

Gallon shook his head. It didn't seem funny to him.

Cosima spoke to Lanier. "It could very well be the Vanessa Kingston business. Could *very* well be. They haven't given up on that."

"How do you know?"

"I still have friends at Hamilton, Schuyler. Vanessa was in their offices a couple of weeks ago. What possible reason could she have had for paying a call at 120 Broadway, unless it had something to do with our confrontation before the subcommittee?"

"Since the bugs are in my office, too—and I'm assuming Bill will find them in yours—the matter could not have anything to do with your effort to prevent the deportation of Svetlana Terasnova," said Lanier.

"I wouldn't be so sure of that," said Cosima. "The sleazeballs behind that effort will use anything they can find. I mean, anything. They think you lied for me at that hearing. If they could prove it—"

"Well," said Lanier. "Let us work with Bill here and feed them some disinformation. Subtly, Cosima, subtly. More subtle than we were before."

* * *

The telephone rang while she was lying in her tub, the tingling stream of bubbles from the Jacuzzi massaging her gently and relaxing the muscles that had come to seem permanently tense and strained. Cosima reached for the phone.

"Hello—" She was not happy to be getting a telephone call at this hour, and she made no effort to put cordiality or enthusiasm in her voice.

"Hey, Cosima baby. Jack. Hey, listen, you *gotta* come out this weekend. C'mon, you just gotta. Christ, it's been two months. More than. Look, I'd be there, but we shoot until too late for me to catch the Friday night red-eye, plus a six A.M. call on Monday. Hey! I'm *lonesome!*"

"So am I," she said quietly.

"Well, then?"

She closed her eyes tight shut. Why not, for god's sake, if he was begging? "Jack . . . All right."

"Same flight? I'll meet it if I can. Otherwise, you've got the key."

"I've got the key, right."

"Hey, I love ya, kid. It's desolate without you."

She wished she could believe it. "Okay, Jack. I love you, too. Tomorrow night."

He did meet her flight. As she came through the concourse he was there, distracted by two teenagers demanding autographs and two adults trying to engage him in conversation. He was wearing faded jeans and a gray sweatshirt, with a black hat. He broke away from the woman and her husband, grabbed Cosima's carry-on bag, and embraced her warmly.

"Oh, my *god!*" squealed the sixty-year-old woman to Cosima. "I've seen every picture you ever made! Every picture! I swear!"

"That would take you about five minutes," said Cosima dryly.

Jack was laughing. "She's my attorney," he said.

"Then you're Cosima Bernardin! My *god!*"

Cosima heard one of the teenagers whisper to the other—"Who the hell's Cosima Bernardin?"

She smiled at them. "I often ask myself that question," she said.

She had dressed to please Jack if he did meet the plane: not in the Levis that would have been most comfortable for a cross-country flight but in her red ribbed-knit Saint Laurent minidress, omitting the flowing red coat that matched it as something she wouldn't need in California. Probably she did look more like an actress than a lawyer.

"Cosima Bernardin!" the woman gulped. "Aww . . . You're his lawyer and . . . Well . . ." She winked. She actually winked!

They extricated themselves from the net the woman and her husband were trying to throw around them—a suggestion that mister and missus would be glad to buy them a drink, or maybe even dinner—and fled to the parking lot.

He drove a Jaguar. "What the hell is this 'You're Cosima Bernardin' business?" she asked as she settled herself in the leather-upholstered seat.

"Welcome to the world of notoriety," he said. "If you didn't know you were famous, you don't look at the tabloids Mr. and Mrs. America devour."

Cosima closed her eyes and pressed her body more comfortably into the redolent leather. "You're going to have to forgive me if I sleep a large part of this short visit. I'm exhausted."

"I saw you and Svetlana on the tube Sunday," he said. "Good show."

"The Senate hearings are going to be expedited," she murmured. "We may get a floor vote in a month or so. The lunatic fringe is so hysterical they are threatening a filibuster."

"I had a Chinese dinner in mind," he said. "You rather just go home?"

"I want to go home," she said. "I don't want anything to eat. I don't want anything to drink. I want to go to bed with you, and ten minutes after we make love I want to be asleep. Tomorrow I'll be a better girl, Jack. I promise.''

"First-class scenario," he said. "I'm worn out myself."

"We're going to make it with *Masquerade,*" she said. "We're going to have enough money to do it. After that, Lana. And after that . . . Damn. Joan has taken on a cause of her own. I hope I can stay out of it. She's entitled, but I've got my own problems."

"Tomorrow night," he said, "we've got to put in an appearance at a producer's party. I was committed to it a month ago. Just an appearance. In the morning . . . *sleep*. Till noon, okay? Then we'll squander the afternoon. We don't have to leave the bed before seven tomorrow evening."

"Sounds wonderful."

She did not fall asleep ten minutes after they made love. Exhaustion does not hasten sleep. When he saw that she was not falling asleep, he suggested they have a drink. She asked him to make a pot of coffee.

He rolled off the bed and ambled into the kitchen, naked. A minute or two later, after she had used cold water on her face and had run a brush over her hair, she joined him, also naked. She sat down on a tall stool at his kitchen counter.

"That'll make a pattern on your bottom," he said, referring to the wicker seat of the stool.

"Obviously you've seen that pattern on some lucky girl," she said. She was thinking of Vanessa.

He shrugged. "Told you I was never celibate."

"Including the last two months?"

He grinned. "Why you think I insisted you come to Los Angeles?"

"You said it was because you love me."

"Hell, yes. If I didn't love you, I'd have been playing around."

"And you haven't played around?"

His grin disappeared, an eyebrow rose, he raised his chin. "Jeez, Cosima. You cross-examining me, counsellor?"

Cosima looked at the coffee maker, at the thin stream of coffee coming down. "You said once that you listened for my voice on your telephone recorder. Well, you might have heard it once, but your telephone recorder didn't answer that call. A woman answered. At six-thirty in the morning."

"When?" he asked grimly.

"Wednesday, March 23," she said. "The day after Vanessa was interviewed at Kennedy Airport, where she was just changing from British Air to United, to hurry on to Los Angeles."

Jack nodded. "It was her. She answered the phone. She didn't tell me, but it had to be her. She was here."

"I guessed that was who it was."

"Do you want to know what happened?"

"If you want to tell me."

Jack sighed. He glanced around the kitchen, and Cosima guessed his impulse was to grab a towel or something, that he had suddenly decided his nakedness was embarrassingly incongruous with the last turn in the conversation. If that was his impulse, no towel was in sight, just paper towels, and he turned to face the counter and the coffee pot, hiding his genitalia from her view but presenting his buns, which was just as incongruous.

"Cosima . . ." he said. He sighed again. "Yeah, Vanessa was here. She spent the night, too. She had a key. You have a key. She had a key. She never gave it back to me. I came home that night—I mean the night she came in from London—and she was in the apartment. She was in my bed. Shnocked out her mind, Cosima, I swear. She'd come in. She'd been in my liquor and got herself stinkin'. I couldn't throw her out. She was so bad I even considered calling a doctor. But Cosima . . . I slept in the other bedroom. I swear that. I never touched her. I made her a pot of coffee before I left for a six o'clock call; and when she got up, she found a pot of coffee and a note from me telling her to clear out. I swear."

402

"Never mind swearing," muttered Cosima.

"Well, d' you believe me?"

"Of course I believe you. It makes all kinds of sense."

He poured two cups of coffee. He spoke as he poured. "No, it doesn't. But it's the truth. Jeez, Cosima, if only what makes sense is true— And what doesn't isn't— I mean, you see what I'm tryin' to say." He handed her a cup of coffee. "Vanessa is spiteful, it turns out. I'd never have suspected it."

Cosima put a finger to her lips and shook her head.

"Hmm?"

She put her cup back on the counter, all the while signalling him to be quiet. "Oh, I doubt she's spiteful," she said. "Probably just in love with you."

"Cosima—"

She put a finger to *his* lips and again shook her head. She beckoned him to follow her, and she led him from the kitchen, through the bedroom and into the bathroom. There, as he stood shaking his head, grinning and grimacing, she twisted the knobs and started water running in the tiled shower stall. She stepped into the shower, invited him in, and closed the glass door.

"Hey, this is romantic, but . . . sort of abrupt, isn't it?"

Cosima stood with her back to the tiles, keeping a little distance between her and Jack—with hot water splashing noisily over her breasts and belly. "Soundproof," she said. "No microphone is going to pick up a conversation we have in here."

Jack laughed. "Hey, are you crazy?"

"I found out yesterday afternoon that my office is bugged. What's more, so is Lawton Lanier's. If we're being bugged, you may be. You see the connection?"

"Jesus Christ!"

"It may mean nothing," she said. "It may relate only to the Terasnova case, and the bugging of Lanier's office could be a coincidence. On the other hand, Vanessa was in the office of Hamilton, Schuyler two weeks ago. Spent more than an hour there. I haven't found out who she saw. But I have my suspicions."

"This is crazy stuff. Who would do a thing like that?"

"Crazy people," she said.

"Because of Svetlana Terasnova?"

"It's brought some crazies out of the woodwork," Cosima said grimly.

"And you figure the connection is they want to make you look bad so as to hurt Lana's case."

"I have to guess," she said. "My guess is that there's some kind of an alliance between certain lawyers at Hamilton, Schuyler who hate me for leaving and taking a good client with me, and the ideologues behind the obsessive campaign to deport Lana."

"That's ridiculous," he said.

"No, it isn't, Jack," she said firmly. "You're naive if you think so."

"I didn't mean it's ridiculous for you to guess there's an alliance," he said. "I meant it would be ridiculous for them to—"

"Did you watch the Iran-Contra hearings?" she asked. "Had you ever before seen the kind of egomaniacal self-righteousness you saw in some of those witnesses? Well, you walk into one of the mega-lawyer firms, in New York or anywhere else, and you're apt to encounter the same kind of personalities. In their own judgment, their superior rectitude justifies lying, evasion of the law, manipulation—"

"And maybe a vendetta against a lawyer who stepped on their toes," said Jack.

"I didn't step on their toes," she said, shaking her head soberly. "I kicked them in the balls."

"Cosima . . ." he murmured with an involuntary grin.

"I have a company in New York checking my apartment for bugs this weekend. In the office, the telephone was tapped, so both ends of the conversation were being transmitted, and a microphone in the air-conditioning vent in

404

the windowsill was picking up every sound and sending it out."

"Well, I'm glad you found out," he said. "I'd hate to think everything we—"

"You'd hate to think everything we say on the phone is being heard," she interrupted. "Well, it *is* being heard. I've left the bugs in place. So we talk accordingly. And when we get out of this shower, I suggest we talk as if this place is bugged, too."

"How long you gonna leave the bugs in place, Cosima?" he asked.

For the first time since this conversation began, she smiled: a cynical smile, just short of a sneer. "I haven't decided," she said. "The felons who bugged my office don't know their bugs have been found. I don't have to explain the advantage that gives me. I'm going to leave the bugs in place as long as I can use them."

Jack, too, was capable of a leering, sarcastic grin. "So, if I'm bugged I should do the same?"

"Yes, but be subtle. You have to be very careful not to tip your hand."

His grin changed to one of genuine amusement. "I like playing games where I've got a devious partner," he said. "I'm glad we're on the same side."

"Lynn . . ." said Claude Graves with enthusiasm a little too great for their relationship. "Good to see you. Have a seat."

Lynn Karadja was a beautiful young woman; he had always thought so. He liked the way she wore her blond hair long, to her shoulders; her face and figure—everything about her, in fact—was enticing, including the revealing simplicity of her clothes. But their relationship was that she was the skilled technician who planted bugs for Americans for the Preservation of American Values.

"I gather you've heard nothing useful."

405

"Nothing, really," she said. "If you want to listen to something, I did bring along a tape."

"Anything interesting?"

"Oh . . . kind of."

She withdrew a small cassette player from her big handbag and switched it on.

"Hello."

"Hey, Cosima baby: Jack. Hey, listen, you gotta come out this weekend. C'mon, you just gotta. Christ, it's been two months. More than. Look, I'd be there, but we shoot until too late for me to catch the Friday night red-eye, plus a six A.M. call on Monday. Hey! I'm lonesome!"

"So am I."

"Well, then?"

"Jack . . . All right."

"Same flight? I'll meet it if I can. Otherwise, you've got the key."

"I've got the key, right."

"Hey, I love ya, kid. It's desolate without you."

"Okay, Jack. I love you, too. Tomorrow night."

"There'll be no activity for a couple of days," said Lynn. "She's gone to California like you hear—to shack up with him."

That was another fascinating feature of Lynn: her direct, earthly speech.

"When will she be back?"

"Sunday evening. I listened to her making the reservation. In the meantime the voice-activated recorders will pick up anything that happens, including telephone calls that come in on her answering machine, but it should be a quiet weekend. I gave the crew the weekend off. Might as well save the money. I suppose Americans for the Preservation of American Values can use it."

Claude Graves nodded. "A good thought," he said. "Anything from Lanier?"

"Talk, talk, talk, no end of it," she said. "I haven't listened to much of it. The monitoring crew reports that none of the key names have been mentioned."

"So everything's in place, right? And now it's just a matter of listening carefully."

"Same old deal," said Lynn. "It may be a month before anybody says anything worth hearing."

"I didn't come out here to go swimming," Cosima had said. "I didn't bring anything I can wear, either in a pool or to lounge around it. Do we have to go shopping?"

Jack had shaken his head. "Not to worry. Uncle Harry will provide. Uncle Harry takes care of every need his guests might have—and I do mean *every* need."

"Sounds like a charming fellow."

"He is, actually," Jack had promised, and now that she met Harry Sigman she found herself agreeing with Jack's estimate of the man. Harry was wealthy, and his money was new, but he retained an innocence that was both charming and disarming. He embraced the most conspicuous gaucheries of the nouveau riche, and he spoke with a Midwestern rasp, but a rival who underestimated him on the basis of his almost rustic speech and manners was in grave peril, for Harry Sigman was as shrewd and ruthless a competitor as any in Hollywood.

"Come in, come in," he said to Cosima. "A pleasure to meet you. I've heard of you. Favorably and unfavorably, I might say."

"I'd be interested in hearing about the unfavorable," she said.

Harry's round, suntanned face spread into a mischievous grin. He was a squat, bowlegged, bald man, with intent dark eyes. He was wearing dark blue shorts, a safari shirt and sandals. "The unfavorable," he said, the wide grin spreading even wider. "Well, you have been negotiating contracts for Jack, and it seems to have made him more expensive."

"Also more reasonable," she said. "More realistic, hmm?"

407

Harry laughed. "Realistic, yes. He wants more money, but he seems a little less insistent on running everything. Anyway, Cosima, we are gathered around the pool. Would you like a swimsuit?"

"Well . . . Is everyone else . . . ?"

"Yes. The pool is under glass, you see, and heated, so it's quite warm in there."

"Jack said you'd provide."

"Yes. There is a room handy where you may change. I'll show you."

He left her to change, not in a bedroom, but in a small sitting room with a large closet and an adjoining powder room. In the closet she found dozens of women's bathing suits in many sizes and a variety of styles—all new, all on hangers and bearing their tags. He must have bought out a bankrupt beach shop. She selected a relatively modest black bikini and a white terrycloth beach jacket.

"Gorgeous!" said Jack when she came out. He had changed into a pair of white boxer trunks with black piping. "Harry has gone back to the pool, 'cause he has other guests. So . . . C'mon with me. Now you're going to see something."

The swimming pool was in a solarium, as Harry had said. One side seemed to have been cut into the living rock of the hillside where the house stood; in any event, the pool had been built to resemble a pond in a tropical forest—a pond with gleaming lights under the water—wildly irregular in shape, with coves and promontories and even a rocky grotto. Water cascaded down from the hillside and fell over a six-foot precipice into the pool. Two thick, hairy palm trees grew inside the solarium, centerpieces of a lush array of tropical vegetation. A few brown birds flitted among the trees and shrubs—not tropical birds, apparently, but probably local birds that had somehow found their way in and of course saw no reason to look for a way out. Soft music sounded from concealed speakers. The self-contained climate was warm, as Harry had suggested—also damp, and all the guests were in swimming clothes. About half of them were in the water.

There were perhaps thirty guests. Cosima recognized none of them, though she would know some of the names when she was introduced. There was a director whose name she didn't recognize, a writer whose name she did, a TV soap opera actress she had never heard of, and a game show host who was disappointed by Cosima's inability to conceal the fact that she hadn't the remotest notion who he might be. Maybe the most prominent name there was Letitia Cummings, who had starred opposite such actors as Ray Milland and David Niven in the fifties and now acted character roles with more talent and verve than she had ever been allowed to show as a leading lady.

Sitting on the edge of the pool, feet dangling in the warm water, were four young women with bare breasts. They worked for Harry, Jack explained—a secretary, a script girl and two gofers—and were there only for decoration; they were not available for visits to the bedroom. They were there also as a suggestion to other young women that if they wanted to take off their swimsuit tops, too, it would be perfectly acceptable.

A long buffet table was set with a rich display of food, and there were two bars. Guests could pick up their own food, but their drinks would be brought by one of the three white-jacketed waiters.

"You know these people?" Cosima asked.

"Some of them," said Jack. "We ought to go over and say hello to Marty Watterman."

"Marty directed *Hidebound* for one. Also *Men Cry Peace*. You oughta remember that one."

"I remember it. Okay. Lead on."

Martin Watterman was a small, thick, hairy man. His pallid face was loose-joweled and puffy, and his prominent lips were red and shiny. His bulging wide eyes were pale blue. A shock of curly red hair added three inches to his height.

"Jack!" he said with a smile, rising from the round, glass-top poolside table where he sat with two women. "And you are Cosima Bernardin, or I am going to be embarrassed by my mistake."

"Hi, Marty," Jack said. "And Pam. And—"

"This is my daughter, Jocelyn," said Marty. "Have a seat, why don't you?"

Pamela was Marty's wife, a stringy-thin woman roughly his own age, which Cosima guessed at forty-five. What color her hair might once have been was a mystery now, since she had long decided to have it stripped periodically and it was butter yellow. Jocelyn, whom Cosima guessed was nine-teen, had put her bikini top aside on the table—possibly, Cosima guessed, to encourage people to look at her naked breasts, not at her plain face with its freckles and protruding teeth.

One of the waiters was at their side immediately and took orders for a Bombay gin martini and a Scotch. Jack told him he could bring them plates from the buffet after he brought their drinks—"Anything, just an assortment, anything at all."

"I've been following your efforts to save Svetlana Ter-asnova from deportation," said Marty. "How's it look?"

Cosima shook her head. "I don't know. The Senate may pass our private bill, though god knows when—but then I'm threatened with a veto."

Marty pursed his lips and nodded. "Figures. We know the prez in this town, this industry."

Harry Sigman had walked up to their table. "The President himself is not the problem," he said. "The problem is with some of the people he appoints. Myself, I never encounter ideologues like that in the ordinary walks of life. Where the hell you suppose he finds them?"

"Maybe the Cincinnati Country Club," suggested Cosima. "There's a supply of them there."

"Cosima'll never forget her visit to Cincinnati," said

410

Jack. "Went down there to a friend's wedding and—" He stopped to laugh.

"Well," said Cosima, smiling wryly. "If you want to know where neo-fascist idiots are supplied from, that's where. In wholesale lots."

"He *will* veto your bill," said Pamela Watterman. "He feels an obligation to his constituency. They support *him* through thick and thin, so he feels an obligation to them."

"Lately we've had to contend with an organization called Americans for the Preservation of American Values," said Harry. "They want movie censorship. They've tried to organize boycotts of pictures they call 'inimical to American values.'"

"Ah, there're always nuts around," said Jack.

"Of course there are," Harry agreed. "And always people to oppose them. Eternal vigilance and so forth."

"They always seem to have money," Jack said. "I wonder why people—"

"I can tell you where APAV's money comes from, chiefly," said Harry. "A little club of multimillionaires. One from Cleveland. One from Lubbock, Texas. One from Denver." He paused and nodded for emphasis. "Oh, yes— and one from Westchester County, New York. Plus, of course, a lot of little people who hand them nickels and dimes—like ten-thousand-dollar checks. Talk about the Cincinnati Country Club. I bet you could find contributors there."

Cosima pulled her chair aside, to make room for Harry Sigman to join them at the table. "You mention four multimillionaires," she said. "Who's the one from Westchester?"

Harry grinned. "You ever hear of a company called Deltafon? You ever hear of a man called Frank Stoner?" He nodded again. "What you might call the Henry Ford of prefabricated buildings and houses—by which I mean a man smart enough to go against the conventional wisdom and make a bunch of money but not smart enough to realize his success does not make him infallible. Frank has never understood why one of the parties had never drafted him for President. You know him, Cosima?''

"I know his lawyer,'' she said.

"P. D. Dougherty,'' said Harry.

"Right.'' She looked at Jack. "My nemesis on the bar subcommittee.''

"They came out here five years ago,'' said Harry. "Wanted someone to do a picture based on the life of Frank Stoner. Unlimited money. They had a script all ready.'' He shook his head. "They couldn't get anyone to do it. The story of Hollywood is that money will buy anything—but it won't. Nemesis, you say? I bet APAV is part of your opposition in the Svetlana Terasnova matter.''

"They haven't come out of the woodwork,'' said Cosima. "But the connection makes sense.''

"The one from Cleveland is Norman Haggard.''

Cosima shook her head. "Uh—''

"Haggard Corporation,'' said Harry. "They make VacuMax lawn mowers. Haggard light helicopters.''

"Oh, yes. I've heard of Haggard,'' she said. Of course she had. Just before she left Hamilton, Schuyler she had been working on the Haggard corporate buyback, a maneuver by the principal owners of the corporation to screw the minority stockholders. She hadn't met Norman Haggard, but she had seen his letters and memos of his phone calls.

"Be careful of those people,'' said Marty Watterman. "They're not playing with a full deck.''

Twenty-one

Lawton Lanier was bored, as any man would be who was watching the same television show for the twentieth or thirtieth time. He relaxed in his chair and tried to look critical and involved. He smiled when he hoped others would, chuckled when he hoped they would laugh. The three other men who watched the big screen of the oversized television set nodded as if they were about to fall asleep. Their faces were professionally noncommittal.

The show on the screen was the pilot for "Rosie's," a two-hour comedy drama that was intended to introduce the series of one-hour shows he hoped would begin to run in the fall. He was going to lose a lot of money if none of the networks was interested in it.

"I can't say it grabs me by the balls," said one of the men.

"It's meant to grow on you," said Lanier. "You're supposed to become involved in the characters and want to know what's going to happen to them."

The Rosie's of the title was a basement wine bar on St. Martin's Lane in London—officially the Bunch of Grapes but known to everyone by the name of the exuberant landlady always to be found behind the bar. Vanessa Kingston

413

played the role of Brenda Riley. Brenda was an American girl, living in London on a work permit that said she was a waitress. Actually she was a hooker, and Rosie allowed her to work from the Bunch of Grapes because she was a quiet, unobtrusive girl who had won Rosie's sympathy by her story of failure and abandonment: the principal story told in the pilot. The story line for each episode was to be initiated by a guest star—Leo McKern was the first one, but most of them would be Americans—someone who wandered into Rosie's and was befriended, either by Rosie or by Brenda, usually by Brenda, who would often leave the bar with the guest star, become emotionally involved with him while he resolved the problem of the story line, and then be abandoned by him at the end.

"Your hooker is too good-looking," said one of the men. "It's hard to accept the idea that a broad that luscious would be selling it. Maybe you ought to give her a habit."

"We didn't give her a habit," said Lanier, "because we felt that audiences may be a little fed up with stories about junkies and pushers and all that. You'll see later here how she's hassled by a vice cop and how Leo there comes to help her out."

"Still . . ." the man said. "She looks too good. I mean, a broad like that wouldn't be sitting on a barstool waiting to be picked up. The part needs somebody a little more shopworn."

"Which you aren't going to cure," said another man, "by changing makeup and costume. Vanessa Kingston's no actress. She's going to play Vanessa Kingston, no matter what role you give her. Suppose instead of a hooker she's an out-of-work showgirl who hangs around the bar between casting calls. That might work. There you'd have Vanessa playing what Vanessa really is. *That* she could handle."

Lanier nodded. This was the third time he had heard this suggestion, or something much like it. Clearly, "Rosie's" wasn't going to play, not next season. He didn't know whether he'd reshoot the pilot or not. It would cost a lot of money. Maybe a cable network . . .

"I have just one question," Vanessa said.

"And that is?" Lanier asked.

They sat in Lanier's office. He had called her in to tell her he was getting no positive answers from the networks about airing "Rosie's" in the autumn, so he feared the pilot was going to fail. She had received the news calmly, saying it did not entirely surprise her. He was not surprised at how cool she was; he had seen her disappointed at casting calls many times and had never seen emotion. She sat with her legs crossed, allowing the short skirts that were fashionable just then to display her dancer's legs. Her dark eyes laid a cool stare on him.

He was, of course, aware that every word they spoke was being transmitted to at least two receivers: one maintained by the people who had bugged his office, the other by Gallon.

"The question," she said, "is how much Jack paid of what it cost you to put me in the pilot."

He answered warily. "I don't know why you ask me that, Vanessa," he said in his crisp British accent. "But I will answer. Jack Putnam had no part whatever in financing the pilot for 'Rosie's.' I have some backers who are going to lose money, and I'm going to lose some myself, but Jack Putnam had nothing to do with it."

"Cosima Bernardin, then," said Vanessa.

"No. Absolutely not. I know what you are driving at. You retained a small-time lawyer, Vanessa, and he made some unfortunate accusations. He made trouble for Cosima, but his speculations were unfounded."

Vanessa drew a deep breath. "I had a decent job," she said. "In *Les Miserables*. I quit to do the pilot."

"You quit to pursue a better opportunity," said Lanier.

415

"You took a risk. So did I. I've lost a great deal of money on this pilot, you know."

"I need a job," she said bluntly.

"I don't have one for you."

"Will you put in a word for me?"

"Yes, of course. And I may tell you, it's not absolutely settled that 'Rosie's' is not going to make it. But I thought you should have a realistic estimate."

"Thanks," she said glumly.

Cosima had not expected Emilie, had not known she was in New York, but she was happy to see her. As Emilie came into her office, Cosima handed her a printed card—

BE CAREFUL WHAT YOU SAY.
THE OFFICE IS BUGGED.

Emilie grinned and frowned at the same time. Her lips formed the question "Seriously?"

Cosima smiled and nodded. "Have a chair, Emilie. It's great to see you. To what do I owe the pleasure?"

"Well . . ." Emilie murmured hesitantly. "I stopped in on the chance you might be available for lunch."

"I'm available," said Cosima. She scribbled a note and handed it to her sister.

Emilie looked at the note and nodded. It said: "Oyster Bar? 12:30?"

"How about the Press Box?" Cosima asked.

"Sounds great."

"At, say, one o'clock?"

"At one o'clock," Emilie agreed, grinning.

At twelve-thirty they sat down in the Oyster Bar, in Grand Central Station.

"Great place for somebody who's the subject of electronic eavesdropping," said Cosima. "The noise level in here is

416

so high that a microphone in a purse or briefcase is going to pick up a babble."

"Tell me what's going on," said Emilie.

"Somebody has done me the compliment of planting microphones and telephone taps in both my condo and office," said Cosima. "Also in Lawton Lanier's office. I suppose you can guess the connection."

"Rats from the White House basement," said Emilie.

"No. I don't think so," said Cosima. "But I think the two sets of rats would know each other."

"And you're not removing the bugs because—"

"Because I haven't yet figured out a way of clobbering them with their own cudgel."

"How did you find out about the bugs?" Emilie asked.

"By accident, actually," said Cosima. "But now that I know, I have a damn good security man working on it."

"It must be spooky, living with microphones that pick up everything you say."

"My guy can check your office—which might not be a bad idea."

"Congressional offices are swept constantly, at irregular intervals," said Emilie. "My New Jersey office is checked, and so is our house, and so is my Washington apartment."

"Odd world we live in, isn't it?" asked Cosima rhetorically. "So . . . how's the bill going?"

"The Senate will pass it," said Emilie. She shook her head. "The veto— Well, I can't tell you."

"Is there anything I can do to help you with the Senate?"

"Bring Svetlana to Washington," said Emilie. "Except for you, she is her own best promoter."

Cosima nodded. "The nut fringe is going to push hard on the man in the White House. So far the evangelicals haven't weighed in, but the haunted anti-communists are in full cry. The moneyed ones."

"They buy congressmen at auction," said Emilie. "The Internal Revenue Service ought to let them depreciate their politicians like any other property. And don't suppose it's all Republican right-wingers. Let's not forget who brokered the 1984 Democrat convention. Our party didn't nominate candidates for President and Vice President in 1984. Those two losers were dictated to us. We can't afford to be righteous, Cosima.''

"How many votes can we count on? In the Senate?''

"Enough. Our problem is with the veto. The President shouldn't veto. He'll have reasons not to. But he may remember the clamor from his archaic allies more vividly than the voices of reason. Can you win in court?''

"I don't think so,'' said Cosima. "Not in the long run.''

"Then why the bugs and phone taps?''

"Our opposition is afflicted with a conspiracy fixation,'' said Cosima. "Seriously. They're not really quite sure they won't hear me talking to a KGB agent. They're not really quite sure Lana herself is not an agent.

Emilie smiled and laughed. "You must be tempted to hire an actor to play a Russian and—''

Cosima nodded. "The thought has crossed my mind. I'm afraid they may be a little too smart for that. Their eavesdropping equipment is quite sophisticated, according to my anti-bugger. And expensive.''

"How are you handling it?''

"We're picking up their transmissions on our own receivers—and recording what they are recording.'' She scowled. "My patience with it is not going to last, Emilie. You can't imagine what a temptation it is to tell them to go fuck themselves, then rip out their little microphones and flush them down the john.''

"Patience, kid sister. In three or four weeks your bill will go to the White House.''

"Yes. And on May 23 the case goes to trial.''

"It hasn't been easy,'' remarked P. D. Dougherty as he sat down with Robert Blyleven at a table in the downstairs dining room at the Harvard Club.

They had carried drinks from the bar and had passed by the buffet to put in their orders for seafood platters. Blyleven stared unhappily around the room: at the scores of men engrossed in weighty conversation, at the somewhat shabby heavy oak tables and chairs, at the paintings of famous Harvard alumni on the walls. The place was to him what it had always been: unfriendly, uncomfortable; he couldn't remember ever having had a pleasant lunch there.

And P. D. Dougherty sat across the little table from him, looking like Henry Stimson. Tall and thin and gray and determinedly dignified, Dougherty wore a dark blue pin-striped suit, and a heavy watch chain hung across his vest. The man had a style about him, and an element of it was a status in life that allowed him to retain all his studied dignity while wearing a broad smear of ash on his vest and a bulging pack of cigarettes in his vest pocket.

"Have there been any developments in the matter of Knightley?" asked Dougherty almost indifferently, with his attention apparently focused on the olive in his martini.

"Not that I know of," said Blyleven. He wished he had accepted Dougherty's suggestion that he bring two Scotches with him from the bar.

As though he had read Blyleven's mind, Dougherty raised a finger to summon a waiter. "I think we'll have another round," he said. "That's Chivas, and this is a Beefeater martini." Returning his attention to Blyleven, he said, "You understand my interests."

Blyleven nodded. "I really haven't anything to tell you." That was what he had decided to say and how he had decided to say it, but he wished he could have said it with more conviction.

"I'm not sure you understand what's involved," said Dougherty smoothly but forcefully. "When this matter started, it was a minor matter, involving the possibility that Miss Bernardin had unethically interfered in the lawyer-client relationship between Miss Kingston and Burton Oliver. When it becomes possible—and I may say even likely—that she or her

419

father attempted to exercise an improper influence on the investigating subcommittee, then—" He smiled wryly and shrugged. "Well, you understand. The matter cannot, and will not, just be allowed to lapse."

Blyleven nodded. He remembered vividly the evening in November when he had been called into the office of Malcolm Stanley, Jr. and given a firm suggestion about how he should conduct himself as a member of the subcommittee investigating the charges against Cosima Bernardin. Stanley was the son of the managing partner in Maxwell, Donovan, Margolin & Stanley. He did not speak officially for the managing committee, but it was understood that often he carried unofficial word that was more weighty than official. He did not say that Leon Bernardin had exerted pressure. He didn't say he hadn't, either. The truth was, Blyleven did not know the answer to the question P. D. Dougherty had called him to the Harvard Club to ask.

Dougherty shook a cigarette from the pack he carried in his vest pocket. He snapped a lighter and lit the cigarette with discernible satisfaction. "In addition," he said, "you should understand that Miss Bernardin is guilty of execrable misconduct apart from what she did to Oliver."

The words "allegedly did" came to Blyleven's mind, for an instant he was minded to point out that the subcommittee had found no credible evidence the allegations were true, but he held his peace. He had something to hide, and there was no point in antagonizing the man from whom he had to hide it.

"She was dismissed from Hamilton, Schuyler for gross insubordination, manifested in a fit of female hysteria, and took a client with her, in complete contempt for her contract and of the canons of ethics. Besides that, Blyleven, you ought to understand that Miss Cosima Bernardin has formed a partnership consisting of another Hamilton, Schuyler lawyer who left with her because he was sleeping with her, plus a bull dyke who was thrown out of Webster, Kent because she tried to seduce a secretary. And that is not all. She is presently abusing the processes of the federal courts in an effort to prevent the deportation of a Russian ballerina who entered this country illegally by concealing her affiliation with Komsomol. I suppose you know what Komsomol is—the youth wing of the Soviet Communist Party."

"Sounds like a bad girl," said Blyleven quietly.

"Something more," Dougherty went on. "Her father has a lifelong record for sharp practice. He does a careful balancing act on the edge of the criminal law."

"I hadn't heard that," said Blyleven.

Dougherty took a deep drag on his cigarette and let the smoke drift slowly from his mouth and nose. "Not very nice people to be allied with," he said.

"Who's allied with them?"

"When you did not disclose to the association that your firm has an indirect but significant financial relationship with Leon Bernardin—that is, that Bernardin can cost your firm a million dollars if he elects to take certain actions with respect to Knightley—you allied yourself with the Bernardins, in effect. To put it another way, it's like dealing with a loan shark—you let them get a grasp on you, they will never let go, and they will use you any way they want."

Blyleven shook his head. The time had come to resist. "I did not disclose to the association an indirect and *in*significant relationship," he said. "*In*significant, Mr. Dougherty."

"Perhaps it will," said Blyleven.

"Which puts my ass in the middle. In the fuckin' *middle*, Loewenstein."

They sat at one of the bar tables in Charlie Brown's, in the Pan Am Building concourse, where they had sat and talked before. Blyleven had just recreated his conversation with P. D. Dougherty, almost word for word. He had telephoned Rick almost as soon as he returned from his lunch at the Harvard Club and had demanded this meeting. Rick had suggested it be in Charlie Brown's instead of either of their offices.

"My senior partners won't back me," said Blyleven. "If it hits the fan, they'll say I acted on my own."

"Why do you tell me this?" Rick asked.

"The question is," said the distraught Blyleven, "did old man Bernardin muscle Maxwell, Donovan? Did Malcolm Stanley give me marching orders about my subcommittee vote because Bernardin had called and threatened or because they were afraid he might?"

Rick shook his head. "I don't know any way to find out."

"Ask him," said Blyleven.

"You ask him. Not me."

"Loewenstein— Jesus! What can I do? What would *you* do if P. D. Dougherty were muscling you?"

"Hang tough," said Rick. "Fuck him. He doesn't have anything against you. If he did, he'd use it, instead of trying to intimidate you."

They glanced around. The small tables at Charlie's were close together, and earnest talk like this attracted notice. A Hispanic girl asked if they wanted another round of drinks, and Blyleven nodded to her. Rick wished he hadn't.

"How about asking Cosima? Did you tell her what I told you a couple of months ago?"

"No, I didn't."

"Why not, for Christ's sake?"

"I had reasons," said Rick. He elected not to tell Blyleven how he and Hugh had decided not to tell Cosima, for fear she would gallop into battle against Dougherty.

"Then she doesn't know Dougherty wants to reopen the case against her—adding a charge of tampering?"

"No, she doesn't. And to hell with Dougherty."

"It isn't that easy!"

Rick leaned over the table, so he could speak more trenchantly without being overheard. "Dougherty has nothing on you, Blyleven," he said. "A client of yours owes money to Bernardin Frères. That's no connection."

"The hell it isn't," Blyleven whispered shrilly. "Mac Stanley thought it was—enough of a connection to lean on me about what to do as a member of the subcommittee."

"Okay. You know that. Stanley knows that. I know it, because you've told me. Who else have you told? Who has Stanley told?"

"No one! God, I've told no one. And I . . . I think I can say for certain that Stanley hasn't."

"Good," said Rick. "Then let Dougherty prove it."

"I voted—"

"Of course you voted to drop the charge. What else could you have done? There was no evidence against her."

"Well—"

"On the other hand," Rick pressed, "P. D. Dougherty voted against her, on the basis of no evidence. *Why?*" He sneered. "To hell with him. I wouldn't let that man lecture *me* on legal ethics."

"You make it sound so easy," said Blyleven disconsolately.

"I've got a question," said Rick. "You told me another member of the subcommittee voted to hold the hearing, even when there very obviously was no foundation to the charge against Cosima. Who was that?"

"Tate," said Blyleven. "When the final vote came, after the hearing, he voted to drop the charge. In the end, only Dougherty voted against Miss Bernardin. Tate was angry—I don't know why—but he voted to terminate the proceedings."

"Why'd they bring in Dan Nash?" Rick asked.

"They wanted to prove she was dishonest—also emotionally unstable. The truth is, they screwed it up. The truth is, they didn't have a case, they weren't prepared."

"Maybe they thought they didn't have to be," Rick suggested.

"What do you mean?"

"Maybe they thought they had enough votes to lynch her," said Rick.

An hour later they sat in Hugh's apartment: Rick and Blyleven. They had arrived unannounced just as Hugh was shaving Adela's head for her club appearance that night, and she had come to the door with globs of shaving cream clinging to her scalp. Blyleven stared at her openmouthed until she left, and only after she was gone did Rick summarize for Hugh what Blyleven had told him at Charlie Brown's.

"Dougherty was going to vote against her," said Rick. "No matter what. It looks as if he was counting on Tate. That's two votes. He needed one more."

"I can't believe that would have been Blocker," said Hugh. "In spite of the fact that he voted to hold the hearing, even when it was obvious there was little or no evidence, I think he did it only out of a sense of fairness, out of a sense that the subcommittee should hear the witnesses before it decided."

"Right," said Rick. "Which leaves the two younger members: James Reardon and Bob Blyleven."

Blyleven had accepted yet another Scotch from Hugh—a heavy one, which he poured himself. He was fuzzy. "Couldn't have been me," he said. "Mac Stanley told me—"

"What Malcolm Stanley told you," Rick interrupted, "came from his father at least and probably from the firm's management committee, and it proves one thing: that your firm is venal, that your firm's vote on the subcommittee was subject to influence. Was Reardon's?"

"Jim Reardon's a *young* fellow," said Blyleven. "Firm of—what?—four, five lawyers. His father's a—" and Blyleven stopped to assemble his thoughts in a more orderly way. He shook his head. "Not part of the *establishment*," he went on. "Graduated from Ohio State law school. He—"

424

"Bob . . ." said Rick. "Is it possible— Is it just possible that Dougherty and Tate were counting on *your* vote?"

"Is it possible," Hugh asked, "that they had it all lined up—and that something happened at the last minute?"

Blyleven sighed loudly. "You're guessing . . ." he mumbled.

"Dougherty told you the Bernardins are not good friends," said Rick. "Let's do a little thinking, Bob, about who are good friends and who are not."

Cosima had been up for an hour. She had made herself a pot of coffee, some toast and marmalade and had read the *Times* as she ate. She had been looking forward to taking this April Saturday as a day of rest, when she might go to the boatyard to see what progress was being made toward readying *Lafayette* for the coming season, or maybe she might go with the Craigs to the airport while they checked out their Piper for the good flying weather they expected. Today was dreary. A low overcast hung over the Sound, dropping a thin drizzle. No sailing, no flying. Maybe some preparation. She had to take Lana to Washington on Monday. The weekend . . . She had not dressed, except to pull on a red silk shirt that covered her hips.

And then the damned doorbell rang.

She peered out through the spy hole. Rick!

When she opened the door, he put his finger to his mouth and shook his head. He beckoned for her to step outside.

"Hugh and I need to talk to you. He's in the car."

She nodded and gestured that she would dress and come out. She stepped back inside the door and said—"Okay. Wait'll I get the keys. I don't think there's anything seriously wrong with it, but you know Porsches." That for the microphones, that for whoever was listening.

She had to wonder if the eavesdroppers were not also watching. Bill Gallon assured her they were not. The listening post, he said, was a mile away, probably in one of the older houses that still stood in Greenwich in spite of its outlandish real-estate prices. If they had binoculars on her, it was not from where they were listening. Well . . . it made no difference now. Rick had come to the door.

She dressed in blue jeans, a sweatshirt and a blue nylon windbreaker that would shed the drizzle. She hurried. There was something ominous about this visit.

They were waiting in a rented Chevrolet, both of them in the front seat, both of them casually dressed in slacks and sweaters and jackets suitable for the weather. She opened a rear door and slid in.

"Where could we go for coffee?" Rick asked.

"Coffee, hell. I want bacon and eggs," Hugh grumbled.

"Anywhere," said Rick, "except the Hyatt or anyplace like that. Just a diner."

She tapped him on the shoulder and pointed to the street outside the parking lot. She would guide him that way, so they could talk without constant interruption for directions.

As they drove rain-wet streets to the Country Squire, a small homey restaurant on the Post Road, Rick recited the conversations of the night before. By the time he was finished and came to a significant pause, they had reached the little restaurant, and Cosima did not respond to what he had told her until they were both inside and had given an order to the waitress.

"He did it," Cosima said then, glumly, staring without seeing the water-beaded cars drawn up almost to the window beside their booth. "My father called that law firm and leaned on them."

"You don't know that," Rick suggested quietly.

"No, I don't know it. Still, I *do* know it. I know him."

"What do we know about Reardon?" Rick asked. "Could his little firm have a client in debt to Bernardin Frères? Could one of the lawyers in the firm—"

Hugh interrupted. "We did our homework before the subcommittee hearing, the same anybody would do. No more, no less. So we knew when we faced Reardon that he

426

was only thirty-seven years old but was the senior partner in his firm."

"Reardon & Smith," said Cosima.

"There are four lawyers in the firm," said Hugh. "They have a good, respectable practice and make a good living, but they have no clients big enough to do banking business with Bernardin Frères. At least I don't think they do—we didn't run a full check on them."

"Blocker?" asked Rick.

"He's a senior partner at Gardner, Finley, Levin & Ferris," said Hugh.

Cosima glanced around the restaurant, which she knew was a favorite with the locals of Cos Cob. The booths were filled this morning with overweight people with bad teeth, some of the men wearing caps. Her attention was taken for a moment by two elderly men who were able to converse only with the aid of a microphone which one held close to his face when he spoke to the other—apparently it was only through the microphone that the other man could get enough amplification to bring his friend's voice to his feeble hearing. They chatted happily in spite of the impediment.

"Gardner, Finley could have clients in debt to the bank," said Rick.

"Why speculate?" Cosima asked. "Why don't we find out?"

"How?" asked Hugh.

"We'll go talk to my father," she said. "I think it's time I had a little talk with Dad. But let's work out a little scenario. Let's understand what we're going to say and who is going to say it."

The rain was falling harder when Rick pulled the Chevrolet to a stop at the door of the house on Round Hill. Leon Bernardin came out immediately, carrying two large black umbrellas, which he offered to his guests so not one drop of rain would fall on them as they entered his house.

"There you are," said Cosima before they opened the car. "Disarming, isn't he? He always is just before he cuts a throat."

"Cosima—" Hugh warned. "Cool it."

She might have responded peevishly to this curt admonition, but her father opened the door and offered Hugh an umbrella. Then he hurried around the car and surprised Rick by offering the second one to him.

Leon led them into the breakfast room, where the table was set for them, with melons and grapefruit, toast and jellies, coffee and tea. If Cosima had not told her father on the telephone from Country Squire that they had eaten their breakfasts already, the table would have included eggs and bacon and sausage. On a clear morning this room was sunny. This morning its broad windows looked out on gray shreds of cloud drifting across the barren hilltop—though the juicy green of swelling buds on the trees beyond the lawn promised a very different view within two weeks.

"I've had a gallon of coffee this morning," Cosima said as they sat down. "I suppose it's too early for a martini."

"I should think so," said her father. "Not, however, too early for champagne."

He left the room to fetch champagne, or to order it brought. Cosima caught Hugh's curious look at her father as he passed through the door. Hugh was guessing, probably, that between their call and their arrival Leon Bernardin had changed his clothes. Cosima knew better. This morning's double-breasted blue blazer, gray flannel slacks, and polished black Gucci loafers were her father's Saturday-morning-casual clothes.

Leon returned without the champagne. It would be brought. He sat down. "Well, it's a pleasure to see each of you. I hope nothing ominous is the occasion for your visit."

Cosima spoke first, as had been agreed. "You remember they tried to disbar me over the Vanessa Kingston-Burton Oliver business."

"An exaggeration . . ."

"Well— Some people wanted my *ass,* Dad."

Leon nodded. "Yes, they did," he said.

"Okay, they still do. P. D. Dougherty is trying to get the case reopened. There's some kind of alliance between him and Hamilton, Schuyler."

Leon rubbed his chin with a bent forefinger. "I suppose the legal principle of double jeopardy doesn't apply," he said.

"The original charge is dead. That's not the problem," she told him. "The problem is, they think they can prove I extended an improper influence over one or more members of the subcommittee."

"By doing what, Cosima?" he asked.

"I haven't been able to find out exactly," she said. "Something to do with threatening to use the economic power of Bernardin Frères."

"Which members of the subcommittee could they have in mind?"

Now Hugh spoke. "We thought maybe you could help us with that. Which member of the subcommittee *could* have been influenced by the financial power of your bank? I'm sure no pressure was brought, but what could Dougherty have in mind?"

"That's very simple," said Leon. "And you could have found out without asking me. It's all public information."

"We know about Knightley International," said Cosima.

Leon turned up the palm of his hands. "All right," he said. "There you have it."

"None of the others?" Rick asked. "In the end, only Dougherty voted against Cosima. Even assuming that Robert Blyleven of Maxwell, Donovan was influenced, he's only one vote."

They were distracted for an instant by the popping of a cork in the kitchen; Leon, who had been about to answer, waited until the main brought in the tray with bottles and glasses, and until he had poured before he spoke.

"The information you are asking me for was available to

you before the hearing," he said. "All you had to do was ask me for it, but no one asked." He tasted the champagne and seemed satisfied. "There is nothing conspiratorial about obtaining information from public sources," he went on. "Contrary to some people's notion, I don't use industrial spies."

"I assume, however, you are confident this house is not bugged as Cosima's condo is," said Rick.

"Entirely confident," said Leon. "I've know about electronic eavesdropping for a long time. When Cosima warned me to be discreet in anything I said to her on the telephone, I offered her the use of my bug sweepers, and it turns out, to our amusement, that we share the same service."

"Gallon keeps secrets so well," said Cosima, "that he's never told me Dad is his client or told Dad that I am."

"Anyway," said Leon, "you want to know about the members of the subcommittee . . . Well, Blyleven is the only one who could have been influenced. Maxwell, Donovan, Margolin & Stanley is financially unsound. Among its problems is that it recruited some high-powered lawyers—stole them from other firms, actually—by offering them extravagant compensation packages—and now it finds it doesn't have the practice to justify what it has obligated itself to pay. Also, as you know, Knightley owes the firm $1,324,000, most of which is never going to be paid. The management of the firm was so desperate to have a client like Knightley that it let the account get far out of hand."

"What do you know about Tate?" Cosima asked.

"Johnson, McNamara, Cohen & Bauman is an old-line, highly traditional firm," said Leon. "Their clients—"he chuckled—"don't owe anybody money. They represent trusts and estates, chiefly. A bank. Some very wealthy people. If William Tate was against you, Cosima, it was because he didn't like you. You do not represent what he thinks a lawyer should be.

"Blocker?"

"Gardner, Finley, Levin & Ferris," said Leon. "They

represent no clients who owe money to Bernardin Frères—if that is your question."

"Then Dougherty," said Cosima. "What moves P. D. Dougherty?"

"Maybe his politics," said Leon. "Or maybe the politics of his principal client. Whatever his motive, it was strong enough to make him *seek* a position on your subcommittee. He went to the chairman of the committee and asked to be appointed to your subcommittee—replacing a man who would otherwise have been on it. He used the Exeter old-boy network."

Hugh settled a skeptical stare on Leon Bernardin. "Uh . . . public information?" he asked.

Leon hesitated for a moment, then remarked dryly, "I made an inquiry or two."

"I think you did more than that," said Cosima.

"What you are involved in, Cosima," her father said, "is not a game played by the rules of games. Yes, I interfered in the matter of the bar association's inquiry into your professional conduct. As I suspected might be the case, they were stacking the cards against you." He allowed himself a smug little smile. "I just reshuffled the deck. As you did, I suspect—by enlisting Lawton Lanier to . . . How shall we say? To create an original version of the arrangement he made with Vanessa Kingston?"

"Who did you call at Maxwell, Donovan?" she asked.

Her father's smile broadened. "No one. They called me. More accurately, they *came* to see me, in the person of Malcolm Stanley. Senior. He told me that one of his younger partners was on the subcommittee that was to hear the complaint against my daughter. He said he was in a position to do me a favor and would like to do one. I didn't ask him to do a thing. Whatever he did, he volunteered."

"Just what did he do?" asked Cosima.

"The favor he meant to do—the only one he specifically mentioned—was to tell me there was a conspiracy to rig the vote so as to embarrass you. They surmised, he said, that when the full committee reviewed the subcommittee's findings, the subcommittee might be reversed, but—''

"Association subcommittees are rarely reversed," said Hugh. "There is a strong sense that the work of volunteers should be respected. I don't know how many times I've heard the old song and dance—'We must never step on one of our subcommittees.' ''

"They needed three votes," said Rick, anxious to bring the conversation back to its main theme. "Dougherty—''

"Dougherty, Tate and Blyleven," said Leon. "That's what Stanley told me. His partner Wilcoxen had had a call from Dougherty. Dougherty had explained the case to Wilcoxen and told him how important it was that the subcommittee make a finding against Cosima. He and Tate, he said, knew what to do, but he was afraid one or two of the younger members of the subcommittee might not. Dougherty asked Wilcoxen to make sure Blyleven knew his duty, as he put it. Wilcoxen was all innocent and said he'd do that. But he mentioned it to Malcolm Stanley first, and Stanley told him he'd be a food to do it. That was when Stanley called me.''

"Why didn't you tell us this before the hearing?" Hugh asked.

Leon Bernardin regarded him intently for a moment, a smile broadening on his face. "I wasn't sure how squeaky clean you might be. Or—'' he glanced at Rick—"how virginal Rick here might be.''

"Blyleven's the one you have to worry about," said Cosima. "He's being pressed by Dougherty, who's threatening to bring charges against him—conflict of interest, since he knew his firm had the problem with Knightley and the bank. Dougherty has got him scared.''

"He also thinks," said Rick, "that if you are accused of using the bank's influence to rig the subcommittee vote, Malcolm Stanley will throw him to the wolves.''

"I'll take care of Malcolm Stanley," said Leon.

"I'm going to ask you not to do that, Dad," said Cos-

432

ima. "Hugh and Rick and I are developing our own way of handling the problem."

"All right," said Leon. "I won't talk to Malcolm Stanley unless you ask me to."

"I doubt I'll be asking you," said Cosima. "If I do, be damned careful."

"I was being careful before you were born," her father responded.

"Not entirely, I think," Cosima laughed.

All of them laughed, and took the moment to sip their almost untouched champagne.

"So, what do you know of Frank Stoner?" Cosima asked her father.

"You know about that connection, do you? I met him once, years ago. He told me he was a member of the John Birch Society and was dedicated to saving the world from the Illuminati: the mysterious master conspirators the Birchers decided were more dangerous than the communists. He owns Dougherty, you know."

"Dougherty's his lawyer," said Hugh.

"No, Hugh. I said it right. Anyone who works for Frank Stoner takes orders, whether a mailroom clerk or a Harvard lawyer. He wanted to borrow from the bank and began to tell me what terms he would accept. I took his application for a twenty-three-million-dollar loan, which he accompanied with a memorandum dictating his terms. I let it sit for a month, then turned him down.

"So Stoner hates you and by extension hates me," said Cosima.

Leon nodded. "And hates your fight to save Svetlana Terasnova from deportation."

"A lot of things come together," said Rick.

Leon nodded. "You have to fight dirty, you want to fight these people."

"I'm capable of that," said Cosima mordantly.

"Well, don't forget," her father said, "the alliance between the Frank Stoners of this world and the creatures you find crawling around if you turn over rocks in Washington."

Twenty-two

Cosima returned her American Express card to her purse. She had just paid for their two tickets, New York to Washington, on the shuttle. Svetlana resumed the conversation:

"He says, we marry, I tell the American authorities I am married to an American citizen, I am entitled to remain in the United States."

Cosima shook her head. "Not automatically. The INS will say it was too convenient—a marriage just as you were about to appear in court to face what may be your final appeal. Marriage does not effect an *automatic* change of status."

Svetlana Terasnova looked past the sleepy man in the window seat, peering out as the airliner banked and turned, showing passengers on the left a view of lower Manhattan and the bay as it swung onto the course to Washington. Cosima did not try to look past her. She had flown this run too many times.

"Understand, Lana," she said. "Marriage to Jerry would not solve all your problems."

"If I am pregnant?" the little ballerina asked timidly.

"Jesus Christ, are you?"

Svetlana shook her head. "Not yet, I don't think. But I can be, when it would help."

Cosima closed her eyes and rested her head against the back of the seat. "God help me," she whispered. "Save me from the likes of Ruggiero Paccinelli."

In a recital arranged by Senator Moynihan and others, Svetlana Terasnova danced at the Kennedy Center on Tuesday night—her perfomance ignored by the White House and boycotted by a small right-wing contingent of the Republican Party in Congress. Sitting with her family in a box—sitting, that is, with her parents, and with Thomas and Emilie McCarthy—Cosima wore a white silk charmeuse gown embroidered with a pattern of silver sequins. She was besieged by cameramen as she entered the Center. Reporters shrieked questions she pretended not to hear.

"Sixty-six years of doing whatever it is I do," complained Elizabeth Bernardin, "plus forty-whatever years of marriage to this notorious banking mogul, and I have never before been jostled by journalists. I have a daughter in Congress and a son who may get a Nobel. I can go anywhere with them, and they're not recognized. Cosima, you attract media coverage like the Mayflower Madam."

"But for dissimilar achievements," said Thomas McCarthy.

Svetlana danced excerpts from *The Firebird, The Rite of Spring,* and *Sleeping Beauty.* The next morning the Washington *Post* review said:

> We may fervently hope the Immigration and Naturalization Service will fail in its attempt to deport this talented young woman—or, better, will drop the attempt. She is an ornament to ballet, a talented, graceful dancer, conspicuously well trained and disciplined. This reviewer is grateful for the opportunity to see her.
>
> Let it be understood, however, that she is not one of the world's greatest. We may assume she is, at

twenty-six years of age, at the peak of her powers. We are seeing the fulfillment of her promise. She is a ballerina of the second rank, not of the very first. Until she became the beneficiary of the notoriety imposed on her by the government's ill-tempered effort to exclude her from our country, she was not called on to dance lead roles, at least not the most difficult ones, and not in leading companies. When her notoriety fades, probably she will not be again. She will, however, always be welcome on any stage where she chooses to perform, assuming only she does not take challenges beyond her powers.

In the Madison Hotel, where Svetlana joined the Bernardins and McCarthys for breakfast in the parents' suite before she and Cosima left for the airport, Leon Bernardin asked a question:

"Why nothing on the editorial page? Why nothing in the *Times* in New York? Can't you arrange more media coverage, Cosima."

"Not timely," said Cosima. "When the time comes, we'll get the thunder."

Svetlana was not pleased with the *Post* review and slipped into a bedroom to make a tearful call to Jerry, who was in San Francisco.

John McGowan knew he was here to be subjected to crude pressure. A senior partner from Quarles & McGrath had not invited him to lunch at the Harvard Club, with a federal judge, only to hear his views on the beauties of spring. They were upstairs, in a private dining room. Judge Hawthorne had not arrived, but a round of drinks had; P. D. Dougherty had just signed the chit and told the waiter to return in fifteen minutes.

John McGowan was a bachelor. Marriage had never interested him. He knew some people guessed he was homosexual, but he wasn't. Rather, he enjoyed the style of life he had arranged for himself: the usually quiet, usually undemanding position of bar-association counsel, which paid him reasonably well, did not often require late hours, and left him time to pursue his interests, which were painting and music. He was a small man. His little face was undistinguished except for its small, dark eyes. He was bald. He spent a great deal of his income on his clothes, all of which, including his shirts, were tailored. Today he was wearing a gray tweed Scottish-wool jacket with black slacks, a white shirt, a black necktie with thin dark red stripes and polished classic loafers.

"Cheers," said Dougherty.

McGowan saluted with his glass of Finlandia vodka on the rocks. He enjoyed lunchtime drinks, but it was an element of his position as bar-association counsel that he should not smell of alcohol when he returned to his office.

"You sat there that day and listened to what she turned into a farce," said Dougherty.

The farce, so far as McGowan was concerned, was that charges of misconduct had ever been brought at all. Burton Oliver was a small-time scrivener of questionable standards, and he had offered no evidence at any point in the proceedings. McGowan dared not say so, but he had rather admired the way Cosima Bernardin and her friend Hugh Hupp had demonstrated that the proceedings were indeed a farce.

"Did you have any doubt that Lanier was lying?" Dougherty demanded.

"It sounded as though he might be," said McGowan.

"We have evidence that he was lying. Unfortunately, our evidence is nothing better than a sworn statement from Vanessa Kingston, and there's nothing to be gained in opposing her word to his. On the other hand . . . Well, suppose I told you a member of the subcommittee voted as he did

438

because Leon Bernardin was in a position to bankrupt his law firm if that member voted against the Bernardin bitch?''

John McGowan put down his glass. This was more serious then he had guessed. "In a position . . . ?" he murmured.

"What if Leon Bernardin called the senior partner of one of the subcommittee members and threatened to do something that would cost the firm more than a million dollars?"

Except for a few years of working in the clerk's office of the United States Court of Appeals, Second Circuit, John McGowan had spent his life as an attorney for one bar association and another. There was a sort of subprofession: association counsel, and he had chosen that subprofession and dedicated himself to it. To succeed in this a lawyer had to become absolutely neutral; he must never take a position on anything; his positions were defined for him by the association committees. McGowan was a success. In this field, survival was success. He had succeeded by never making a suggestion, much less a recommendation. He heard facts and reported them, exactly as he heard them, with careful, quiet objectivity. It frightened him when anyone tried to maneuver him into taking a position, when anyone tried to make him an ally. And that was just what P. D. Dougherty was doing now.

"If there is evidence . . ." he said in a weak, low voice.

Dougherty nodded. "Evidence. We'll have the evidence."

"A member of the subcommittee . . ." said McGowan. It had to be Blyleven. Dougherty had mentioned senior partner. Blyleven was the only subcommittee member who was not himself a senior partner. Reardon's firm was small, but no one in it was more senior than he. "Not a small matter. Uh . . . what evidence is there?"

"We'll call it a confession," said Dougherty.

"The member has . . . *admitted* he was improperly influenced?"

"Not yet. But he will."

McGowan was relieved. He had heard it a hundred times. There will be an admission, there *will* be evidence. "I will of course be very interested in the evidence," he said.

"I'd like to have your help in getting it."

Oh-ho. Yes. Wouldn't they all? McGowan nodded and made the statement he had made a hundred times. "Of course: I'll be happy to do whatever I can. Now . . . your procedure, Mr. Dougherty, is to speak to the chairman of the full committee. He may ask you for a written statement. Then he will present the matter to the ethics committee, which will authorize me to initiate an inquiry."

"Do we have to do that? Can't we just go forward?"

McGowan offered a small, noncommunicative smile. "I work for the association, Mr. Dougherty. I can't initiate any sort of proceedings except in accordance with the by-laws and pursuant to specific authorization. That's how my job is defined."

Dougherty cloaked his annoyance behind the business of lighting a cigarette. "I'm not talking about a case against the subcommittee member," he said. "I'm talking about a case against Cosima Bernardin for exerting an improper influence on a member of the subcommittee."

McGowan's neutral comment would have been that that would be a more difficult case to prove, but he did not have to make it because at this moment Judge Ralph Hawthorne walked in, followed by the waiter bearing a tray of fresh drinks.

Introductions were not necessary; they all knew each other. The association had presented findings against Attorney Ralph Hawthorne in 1968, and the Appellate Division of the Supreme Court of New York had privately reprimanded him. His offense had been depositing a client's funds to his personal bank account. Though the money had been paid to the client with interest, during the time it had been in Hawthorne's account it had given his bank balance an appearance that supported a loan application that would probably have been otherwise denied. McGowan had not

440

been counsel then. A note in the file, left by his predecessor, said that Hawthorne had wept before the subcommittee that heard the complaint against him. When the President nominated Hawthorne for judgeship, Hawthorne had come to McGowan to ask if the private reprimand were still on record and if that record had to be turned over to the F.B.I. McGowan had said he would follow standard procedure— if the F.B.I. didn't ask, he wouldn't volunteer the report of the private reprimand. He did hand a copy to the committee on judicial qualifications, which also was standard procedure. The committee did not see fit to make it public. The committee found Hawthorne marginally qualified, and the Senate confirmed him. Judge Hawthorne seemed to have believed John McGowan had done him a favor.

And he seemed still to think so. He shook McGowan's hand, smiled warmly and said it was good to see him again.

"We're talking about Cosima Bernardin," Dougherty said.

The judge's smile disappeared, and he nodded somberly. "John," he said to McGowan, "we're going to have to do something about that young woman."

McGowan retreated into his reserve. He nodded ambiguously.

"She is abusing the processes of the federal courts," said Judge Hawthorne. "I mean in this Terasnova deportation case. Frankly, I've been letting her have her way. As the old chiché goes, if we give her enough rope she'll hang herself. But we're making a record. And when the dancer is finally deported, I'm very likely going to cite Cosima Bernardin for contempt. I'll turn the whole record over to you. With some of the other things that have come up, I'd think she's on her way to disbarment."

"We may have come up with something," said Lynn Karadja to Claude Graves.

She had come to his office on East 34th Street, the head-

441

quarters of Americans for the Preservation of American Values; and as she sat down on the couch that faced his desk, Graves ran his eyes up and down over her as he always did, bluntly appraising and speculating. On a warm spring day she was lightly dressed, in a yellow blouse and short black skirt; her breasts were spectacular, thrust out against the light yellow silk, and her legs were erotically sleek. For some time she had anticipated a proposition from Graves. She was only surprised she had not heard it yet.

He was smoking one of his stinking little cigars—which was something he was not going to do if she went out with him. He carried his weight loosely, so his clothes didn't fit well. Though APAV paid well and promptly, they kept shabby offices on the third floor of what had been a brick house—above a beautician's shop and a language school. She had guessed that APAV's millionaires were quite miserly about administrative expenses, about any money in fact they could not see as spent directly for their purposes.

"You have a tape?" Graves asked.

She nodded. She put the player on the edge of his desk. "This is from the telephone tap on Lanier." She smiled. "He's calling Cosima Bernardin, so we'll have the same conversation from the other end. Okay—"

"Bernardin, Loewenstein & Salomon, good morning."

"Lawton Lanier for Miss Bernardin, please."

"One moment, please."

"Good morning, Lawton. How's everything?"

"Couldn't be better. And all's well with you, I hope. Uh . . . The reason for my call—Lunch?"

"Today? I wish I could. I'm afraid I can't today."

"Ah. Well . . . Sorry to hear it. I do have a bit of news that might interest you. Has to do with Vanessa Kingston."

"I'm listening."

"When I gave her the discouraging news about 'Rosie's,' she asked if I could help find her another job. Well, I've got a possibility. How would it be if Vanessa went to Australia for a while?"

442

"I suppose that would be all right. What's she going to do in Australia, go swimming with the great white sharks?"

"I had a wire from an Australian company, asking if we might be interested in shooting 'Rosie's' in Sydney, changing the locale to down there, and putting it on Australian television. They'd want to use Australian actors mostly, but they think they'd want to use the original Rosie and Brenda. In any event they'll broadcast the pilot. I could possibly arrange to send Vanessa down there. She could work with them on setting up the scenes and scripts, in preparation for shooting some episodes. She'd have to be gone three or four months, I should think. And the Australians can be prevailed on, I'm almost certain, to pay her salary and expenses."

"Sounds good, Lawton. Good for Vanessa, actually."

"I thought so. I'll go ahead and explore it."

"Good luck, Lawton. And thanks for calling."

"I'm glad you brought the wine," said Joel to Rick. "Otherwise you might have been drinking Mogen David."

Rick was seated at his sister's dinner table, in her apartment uptown. Her children by this marriage were in the living room, their attention fastened to the television set—which Martha had repeatedly told them to turn down—leaving only the adults at the table: Martha, Joel, another Martha, nineteen years old, the only child of his sister's first marriage who was still at home—and Sally Lugar.

Sally was there "by chance," as Martha had put it. "Your sister the matchmaker," Joel had said in the kitchen where he had asked Rick to join him for before-dinner drinks.

Sitting first in his sister's living room, then at her table, Rick was oppressed with memories of the flat where he grew up, of his parents' life-habits and mannerisms. He and his sister had been the same noisy children her younger two were now, and his parents had tried with the same indifferent success to entertain without their raucous interruptions. Like Joel, Rick's father had guided men to the kitchen for shots of rye or vodka, while the women chatted in the living room, maybe sipping small glasses of wine, without the least resentment at their exclusion from the rude male ritual of tossing back a shot or two before dinner. These were his mother's dishes, left behind when father and mother moved into their tiny flat eight blocks from the water in Miami Beach. In fact, much of the furniture was what he had grown up with. And Martha cooked like his mother: with more attention to quantity than quality.

Sally. She was very small, not more than five-feet-two, and surely there was not more than ninety pounds of her. She was shy and quiet. Her hair and eyes were dark and her skin olive. She was plainly embarrassed by the situation; yet, he understood, she had accepted the invitation and was here to see Martha's younger brother, the lawyer, and to be seen by him. From time to time he noticed her big, solemn eyes looking at him. He had never before experienced such an arranged confrontation, and he was surprised to discover he found something erotic in it.

"That lawyer who's your partner, she's a real superstar, isn't she?" his sister said. "You can hardly turn on the TV that she's not on, with the dancer. Sometimes without the dancer. Tell us about her."

"Well, uh . . . She's very beautiful. Very smart. Very rich."

"You got a thing for her?" the younger Martha asked.

Rick lied. "No way. She's engaged to Jack Putnam."

"And you're lawyer for people like Jerry Patchen and Adela Drake," his sister said.

"Well . . . I do some work for them. On their tax problems." He knew what his sister was doing, exactly what his mother would have done: prompting him to parade his accomplishments, his association with famous people. It was most awkward.

Sally rescued him. "My brother wanted to be a lawyer," she said quietly. "He started the course at Brooklyn, but he dropped out after a few months and went to work for a brokerage firm. It was a bad decision. When the market fell, he lost his job. But it all works out in the end. His real ambition was to be a singer, so he's cutting sandwiches in a deli while he studies voice."

"Sally is a secretary," said Martha. "More than that, actually. She studied at Catherine Gibbs."

"Where do you work, Sally?" Rick asked.

"At Doyle Dane Bernbach," she said. "The advertising agency."

"It must be nice to work in an office," said the younger Martha. She herself worked on an assembly line, soldering two wires to two terminals, on hundreds of subassemblies every day; she was not entirely sure what the subassembly became part of. She went to night school, though, and was studying to become an elementary-school teacher.

When dinner was over they went to the living room, carrying chairs from the dining room. Martha made her children give up the couch to their Uncle Rick and Sally; but she did not tell them to turn off the television set, and for half an hour conversation competed with the police-show noise blaring from beneath the flashing picture. Rick endured as long as he could, then remarked that he hated having to leave so soon but had worked a long day. Then everyone said the appropriate things, and everyone but the children rose and gathered near the door.

"Oh, Rick, I'd appreciate it if you'd walk Sally home. It's just a block and a half, and it isn't really safe for a girl—"

"Martha, I—"

"I'll be happy to."

On the street outside, she looked up and said, "You're really under no obligation to—"

"That's right," he interrupted. "It's no obligation. It's a privilege."

On the stoop before the door to her building, she said, "Do you want to come up for a drink? Your sister went to a great deal of trouble to get us acquainted, and we're not

445

really acquainted. We might spend a few minutes together before we decide she had a dumb idea."

"I'd like to, Sally," he said. "With the understanding that you're under no obligation—"

"No obligation," she said with a little smile. "It's a privilege."

Cosima and Susanne handled the lines, and their father brought *Lafayette* alongside the dock. They had taken the sloop out for an hour's swing around the islands off Greenwich, a sort of shakedown cruise to see if any part of her had developed a flaw that had to be corrected—or if any of them had allowed their skills to lapse over the winter. It had gone smoothly. The weather on the last day of April was warm, with a fresh northeast wind that raised three-foot seas on the Sound and provided a sailor with enough to keep him busy.

Leon was pleased with his two daughters, so far as their crew work was concerned. He was a little annoyed with Cosima. She had made some comment about his interference in her bar-association problem: that he might do more harm than good and that anyway she had to handle her own problems. He could be tolerant of that kind of talk; young people always thought that way; but he saw no reason why she should have brought it up while they were out sailing.

Now she was returning to her condominium. She would be at the house for dinner. He would have suggested she telephone Jack while she was at home, but she could be a bit touchy on that subject, too. He did his share of making the boat secure, while the girls did theirs, and they went their ways: he and Susanne to the house on Round Hill, Cosima to her condo on the water.

In her living room she found the red light burning on her telephone recorder. She played the message.

"Hi. Jack. Just checkin' in. Nothing in particular to say, except that I love you very much. You don't need to try to return this call. I'm going to be out for a while. I'll try to get back to you about six, your time."

It was a message they had arranged. They couldn't talk on her tapped telephone, but he needed to talk to her and would be expecting her to call him about six.

It was four-thirty. She bathed, took a short nap, and twenty minutes before six she slipped out of the condo and drove to the Howard Johnson's Motel on the Post Road. There, on a pay telephone in the lobby, she placed a call to Jack.

"We'll make this quick," she told him. "Then I'll zip back home, and you can make your call 'about six.'"

"Okay. Listen, I got some news for you. Had a call from Vanessa. Happy as a bug in a rug. Some company's hired her on a six-month renewable contract to do some television commercials. They'll be shooting them in Florida at first, then on Long Island, and she's leaving for the first shooting next week. You asked me to let you know if she called with that kind of news. Well, she did."

"She name the company?"

"No, but she named the product. You won't believe this, Cosima, but Vanessa is going to appear in skimpy white shorts mowing lawns with VacuMax lawnmowers."

"Bingo!"

"Hmm?"

"A setup, Jack, and it seems to have worked like a charm. Lawton and I let our buggy friends hear a conversation in which Lawton said he was thinking of sending Vanessa to Australia. Of course, he had no such idea. We wanted to see if the buggers would react. And they have. A job for Vanessa. Sure. Keep her in this country. Keep her available."

"Aw . . . Poor kid."

"Poor kid, hell. She gets to make the commercials, right?

447

And she gets paid generously from them. Don't let's worry about Vanessa.''

"I guess that's right . . ." said Jack hesitantly.

"Okay. It is right. So thanks for good news. It will take me about ten minutes to get back to the condo. Call me, say, six-fifteen.''

A message waited for Leon, too, when he returned from his afternoon on the Sound. Malcolm Stanley had called and, like Jack calling Cosima, would call again about six.

He was prompt. "I'm glad to reach you. May I hope I'm not interrupting anything?''

"In the past," said Leon, "I've had some unfortunate experiences resulting from taps on telephone lines. Are you sure this line is secure?''

A little chuckle rippled under Stanley's words as he replied. "From where I'm calling . . . don't worry. And you?''

"Secure on my end.''

"Ah, good. Well look, Mr. Bernardin, as I said to you before, I would like to do you a favor if I can. No point in my being coy as to why. I don't know whether I did you one before or not. The report I got from the hearing was that the charges against your daughter were so patently ridiculous that no honest lawyer could have voted against her.''

"One did," said Leon coldly.

"I said what I meant. Now, my young man is being pressured to make a statement to the effect that our firm dictated his vote as a favor to you. Okay. I've had an earnest conversation with the boy. He knows the score, if he didn't before. You'll have his complete cooperation.''

"We may not need it.''

"I hope you don't. I hope I'm offering a favor you won't need. Indeed, I can't imagine you'll need it. But it is there for you if you need it.''

"I appreciate that," said Leon.

Three cool words—"I appreciate that"—were all Malcolm Stanley had hoped for. It is with baubles that men are led, Napoleon said. Yes, and they can be more than led, with a few significant words.

On her way from the condo to the house, Cosima stopped again at the Howard Johnson's and placed a call to Rick. He didn't answer. She tried Hugh. He did.

"Success!" she exhorted. "We know who's listening. They bought the little chat between Lawton and me. They really thought he was about to send her to Australia, and to keep her here on the hook they gave her a job. That establishes the connection."

"Specifically . . ." said Hugh quietly. He and Adela had just sat down to a Chinese dinner that had been delivered.

"She's going to make commercials for VacuMax lawnmowers. VacuMax is a trademark of Haggard Corporation in Cleveland, and Norman Haggard, its chief stockholder, is one of the millionaire supporters of APAV."

"Success is the word, kid," said Hugh. "Now I'm going to get back to my diner. You do the same. Monday we'll set to work on giving Mr. Haggard and his bugger friends a royal screwing."

Cosima had been unable to reach Rick at his apartment because he had not returned there. On this Saturday night, while Cosima dined at the house on Round Hill and Hugh shared cartons of Chinese food with Adela, Rick had brought Sally Lugar to Four Seasons—in celebration.

He was in love with her. And she was with him. So they had promised each other in the early hours of Saturday morning; and as they sat in the pool room of Four Seasons, her innocent wonder in the decor, in the menu, in speculation over the identities of people at tables around them,

449

touched him as he had never been touched before. He was chary of new love. He had experienced it before; and so, she said, had she; they both knew what disappointment might lie in it. But for now, for still another night, he would enjoy it uncritically.

Last night had been astonishing. She had made coffee. She had sat down close to him on the couch. Her signal had been unmistakable—and to him wholly surprising. But he welcomed it, and within a minute she had been in his arms, their tongues were exploring each other's mouths and she was guiding his hand to her breasts. And he had undressed her. He had been surprised at her underwear: the very cheapest white rayon, likely from Woolworth—which made no difference anyway, since her simple white brassiere hung loosely over her tiny breasts. She wore neither deodorant or perfume, shaved her legs but not under her arms or in her crotch and smelled of soap and maybe a little talcum powder, plus sweat. A little line of dark hair marked her belly from her navel to the edge of her thick, dark bush of pubic hair. Half a dozen hairs grew on her breasts, including one from her left aureole, which in the early light of morning he was tempted to pluck but didn't for fear the sharp small pain might alter her mood.

She was so small he could hardly believe she could take all of him into her, but when the time came she had seized his shaft and guided it, then urged him down, gasping and grunting, until his coarse hair was entangled in hers and their pubes were pressed tightly together. She wanted all he had—flesh and vigor and spirit. He had given, and she reciprocated with all she could give. When they finished the first time, they were sated, winded, and sweating.

As soon as she detected the first sign of a returning erection, she threw herself over him, pressed her face to his crotch and sucked his penis into her mouth. His hard returned, and another eruption came within two minutes. He repaid the favor, and for a little while he was afraid her cries would rouse the neighbors.

About nine she had gone out to a neighborhood bakery where she bought their breakfast. He had offered to go with her, but she had insisted he stay in bed. He had stood at the window and watched her walk up the street, modestly dressed in a black skirt and white blouse, with a little square of blue-and-white rayon folded into a triangle and tied neatly under her chin and over her hair. It was an interesting contradiction. The tradition in which she had been reared required her to cover her head when she went on the streets, and she was keeping that tradition on this Shabbat morning. It also forbade her to handle money today, but she was on her way to the bakery with money in her purse. The Jews of this neighborhood would notice the scarf over her head and would approve; at the same time they would not condemn her doing a bit of shopping on the Shabbat. In the Brooklyn neighborhood where she was reared, she would have been scorned, if not shunned, for breaking the Shabbat, yes, but more for being an unmarried, childless woman at twenty-seven.

They had talked about things like this—already. In the afternoon, Sally had telephoned Martha.

Now, in Four Seasons, she said—"It's very expensive here. But I could have afforded it, occasionally. Why didn't I, Rick?"

"It's not a question of money," he said. "It's a question of venturing into an environment you suppose may be hostile. And you never know. It may be."

Twenty-three

"I appreciate your coming out here," said Bill Gallon. "It's not the most convenient place in the world; still, it serves well for our purposes."

Cosima, Hugh and Rick were sitting inside a conference room in a building in Westchester County, south of White Plains. The car Gallon had sent for them had left the highways and driven the last few hundred yards on an unmarked road through a grove of trees, to the top of a low hill. The headquarters of William A. Gallon & Associates, Security Consultants, was not identified by any sign, and only the array of antennas on a steel tower above the squat, ugly, concrete-block building offered any hint as to what kind of business was conducted there. The conference room itself had the aspect of a city-university seminar room: spare, lighted with glaring fluorescents, windowless, without carpets on the tile floor.

"Let me get immediately to what I want you to hear," said Gallon. "Then we can discuss what it means and what you want to do about it."

He reached for the switch on a bulky reel-to-reel tape recorder, and the reels began to turn.

"You sat there that day and listened to what she turned into a farce. Did you have any doubts that Lanier was lying?"

"It sounded as though he might be."

"We have evidence that he was lying. Unfortunately, our evidence is nothing better than a sworn statement from Vanessa Kingston; and there's nothing to be gained in opposing her word to his. On the other hand . . . Well, suppose I told you a member of the subcommittee voted as he did because Leon Bernardin was in a position to bankrupt his law firm if that member voted against the Bernardin bitch?"

"In a position . . . ?"

"What if Leon Bernardin called the senior partner of one of the subcommittee members and threatened to do something that would cost the firm more than a million dollars?"

"If there is evidence . . ."

"Evidence. We'll have the evidence."

"A member of the subcommittee . . . Not a small matter. Uh . . . what evidence is there?"

"We'll call it a confession."

"The member has . . . admitted he was improperly influenced?"

"Not yet. But he will."

"I will of course be very interested in the evidence."

"I'd like to have your help in getting it."

Gallon stopped the tape. He turned the reels with his hand, rolling forward to a mark. "Another man joined them," he said. "And a waiter brought drinks. We can omit the sociability. It goes on—"

"We're talking about Cosima Bernardin."

"John, we're going to have to do something about that young woman. She is abusing the processes of the federal courts. I mean in this Terasnova deportation case. Frankly, I've been letting her have her way. As the old clichée goes, if we give her enough rope she'll hang herself. But we're making a record. And when the dancer is finally deported, I'm very likely going to cite Cosima Bernardin for contempt. I'll turn the whole record over to you. With some of the other things that have come up, I'd think she's on her way to disbarment."

"Where'd you get this tape?" Rick asked apprehensively.

"That conversation was in the Harvard Club last Thursday," said Gallon.

"You bugged the Harvard Club?"

"No—No," Gallon hurried to say. "We picked that up with our ECR."

"But—"

"It was Miss Bernardin's idea," said Gallon.

"A shot in the dark," said Cosima. "I guessed that whoever bugged my home and office might be carrying a transmitter and sending his various business conferences to a recorder. I asked Bill if there were any way to find out. Turns out there is."

"Yes," said Gallon. "Bugs transmit on a limited number of FM frequencies and carry a very limited distance. But if you suspect someone and can get your ECR close enough to him, you can find out if he's transmitting. If you use a couple of ECRs you can also locate the transmitter, by triangulating. Sometimes that's all you can find out, because some of the transmitters include rather sophisticated scramblers. We checked on Mr. Dougherty and Mr. Nash. Both of them carry transmitters in their briefcases. At least sometimes. Both of them occasionally transmit their business meetings. This is the first time we picked up anything that related to Miss Bernardin."

"In other words," said Rick, "you didn't bug the Harvard Club, Dougherty bugged it himself—you just picked up and recorded the transmissions from his bug."

Gallon nodded. "Precisely," he said with evident self-satisfaction. "I might tell you, incidentally, that was only one of three bugs transmitting from the Harvard Club during that lunch hour."

"God, can I talk anywhere without being recorded?"

"Yes, you can. I make my living providing people with assurance that they can. In a situation like this one, you can, for example, jam their frequency."

Hugh sighed. "I wish Dougherty had taken that briefcase to his lunch with Blyleven."

454

"Oddly, he did," said Gallon. "But he left it in the checkroom, maybe because it would have been too conspicuous in the public dining room. We picked up a lot of chit-chat between members of the club and the checkroom attendant."

"We have acquired another advantage, gentlemen," said Cosima. "I don't like the ethics of bugging. Bill and I talked about wiring Blyleven when he next meets with Dougherty, and I was very reluctant to do it. But if we can continue to intercept the transmissions from Dougherty's own wired briefcase, and Nash's, we can castrate these bastards with their own knife."

"I like the metaphor," said Hugh.

"I hate to ask the question," Rick said in the car as they were driven back to the City, "but who is paying Gallon & Associates? They are competent, I have no doubt, but—"

"Not the partnership," said Cosima crisply. "I'm paying the fee partly out of the funds my mother raised to help Lana, partly out of personal funds. I think that's a good mix. In part, we are fighting back against a clique of infallible patriots who want to deport Lana, and in part I am still contending with the consequences of leaving Hamilton, Schuyler and taking a big client with me. It's not coming out of the money you and Joan and I will divide at the end of the year."

"Cosima, I apologize," said Rick. "That wasn't my question. I . . . Well, I really wanted to think you weren't paying the whole bill yourself."

Cosima squeezed his arm. "I understand."

"I'll bill as little as I can," said Gallon from the front seat. "I like this case. I like working for people I can identify as the good guys, and I don't often get the chance."

"We've got a federal judge on the bad side, don't forget," said Cosima. "Plus the Justice Department."

The normally sober, often expressionless Gallon smiled. "No challenge," he said.

"I am really opposed to wiring Blyleven," said Rick. "Even assuming he'd go along with it. Are you confident you can pick up the signals from Dougherty's briefcase?"

"Yes," said Gallon. "Of course, he has to have it with him when he says the kind of things we want to hear. If he decides not to transmit, then there's nothing for us to pick up."

"There is another problem," said Cosima. "If we wire Blyleven, he'll have to know about it. He drinks and talks. I don't want to have to trust him."

"It'll be damned interesting to know what he says," Hugh said with a grunt.

"I don't want to wire him," said Cosima decisively. "We'll have to take our chances with Dougherty. Since he carried his briefcase to his meeting with McGowan, why wouldn't he carry it to his meeting with Blyleven? So . . . Next question—What disinformation do we feed through the bugs they've planted on us?"

"That's a resource you may want to hold in reserve," said Gallon. "You really only get one chance, you know. Once you cut them with their own knife—to adopt your metaphor, Miss Bernardin—they are very likely to realize they are being had."

"Agreed," said Cosima. "Trial in three weeks. We'll live with the bugs until then and wait and see how to use them."

"I want to cancel it," said Adela.

Hugh shook his head. "I don't want you to cancel it."

Adela sighed sorrowfully. "I don't want to go, Hugh."

"I don't want you to go. But you can't quit, you can't stop, you can't . . . Hell, girl, spare me from reciting a litany of clichés."

"I love you, Hugh," she said simply.

"Yeah," he nodded, muttering through clenched teeth. "I love you, too."

They were sitting in a tiny Hungarian restaurant within walking distance—Hugh's walking distance—of his apartment, drinking red wine, dining on food she could not name and maybe he couldn't either. She was not performing tonight. It afforded them an opportunity to eat out, at a normal hour, without thought of her schedule—

Except that their conversation, and all that was on their minds, was her schedule. She opened tomorrow night in Boston: The Infinite Adela, in concert. Then she went on to Rochester, Buffalo, Cleveland, Columbus, Indianapolis, St. Louis, Chicago, Kansas City, Denver, San Francisco, Los Angeles, Dallas, Houston, New Orleans, Miami, Washington, Baltimore and Philadelphia—before returning to New York toward the end of June.

"Who's gonna shave my head?" she asked tearfully.

"You're going to do it yourself, I sincerely hope."

She swallowed back a sob, then nodded. "I wouldn't let anyone else touch it."

"You can't throw away achievement and success, Adela," he said gravely. "They're too damned rare and too damned precious."

"So's love," she whispered.

"For a pair like us, I suppose so," he said. "But not as rare as what you've got. There's also talent. And, hell kid, there's also money. You'll be hard put to carry back what you get from this tour. Plus, think of the alternative. If you don't go, you'll be sitting around our apartment the next six weeks, wondering why the hell you didn't go on the concert tour any performer would give her life for. Hell . . . Like I said, don't force me to recite a litany of clichés."

She used her fingers to wipe tears from her eyes. "Love's a cliché, too, isn't it?"

He shook his head. "Not when it's between a pair of oddballs like us, Adela. And it'll last out a six-week tour. It isn't worth a hell of a lot if it doesn't."

* * *

"I usually try to go into Hugh's office, rather than ask him to come in here," Cosima said to Jerry Patchen. "Courtesy to his seniority, you know."

"Sure," said Jerry.

She glanced at the lights on her telephone. "He's on the line right now. Soon as he's off—"

"Right."

It had been difficult for Cosima to conduct business in her office, knowing that everything said there was being transmitted to a recorder somewhere and reviewed by strangers. On the other hand, it was important that she do some business there, to maintain the image of a working law office, not one abandoned because it was bugged. She had to warn people not to say anything in her office that they would not want overheard outside. That had been easy enough, but to interrupt telephone callers when they began to talk too easily had been more difficult. ("Excuse me a sec, Watson. Look, I—Listen, I'm going to have to get back to you.")

"Adela's off on her concert tour," said Jerry. "Hugh must be feeling pretty low."

Cosima frowned. She would just as soon Jerry not discuss Hugh's relationship with The Infinite Adela for consumption by the warlocks of APAV. "She's going to make a bundle," she said, trying to turn the conversation to the economics of the tour.

"I want you guys to write me a new set of contracts for people I hire in the future," Jerry said. "I made Adela a star. And what the hell good's it going to do me?"

"Hugh is off his line," said Cosima.

They sat down in Hugh's office. Here, high in the Pan Am Building, Hugh kept almost a replica of the office he had occupied at 866 Third Avenue: a cluttered, determinedly functional room, equipped with a desktop computer that emitted an incessant whirring sound (which was

458

the spinning hard-disk drive) and decorated with the same old diplomas, certificates and Spy prints. Hugh sat in his shirtsleeves, behind heaps of books and files that covered his desk; his morning cigar was in his hand.

"You're going to have to make your choice, Jerry," Hugh said without preliminaries. "You can make a video-tape that is non-copyable. Kids who buy it can play it but can't—to use their word—'dub' it. Or you can accept the offer from HBO and let them broadcast your show. If you do that, you can't prevent copying. Anyone can tape a tele-vision show off the air, and when they do they have a tape that can be dubbed as many times as they want. I'm talking about both law and technology."

"If I produce the videotape myself," said Jerry. "I can put it on the market for less than eight dollars, cost—that is, assuming I can spread production costs over a minimum of two hundred thousand sales. I can sell it to the stores for, like, fifteen dollars, and they can market it retail for what-ever they want, say, $34.95 list, discounted to $21.95. Any-way, I'm gonna net, say, seven dollars a copy. Sell a million—No network is going to pay me seven million for the show."

"Let me suggest a possibility," said Hugh. "Make two tapes. Announce on the broadcast tape that a video of the *full* concert will be available in stores the morning after the broadcast. Then float a rumor that the tape in the stores not only contains songs that weren't included in the broad-cast versions but that the broadcast was a 'cleaned up' ver-sion: censored."

"HBO would never go for that," said Jerry.

"Maybe," said Hugh. "Depends on how you do it. You can do it so as to make you look good and HBO look good, too—at the expense of the 'clean-lyrics' harpies."

Jerry grinned. "You're a clever man, Hugh."

"Maybe," said Cosima. "But let me throw some cold water. Bull Dog Fangs appeals to a highly specific group of fans—wildly enthusiastic and intensely loyal—but their enthusiasm and loyalty are fragile, as you well know. Video-tape is part of their lives, part of their culture. *Dubbing* video-tapes is part of their culture. They all do it, they've always done it, and they see nothing wrong with it. You try to sell them a non-copyable tape, they'll think you're cheap-shotting them. It's a hell of a risk. You could kill the goose."

"You're saying copyright is a dead issue, so far as video-tapes are concerned," said Hugh, irritated.

"Remember what happened with personal-computer software," she said. "Copy protection was put in the best programs. Then came software to break the copy protection. Then copy protection was made more rigid. One copy protection scheme actually damaged your computer if you tried to copy the software it guarded. And you remember what happened? Software buyers *resented* copy protection. Protected programs lost their market share. Something close to a boycott developed. Today, there's hardly a protected program left. Companies that wanted to survive dropped protection—and made a big point of announcing they were dropping it."

Jerry shrugged. "Maybe there's not enough money in videotapes to justify doing it."

"How much money does it take?" Cosima asked. "Remember something else. Remember the football strike. I thought the players had a good case, but the fans didn't. They resent the amount of money professional athletes make. They're wrong, in my opinion, but they made their feelings very clear. If you made your videotape noncopyable so you can make ten million from it instead of four million, you may get the same reaction."

"Ah, but the fans came back and filled the stadium again, as soon as the strike was over," said Jerry.

"Because the NFL is the only game in town," said Cosima. "Bull Dog Fang isn't. I wouldn't throw a challenge at my fans, if I were you. You of all people ought to know how quickly they can take their enthusiasm and loyalty somewhere else."

460

Jerry smiled wryly at Hugh, who was glowering. "What have I got here?" he asked. "A lawyer or a guru?"

Hugh shrugged. "She's going what we lawyers are constantly accused of doing—shooting holes in people's happiest schemes."

"Exactly," said Cosima. "I've shot holes in your blimp, Jerry; I haven't shot it down. I'm just telling you—you better think carefully about this thing."

"Yeah," he said glumly. "I guess that's what I pay you for."

"We'll send you a bill," said Cosima.

She went to lunch with Jerry. She thought she had become perhaps even a little paranoid about the eavesdropping, but she had developed habits like the one she followed today: skipping around among restaurants, not letting anyone perceive a pattern in her choices—to make it impossible for someone to establish surveillance over her at her lunch. So, she and Jerry went to Nanni, where they sat down in the close, crowded dining room over platters of Italian food and a bottle of Italian wine.

"If you marry her, the government will argue it is only a marriage of convenience, to save her from deportation. If you get her pregnant, they will say even worse."

"Would anyone think of conceding Lana and I might be in love with each other?" he asked.

"The people who'd like to be rid of her would like to be rid of you, too—except that you're an American citizen and they can't. Association of your name with Lana's can only hurt her right now. Later, one way or the other, it won't make any difference."

His lips were hard and tight, and he looked away and spat his words at the corner of the table—"I don't believe it."

Cosima sighed. She lifted her chin high. "For the moment, Jerry—for the moment—this country is in the grip of

461

the Baptists, Methodists and Presbyterians, the Rotarians, Kiwanians and Civitans—Main Street run wild. It's a phase. It will end. But while it lasts . . ."

"All right. But I'm going to tell you something, Cosima. Lana is not going back to Russia. *Not,* you understand? Fuck the law. Fuck the federal government. She's not going."

Cosima shook her head. "Don't do something stupid, Jerry. Don't make Lana do something stupid. I may be able to drag out the court case for a long time yet. The Senate is going to pass the bill. There'll be an election in November. There are a lot of options still open. Don't foul everything up by doing something stupid."

Robert Blyleven climbed the stairs heavily and trudged across the thin-carpeted floor of the Harvard Club to the confrontation he dreaded. He opened the door of the private dining room to which he had been summoned. He was surprised. He was the first one there.

The table was set for four. A bar had been set up in a corner, with bottles of Scotch, gin, vermouth and vodka, plus ice and soda. He frowned at the bottles, then decided not to pour himself a drink. He would need a clear head.

Malcolm Stanley himself—Stanley, Senior, not Stanley, Junior—had spoken to him last evening just before he left the office—"Don't let 'em intimidate you, Bob. Leon Bernardin did *not* ask us for a favor. You voted on the basis of the evidence that was before the subcommittee. That's all there is to it. You're clean. But, just remember, *they're not.* Their motives won't stand examination."

He did not know how to defy P. D. Dougherty and whoever else was taking the extra places at this table—god knew who. He had effected a little essay at boldness, by wearing a brown tweed jacket and dark brown slacks to the meeting. Maybe he *should* take a drink—what the hell.

The next to arrive was Daniel Nash. He was a busy little

man, with reddish hair, a fixed, ostensibly optimistic smile, and businesslike small round glasses.

Nash introduced himself. "Dan Nash. Hamilton, Schuyler, Depew & Chase. You sitting here? I'll sit beside you." He shoved his briefcase under the table beside the chair he had chosen. "Well . . . Drink?"

Blyleven let Nash pour him a Scotch, noticing it was a heavy one and deciding to nurse it.

"I guess you know what we want to talk about," Nash said briskly. He lit a small cigar. "Cosima Bernardin. We had trouble with her at our firm. All the characteristics that have come out in various ways in the past year were sadly apparent while she was with us."

Bill Gallon himself was in charge of the electronic countermeasures receiver. The young woman beside him wore earphones and was listening on a second ECR.

"Nash's frequency," he said. "So that *was* him going into the Harvard Club."

"You want me to record on this frequency?" the young woman asked.

"Uh . . . Yeah, I'll record Dougherty's."

The young woman grinned. "You suppose either one of those bastards knows the other is transmitting?"

"I doubt it," said Gallon. "One thing's sure, Blyleven doesn't know."

"Shouldn't someone have told him?"

Gallon shook his head. "He's nervous enough as it is."

P. D. Dougherty arrived next, carrying his briefcase and depositing it under his chair as Nash had done. He stepped to the bar and poured himself a big drink, after which he lit a cigarette.

Blyleven noticed Dougherty's openly disapproving assessment of his jacket and slacks. At Quarles & McGrath there was no doubt a dress code, which Dougherty conformed in his dark-blue pin-striped suit with gold watch chain hanging across his vest.

Nash returned to the subject of Cosima Bernardin. "She was insubordinate. She refused to accept supervision. She took the attitude that, as the daughter of Leon Bernardin, she was not required to conduct herself as an associate and junior partner, and she made it very clear to us that what we paid her was not her chief source of income. She—"

"There is another point," Dougherty interrupted. "We are talking about how Bernardin uses his financial clout. Well, that's how the lovely Cosima got her job with Hamilton, Schuyler."

"True," said Nash. "He telephones Clarence Paul Davidson, our most senior partner, and called in an obligation. She was eighth in her class at Harvard and not qualified for our firm unless there were some other persuasive reason, and—"

"And there was definitely a persuasive reason," said Dougherty. "Her father was in a position to lean on the firm—and he did."

"They use their money and power," said Nash, "in ways wholly inconsistent with the ethics of the profession."

Blyleven nodded ambiguously and sipped from his Scotch.

"Ah. Here's the judge. Judge, have you met Bob Blyleven? Bob, this is Judge Ralph Hawthorne, United States District Court."

This was a disturbing surprise. A federal judge . . . Not only that, Judge Ralph Hawthorne. Blyleven had heard bad things about Judge Hawthorne: that he was hot-tempered, arbitrary, and not the most knowledgeable judge on the District Court. He had never met him. He was a personable sort of fellow, with a quick but reserved smile—in fact, an artificial smile—conceded for the occasion and rapidly withdrawn. He was brisk of manner. He accepted a drink and sat down at the table, glancing around as if to suggest his time was valuable and he hoped people would get on with whatever it was they wanted to talk about.

He was not to have his way. The talk returned to Cosima Bernardin but skirted around the main point until the waiter had been in to take their orders for lunch.

Then Dougherty assumed command of the meeting. "Gentlemen," he said, "we've met with counsel for the Association of the Bar, and we are going to initiate new charges against Miss Cosima Bernardin. Two sets of charges, probably. The first will be that she, through her father, attempted to corrupt the subcommittee that heard the last charges brought against her. The second will be that she has abused the processes of the federal courts, by dishonesty and the use of admittedly manipulatory and dilatory tactics. I might say that none of us here will be members of the new subcommittee that will take up these charges. I've already talked to the chairman of the full committee, and he will appoint an entirely new subcommittee. That subcommittee will not have prior experience with this young woman, so we will have to develop the case against her with considerable care. Now— It starts with you, Bob. We will need your statement of exactly how Leon Bernardin contacted your firm, what he said, and what instructions your firm gave you."

Blyleven pushed down on the arms of his chair, straightening his back. Okay. He had rehearsed. "Our firm," he said quietly, "represents Knightley International. Knightley owes the firm more than a million and a quarter in unpaid fees and expenses. Knightley is insolvent. The principal secured creditor is Bernardin Frères. If Bernardin et Frères decides to liquidate Knightley, its preferred status as a secured creditor will take every dollar the liquidation produces, leaving our firm stuck with a million and a quarter in fees and expenses it can't collect."

"You have an attorneys' lien," said Judge Hawthorne.

Blyleven shook his head. "We waived it. Maxwell, Donovan was so anxious to keep the account that we not only extended credit far too fully but also waived our priority rights."

"Which puts your firm on Leon Bernardin's hook," said Dougherty.

Blyleven shrugged. "I knew all this when I accepted a position on the subcommittee. I suppose I should have declined to serve."

"Questionable conduct," said Judge Hawthorne sepulchrally—thereby signalling Blyleven that he too was part of the intimidation.

Blyleven decided to stop, to wait for them to prompt him.

"And why—*specifically*—did you vote in subcommittee, first not to hear the charges against Cosima Bernardin at all, then when the evidence had been heard, to recommend the charges be dropped?" Dougherty asked.

"Because the charge against her was fanciful to begin with," said Blyleven evenly, using the words he had rehearsed over and over in his mind for a week, "and the evidence against her was nonexistent."

"Oh, really?" sneered Dougherty. "Then why did *I* vote to find her guilty?"

Blyleven smiled, though almost imperceptibly. This was the very question for which he had rehearsed an answer. "I'd be curious to know," he said.

"Uh . . . Let me ask—" Nash intervened. He put his little cigar aside in an ashtray. "What we need from you, Bob," he said, "is an account of what Leon Bernardin said or did."

"I understand that," said Blyleven. "And after my last meeting with Mr. Dougherty, I inquired of several of my senior partners. So far as I can learn, Mr. Bernardin did not call our firm. If he did, no one has told me."

"Question, Mr. Blyleven," said Judge Hawthorne, stabbing the table with his right forefinger. "Did anyone at your firm instruct you as to how you should vote in the subcommittee? Did anyone try in any way to influence you?"

This moment, too, Blyleven had rehearsed. Turning his

head, he met the eyes of each one of them. Then he said—
"No. No one, in my firm or out of it, tried to influence my vote."

P. D. Dougherty pushed his chair back and swung around on it, facing the window. "I don't think you're telling the truth," he said bluntly.

"I don't think you are either," replied Blyleven, his labored effort to appear calm so intense as to be almost convincing.

Dougherty swung back toward Blyleven, his face darkened. "I've practiced law in this city for thirty-five years, and until this moment no one ever suggested I am a liar."

"I doubt that, too," said Blyleven.

"Now, just a goddamned minute—"

"Just a goddamned minute is right!" shouted Judge Hawthorne. "Why am I here? To listen to a lot of bullshit? If you two want to go over on the Jersey side of the Hudson and blaze away at each other with pistols like Hamilton and Burr, go ahead, but don't ask a judge of the United States District Court to waste his time witnessing the spectacle. Frankly, I don't care which of you wings the other. It looks to me, Dougherty, like you can't make this charge stick."

"She hired Lanier to lie for her in the hearing," growled Dougherty, "and now she's hired this little shyster to lie for her here."

"Maybe," said the judge. "And if so she's ramming it up your ass—'cause you can't prove a thing."

"Judge Hawthorne," said Nash, trying to be cool, though his voice was thin with indignation, "we were counting on you. You are a judge now, but you weren't two years ago when some of us stuck our necks out pretty far to support your nomination."

"The part of this that you're counting on me for is going to come out all right," said the judge. "I won't have to rely on testimony I can't get, or perjury, to sustain my charges. My evidence will be on record, the transcript of proceedings in open court, where that bitch has lied and—"

"Good," Nash interrupted. "Then we can count on you? Fine. And what are you going to do about Svetlana Terasnova?"

Judge Hawthorne reached for his glass and took a swallow of Scotch. "I'm going to find against her, what the hell you think? And I'm not going to continue her bail. She's going to the detention center and she's going on a plane to Moscow, I promise you. And as soon as I announce that order, I'm going to order Cosima Bernardin held for contempt. Those two cunts are going out of my courtroom in handcuffs, gentlemen."

"They'll run straight to the Court of Appeals," said Nash.

"Which won't get the toe dancer out of the detention center," said Judge Hawthorne. "And as for glamourous Cosima . . . Well, at least she's gonna get a ride in the paddy wagon, a strip search, and a day or two in the slammer. Then we'll see. She may be a little less cocky the next time she appears before your subcommittee."

Twenty-four

"Then we can count on you? Fine. And what are you going to do about Svetlana Terasnova?"

"I'm going to find against her, what the hell you think? And I'm not going to continue her bail. She's going to the detention center and she's going on a plane to Moscow, I promise you. And as soon as I announce that order, I'm going to order Cosima Bernardin held for contempt. Those two cunts are going out of my courtroom in handcuffs, gentlemen."

"They'll run straight to the Court of Appeals."

"Which won't get the toe dancer out of the detention center. And as for glamorous Cosima . . . Well, at least she's gonna get a ride in the paddy wagon, a strip search and a day or two in the slammer. Then we'll see. She may be a little less cocky the next time she appears before your subcommittee."

They sat in Hugh's apartment—Hugh, Cosima and Blyleven—all of them grim as they listened to the tape.

"We would like to have your affidavit, Bob," said Cosima. "To the effect you have heard this tape and that it accurately represents what you heard live at the meeting."

Blyleven nodded.

"I'd like to have a second affidavit, if you don't mind," said Hugh. "Forgetting the tape for the moment, let's have

469

an affidavit telling in narrative form the circumstances of the meeting and what you heard."

Blyleven sighed. "I've been instructed to cooperate with you in any way you want."

Cosima sat down with Blyleven alone in the Hungarian restaurant where Hugh and Adela had eaten their dinner the night before she left for her tour. They'd had dinner, so they ordered a bottle of wine and sat at a quiet corner table. Casual observers—and there were no other observers—probably took them for a pair of lovers having a soulful conversation. She had seized him by the arm as they left Hugh's apartment and told him she wanted a private talk with him.

"You must know," he said.

"Maybe you'll feel better if I tell you I *don't* know," she said. "But I want to know."

Blyleven was intensely uncomfortable sitting opposite this young woman, at a small table in an intimate restaurant. At the moment she was one of the most recognizable women in New York; her face was in print everywhere, on television constantly. Only this evening she had made a quick statement to a television reporter at LaGuardia as she returned on the shuttle from Washington. Yes, she was optimistic that the Senate would pass the bill to grant citizenship to Svetlana Terasnova. Yes, she thought the President would sign it. The Senate might in fact reach the bill yet this week. The trial started next week. Yes, she was confident the judge would rule in her favor. Anyone who looked at this table twice was going to recognize her.

Then what? What if a news story appeared saying he was seen enjoying a quiet, even romantic, tête-à-tête with Cosima Bernardin? If Dougherty and Nash had nothing on him so far, this would— But, worse than that maybe, how would he explain it to his wife? Cosima—and she had insisted he use her first name—was beautiful. She was stylish, glamorous. Right now, she sat here in what was probably a designer outfit: a short bright-red skirt, a matching zipped-up red jacket, exhibiting a confident flare his wife could not even imagine.

While he assessed her, she assessed him: deeply troubled, a reluctant witness.

"Seriously, Bob," she prompted him. "I'd like to know what you meant when you said you'd been instructed to cooperate."

"You know about Knightley and all that," he said.

"I know, of course. I also know my father did not call your firm and ask for any favors."

"That's not exactly true, Cosima," said Blyleven. "I don't know how the conversations have gone, but your father and my senior partners have discussed the way I voted on the Oliver charges and how I was to handle myself in the meeting you recorded."

"You understand we did not bug that meeting room? That tape is a recording of transmissions from two briefcases—Dougherty's and Nash's."

"I guess that makes a difference," he said. "Pretty clever, too."

She sighed. "All right. You say somebody told you how to handle yourself in that meeting?"

He nodded. "Yes. And I was assured the firm would stand behind me."

"Your firm told you to lie?"

He shrugged. "Obviously."

"You think my father asked your firm to instruct you to lie?"

"I can't say that. I only know your father talked to Mr. Stanley."

"I know about that," she said. "First you were told to vote against me, then to vote for me. Isn't that right?"

"Something like that."

"My father didn't call and ask for that," she said. "Malcom Stanley, Senior, called my father and told him he would tell you to vote for me. My father didn't tell him not to, but he didn't ask him to do it."

"Distinction without a difference," Blyleven muttered.

"Maybe. But what about instructing you to lie in the meeting we recorded? I thought you had your own reasons for doing that."

"I did, of course," he said. "But it was discussed between your father and Mr. Stanley."

"When?"

"Sometime last week, I think."

"Are you sure about this?"

Blyleven nodded.

Cosima drew a deep breath and let it out slowly. "How would you have voted in the subcommittee if nobody had told you what to do?"

He smiled faintly. "I'd have voted for you. There was no case."

Cosima shook her head. "I don't know what my father has done," she said quietly, staring at the tablecloth. "Maybe we've corrupted the processes. On the other hand, Bob, you've seen what's being done by the other side. How the hell do I defend myself? How the hell do I defend my client?"

Blyleven smiled. "You and I rationalize the same way," he said.

She reached for his hand and squeezed it. "I liked what you said to P. D. Dougherty," she said. "When he said he'd never been called a liar, you said you doubted it."

"That sanctified son of a bitch," said Blyleven.

"And what about the judge?"

"I was shocked. Honest to god, Cosima. I was shocked. A federal judge!"

"Yeah . . . And I have to appear before him next week."

She confronted her father, in his paneled office at Bernardin Frères.

"It's got to stop, Dad," she said to him. "For all kinds of reasons. I love you, and I know you love me, and I understand your motives. But I cannot practice law with you working in the background to assure me of winning, to keep me out of trouble.''

"I did not call Malcolm Stanley," her father said rigidly. "He called me. He called to tell me what he had already done, not to ask if I wanted him to do it."

"When?"

"Well . . . Whenever it was. January."

"What about last week?"

Her father pressed his lips together tightly. They turned white and wrinkled. "Well," he said curtly. "It was the same. He called to tell me what he had *already* said to his young partner."

"Why didn't you tell me?"

He shrugged. It was a shrug of dismissal, meant to conclude the exchange.

"It could have fucked me up, Dad. I—"

"Don't use that kind of language."

"It could have fucked me up. I have my own arrangements for defeating those bastards. I don't need lies arranged for me by Malcom Stanley. In any event, I need to know."

"I acknowledge error," he said brusquely. Once again, it was a dismissal, one she had heard before.

"I'm not sure I can practice law in New York," she said. "I'm not sure you will ever let me. Maybe I'll move to Los Angeles—marry Jack and move to Los Angeles."

"I like the part about marrying Jack."

"Will you like it as much when I tell you Rick is about to marry someone else?"

"What's that got to do with it?"

She smiled. "Never mind. You know Jack is not Catholic."

"That's unfortunate."

"No, it's fortunate, because neither am I, not in my heart. And neither are you, for that matter. You go through the motions—and the devout know it, and resent it."

"I'd like to drop this subject, Cosima."

"So would I."

"In fact, is the conversation over?"

"Almost." She stood. "Next week I am taking the Terasnova case to trial. There's going to be an angry confrontation. With threats. I warn you, it's possible I may even
wind up in jail for a few hours. Even overnight. I—"

"You're going to commit contempt?"

"I may have to. But whatever happens, *stay out of it, Dad.*
If I need your help, I'll call for it. If I don't, don't try to
give it to me. I know what I'm doing. Don't butt in."

Leon Bernardin swelled. "I shall be governed by your
present admonition," he said stiffly.

"Jack? This is Leon Bernardin."

"Oh, hi there, Mr. Bernardin. Everything okay?"

"A crisis may be developing, Jack. I—"

"Let me interrupt you, Mr. B. I'm a jump ahead of you.
Already got my reservations. Comin' in on the red-eye Sunday night. Got a room at the Waldorf. Gonna stay out of
sight, but I'll be there if she needs me."

"I'll be grateful, Jack."

The Wall Street Journal editorialized:

From all we hear, Svetlana Terasnova is a talented
ballerina. It might be to this nation's artistic advantage if she were allowed to remain in the United States,
perhaps even to receive citizenship. On the other hand,
in order to gain admission to this country she lied
about her youthful affiliation with Komsomol, so she
entered the United States in violation of our immigration laws and is subject to deportation.

Our point is that the officers of the Immigration and
Naturalization Service and the Justice Department,
who are trying to deport her, have legitimate cause.

They are not a crowd of Philistines persecuting an artist. Their judgment of the values involved in this ballyhooed matter is just as sound as the judgment of the powerful allies Miss Cosima Bernardin has rallied to her client's cause.

On balance, we had just as soon Miss Terasnova were allowed to stay. We see no great harm in it. On the other hand, the pious attitude of professional liberals, who have tried to make her case something of a humanitarian cause, does not ring true. It is really a rather practical matter. Miss Terasnova broke our laws and is subject to deportation. Whether she should be given leave to stay here under the circumstances is a matter on which reasonable people can honestly differ.

They met again in Hugh's apartment—after another careful sweeping by Gallon's technicians. This time it was Cosima, Hugh and Rick, plus Jerry and Lana. Hugh poured champagne, and they drank a somewhat subdued toast. The toast was in celebration of the Senate's passage of the private bill. It had passed late in the morning, 61 to 34.

"It passed, but I'm not pleased," Emilie had said to Cosima on the telephone. "We had thirty-one Republicans and three Democrats on the nay side. That means that what's left of the President's constituency rallied to oppose us. It means we couldn't override a veto—"

"Which we wouldn't try, anyway," Cosima had said.

"No. There's a limit, as we've understood all along. Anyway, the President has just been handed assurance that he can veto without embarrassment. He can veto without appearing to ally himself with the lunatic fringe—a respectable bloc opposed the bill."

Cosima did not explain this to Lana and Jerry—or for that matter to Rick and Hugh, whose political instincts might or might not be sharp enough for them to understand it.

"We want to hear the tape," Jerry said.

"I don't think you should," said Cosima.

"She's the client," said Jerry, nodding at Lana, "and she wants to hear it."

Cosima shrugged. "All right . . . If you insist. But don't get too excited. It isn't as discouraging as it sounds."

"I'm going to find against her, what the hell you think? And I'm not going to continue her bail. She's going to the detention center and she's going on a plane to Moscow, I promise you. And as soon as I announce that order, I'm going to order Cosima Bernardin held for contempt. Those two cunts are going out of my courtroom in handcuffs, gentlemen."

Lana blanched.

Jerry flushed and clenched his fists. "This is the *judge* who's gonna hear her case?" His voice broke in fury.

"He's stepped on his cock, Jerry," said Cosima. "Let us handle him. We know what we're doing."

"I appreciate your coming," said Cosima.

"Lady," said Sheldon White, reporter for the New York *Times*, "any reporter you called would come running."

"I called the three of you for an important reason," said Cosima. "I'm going to put you in an uncomfortable spot. On the other hand, I may be giving you a very big story. I'm sorry we couldn't meet at my office. Unfortunately, it is bugged. There is a hidden microphone in my office and one in my condominium in Greenwich, and my telephones are tapped. And these microphones and taps are one-hundred-percent illegal, I may tell you—not there by court order. That gives you some idea why I asked you to meet with me—and why I asked you to come here, not to my office."

"Damn interesting," remarked Della Rosario. She was now with New York *Newsday*.

"Okay, but I'm asking you not to mention it. Not yet."

The third journalist there was Max Wilmot. It was he who had brought Sheldon White, who until three years ago had been a reporter for *The National Law Journal.* Max had assured Cosima that White could be trusted to hold a confidence. It was Max who had arranged the meeting place, too, on what he called neutral ground, the bar of the Overseas Press Club, where they sat around a table in midafternoon, munching peanuts and sipping the dark German beer Max had recommended.

"What I propose to do," said Cosima, "is hand each of you a sealed package. I will ask you not to open it except on two conditions. I may ask you later to return it to me, unopened. As I said, I'm putting you on the spot. If you feel you can't do this—as a matter of ethics or your obligations as journalists—we can drop the whole matter."

"It's all right with me," said Max immediately.

Sheldon White was a diminutive man, with dark curly hair and a big sharp nose in the middle of an otherwise puckish little face. "What's in the package is not a news release, I hope," he said.

"What's in the package is a set of affidavits and two audiotape cartridges. There is also a memorandum from me, explaining what the tapes are and how they were obtained. That's for your convenience. The affidavits and tapes are essentially self-explanatory."

"What are the conditions?" White asked.

Cosima was tired. She arched her back and flexed her shoulders to relieve the fatigue in her muscles. "Two conditions," she said. "You may open the packages and use the materials they contain in any way you see fit, *if,* one, I give you specific authorization, or, two, I go to jail."

White smiled. "This gets highly dramatic," he said.

"I accept your conditions, Cosima," said Della Rosario. She spoke to White. "I've worked with Cosima before. I trust her, and so can you."

"Why the three of us?" White asked.

"Max because he's a friend and because his papers are for lawyers and this is a legal matter," said Cosima. "Della because I trust her and she trusts me—and she works for a paper with wide circulation. You because Max recommended you—and because the *Times* is the most influential paper in town."

"No broadcast people?" White asked.

"The matter is too complex to be covered in a thirty-second bit on a television news show," said Cosima.

White glanced at Max, then at Della. "You've been accused of having a finely tuned sense of public relations, Miss Bernardin," he said.

"I take that as a compliment."

"But you are assuring me that what is in this package you propose to give me is hard information?"

"If you don't like it, don't use it," said Cosima. "In the package is source material, plus a brief explanation I've written. You don't have to accept my explanation. You don't have to believe the source material. You can reject what you find in the package and not publish a word about it. All I ask is that you don't open the package or use what's in it until one of my two conditions is met."

White sighed. "Okay. I guess I have nothing much to lose. And you are the biggest story in town right now. Okay. You have my word, I'll treat your package as you say."

Cosima reached into her briefcase and withdrew the three sealed packages. "I'll see you in court, then. Monday morning."

Twenty-five

The hundred-or-so seats in the courtroom were filled with reporters and celebrity watchers. At least a hundred others shoved and complained in the hall just outside the doors. United States marshals supplemented the bailiffs, keeping order inside and outside.

The front rows of seats, reserved for the news media, were not jut filled but jammed, with reporters elbowing each other. Cosima looked for Max, Della and Sheldon White. They were there.

Hugh was with Cosima at the defense table in the well of the courtroom. Rick, as had been agreed, was in the office, available on a special clean telephone line that had been installed over the weekend.

Layman Langley stepped over to the defense table. "Nothing personal, Cosima," he said quietly.

She smiled at him. "How's your head?"

He closed his eyes tight. "Ohh . . ." he said. "Annihilatory."

"Sorry," she said.

She was wearing a dark-gray wool skirt, almost to her knees, and so perhaps long enough not to offend Judge Hawthorne, but tailored to cling to her hips and thighs. She

479

wore also a light gray turtleneck and a jacket of crisp checks over gray.

The door to the judge's chamber opened.

"Oyez, oyez, oyez! The United States District Court for the Southern District of New York is now in session pursuant to adjournment. Honorable Ralph Hawthorne presiding. All persons having business before the Court draw near and give attention. God save the United States of America and this Honorable Court!"

Judge Hawthorne strode briskly across the front of the room, his black robe swirling around and behind him, and took his seat on the bench.

"Be seated."

Few had stood, apart from the attorneys in the well and the officials of the court. Judge Hawthorne glanced over the courtroom, his disdain—perhaps he thought it was appropriate judicial hauteur—visible on his tight face.

The judge nodded at the clerk, who rose and intoned, "Svetlana Terasnova versus Thomas Eberhard, District Director of Immigration, action in habeas corpus."

Judge Hawthorne looked at Layman Langley. "Is the government ready to proceed?"

Langley stood. "The United States is ready, Your Honor."

"Miss Bernardin?"

"The petitioner is ready to proceed, Your Honor."

The judge glared at her. "I don't think so, Miss Bernardin. Unless my eyesight is failing, I don't believe I see the petitioner. Where is Miss Terasnova?"

Cosima drew a breath, sighed, glanced down at Hugh. "I regret to say I don't know, Your Honor. I expected her. She is not here. I have people making inquiry. But at the moment I don't know where she is."

Judge Hawthorne played out a little mime. He glanced at his watch, checked it against the clock, glanced over the papers before him, looked at Langley, then at the clerk, then at the bailiff, then at Cosima and again compared his watch to the clock. "You, uh . . . you will understand, Miss Bernardin, when I tell you I find your statement difficult to believe."

"I do understand, Your Honor."

"This court's time is valuable, Miss Bernardin!"

"If Your Honor please, we can proceed to present certain evidence, so as not to waste the Court's time, and—"

"Miss Bernardin! I have no intention of going on with this proceeding without the petitioner. I want her here, and I want her *now."*

"I sincerely wish I could comply with Your Honor's order," said Cosima, feigning impassivity she did not feel.

"Where is she, Miss Bernardin?"

Cosima shook her head. "I honestly don't know, Your Honor."

The judge nodded sarcastically. "You don't know . . . You don't know! This hearing has been scheduled for two months, Miss Bernardin. Do you know where she was yesterday? Saturday?"

"I saw her Friday evening, Your Honor. I've had no contact with her since."

Judge Hawthorne stared at Cosima, as if he could not believe her impudence. He tapped his fingers together. He nodded again, again sarcastically. "Well . . ." he said finally, "I could, I suppose, just deny the petition and let the matter go at that. But you and your client have invoked the jurisdiction of this Court, Miss Bernardin, you have prayed for an order from this bench, and I am not going to let you pursue whatever tactic you now have in mind by keeping your client away from this hearing. I'm not quite sure what you have in mind, but whatever it is I have no intention of letting you *use* a federal court as a pawn in your scheme."

"Your Honor—"

"Miss Bernardin! Miss Bernardin, I am forfeiting your client's bond. Forfeit, you understand—I am not continuing the bond. I am issuing immediately a warrant for the arrest of Miss Svetlana Terasnova. And I am ordering you, Miss Bernardin, to produce your client before this Court at this hour tomorrow morning. If you appear here tomorrow morning without Miss Terasnova, bring your toothbrush, Miss Bernardin, because I will then commit you for contempt!"

"I understand, Your Honor," she said quietly.

"I doubt it," he said. "I very much doubt that you do understand. But understand this—either you bring Miss Terasnova into this courtroom tomorrow morning at nine A.M. or be prepared to go to jail. You have no alternative."

Max Wilmot somehow managed to penetrate the crush and reach her side as she and Hugh left the courtroom. "Where is she?" he asked quietly in her ear. Maybe no one else heard.

Cosima shook her head. "I don't know," she muttered between clenched teeth.

But in their rented limousine a couple of minutes later, as soon as the door was closed, Hugh said angrily, "By god, I do. She's with the wop, is where she is. Find Paccinelli, you'll find Lana. And neither one of them is worth a shit. As far as I'm concerned, they can damned well deport her. She'll let you go to jail to save her own ass. And he'll let you—"

"Not necessarily," said Cosima. The driver was having difficulty getting the limousine through the crowd that pressed around it. She tried to smile at the cameras pressed to the windows of the car. "She was scared to death. I shouldn't have let her hear the tape. He said he'd send her to jail in handcuffs. She's *been* handcuffed—she knows what it's like."

"Well, maybe *you're* about to find out."

Cosima sighed. "Sydney Biddle Barrows survived it," she said, with more courage than she felt.

482

"Lana's fouled up everything," Hugh complained angrily. "She and Paccinelli. I never did trust that son of a bitch, even before Adela told me a few things about him."

They had ordered a limousine with a telephone in it. Cosima picked up the cellular telephone and called the new number they had installed in the office. Rick answered.

"Any word from Lana?"

"No. Didn't she show up?"

"She did not show up. He forfeited her bond and issued a warrant for her. If she doesn't appear tomorrow morning, *I* go to jail. Call Jerry. If you can't reach him— No. Never mind. Try her agent."

"We fall back on plan two, I'd judge," said Rick.

"Not yet. Just try to reach Jerry."

"On top of every other goddamned thing," said Hugh as soon as she'd hung up the phone, "it gives the President another excuse to veto. I can hear his pious little statement now—'Broke our law to enter the country, defied the orders of our courts . . .' Shit!"

"Jesus Christ, Hugh . . . Let me think."

She stared without seeing, at the streets, at crowds, at traffic, as the driver took them uptown, toward the Pan Am Building. She had not taken seriously what Judge Hawthorne had said on the tape about sending her to jail. She had known he had no grounds. Now he did—at least "colorably," as a lawyer might say—and tomorrow morning she might very well leave the federal courthouse in handcuffs, might before the end of the morning find herself locked inside a grimy crowded cage in the women's house of detention. He *had* the power to commit her until she obeyed his order—which was, after all, ostensibly a lawful order, since he actually didn't know she was not defying him but really could not produce Lana. She had told her father she might be jailed a few hours, or even overnight. It could be . . . She tried to remember. A woman in South Carolina—

she thought it was South Carolina—had spent six months in jail for continuing to defy the order of a federal judge and in fact might still be there. Damn Lana! She *had* to appear.

She reached for the phone. In a moment she had her father on the line.

"No, she did not appear. I don't know where she is. I told you I'd call if I needed help. Do one thing for me. Just this one. Call Basilio Paccinelli. Tell him he must get word to Jerry. They've done the wrong thing. I can go to jail indefinitely—until Lana shows up or is found."

"You think Basilio Paccinelli will care?" her father asked.

"Jerry will. Lana will. In fact, if they read the newspapers, watch the television news— Listen. Take down this number. It's a secure line in our offices. They can call in on that. They must not call on the regular number. You know why."

"Release the packages you gave to the newspaper people," were Rick's first words when she returned to the office and they were inside his room which had been swept this morning and was free of bugs. "The best defense is offense."

"The best defense is *timely* offense," said Cosima.

"Timely is before we're in checkmate," said Hugh.

"I've heard Bill Craig recite something about flying an airplane," she said. " 'Plan your flight, and fly your plan.' "

"For every cliché there's an equal and opposite cliché," said Rick. "Haste makes waste, but he who hesitates is lost."

"I have an idea, Hugh," said Cosima. "Something useful we can do while we sit around waiting to hear from Lana. How about you going home about the middle of the afternoon. I'll call you. And here's what I want you to say . . ."

484

SVETLANA DOESN'T SHOW!
COSIMA TO JAIL TOMORROW!

Judge Tells Her, "Bring your toothbrush."

WCBS news:

"Russian ballerina Svetlana Terasnova did not appear in Manhattan federal court this morning for the long-awaited hearing on her application to be saved from deportation by habeas corpus. From the federal courthouse, here's a report from Julia Harris—"

"Yes, Frank, it's true. When the judge entered the courtroom this morning, he took one look at the table where Svetlana Terasnova was supposed to be sitting with her lawyer, Cosima Bernardin, and flushed red with anger. The ballerina was not there. He lectured Miss Bernardin for a few minutes and then gave her until nine o'clock tomorrow morning to produce her client in court or face immediate commitment to jail. Judge Ralph Hawthorne obviously did not believe Miss Bernardin's protest that she did not know where her client was. 'If you show up here without her tomorrow morning, bring your toothbrush,' said the judge as he warned Miss Bernardin that she would go to jail. He also revoked Miss Terasnova's bond and issued a bench warrant for her arrest. This is Julia Harris at the federal courthouse. Back to you, Frank, at the studio."

WINS news:

"WINS Wins News, all news, all the time. Give us twenty-two minutes, we'll give you the *world.*

"Glamour-girl criminal lawyer Cosima Bernardin faces jail tomorrow if she fails to produce her client, Russian ballerina Svetlana Terasnova, before the

United States District Court for the Southern District of New York. The expected dramatic fireworks in the federal courtroom were real but brief this morning as Judge Ralph Hawthorne refused to accept Bernardin's statement that she does not know where her client is and threatened to jail her if the ballerina is not in court tomorrow morning. The judge was obviously angry. The lawyer was obviously off balance. The ballerina was absent.''

Hugh sat down in his bedroom, removed his prosthesis, glad of the opportunity to take it off earlier than usual, and began the process that Adela had been helping him with so competently. She called every night, sometimes very late, after her performance. She kept saying she loved him. He believed it. A twenty-nine-year-old girl was in love with him! Life had its compensations.

The telephone rang before he was quite ready to answer it. Cosima—

''Hugh?''

''Yeah, who's this?''

''Paccinelli. Christ, man, I've been calling your number every fifteen minutes—I can't call the goddamned office, you know. Is this line safe?''

''Was this morning,'' said Hugh dryly. It was in fact now; a lovely miss in the employ of Gallon had come home with him and taken five minutes to sweep the place. ''Yeah, it's safe. Where the hell are you? Where the hell's Lana? Do you have any *idea* how you've fucked up?''

''What am I supposed to do, let Lana walk into the lion's den? What that judge said on that tape, he said in public this morning! The papers—Radio. Television. Hey!''

''So you two are gonna let Cosima take the rap for Lana, is that it?'' Hugh asked scornfully. ''Let *her* go to jail.''

''That judge bastard is bluffing . . . isn't he? Hell, he *can't!* I mean, he can't—''

''Yes, he can,'' Hugh interrupted. ''Paccinelli, I can't

begin to tell you how much you've fucked up. You may have killed whatever little chance we had to get the bill signed. In the morning, Cosima's going into the slammer—and don't you think she isn't. And not for a few hours or overnight, either."

"Hey, I—"

"Let me tell you something, you guinea asshole. As a copyright lawyer I know every goddamned thing there is to know about copyright law. At the same time, I know nothing about music. Or drama. Or literature. I'll represent you as a copyright lawyer, but I wouldn't by god *think* of telling you how to write a piece or how to play it. What do I know from that? About as much as you and Lana know about law. Cosima had planned a damned good defense for Lana. And you— You, you idiot, you egomaniacal dimwit, have fucked it up—maybe beyond repair."

"Jesus Christ, Hugh! What can we do?"

"You listen to me, Paccinelli. You've got to come up with a story. And between now and tomorrow morning, you rehearse Lana in this story. It may help. *May.* Not for sure will, but may. Shit. Never before in my professional life have I advised a client to lie."

"Hugh?"

Ten minutes later. It was Cosima on the line, the call he'd expected. They had rehearsed what they would say:

"Yeah, Cosima."

"Everything okay? She okay?"

"The guinea showed up."

"Huh?"

"Everything's okay, Cosima. Lana's in the bathtub, in fact."

"Fine. Send out for food. Don't let the delivery boy see her. And send the guinea to talk to me."

"You got it, kid."

487

* * *

"Honey . . ."

"Uh . . . Jack, for god's sake!"

"I'm in town, baby. Thought you might need me."

"Yeah. Yeah, I sure as hell do. But I can't talk to you right now. Uh . . . Could you come up to the office?"

"Be there in fifteen minutes."

"This is apeshit, Cosima. I can get you out of here. Look, I may have a conniving frame of mind, but I've got a private plane leased. If we need it. To Toronto in a couple of hours. Air Canada to London. Who's gonna extradite?"

For the first time all day, she could laugh. They had gone to his suite at the Waldorf, from which she had given Hugh and Rick her number. "You wonderful man," she chuckled. "It's not going to be so bad. You don't need to hire a helicopter to snatch me off the roof of the detention center. I haven't played all my cards yet." Then she tipped her head and sighed. "Strike that last. I might need the helicopter."

"Jeez, Cosima. I mean, I'm used to being the big strong man that makes things happen."

She could laugh again. "Get used to something, Jack," she said. "This girl likes to make things happen herself sometimes."

Hugh sat in his silk robe, listening to a compact disk of the London cast album of *Les Misérables*. Someone knocked on the door. Didn't ring the bell. Knocked on the door.

He picked himself up with his crutches and went to the door. "Who is it?"

"Federal officers. We have a warrant to search the premises."

He opened the door. There they were all right: four fed-

488

eral officers, three men and woman. "I'm a lawyer," he said. "Let me see this warrant."

It was a warrant, in order, signed by Judge Ralph Hawthorne. These officers were authorized to search his residential premises in search of a fugitive from federal custody, one Svetlana Terasnova. He was entitled to keep the warrant, and he folded it and put it in the pocket of his robe.

"Any problem?" the chief officer asked.

"None at all," said Hugh. "Be my guests. Do your damnedest. There is no such person here, and never has been, but have a look for yourself."

"The warrant was issued on good information, sir."

Hugh grinned. "When you return the warrant, tell Judge Ralph he's been schnooked—which isn't difficult to do, considering the level of his intelligence. So, if you have no more business with me, I'll sit down while you do your job. I left a leg on a beach in Normandy some forty-four years ago, and standing on crutches is no great privilege."

"I'm sorry, sir," said the officer. "You know we're only doing our job."

"Sure. But searching for a full-grown person, little girl though she is, you won't need to go through my drawers or the boxes in my closets, no?"

The chief officer sat down in the living room with Hugh while his subordinates made their search. Hugh had not turned off the music, or even turned it down. *"Les Miserables,* right?" the officer said.

Hugh nodded.

"I took the wife. Great show. I wish, though, I'd seen Miss Terasnova dance before she's deported."

"Oh, I wouldn't worry about that," said Hugh insouciantly. "With nothing better than Judge Ralph Hawthorne determined to deport her, I don't think she's in any great danger."

"You have no respect for the judge, then?"

"Should I?" Hugh shrugged. "The Attorney General arranged his appointment," he said.

* * *

"Oyez, oyez, oyez! The United States District Court for the Southern District of New York is now in session pursuant to adjournment. Honorable Ralph Hawthorne presiding. All persons having business before the Court draw near and give attention. God save the United States of America and this Honorable Court!"

Cosima stood at her table, Hugh beside her. Lana was not there.

The judge did not even sit down. "Your client is not present, Miss Bernardin," he said. "Let the record show that the petitioner, Svetlana Terasnova, is not present in the courtroom."

"If the Court please," said Cosima. "I can produce my client within five minutes. I know where she is, and I can send for her. I—"

"Miss Bernardin, you have played games with this Court for five months. Your contempt, not just for this Court, but for the processes of law is manifest. I—"

"If Your Honor please—"

The confrontation crackled across the courtroom, which had fallen dead silent. The reporters, the spectators, had seen that Svetlana Terasnova was not present beside Cosima Bernardin; they expected an angry decisive reaction from Judge Hawthorne. People in the rear seats rose to their feet, perhaps unconsciously. The tension was palpable.

"If you have a statement, Miss Bernardin, make it brief."

"I respectfully request a brief conference in chambers," she said.

He raised his chin high. "To what purpose?"

"Useful purpose, Your Honor."

The judge glared at Layman Langley, as if he thought Langley knew why she had asked for a conference and had not told him. "Objection, Mr. Langley?" he asked.

"Conference in my presence, Miss Bernardin?" Langley asked.

"Yes. Of course."

"No objection, Your Honor," said Langley.

The judge nodded. "I hope this is indeed to some useful purpose," he said. "If it is for the purpose of further delay, Miss Bernardin, this Court will take notice."

Chambers may have been an appropriate word for the offices occupied by distinguished judges of high court in past decades; it was a mockery of the spare offices provided by the federal government for judges of the District Court. Ralph Hawthorne threw his black robe over a chair and sat down in his shirtsleeves behind a green steel desk.

"All right," he snapped. "What is it?"

"I have an affidavit here, Your Honor. I will ask you to read it."

"Whose affidavit?"

"It is the affidavit of Robert Blyleven," she said as she put the document in front of the judge. "You've met him."

"Uh . . . copy?" asked Langley.

Cosima nodded and handed him a copy.

Judge Hawthorne frowned hard and read—

"The Affiant states that on the 11th day of May he was present during a meeting in a private dining room at the Harvard Club, in the City of New York, at which meeting also present were Mr. P. D. Dougherty and Mr. Daniel Nash, attorneys in the City of New York, and United States District Judge Ralph W. Hawthorne; that the Affiant was present at said meeting at the behest of the aforementioned Dougherty, who demanded of him then and at another time and place that he make certain statements detrimental to the professional reputation of another attorney, Cosima Bernardin, which the Affiant refused to do, having no reason to believe the demanded statements were true.

"The Affiant further states that during the course

of the conversation during the aforesaid meeting Judge Ralph W. E. Hawthorne stated that he intended to find against Svetlana Terasnova on her application for a writ of habeas corpus. He stated further that he intended to order Miss Terasnova's attorney, Miss Bernardin, held for contempt and that both she and Miss Terasnova would leave his courtroom in handcuffs, or words to that effect. In referring to Miss Terasnova and Miss Bernardin, Judge Ralph W. E. Hawthorne used a vulgar word, to wit, the word 'cunt.' The Affiant states further that Judge Ralph W. E. Hawthorne, by his words, tone and manner, exhibited a strong emotional hostility toward Miss Svetlana Terasnova and Miss Cosima Bernardin.

"And further Affiant sayeth not."

Judge Hawthorne shoved the affidavit across his desk, toward Cosima. "So what the hell? Is somebody going to take the word of this two-bit little shyster against my word and Dougherty's and Nash's? What the hell are you trying to pull?"

"I am going to move that you recuse yourself," said Cosima. "On the ground of prejudice against Miss Terasnova and me. I want you to step aside and let the case be heard by another judge."

"You're damned well out of your mind, Bernardin. Another *judge?* What your client is gonna have to have is another *lawyer.* You're going into a cell! From this office, you're going! You're trying to blackmail me! I'm putting you in the custody of the bailiff, right now."

"Yes, you said I'm going out of here in handcuffs. Well, I did bring a toothbrush. And the moment I'm seen going out of here in handcuffs, this affidavit and some other evidence more dramatic than this will be released to the newspapers."

Judge Hawthorne stood, as if he were about to bolt for the door and summon the bailiff. But he paused. "You're

a witness to this, Langley! She's threatening me! She's—
This is no longer just contempt. This is a felony!''

Layman Langley sat rigidly, as though he were afraid to
move, afraid to show any expression. His copy of the affidavit lay on his lap. He picked it up then dropped it
abruptly, as if he didn't want his fingerprints on it.

''I have other evidence here in my briefcase,'' she said.
''Copies, that is, not the original. And let me point out
something else, Your Honor. Last night federal agents appeared at Hugh Hupp's door, with a warrant signed by
you, and—''

''Somebody was playing games,'' the judge interrupted.

''What made you think Svetlana Terasnova could be
found in that apartment, Your Honor? You don't need to
tell me, I know what made you think so. Somebody told
you so. And where did that somebody get the idea that Lana
was in Hugh's apartment? He listened to a tape from an
illegal tap on my telephone. Maybe you listened to it. Uh
. . . Is that correct judicial conduct?''

''You're just diggin' yourself a deeper hole, sister.''

''Okay. So, would you like to know what the other evidence is? Before you have me arrested?'' She controlled her
voice, but only barely. In truth, she was afraid. She'd had
a nightmare about going to jail. She had not slept much;
the nightmare kept coming back. ''It won't take a minute.''

''Another affidavit?'' the judge sneered.

Cosima nodded. ''I have another affidavit,'' she said.
''Then a tape you should hear.''

The judge sat down. ''Let me see your goddamned affidavit.''

She pushed one copy across his desk and handed another
copy to Langley.

''William A. Gallon, being duly cautioned and
sworn, says that he is President of William A. Gallon,
Security Consultants; he states further that on April
14 his firm was engaged by the law firm of Bernardin,

493

Loewenstein & Salomon to determine whether their offices were 'bugged'—that is, to determine if any electronic eavesdropping devices were present in their offices; he states further that an electronic sweep of the said office, at 200 Park Avenue in the City of New York, detected a hidden microphone and FM transmitter capable of transmitting to a receiver at some distance all sounds, particularly conversation, in the office of Miss Cosima Bernardin; he states further that Miss Bernardin's telephone line had been tapped; and he states further that identical equipment, that is, a 'bug' and a tap were found in Miss Bernardin's personal residence in Greenwich, Connecticut.

"The Affiant further states that at the request of Miss Bernardin his firm conducted an electronic sweep to determine whether or not two individuals, to wit, Attorney P. D. Dougherty and Attorney Daniel Nash, carried FM transmitters concealed in their briefcases; Affiant states that the technique used to determine if these two individuals carried transmitters was to activate an electronic countermeasures receiver in the vicinity of locations where these individuals were known to be; Affiant states that the said receiver did detect transmissions from FM radio transmitters concealed in the briefcases of the two named individuals; and Affiant states that for a period of time beginning April 20 and continuing to the present the Affiant's firm has regularly received and recorded transmissions from the briefcases carried by the two named individuals and other lawyers, discussions with clients, claimants, and others, and other meetings and conversations, all unlawfully transmitted.

"Affiant states further that on May 11 he and a member of his staff operated two electronic countermeasures receivers in a building in the vicinity of the Harvard Club on East 44th Street in the City of New York; Affiant states that both receivers detected transmissions which proved to be from the briefcases of Mr. Dougherty and Mr. Nash; Affiant states that these transmissions were recorded; and Affiant states that the tapes provided by his firm to the firm of Bernardin, Loewenstein & Salomon are true and accurate recordings of conversation picked up by microphones in the briefcases of the said Dougherty and Nash, transmitted by associated FM transmitters, and received on the said electronic countermeasures receivers.''

Judge Hawthorne's face had turned red, so darkly red that Langley involuntarily rose and stared closely at him.

Cosima had lifted her little recorder from her briefcase, and without a word she pushed down the PLAY key:

"Then we can count on you? Fine. And what are you going to do about Svetlana Terasnova?"

"I'm going to find against her, what the hell do you think? And I'm not going to continue her bail. She's going to the detention center and she's going on a plane to Moscow, I promise you. And as soon as I announce that order, I'm going to order Cosima Bernardin held for contempt. Those two cunts are going out of my courtroom in handcuffs, gentlemen."

"They'll run straight to the Court of Appeals."

"Which won't get the toe dancer out of the detention center. And as for glamourous Cosima . . . Well, at least she's gonna get a ride in the paddy wagon, a strip search and a day or two in the slammer. Then we'll see. She may be a little less cocky the next time she appears before your subcommittee."

Langley dropped back into his chair as the voices spoke from the little machine. He looked at Cosima and shook his head.

Judge Hawthorne licked his lips. "Okay," he muttered. "You've got me by the short hairs. What do you want?"

"I want you to recuse yourself," she said coldly, pulling his copy of the affidavit back across his desk and replacing

495

it in her briefcase with the tape recorder. She reached for Langley's copy. "I don't think you're impartial."

The judge drew a deep breath. "And if I do, what happens to those affidavits and those tapes?"

Cosima shrugged.

"They don't go to the newspapers? They are, uh, as we might say, sealed?"

"Well . . . What about this business of contempt? Blackmail? Felony charges? What about the warrant for Lana's arrest? What about continuing Lana's bond?"

He sighed. "You've got me by the short hairs."

She looked at Langley. "What's your position? What about the Justice Department?"

Langley shook his head and gestured nervously, throwing his hands about in front of him. "I disassociate myself from this whole thing," he said. "I'll raise no objection. Judge Hawthorne recuses himself. Bond is continued. Obviously there's no contempt. And the case . . . It may be months before it is heard again."

"Maybe it can be dropped," she suggested.

"Not my decision."

They returned to the courtroom. Lana was at the table, sitting beside Hugh. Jerry was immediately behind her, in the first row of press seats. Jack Putnam sat beside him.

Judge Ralph Hawthorne mounted the bench, moving heavily. He sat down.

"During our conference in chambers," he said quietly, "Miss Bernardin brought to my attention certain statements I made in private conversation a week or so ago which might be interpreted as evidencing a predisposition on my part to find against her client. It is, of course, essential that judicial proceedings not only *be* impartial but that they have the appearance of impartiality, with no . . . hint or suggestion of, uh, any preconceived ideas about a case. Uh . . . We conferred. Discussed the matter. And we agreed, Miss Bernardin, Mr. Langley and I, that it would be better if I step aside and allow another judge to hear this case."

"Jesus Christ!" Jerry whispered, loudly enough that the whole courtroom heard him.

"Uh . . . Accordingly," the judge went on, "I recuse myself, as the legal term is. The warrant for the arrest of the petitioner is voided. The petitioner's bond is continued until such time as another judge assumes control of the case. And, uh, this Court now stands adjourned."

"All rise!" yelled the bailiff as Judge Hawthorne retreated from a courtroom that had now dissolved into chaos.

Marshals moved in to try to restore order. Only with difficulty did they keep the reporters behind the rail. Shouting questions, men and women crushed against Jerry Patchen and Jack Putnam, as many as pressed to the rail and shouted at Cosima and Lana.

Cosima located Max Wilmot, Della Rosario and Sheldon White, back in the crush. She waved at them and quickly had their attention. "Okay!" she called to them, relying on their reading her lips to understand what she was saying to them over the pandemonium. "Open your packages. *Publish!"*

Their exhilaration died quickly—in the limousine on the way to the Waldorf. When Lana asked if this was the end or would the Justice Department go on pressing the case, Cosima had to shake her head. She didn't know what the Department would do. She couldn't answer Jack's question as to whether the humiliation of Judge Hawthorne would make the President more or less likely to sign Lana's bill. They retreated to Jack's suite, where they agreed to go, to find refuge and quiet. Cosima called Teresa and told her to close the office, to come to the suite and screen calls. Jack ordered champagne. There was something to celebrate anyway, he said. Cosima, Lana, Jerry, Jack, Hugh, Rick and Teresa toasted the morning's exploit.

Others arrived—Bill Gallon, who would not accept a glass of champagne until he had hastily swept the suite for bugs and taps, then Lana's manager, Aleksandr Khvostov, who was ebullient about what he insisted was a great victory. Leon Bernardin called from the bank and announced he was coming to the suite to hear firsthand what was already being reported on the radio.

They listened to WCBS:

"Yesterday Judge Ralph Hawthorne threatened to jail lawyer Cosima Bernardin if her client did not appear in court this morning. This morning the Russian ballerina did not appear. For a report on the confrontation between the lawyer and the judge, we go to Julia Harris, who is still at the federal courthouse—"

"Things are still in confusion here, an hour after Svetlana Terasnova either did or didn't—depending on how you look at it—appear for her habeas corpus hearing before the federal court. In fact, she wasn't here when the judge entered the courtroom. He had threatened to commit Miss Terasnova's attorney, Cosima Bernardin, to jail if the Russian dancer did not appear, and for a moment it appeared as if that was exactly what he was about to do. Then Miss Bernardin demanded a conference in chambers. Everyone waited for about half an hour, while judge and lawyers conferred in the judge's office just outside the courtroom. What happened next was an immense surprise. The judge returned to the courtroom and announced he was—to use a lawyer's word—'recusing' himself, that is, he was stepping down and would turn the case over to another judge.

"Why? What's going on here? There are a thousand rumors. Judge Ralph Hawthorne said he was stepping aside because Miss Bernardin had brought to his attention a statement of his in which he apparently expressed a prejudice about the case. Rumor has it, though, that the matter is more serious than that. Rumor has it that Judge Hawthorne may have committed some judicial impropriety that made it impossible for him to continue on the case. For now, nobody is talking. The judge is unavailable. Cosima Bernardin and her client left here in a limousine shortly after the judge adjourned the court. Justice Department attorney Layman Langley refused to comment.

"An interesting sidelight. Miss Terasnova did appear while the conference in chambers was going on—accompanied by a most protective and affectionate Jerry Patchen, leader of Bull Dog Fangs. And with the couple came Hollywood actor Jack Putnam, whose name has long been linked with Miss Bernardin's. The three of them left in Miss Bernardin's limousine, and no one got a chance to talk to them either.

"Julia Harris, at the federal courthouse."

A strategy huddle would have been futile. Rick's cliché spoke the truth. "The ball's in their court now." All they could do was wait for reaction.

Rick had telephoned Sally at her office and told her to come to the Waldorf on her lunch break. She arrived a little after one, carrying two copies of *The Daily News*. The front-page headline:

I'LL PUT THOSE TWO C-NTS IN HANDCUFFS,
JUDGE THREATENS!

Obscene Words Promise As To How He
Would Decide Ballerina's Case!

The first paragraph of the story was:

Federal Judge Ralph Hawthorne should have been more careful in choosing his friends and then a great deal more careful about what he said in front of them.

499

When he shot off his judicial mouth at the Harvard Club two weeks ago, he did not guess, apparently, that two of the big-firm lawyers he was talking to carried hidden microphones and FM radio transmitters in their briefcases and were in the habit of transmitting and recording even the most confidential conversations. And they in turn didn't seem to realize their illegal eavesdropping could be picked up by others.

"Where the hell were you two?" Leon Bernardin demanded of Jerry Patchen.

"You want the truth or the official version?" Jerry asked.

"Both."

"We were in Westport," said Jerry. "Home of a friend. That's the truth. But that wouldn't explain why we didn't show up when we were supposed to, so we had another story ready. If we'd had to say in court where we were, we'd have sworn we were on a fishing trip in New Hampshire, staying in a little lakeside cabin my father owns—where there's no phone—and that I had to work three hours on the car to get it started—either that or walk out to a station for help. So we couldn't make it to court on time and couldn't call to say why."

"I asked your father where you were."

"He didn't know," said Jerry.

Hugh had walked up. "You can get a new lawyer if you don't like the way I talked to you."

"I ought to, you peg-leg son of a bitch. Here, your glass is empty."

Cosima had placed a call to Emilie as soon as they returned to the suite. In midafternoon, Emilie returned it:

"I've heard how it came out," said Emilie.

"No word from the White House?"

"No. He's had the bill since Thursday. He has till next Tuesday, the thirty-first, to sign it. Or veto it. And there's not a word. They're keeping their counsel."

"Well, we've routed their forces here," said Cosima.

"It's possible, I suppose just possible, the Justice Department will drop the case. But I don't count on it."

"Hang in there long enough, we'll get a new President, new Attorney General."

"It's almost ten months since Lana was ordered to report for deportation," said Cosima. "Maybe . . ."

"Stir the pot all you can," said Emilie. "The more embarrassment for the White House, the better."

Cosima looked around the suite. "I wish you could be here," she said. "Dad's here. The way everyone's drinking champagne and giggling, you'd think we'd won."

The Times the next morning, then the New York *Law Journal* and later *The National Law Journal* covered the courtroom debacle in the Terasnova case in exhaustive detail.

From the *Times* story, by Sheldon White:

Embarrassing to Judge Hawthorne as his intemperate language may be, far more serious is his violation of the standards of judicial ethics in meeting *ex parte* with an attorney for the Justice Department to discuss a case that was then pending before his court. Still worse, he announced how he intended to decide the case, having as yet heard nothing of the evidence Miss Terasnova's counsel was preparing to offer.

What is more, the discussion transmitted out of the Harvard Club meeting by the two briefcase radios seems rather clearly to support Miss Bernardin's charge that the judge lent himself and his judicial office to a conspiracy to damage her professional reputation, perhaps to disbar her.

The two law firms involved, Quarles & McGrath and Hamilton, Schuyler, Depew & Chase, issued statements late yesterday afternoon saying they had never authorized any of their personnel to use unlawful eavesdropping equipment in any way, and both insisted, through their spokespersons, that they had no idea Dougherty and Nash were engaged in such conduct.

An attorney for the Association of the Bar of the City of New York indicated the Association's committee on lawyer ethics will initiate an immediate investigation into "improper disclosures of confidential information" by Dougherty and Nash.

* * *

The illegal eavesdropping equipment has not been removed from Miss Bernardin's office or home. Federal agents are expected to remove it today. A spokesman for the office of the United States District Attorney said those who installed it will be prosecuted if they can be identified.

From the New York *Law Journal*:

Clarence Paul Davidson, senior partner at Hamilton, Schuyler, Depew & Chase, said this morning he would ask partner Daniel Nash to resign from the firm if it is true that he has been carrying an illegal radio transmitter in his briefcase. Davidson acknowledged that the firm has received "some" calls from lawyers at other firms, who demand to know if their conversations with Hamilton, Schuyler lawyers have been broadcast and recorded.

* * *

Judge Ralph W. E. Hawthorne remains unavailable for comment. One judge, who asked not to be named, said he "would expect" Judge Hawthorne to resign unless the tape proves to be a fraud. He added that the judge's alleged misconduct would be grounds for

502

impeachment if the facts alleged against him prove to be true.

The story was picked up by all the television networks, by *Time* and *Newsweek*, and by newspapers all across the country. On Sunday morning, Cosima appeared on the weekly David Brinkley news show from Washington, as participant in a segment devoted to the illicit tactics of super-patriot infallibles.

On Monday, May 30, Emilie called Cosima in New York. A rumor was floating that the President had vetoed Lana's bill. Emilie had called the White House and got a denial.

On Tuesday, Lana came to Cosima's office and sat there with her, waiting for the call from Washington—which had to come; the President had to act before midnight. Jerry was meeting a commitment in Boston. Jack had returned to California; he was committed to a schedule of filming. Hugh and Rick tried to keep busy all day; Joan really was busy; but all three of them looked in four or five times an hour to ask if there was any word.

Emilie called at six. There was no word from the White House. Everyone went to Hugh's apartment then, because Cosima did not want to be out of touch as long as it would take to go home. They had food brought in. Cosima mixed martinis with the Bombay gin Hugh had had delivered just for her, and by mid-evening she had sipped a little too much of it. She ate more than she wanted to, to oppose the alcohol. Rick made coffee. Hugh suggested he call Sally, which he did, and Sally arrived. Adela called. Hugh told her he had to keep the telephone available for the call from Washington but that he would call her as soon as there was word.

They had run out of things to say. They tried to make conversation about other subjects, but their minds came back to the veto, and their other talk was unfocused. Hugh went to his bedroom and removed his prosthesis. He put on his long robe, so they wouldn't see his pinned-up trouser leg, and he returned to the living room on crutches, looking

503

tired. The gin had dulled Cosima. She sat beside him on the couch, staring first at the floor, then at the telephone, then at the floor again.

At five minutes after midnight the telephone rang at last. Cosima reached for it. Emilie was on the line, and Cosima switched on the telephone speaker, so everyone could hear.

"He didn't veto it," said Emilie, her voice echoing metallically through the room. "He didn't sign it either. He let the bill become law without his signature. A grudging concession, I suppose, but it's as good as if he'd signed it. Is Lana there? Congratulations, citizen. And Cosima . . . You're one hell of a lawyer. You know that? You're one hell of a lawyer."

Hugh grabbed his glass of Scotch and struggled to rise. He let Rick help him; and, standing, he raised his glass. The others raised theirs. "Amen," said Hugh. "One hell of a lawyer. You'd never guess it to look at her, and when I first met her I didn't think it was possible. But— There you are. One hell of a lawyer."

Lana wept, but she managed to whisper, "Thank you, Cosima."

Twenty-six

At the end of the week, Rick and Sally were married. Everyone who had shared the vigil in Hugh's apartment went to the simple wedding, which was not attended by her parents.

On the 25th of June, Cosima married Jack Putnam. She retained her name, and the firm remained Bernardin, Loewenstein & Salomon. She and Jack had kept a secret. They expected a child by Christmas.

Jack closed his apartment in Los Angeles and declared himself a resident of Connecticut. He and Cosima sold her condominium and bought a back-country house, two miles from her parents. The two miles, Jack said, was the least they could tolerate. He signed a contract to produce and direct a picture, one in which he would play only a cameo role.

Jerry married Lana. He wrote a show for her. She had been a ballerina of the second rank. She would be a Broadway star of the first rank, he promised; and those who saw the script and her first rehearsals expected the promise to be redeemed.

Hugh and Adela agreed to go on sharing intimacy and his apartment but not to marry. They were happy with things as they were, they said. She said she expected The Infinite Adela fad to last less than a year—in which time she would make more money than she could spend in the rest of her life. Soon, she told Hugh, she would let her hair grow back; then she would return to what she had been trained for: serious piano.

Joan Salomon, with help from Cosima and Hugh, obtained a large settlement for Vicky Edsel, the young woman fired by Hobson, Tillman. Vicky moved in with Joan, who had been abandoned by Patricia Larouche, and Cosima, Hugh and Rick attended a small private party in the two women's apartment and heard them pledge to live together permanently and give themselves to no others.

Masquerade opened in London, closed there after three weeks and never opened in New York. Cosima lost her investment. Watson Waugh retained her permanently as his counsel, just the same, saying he liked the way she had raised the money, even if they did lose it.

Layman Langley left the Justice Department shortly after the abortive Terasnova hearing. He came to see Cosima and asked if she had an opening at Bernardin, Loewenstein & Salomon. Even if she had respected his ability, she had no opening; so she told him how sorry she was not to be able to take him into the firm. Langley accepted a position he had already been offered: partnership in a small firm in Jersey City.

Daniel Nash resigned from Hamilton, Schuyler. Criminal charges were brought against him for his illegal use of radio equipment to transmit confidential communications to persons not authorized to hear them. The bar association initiated disbarment proceedings. The charges and proceedings were dropped when he resigned his license to practice law. Norman Haggard, the Cleveland contributor to APAV, employed him as office manager for the VacuMax division of Haggard Manufacturing. He moved to Cleveland.

Hamilton, Schuyler settled the lawsuits arising out of his electronic eavesdropping for a quarter of a million dollars.

P. D. Dougherty resigned his partnership and license in the same circumstances. Claude Graves was sentenced to a year in prison for tapping Cosima's phones and bugging her office and home, so APAV needed a new executive director. Dougherty was appointed.

Lynn Karadja was sentenced to six months in the federal detention center for women for her part in the tapping and bugging. She served two months and eighteen days.

Judge Ralph W. E. Hawthorne resigned his judgeship five weeks after the Terasnova hearing. The House Judiciary Committee had initiated proceedings to impeach him.

Toward the end of August the Bernardins gathered on the terrace behind the Round Hill house—Leon and Elizabeth, Cosima and Susanne and their husbands, and Emilie. They had taken *Lafayette* out during the afternoon, and had enjoyed sailing, though Jack and Emilie together had been strained to do the work Cosima usually did and was not doing because she was six months pregnant. She had sat in the cockpit beside her father, taking the wheel part of the time, but enjoying the luxury of pregnancy: relief from the jumping, tugging, and hauling Susanne, Emilie and Jack were doing.

"I was afraid you would never bear a child, Cosima," her father had said.

She shrugged. "I wasn't," she had said. "And don't count on more. I'm thirty-three."

On the terrace, as the sun set over the western neck of the Sound, Leon Bernardin sipped from his Bombay gin martini and nodded. "A woman's fulfillment," he said, "is in her children. I'm glad that all my daughters—"

"And what's a man's fulfillment, Dad?" Cosima interrupted.

"His success," said her father simply.

Cosima shook her head and opened her mouth to respond, but Jack interjected:

"Jeez, Cosima, you're a success both ways."

Cosima threw an olive at him.

ED MCBAIN'S MYSTERIES

JACK AND THE BEANSTALK (17-083, $3.95)
Jack's dead, stabbed fourteen times. And thirty-six thousand's missing in cash. Matthew's questions are turning up some long-buried pasts, a second dead body, and some beautiful suspects. Like Sunny, Jack's sister, a surfer boy's fantasy, a delicious girl with some unsavory secrets.

BEAUTY AND THE BEAST (17-134, $3.95)
She was spectacular—an unforgettable beauty with exquisite features. On Monday, the same woman appeared in Hope's law office to file a complaint. She had been badly beaten—a mass of purple bruises with one eye swollen completely shut. And she wanted her husband put away before something worse happened. Her body was discovered on Tuesday, bound with wire coat hangers and burned to a crisp. But her husband—big, and monstrously ugly—denies the charge.

Available wherever paperbacks are sold, or order direct from the Publisher. Send cover price plus 50¢ per copy for mailing and handling to Pinnacle Books, Dept.17-303 475 Park Avenue South, New York, N.Y. 10016. Residents of New York, New Jersey and Pennsylvania must include sales tax. DO NOT SEND CASH.

BLOCKBUSTER FICTION FROM PINNACLE BOOKS!

THE FINAL VOYAGE OF THE S.S.N. SKATE (17-157, $3.95)
by Stephen Cassell
The "leper" of the U.S. Pacific Fleet, SSN 578 nuclear attack sub SKATE, has one final mission to perform—an impossible act of piracy that will pit the underwater deathtrap and its inexperienced crew against the combined might of the Soviet Navy's finest!

QUEENS GATE RECKONING (17-164, $3.95)
by Lewis Purdue
Only a wounded CIA operative and a defecting Soviet ballerina stand in the way of a vast consortium of treason that speeds toward the hour of mankind's ultimate reckoning! From the bestselling author of THE LINZ TESTAMENT.

FAREWELL TO RUSSIA (17-165, $4.50)
by Richard Hugo
A KGB agent must race against time to infiltrate the confines of U.S. nuclear technology after a terrifying accident threatens to unleash unmitigated devastation!

THE NICODEMUS CODE (17-133, $3.95)
by Graham N. Smith and Donna Smith
A two-thousand-year-old parchment has been unearthed, unleashing a terrifying conspiracy unlike any the world has previously known, one that threatens the life of the Pope himself, and the ultimate destruction of Christianity!

Available wherever paperbacks are sold, or order direct from the Publisher. Send cover price plus 50¢ per copy for mailing and handling to Pinnacle Books, Dept. 17-303, 475 Park Avenue South, New York, N.Y. 10016. Residents of New York, New Jersey and Pennsylvania must include sales tax. DO NOT SEND CASH.